FIRST SONG BOOK ONE

A BARD STORY

BLAISE CORVIN
OUTSPAN FOSTER

TABLE OF CONTENTS

ALSO BY BLAISE CORVIN

*Note: Some titles are scheduled for launch in 2018 or 2019

For Steve, who is a bad influence, motivating me to spend money on stuff I will probably never use.

FOREWORD

From BC:

Hello readers! This book is classified as GameLit or RPG GameLit.

You might be curious what RPG GameLit actually is. GameLit, the larger genre umbrella, is any fiction with game mechanics or that takes place in a game. RPG GameLit is a subgenre of GameLit where stories include some sort of linear progression for characters, significant to the plot of the story. These types of stories have been extremely popular in Russia and other countries where they are called LitRPG. They're just now making an impact in the West!

RPG GameLit is usually a funky mix of Fantasy and Sci Fi. The settings can vary, but what most GameLit novels have in common is a world that most gamers can immediately relate to.

***

Anthem of Infinity has been a weird project. Outspan Foster and I decided we wanted to do a series together, and in the process of developing our story, kept brainstorming crazier, more difficult ideas to actually write.

"A Young Adult, post-apocalypse, bushcraft/preparedness, coming of age, hero's journey, LitRPG bard story with aliens? Sure why not? Actually, let's make the MC super unlikeable at first!"

So...yeah. That's kind of how it happened. Outspan in particular thrives on a challenge.

Speaking of Outspan, we've known each other from way back during my web serial writing days. He was part of my original writing group, the LitRPG Society, and it's been really fun to work with him again!

This story represents a lot of effort, many revisions, and I really hope everyone enjoys it. Please remember to leave a review, even if you only want to post a few words. Every little bit helps!

***

I really had a lot of fun writing this book. If you'd like to visit my website, the URL is http://blaise-corvin.com/

I also have a writer's note in the back of the book with a whole mess of links.

If you'd like to connect with me on Patreon, the link is http://www.patreon.com/BlaiseCorvin.

My reader group on FB is at:

http://www.facebook.com/groups/BlaiseCorvinBooks/

I hope you enjoy your time with Noah!

From Outspan Foster:

The book you are reading was, in scientific terms, a blasty blast to write. It challenged me in every way imaginable—having to turn down fun to stay up all night and finish a chapter, getting haircuts because I might as well since I pulled most of my hair out anyway, and sounding like a crazy person to my friends and family.

You get the idea.

But in the end, making the best thing I've ever written with my friend and mentor made the journey more than worth it. Speaking of Blaise Corvin, let me tell you from someone who talks to him on a daily basis that he is a tough son of a gun who will cut you so deep with his honesty that you will cry in a corner until you come back for more punishment.

I wouldn't trade him for anything in the world.

He'll say how he has only a little talent and he got here because he worked his butt off. That's all well and true, but he is a damn genius. Working with him has forced me to step up my game and grow at an exponential rate. And isn't challenge and self-growth what GameLit is all about?

It is for me.

At the time of writing foreword, I've been a full time writer for about half a year. It's been a wild ride full of fun and growth. I've used the word 'growth' twice now because becoming better at my craft and being a better person is at the core of who I am. I am addicted to growth, and I hope this book reflects that.

I want to take this space to thank the important people who helped shaped me to become the author you see today. So, thank you Mom for reading Harry Potter to me and quenching my thirst for Young Adult books. Thank you Dad for teaching me how to listen to people, allowing me to write characters with depth and real flaws. Thank you to my Auntie, who was always my champion and who told me to write every day, even if it was just a single word.

Thank you to Blaise Corvin for putting up with my late night ramblings and reining me in. I definitely needed it. And finally, thank you to my readers, who have supported me all the way. You rock.

Okay. Time to reign myself in. I can go on forever with all the gratitude I feel.

Peace and love,

Outspan

https://www.outspanfoster.com/

From BC again: (˙ _ ˙)

CHAPTER 1

Noah felt a burning need to yell, to shout a warning to his small group of surrounded travelers, but as usual, he couldn't find his voice. Then the tired old guilt set in, familiar self-loathing—he was a coward, his mind drowning in fear.

Hints of a red banner flying in the deep woods, past his open clearing, gave him a good idea of what was happening. A hand pressed on his shoulder with a decent amount of force, and Noah knew what the signal meant. Combined with a whistle, it meant one thing: Down.

He fell to the cushioning grass like a sack of potatoes, then turned to the owner of the hand. Yusef gave him a weary smile. "I don't think Allah will count this as one of my five prayers for the day."

"Th—the Red Chain," Noah managed to whisper. He noticed the others in the group were down low in the high grass as well. It had been two years since the Shift - when all the electronics and technology in the world had largely become useless. Not many lawns had been mown in the last two years, or grass trimmed, which everyone in Noah's group was deeply thankful for. Unfortunately, the high grass had kept both their group and the incoming raiders hidden from each other's view.

Still, that didn't change the fact that the Red Chain, the most notorious raider gang in the area, had spotted his group and were closing in on them. Prayers to the Muslim Allah were quickly murmured by everyone hugging the ground, except for Noah. He had been their newest addition. The only thing he believed in was survival.

Noah had known this might happen, that a raider gang might come to kill or hurt or enslave them. But the reality of it, the entire transition to this...world after the Shift, was still foreign to everyone. Where rules and laws were once commonplace, brutality had rushed in to fill the vacuum after societies had collapsed.

The sandy-haired young man began to breathe heavily. He said, "Yusef. We can't win."

Yusef's fragile smile collapsed into a serious frown. "Enduring is winning. Our lives aren't our own. Inshallah."

Noah's anger rose. He was grateful the group of people had taken him in and fed him, but their insistence that a higher power could save them made Noah even more bitter about his life. *Some existence this is*, Noah thought for at least the hundredth time. "I don't care what God's plan is. What is *our* plan? You must have planned for this right? Do we fight or run?"

Yusef only had about twenty years on the twenty-year-old Noah, but his hair and beard had greyed. Noah wanted to scream the words everyone was thinking. *Run. Run. Run.*

Whatever deliberation Yusef was going through in his head must have come to a dead end. A second later, he completely contradicted everything he'd just said earlier and screamed, "Run!"

It took a moment for the ten people in the group to realize Yusef, the de facto leader of their group who had promised to lead them to Smalltown, the closest safe fortress, had just told them to break up and scatter. Smalltown…where Yusef had said his family lived.

The group had known that this had been a possibility, but none of them had probably actually been truly prepared for it. They'd believed that Allah would protect them.

Noah's eyes widened and he sprang up, sprinting after Yusef. Chaos broke in the tree line as the men and women in the small group began running in different directions. The frightened young man didn't dare look back. Even as he sprinted, he could hear the laughter of the Red Chain, their horses neighing as they cut off their prey's escape. Noah's heart beat a river of fear into the rest of his body.

As he ran, he focused on following Yusef. Over the past two weeks, since the man had taken Noah in, Yusef had always seemed so controlled, like he always had a plan. The truth of the matter had dawned on Noah in that moment with terrifying clarity. In fact, the whole nature of the world had become clear—humanity was divided between cowards, prey, and predators.

Maybe inside fortresses, people had the luxury to be strong and lead with a calm mind, but out in the wilds, there was only survival. He was not disappointed in Yusef for failing to protect his group, but rather because he'd proven to be no better than Noah, a coward. For the past few days, Noah had stupidly allowed himself to believe in the man. The truth was, the world hadn't just changed from the Shift, people had changed as well. *Strip away all safety and comfort, and the only thing that's left is either a coward or a beast,* Noah thought.

They darted through the woods, and Noah's breath became more ragged. Screams behind him grew muted through the thick trees. He didn't know if it was because the Red Chain had caught the travelers or because he'd created enough distance not to hear them anymore.

Noah stumbled on something hard and tumbled head over heels, crashing into a tree. He quickly got up and realized he had fallen with Yusef, who had tripped on a root. The older man shook his head. "The woods here are different than Boston," he remarked with an odd tone in his voice, as if he were observing the whole thing as an outsider.

They both got up, and Noah saw dawning horror on the other

man's face. Yusef shivered as he looked back the way they'd come. He said something Noah didn't understand, probably in Arabic, but he recognized the tone - an apology filled with guilt. The same feelings were welling up within himself. He too had left the others behind.

Yusef turned, clenching his jaw. He ordered, "Survive. Endure. Don't let this world break you."

Before Noah could say anything, something cracked in the woods behind them. A man in a black leather jacket, holding a crossbow stepped out from behind a tree, aiming his weapon at Yusef. "End of the road, boys," he said. The man's mannerisms reminded Noah of a wolf, and he immediately recalled that wolves rarely hunted alone.

Yusef tensed to run, probably to take the bolt so Noah could escape, but as he bent his knees, another man stepped out from behind him. Noah tried to shout a warning, "Yu-"

Suddenly, something cracked against Noah's temple. He tasted dirt and blood before the black swallowed his world.

***

Laughter. Crying. Something heavy clamped against Noah's wrists. When he opened his eyes, he found himself lying with half his face in the grass. Men wearing black jackets surrounded him, each of them holding weapons, and half were riding horses. They all had the letter "R" patched on their jackets. *The Red Chain,* Noah thought beneath the fog on his mind. *The wandering slaver gang.*

Noah got up slowly and felt the weight of the clamps and chains on his wrists. *That's about right*, he thought. He was a slave now, and some part of him had known this would happen. The promise of safety behind the walls of a fortress had been fantastical, too good to be true. Sure, towns were safe...until a raider gang attacked—or worse. Some part of him felt resigned to his situation. The ring of raiders that had formed around him began passing strips of meat around.

He realized Yusef was restrained, facing Noah. They had both been chained. Noah looked around and saw cages with people inside being carted by horses. He recognized most of the new slaves, people he had been travelling with the past few weeks. They'd been beaten and bruised.

A large, bald man with a scar across his upper lip stepped out from the ring of raiders surrounding Noah and Yusef. The man raised his hands in the air, each holding a knife. The crowd hushed.

"We don't need either of you for our next shipment. Our sellers want families. Easier to control," said the man. His voice was low and gravelly. The scar on his upper lip seemed open whenever he moved it. "You two are the loners in this group, but I'm feeling mighty generous."

He tossed the two knives between Noah and Yusef. Noah's heart dropped.

The bald man continued, "Fight. Survivor gets to live with us. We feed you, clothe you, and you live, as long as you keep your mouth shut and keep yourself useful. Maybe one day, you'll get a jacket."

Noah's eyes were transfixed on the two knives between them, lying in the grass. He found himself breathing heavily, his body tilting side to side as he levered himself up. Neither he nor Yusef needed to speak. At this point, words would be meaningless.

The bald man nodded in approval, no smile on his face. "When one of you takes your last breath, remember it was Redford Vaillancourt who gave you a chance to live." He raised a hand in the air and let it fall like a guillotine. "Fight."

Neither Yusef or Noah moved right away. *I have to kill a man to survive*, Noah realized. He tasted the words on his mind, and they didn't feel real. Just a few years ago, his biggest problem had been deciding whether or not he should drop out of college. And now, he had to kill someone.

Noah stared at the man before him. Yusef. What did Noah know about Yusef? Not much, except it had been Yusef who'd insisted the group of Muslim travelers allow the white kid into their group. Like the others, he'd prayed five times a day, and he had made an unprompted confession to Noah about having once eaten a slice of bacon. *His family*, Noah remembered. *That was why Yusef was going to Smalltown, to reunite with his family.* Noah didn't have any family left. Maybe he was the one who should die here.

Everyone in the group had mattered except Noah. Some part of him felt like he deserved to die–he didn't really have anything to live for. His body wasn't listening, though. He found himself sluggishly picking up the knife from the ground, gripping it awkwardly because of the clamps on his wrists. The ugly knife seemed appropriate; just a cheap kitchen knife from a department store. Every inch of Noah felt heavy with guilt, but a feral growl in his chest forced him to survive. Fear for his life ruled him, now. He had become nothing more than a rat.

Yusef shook his head solemnly and made a prayer Noah couldn't understand as he picked up his own knife. The man looked eerily at peace. After both men were armed, the fifty or so members of the Red Chain began hooting and hollering. Noah didn't know what to do. He stumbled and made an awkward thrust with his knife, both hands around the handle, missing Yusef as the man spun away.

Noah fell to his knees and scrambled back up. "I'm not gonna die," he said to himself, repeating it over and over. He looked at the man he was supposed to kill, gazing directly into his eyes, and saw nothing but peace. Something about the older man's calm startled Noah and made him feel wary.

Had he killed before? Noah wondered.

In a blink, Yusef's face was suddenly an inch apart from his. Noah screamed in surprise, thrusting his knife once more. He struck something hard and felt a crack, but he saw no blood when he glanced down. Noah had torn Yusef's pants, and a small purple orb fell out of the tear, tumbling to the ground. The strange sphere had a crack in it. The orb might have saved Yusef's life.

Noah looked back at the older man's face. They were so close now. Yusef gave him a calm smile and whispered, "My family isn't in Smalltown, Noah. They died years ago in the Gaza Strip."

The youth tried jumping back, aware that his strike had missed actually injuring Yusef and that the man could counterattack, but Yusef's grip held firm on Noah's sweater like they were almost hugging. The surrounding Red Chain members made more noise and banged metal together, thinking that the two combatants were struggling with controlling each other's knives. Noah asked, "Why are you telling me this?"

Yusef's face had begun growing pale, and he gave Noah a nod to look down again. The man's knife had been plunged into his own stomach, blood beginning to spill all over both of their clothes. Noah didn't know what was happening. Why had the other man stabbed himself?

His voice not much more than a whisper, Yusef said, "Do not fool yourself. There was never any peace on this world to begin with. Take the orb with you. It is the closest thing to peace you will find before you die. Salaam."

The man slumped against the confused and terrified Noah, his consciousness fading as he bled out. It was only then that Noah realized he had lived. Noah hadn't killed the other man, but he had tried. His hand might have even been on the knife. Had it? He couldn't remember. Maybe Yusef hadn't technically committed suicide after all...he wasn't sure. He wasn't sure about anything. The crowd of raiders seemed confused by the outcome until Noah pushed Yusef's body off of him. After they saw the blood on his hands, the slavers all cheered.

A shadow fell over Noah. Redford Vaillancourt put on a hand on Noah's shoulder and said, "Today, you survive. But you aren't one of us yet. What's your name, kid?"

After a moment, Noah gathered himself and forced his dry tongue to scrape out his name. "Noah. Noah Henson."

Redford's giant hand smacked against Noah's face like a sledgehammer, splitting his lip and making Noah see stars. The surrounding crowd laughed. Redford frowned and growled, "Wrong answer. From now on, your name is Worm. We feed you. You live. You do what we say, got it, Worm?"

Noah massaged his face, staring at the bloody, lifeless body that had once been Yusef, the last person who had shown Noah any kind of kindness. So now Noah was neither a slave nor a raider, but something in between. It would be something he would need to get used to. He'd made his choice—he wanted to live. "I understand." The young man savagely suppressed tears, refusing to give the slavers any further satisfaction.

His knees suddenly gave out, and he fell on his butt, one of his hands falling on something round and cracked - the purple orb. Something like static electricity rushed up Noah's arm at the touch, and he quickly pocketed the object. One of Redford's men walked over and unlocked Noah's manacles. None of them had seen him take the orb.

Redford crossed his arms and measured the lanky Noah with his gaze. "Once more," Redford said. "What is your name?"

Noah winced. He didn't want to be Noah anymore. He had had to make decisions about how to be decent in a terrible world, to choose between survival and honesty. But Worm? Worm could do whatever the heck they told him to do. It wasn't ideal, but he would live…and he was a rat now, after all.

"Worm, sir. My name is Worm."

CHAPTER 2

"He's useless," muttered Talbot, and Redford nodded.

It had been a couple weeks since the Red Chain had taken Noah in. He had been their gopher, the guy who did everything for anyone in the group without question. In return, he was allowed to survive and eat scraps of venison. Most of the raiders in the group were skilled hunters, dragging in deer for food and exchanging slaves with fortresses they encountered for weaponry and other items. Noah had heard that the slavers' largest and most consistent customers had been the Iron Wolves, and now they were on the way to Iron Wolf Fortress with the new haul of slaves.

Talbot, a leader of the Red Chain, called a "foreman" by the others, seemed to despise Noah personally. The man wore a goatee, had a gold tooth, and his tattoos under one eye and on one side of his neck were crude, almost unfinished looking. His rough skin had a red hue, and he kept his stringy hair tied into a ponytail.

His leather jacket had a patch sewn on, a biker gang sign or something, maybe a reminder of the days before the Shift. Talbot and Redford conversed openly about Noah. In fact, he could tell they were making it a point for him to hear what they were saying. He got the message loud and clear: *Make yourself useful or we get rid of you.*

Noah kept his hands in his pockets, his right hand idly toying with the broken purple orb. Yusef's last words to Noah had been that the orb would give him peace. At that time, he hadn't known what that had meant, but now he had a better understanding.

Thinking about the orb allowed him to ignore his surroundings. Some of the slaves were allowed to walk, especially the meeker or weaker ones. Mothers with children were allowed to walk alongside their caravan too, the young ones carrying heavy chains. Some of the women actually helped support the chains of the littlest kids. Noah tried not to see them, tried to look past them, but sometimes his gaze alighted on the barred wagons.

He didn't want to dwell on the fact that he walked alongside a cage full of captured people, all to be sold into slavery. Their cries, their whispers for his help were unwelcome. He didn't want to think about the silence he gave to them in return.

What did they expect? That he would unlatch their cages and let them go free? Nothing was that easy. He had no power of his own, so the best he could have done was just pop the locks and run along with the escapees. Of course, only half of them would probably survive as the Red Chain hunted them down once more. There would be a chance for freedom, but the price would be high.

I'm a coward, Noah thought. He mentally hummed a tune in his head to drown out other thoughts. It was strange that he couldn't remember what song the music actually came from. He hadn't heard any real music in years, so his fuzzy memory didn't exactly raise any flags. Somehow, the orb pulsed in time with his mental humming.

The orb's strange behavior was one of the first discoveries he'd made about the mysterious object. Noah blinked and his vision blurred a little as something like a blue rectangle appeared in front of him. He looked around warily, but none of the other raiders made any indication they could see the shape.

The blue, rectangular box floated wherever Noah looked as long as he held the purple orb and mentally willed it to appear. Noah knew what the shape looked like, but it was impossible. He must be crazy. There were words on the box, the screen, but they were fuzzed out. He had tried several times to read the text but hadn't made any headway with deciphering it. He willed the box away, and it disappeared.

"Seriously, am I going crazy?" Noah whispered. Talking to himself was already not exactly normal behavior but seeing things that weren't there took it to another level.

He stole a glance at Redford, the leader of the Red Chain. Some of the Chains called him Red, but everyone else referred to the bald man as Boss. The man sneered at Noah with his scarred upper lip, and Noah flinched. This wasn't the first time Talbot, Red's second in command, had voiced his frustration with their new worm's uselessness. They had been talking about it for a week, but luckily, Noah was still being allowed to live.

The sandy-haired youth was too afraid to run, too scared that weak, exhausted legs wouldn't take him far away, fast enough. *The orb. Just think about the orb.* He rubbed his fingers against the smooth surface, stopping against the crack.

Noah massaged a new bruise on his face with his other hand. Every new scrape or bruise that Talbot, Red, or any other Chain had given him for failing a task or not doing something fast enough had been healing fast. In fact, he'd been healing abnormally fast. It was lucky that his body was repairing itself so quickly, but was getting seriously tired of being hit. In fact, half the time he couldn't tell if he was actually useless to the Red Chain or if they said that about any new recruit. Either way, Noah didn't like his position–he needed to change something and fast.

Gentle probing of his face revealed that the bruise had already almost healed. *The orb. It had to be the orb. This thing is healing me,* Noah realized. Whatever the orb was, it wasn't like anything he had ever experienced before. Just touching it gave him a sense of calm he hadn't felt since before the Shift.

"Hey," someone whispered.

By the voice, Noah knew it was one of the prisoners, a woman who had been caught with her young daughter. The woman was middle-aged and skinny, but her face was lumpy with the telltale marks of someone that had used be overweight, then starved. Her olive skin was scratched, dirty. The only jewelry she wore was a plastic bracelet people could buy in gas stations before the entire world had gone crazy. The woman would probably be sold to make weapons for the Iron Wolves, threats made against her daughter to keep her in line. Noah ignored her. The last thing he needed was Red knowing he'd spoken to the prisoners.

"Worm, right?" the woman insisted just above a whisper.

Noah frowned. "My name is Noah to you. Only the Chain calls me Worm."

The woman's curiosity flashed into anger. She spat at his feet. "You think you're better than us? You're worse. You could help us escape, but you don't. I can see the guilt on your face. Do you think you aren't scum because of that guilt? Because you aren't. You're even worse because you don't act on it. You don—"

A young girl, probably eight or nine pulled on the woman's leg. The tired-looking slave-to-be angrily turned from Noah and began to cry into her daughter's hair.

"She's right, you know," said a voice from above. Talbot had slowed his horse down from ahead. His battered, steel-toed work boots were covered in mud. "You are worse than a piece of trash. All you do is carry packs, but what purpose does that even serve? We could just tie that stuff to another horse or put them on the prisoner carts. What good are you, Worm?'

Talbot kicked Noah's back, and he fell to the ground. The miserable young man felt people stepping past him, pretending to ignore his weakness and humiliation. He heard their snickers. Noah fought down the tears welling up in his eyes, and his hand instinctively went for the orb. He held the precious object and hummed the usual song in his head. The orb responded.

Suddenly, strangely, he could hear everything around in the general area. He caught Red's grunt of agreement when Talbot said they should probably get rid of Noah that night after they dropped off their shipment. A few Chains laughed at that. Sobbing from the people he had helped enslave, people he did nothing to comfort haunted him.

Then there was a new sound, a snapping of twigs in the woods.

Noah's head snapped up. He held his breath and focused everything on his strange new hearing. The horses neighed, their hooves clopping at a slow walk. Leather jackets brushed against the tall grass. People whispered in the distance, closing in on them.

"Come on, Worm!" Talbot yelled. "Keep up, or we stick a bolt in you."

"I can hear it all," Noah said to himself as he got up. He wanted to say more, to warn someone about what he had heard, but he stopped himself.

All the sounds around him had become crystal clear as he pressed his fingers on the orb. Quickly, he put the orb back in his pocket, and his hearing went back to normal. Again, he put his hand back in his pocket. The surrounding noises were clear again.

His senses were so sharp; he could even distinguish the different breathing patterns of all the people around him. The world hadn't gotten louder, just *clearer*, like he had mistaken the lyrics to a song for years and had just now realized the right words. Each sound rang in isolation, and every noise was familiar to him except for the whispers in the forest.

The soft, unfamiliar sounds were not coming from the prisoners or the fifty-odd members of the Red Chain. Noah suddenly realized the group was about to be ambushed.

The blue screen he'd seen before suddenly popped into view. The entire thing was still fuzzy, like it was out of focus, and Noah couldn't make out what the writing said, if it even said anything. This was the first time the object had manifested on its own— something was wrong. To Noah, its appearance confirmed that something was about to happen.

Maybe *I could be free from the Red Chain*, he realized. If he let whoever was ambushing them attack without warning, Noah could survive and slip away—risk, reward. *Maybe even Talbot and Redford won't notice*. After pondering for a few seconds, Noah realized he'd been too obvious when Talbot stopped his horse and gave him a glare. "If I have to ask one more time, Worm, you're dead."

Noah jumped up and nodded. "Sorry, sir."

The attackers were closing in, picking up their pace. If Noah didn't say anything now, the Red Chain could take the attack head-on. Even if half the members died in the attack, it would be impossible for them to have the strength they'd had before.

Noah sneaked glances at the members, most of whom were only a little older than him. He wondered if they had all been given the 'Worm' treatment once too. Was it was part of a regular hazing process? However they'd gotten one, they all had jackets now. Noah frowned as something churned in his stomach. *What they're doing is wrong*, he reminded himself. *What you're doing is wrong.* He wasn't any better than they were. If anything, he was worse, never speaking out against slavery, sticking his neck out. The Red Chain didn't starve or rape slaves, who were property, but they did sell people to the Iron Wolves. Things Noah had heard about them made the Red Chain look like boy scouts. At least the Chain only killed people.

Another thought came to him and it froze whatever fantasies he had about escaping. *What if the attackers are worse?* he thought. So many things had to go right in order to escape. First, the attackers had to be successful in taking down the Red Chain as a group. Second, they had to specifically take down, kill or incapacitate both Talbot and Redford. Third, Noah would have to convince the attackers that he wasn't one of the Chains, just another victim in all this.

But am I a victim? He played with the hope that he might have some shred of decency left in him, enough to deserve freedom.

Then he thought about the last two weeks of fear for his own survival, his drive to make himself useful. It made him sick. *Was this how Talbot and Redford made such a loyal raider gang, with this fear?* Maybe one day, Noah would stop feeling sick, but if that happened, he wouldn't be Noah anymore—he'd just be Worm.

The Red Chain deserved to die. *He* deserved to die. Noah could still hear the attackers' footsteps. They were so close now, in the cover of the tall grass and high trees. The potential for freedom was so close. But... "Am-ambush!" he shouted, the sound coming out like a hiccup.

Talbot and Redford stopped and spun back toward Noah. Talbot growled, "What did you just say, Worm?"

Redford calmly raised his hands in a fist, and the entire party stopped. He moved his hand in a circle, and all the members formed a defensive perimeter, the crossbowmen setting themselves up for an attack. The deadly, modern sports crossbows manufactured before the Shift whispered as they were cocked. Other than weapons being readied, no one made a sound, not even the prisoners. All the slaves-to-be knew that punishment would be swift if they spoke out of turn. Mothers clamped hands over the mouths of children. Fear ruled them too, they attached their own chains, just like Noah had.

The leader of the Red Chain scanned the tall grass and tree line for a few seconds, and Noah felt like his entire life stretched in that silence. He had made the decision without even thinking.

Even the touch of the orb didn't stop the tight knots that grew in his stomach. He felt like a coward through and through, and actually, truly hated himself for the first time in his life.

Redford's scar on his upper lip warped as he frowned at Talbot. Then he gave Noah a hard look, studying the Chain's Worm and nodded. In that nod, Noah knew he would survive, that he had bought himself his way into the Red Chain's trust. But at what cost? Redford spoke loud, but calmly to Noah, "Get down, Worm. Time for the big boys to play." The man waited a few more second, before ordering, "Fire."

From his spot on the ground, Noah watched as each member of the Chain with missile weapons attacked at once, aiming at targets that Noah couldn't see.

Then the screams began.

Arrows, bolts, and shouts flew above him. Noah could hear everything. Some of the slaves couldn't hold in their fear and began to wail. Meanwhile, men and women on both sides died, but mostly the attackers. The Chain had been prepared. The Red Chain were well-trained and had great gear—their cohesion was top-notch. The unknown attackers had had the element of surprised, but Noah had ruined it. In only a few minutes, the skirmish ended, and a number of the attackers fled.

Noah's head scraped against the dirt the entire time, staying low and stewing in shame. *I might as well stay in the dirt*, Noah thought. *I'm nothing but a Worm.*

CHAPTER 3

"Worm," Talbot asked, "do you hear anything?"

Noah reached into his worn, Red Chain leather jacket. The jacket signified he was part of the raider gang, but just because he'd been given one didn't mean he was actually accepted yet. When his hand touched the cracked orb, sounds instantly became sharper, clearer. He no longer had to hold it as long to experience the hearing effect.

"No, sir," Noah confirmed. He quickly pulled his hand free of his jacket to help balance the large pack he'd been forced to carry. Talbot moved ahead with Redford, and Noah dispassionately examined the slaves in the wagon-cages.

His duties hadn't changed in the three months since he warned the raiders about the ambush. He was still in charge of watching the slaves and carrying whatever Talbot told him to. But ever since his timely warning, Redford had used Noah's unusual hearing to the group's benefit. Noah had prevented a couple more attacks since then, but this was good. He was being useful.

Noah was surviving as Worm, the spineless fool who kept his ear to the ground, kept everyone safe, kept *himself* safe. But when they used him as a hound dog, used his hearing to listen for the ragged breaths and scared whimpers of potential slaves, he hated his life. Sometimes he was brave enough to lie, say that he couldn't hear anything, but he had to give up real information occasionally or they would start suspecting him. It usually didn't work.

They are always testing me, Noah thought. Even when he lied, Redford was usually able to find his targets without Noah's help. The man seemed to have a sense for smelling out fear. Whenever the Red Chain suspected he'd lied, Talbot would dish out the beatings, saying pain was the only discipline left in this world. Luckily, the orb helped Noah heal faster than ever, but not at an obviously inhuman rate, just a little faster than normal.

Noah watched Redford get off his horse and open a cabin door without knocking. Noah didn't reach for the orb to listen in on their conversation. He knew what Redford and the cabin owner would be talking about—why the raiders were here. Besides, the pack on his back was getting too heavy to balance one-handed. The presence of the cabin meant the band would probably rest, and he was looking forward to it.

The young man watched Talbot's eyes dart across the tree line in the nearby woods. The man's unibrow made it look like he had a caterpillar on his face at all time. The facial hair somehow came across both ridiculous and threatening at the same time. Despite the beatings, Noah had learned not to hate Talbot as much as he had before. The man was just following orders. Even with Noah's earlier confirmation that no threatening noises had come from the cabin, Talbot's paranoia was on display as he scanned the woods. Noah caught a frantic look in the goateed man's eyes, and he realized that Talbot was probably actually just like him—a man full of fear.

Redford eventually came out of the large cabin followed by a thin man in a plaid button-down shirt and overalls. Unlike all the newcomers, the man in overalls was completely clean shaven. *He probably shaves in the nearby* creek, Noah realized. Despite his well-groomed appearance, the man, Doc, came across like a mountain man or something. A few nods flashed among members of the Red Chain, making it obvious that the majority of the gang recognized him. Noah knew him too.

The plaid-shirted man walked with a bouncy gait toward the prisoners, ignoring Talbot. Noah reported, "Doc, there are five prisoners total. I've been trying to keep them dry this time like you told me to the last visit, but the winds brought rain in from every direction. It was hard to keep them dry from—"

Doc put his hand up and gave Noah a warm smile. "I'll be the judge of that, Noah. I'm glad you tried. That's really all we can do, isn't it—our best? Send the walking prisoners inside right away, and get the others inside before the evening dark comes. Hypothermia is bad. I'll see what I can do."

Noah suppressed the emotion that swelled in his throat. Doc was the only one who called Noah by his name anymore. The thin man turned around and asked Talbot, "Did you get that supply of antibiotics from the Iron Wolves like I asked?"

Talbot's eyes stayed glued to the trees. "Yeah. Worm's got them in the pack."

Doc smiled at that, pulled out a pack of smokes—valuable after the Shift—and lit a cigarette in his mouth. One of the slaves, a man with wiry muscles, gave Doc a pleading look. "Please. Help us."

Noah shivered. The slaves—no, the people that had been caught—used to ask Noah to help them escape. They might have been able to sense the small grain of humanity left inside him. But now, the only person the slaves ever pleaded with was Doc. With Doc's kind smile and easy demeanor, he was like everyone's best friend's dad, like he might crack a corny joke any minute.

The thin man in overalls puffed out a puff of smoke, his eyes closed, enjoying the slow burn between his lips. "Just what the Doc ordered." Then he regarded the man inside the cage and gave him a sad smile. "That's what I'm here for. To help."

***

Christopher Broad watched Noah usher the prisoners inside his cabin. The young man brought a few of them to the medical beds that the Red Chain had hauled in from nearby hospitals.

After killing his cigarette and crushing it under his heel, Chris sighed. The Red Chain called him Doc—everyone did. He'd never liked the nickname because he wasn't technically a doctor. Chris had never gotten his test results back or begun residency. He did come from a family of doctors, though. His father, grandfather, brothers, and sisters had all been doctors. After the Shift they had all died in various ways, most in raider attacks. It was ironic now how he was helping a group of raiders. They had him by the balls, though—he'd always heal and help anybody he could regardless of their current circumstances. Chris watched Noah, shaking his head at the weight of fear the boy carried— Red's doing. Redford was definitely not Chris' favorite person.

Men like Redford always ruled through fear. Talbot was a perfect example of its effect. Chris had watched Talbot morph from a man more like Noah to Redford's ruthless second in command. There was a real possibility that one day Talbot might become a new Redford, and Noah would be Talbot's replacement. Over the past few months that Chris had known Noah, he had learned to like the young man. The way he guided the prisoners to their medical beds without touching them, offered them blankets, and asked them if they felt any pain, were indicators that Noah probably carried as much guilt as he did fear. No mean feat. The boy was decent, just trapped.

He and Noah had chatted every time the Chain brought new

prisoners to the cabin for a fix-up. The raider gang always needed Christopher to clean up their merchandise before they were sold to the Iron Wolves. The people would be worth more if they were in the best condition possible. Chris hated it. Every single time Redford paid a visit, his ethical dilemma grew.

Chris wanted more alone time with Noah so he could break through the hard exterior the young man had been building...just like Talbot had. Healing the spirit could be as important as the body, sometimes more. Luckily, he'd been able to help Noah in a way he'd never thought to help Talbot. Proof of the headway he'd been making lately had come when Noah had entrusted him with knowledge of his orb and its properties.

He'd been shocked by the boy's claims at first, but after seeing its healing effects first-hand, the orb's powers had been undeniable. He had gained Noah's trust—listening about the orb and never telling the rest of the Red Chain about it.

Chris snapped out of his memories and came back to the present. He still had patients, after all. Going through his normal procedure, diagnosing and treating the prisoners was a matter of routine, now. As usual, at first the prisoners were confused, wondering why the Red Chain had brought them to a doctor. Then as they always did, they eventually realized that they were just being cleaned up before being sold.

A few more hours passed before night. His work done, he and Noah sat on the back porch of the cabin alone. The rest of the Red

Chain were busy eating their game they had hunted or were standing guard around the front of the cabin. Noah would eat last since he was the newest member.

The young man looked into the night sky using a telescope that Chris had propped up with old gaming consoles. Most of them had been side projects, things to pick apart over the years before the Shift. He'd grabbed them from his lab inside the cabin—they weren't worth anything anymore. Noah glanced back and forth between a candle-lit astronomy book and the telescope. His face scrunched in confusion, he asked, "Hey, Doc. I can't find Ursa Major. I never really cared about constellations before—like, astronomy stuff."

Chris nodded as he drew on his Marlboro Red. "Yes, I understand. I never looked at the stars before the Shift, but after that, there wasn't much to do without electricity. I guess the brightest things at night now are the stars, just like when our ancestors lived. That's probably why we have so many songs and stories about the heavens from the past, when you think about it. Anyway, to answer your question, I recognized the same thing about a few months ago—you're not seeing things. I don't know if it has anything to do with the Shift or if that book is outdated, but there's something wrong with the stars."

Noah's eyes widened, his interest plain before he went back to the telescope with renewed concentration. Nervousness tap danced on Chris' heart as he thought about the request he was about to make. What he had to ask Noah. This was serious. Finally, he cleared his throat and first asked, "Noah, is anyone here right now other than us?"

The kid reached into his leather jacket, then shook his head. "No, we're alone. Why do you ask?"

Chris absent-mindedly blew smoke out through his nose. *Might as well get straight to the point,* he thought. "I need you to give me the orb. Just for a few weeks."

Noah froze like a deer in the headlights. He backed away slowly from the telescope and folded his arms. Chris saw a flurry of emotions pass over Noah's face—confusion, then trust warring with skepticism. Finally, the young man seemed to come to a decision. To Chris' relief, Noah asked, "Why are you asking me this, Doc?"

"My name isn't Doc. It's Chris Broad. If that's too much for you, Doc Broad will do. Take this as a sign of trust. So, yeah, I'm not going to beat around the bush about the orb. I believe it's capable of great good. My theory is that it can be used as a power source. I still remember when I was a kid and I pulled apart my first PC to see how it worked. I learned how to power it by combining solar power panels and a potato. "

"Okay, I already know you're smart, Doc—Chris—Doc Broad."

"That wasn't the point."

"No, I know that." Noah shook his head and said, "Come to

think of it, I don't know why I spilled everything about the orb before. I think I just needed someone to talk to. I mean, I trusted you. Well, I still trust you."

"I really appreciate that, and—"

Noah slashed his hand through the air. "No, you don't know what you're asking of me. I told you before that the orb is the only thing keeping me alive. It's the only reason the Red Chain see me as valuable. I'm not just a useless pack mule to them anymore. I'm the reason that some of them are still alive. Well, the orb is the reason."

Chris put out the butt of his cigarette. The only light left on the porch was from a couple candles. Moonlight fell on the porch steps; a dome of stars covered the entire world. He scratched his head in thought and finally said, "Just a few weeks. Can you survive for...two weeks without the orb? When was the last ambush you warned the Chain about?"

"Two weeks ago," said a deep baritone from the shadows. Chris froze in place and saw Noah do the same. A serious-faced Redford stepped out of the shadow and into the moonlight. "Tell me about this orb," he ordered.

CHAPTER 4

"Hand me the orb, Worm," ordered Redford. Noah pleaded with Doc Broad for help with his eyes, but the clean-shaven man just shook his head. With a sinking heart, Noah walked over to Redford and handed him the orb.

The Crimson Chain leader gently traced the crack in the otherwise perfect sphere with his thumb. He seemed to be concentrating but finally looked up in annoyance. "I can't hear anything." Redford frowned. "This thing is probably something from the Aelves." He spat. "Bah...magic. As useless as it is evil. Alien bastards are probably just seeding poison for idiots to pick up."

Noah felt like a million stones were suddenly dropped into his stomach. He no longer knew if he would survive the next day, not without the orb. Redford must have noticed his stress, because, in a rare show of reassurance, he gruffed, "You have a jacket. You're one of us, Worm." The man was still obviously irritated, though.

Redford sneered at the orb, and Noah thought he might throw it out into the darkness before Doc Broad stepped forward, saying, "In time, I could make your group the most powerful in the area with that orb. We could have electricity, Red."

Based on Redford's reaction, that had caught his attention. Instead of hurling the precious sphere, he pocketed the orb inside his own leather jacket. Then the Red Chain leader towered over the thin and wiry doctor. He growled, "Is that a guarantee?"

Doc Broad calmly pulled out another cigarette, making Redford wait while he lit it. Noah goggled at the man's sub-zero calm. Finally, Doc said, "There is no guarantee. But like I was telling Noah, I have had experience with alternative power sources in the past. All the broken solar panels and extra video game equipment on one side of the cabin were from my hobbies.

"I used to come out here to work. My family owned the place. It seemed like a good place to hole up after the world ended, and all my old junk was still there. Heck, most of my not-so-secret lab you saw before was just set up to break apart video game consoles for experiments. After I made this place home, after the Shift, I spent a lot of time trying to make electricity work again."

"That doesn't tell me anything," Radford growled. He took a threatening step forward, but Doc didn't move.

The smaller man said, "Give me two weeks, and I'll see what I can do. I'm no genius, but like I said, I feel certain that this is important and we can get results. Even if I was only able to use that thing to power basic, low-level electronics, you would still be the most powerful group in the entire area. With electricity, you could have radios. You could also have flashlights and other things that no one else has now. Maybe your group might even have a chance against a group of Aelves."

How did he do that, Noah wondered. *How can the Doc just look at Redford straight in the eyes without folding?*

"The Aelves, huh?" Redford's hands tightened into fists as he stared Doc down. Noah could practically see wheels spinning in the brutish man's mind. Trust didn't matter in this situation; Red just weighed the pros and cons, deciding who and what was valuable for his own survival and wealth.

After a long, uncomfortable silence, Redford finally decreed, "You have two weeks with the orb. If you don't produce electricity for us by then, you're dead. I can't have you running around sharing secrets or helping other groups, not after you know about this. As another safety measure, I will have one of my lieutenants stay here with you to keep an eye on you. This is an investment after all."

Noah mentally sighed in relief. He hadn't realized how stressed he'd been about Doc's safety until Redford had finally backed down. However, the leader of the Red Chain turned his head slowly to Noah and frowned, and in that moment, Noah recognized the future beating he'd have to endure. He also knew there wasn't any way to avoid it, not now. One of Noah's nightmares had come to pass–Redford knew about the orb and knew that Noah had been keeping secrets.

***

In the past, Noah had thought he might actually get used to the taste of blood in his mouth, or become accustomed to pain. However, every new beating Talbot had given him always brought new agony and additional ways to hit rock bottom. This time around, Redford had watched the whole time, repeating his senseless mantra, "Pain is the only discipline."

Noah must have blacked out at some point. After waking up sometime later, he overheard voices.

"What do you think has the boss in such a flurry?" one person asked. Noah recognized the voice, a high tenor. The Red Chain wasn't a talkative group, especially with Redford around, but Noah had heard snippets of conversation over the last couple months. He didn't really know many of the raiders' names, though. Other than Talbot and Redford, most of them didn't have a direct impact on his life, and it wasn't like he wanted to bond with them. Noah was like them now, but he didn't want to try to *be* like them. At least, that's what he always told himself.

A second voice, a scratched with a husky baritone answered, "No clue. Whatever it is, I've never seen him excited before. I mean, I saw him smile, and it gave me the creeps."

"I think it has to do with the Doc," said the high tenor. "I overheard Talbot and the boss talking about getting rid of him in a couple of weeks once whatever he was doing for the boss was finished."

Oh no, Noah thought. *Red is going to kill Doc once he creates electricity.*

In a ruthless way, it kind of made sense. Redford would never want knowledge spreading that he could use for himself.

Several memories passed through Noah's mind all at once, and it was hard for him to focus on anything, his brain still addled from the recent beating. Instinctively, he searched for the orb, longing for the familiar warm feeling and a respite from his aches and pains, but then remembered he no longer had it.

As his head cleared, Noah kept repeating one thing over and over in his mind—the bastards wanted to kill Doc, the only person that had treated him with any sort of respect or dignity in months. The last man who had treated him like a person before Doc, Noah had either directly or indirectly killed. He hadn't thought about Yusef for a while, but all the old guilt came rushing back in, unaffected by time.

None of The Red Chain cared about Noah as a person. None of them knew about his past, or how his family had died on their journey from the outskirts of Grand Rapids to a fortress in Indiana. They hadn't asked, and he hadn't told them the story of how it had already been too late when his remaining family and friends reached the so-called fortress.

Fear of the Aelves had brought humanity's baser instincts to the fore, turned people into animals. Of course, he would never need to explain that part to the Red Chain; they were already a perfect example of the lows some people would go to for survival.

Noah was part of that cycle now—he couldn't deny it.

These days, after the Shift, some of the only places with any remaining sense of community left were small towns, but they were becoming less common, destroyed over time by raiders, or competing factions...or the Aelves.

All of this had begun warping Noah, turning him more into someone he couldn't recognize. The Chain had given him a name. They had given a title to the spineless thing that he was becoming, Worm. But Doc, Doc Broad, had taken the last speck of humanity inside Noah and given it some room to grow. He'd helped Noah remember who he really was.

There was no escaping the fact that Noah owed Doc his continued humanity, something he had just realized was perhaps worth more than his life. If Noah kept falling deeper, becoming more Worm than himself, he might end up a true member of the Red Chain. In the past, he had wondered if other members of the Red Chain had started out like him, and now he was sure of it.

Right now, Noah didn't have any power, but he knew where he might be able to get some. He had another important, life-shaking choice to make now, but the decision was obvious. Even if he failed at claiming power for himself, or for his friend, he had to make sure Redford didn't gain any more.

The young man had made up his mind—he needed to steal the orb back.

CHAPTER 5

Noah waited silently, watching the rest of the Red Chain pack. The raiders were preparing to travel the last leg of their trip to trade with the Iron Wolves. Luckily, he'd already had months of practice at staying practically invisible. His chores were done–he had already chained up the new slaves-to-be, some of whom seemed to be amused, or satisfied that Noah looked far worse than they did. They were more valuable to the Chain now than he was. None of the raiders were asking why one of their lieutenants had been ordered to stay behind with Doc, though the tense atmosphere was thick with the unasked question.

How the heck am I going to get that orb? Noah asked himself for the hundredth time. At least everyone was distracted at the moment. Still, if he didn't steal the orb, Redford was going to kill Doc - one way or the other. The man's days were numbered—two weeks more to live. Noah hadn't wanted to believe that Redford would risk the life of the Red Chain's only medical professional on such a gambit. But the look he'd seen in the raider leader's eyes when Doc had mentioned the Aelves, had forced him to admit the truth. That glimmer in the other man's eyes had been haunting–fascination mixed with a relentless hunger for survival.

Noah quietly witnessed Redford giving another 'lecture' accompanied with a beating to another member of the Red Chain. If Noah was going to do anything he had to do it while the leader of the Red Chain was otherwise occupied. The big man moved silently, like a ninja, and always seemed to turn up where he was least expected.

The young man had achieved clarity...he had a goal. Now he knew the "what" but was still working out the "how." After his conversations with Doc, Noah couldn't tolerate being Worm anymore. He hated being Worm. Worm didn't hurt people directly but might as well.

I can use Worm to my advantage. Noah thought. *I have to.* As Worm, he was normally invisible to the others unless a lieutenant or a foreman needed something from him, but people paid even less attention to Worm after he took a beating.

Noah imagined the rest of his life playing out if he didn't go through with his convictions. Doc would die and 'Noah' with him, only Worm would remain. *He* would become a true Red Chain member, maybe even being like Redford one day, spouting nonsense about pain to justify beating on new members of his group. Noah had thought he'd hit rock bottom before, but Doc Broad's situation made him realize that he had further to go. Honestly, now was his last chance to do something, *anything* that would give him a different path.

He had no plan, only a need to take the orb. Enough thought turned into action, and his legs began carrying him forward. Noah didn't think through what he was doing, so it was almost with a bit of surprise that he suddenly found himself standing in front of Talbot. Curiously, Noah felt a weird, alien sort of confidence.

Talbot turned to him and demanded, "Do you need another beating, Worm? "

"No, sir," Noah replied, letting the words come out smooth. He'd just quickly realized that he'd spent most of his life lying to himself. Maybe now he could deceive someone else, channel it. "I was just going to ask Doc if I could borrow a book. I've been reading the astronomy book about stars. Maybe I can learn more about it while we're away from the cabin."

"Why the heck would I allow you to do that?" Talbot snarled.

That's a good question, Noah realized. He also saw the perpetual paranoia crossing Talbot's face, his unibrow curling at the center. However, in the man's eyes, Noah noticed a glimmer of disdain borne from understanding, maybe a little echo of something. Talbot had once been in a similar position as himself, a Worm, useless. Noah could use it.

"Sir," Noah responded, "You and Boss have kept me alive

since I came in, and I want to be more useful. Nobody ever needed to give me a leather jacket, and I appreciate that. You were right before about my bad attitude. I just thought that by studying the stars and learning how to navigate them, it could help me learn to be a scout, you know, let us know what our position is. Maybe it could help us navigate faster, or even find new water sources faster. I just don't want to be useless, and this is one way I can help, I think."

He said it in a way that made him sound nervous, but it didn't require much acting. Noah was improvising on the spot, something he hadn't done in years. Before the Shift, his parents had always told them him that he should be a politician one day. Apparently, he'd had a reputation as a teen for all the bullshit he could come up with.

Noah let the silence hang between them as Talbot searched his face. Finally, the goateed man growled and looked away. "Screw it," he said. "Just grab the darn thing and hurry back, or else Boss won't even have to tell me to beat the shit out of you. I'll crack you so hard you'll never get back up. You think you're useless now? Piss me off one more time…"

"Understood, sir," Noah said, surprised by the Red Chain foreman's response. Noah didn't thank the man as he walked past, realizing that would have been laying it on a little too thick. Talbot's paranoia was probably even higher than normal with the change between Doc and Redford, so he had to be even more keyed up than usual.

On the back porch, Noah found Doc smoking a cigarette as he rolled the orb in his hand. The thin man gave Noah an odd look as his babysitting Red Chain foreman stopped Worm in his tracks, standing in his way. Talbot was the number one foreman, but this man was one of the other two leaders of the Red Chain under Red. The black man standing in Noah's way was the tallest member of the Chain, his hands riddled with scars. Noah didn't know his name, just his reputation for being joyless and decisive. This would be his first time ever talking with the guy.

The man barked, "What are you doing here?" Light glinted from his freshly-shaved scalp, and his hands flexed.

"Talbot told me to get the astronomy book from the Doc, so I could learn more about the stars and help us navigate easier. He said that we need better scouts, sir. Should I get him for you?"

The Red Chain foreman glanced at the closed door behind Noah that led back to where his superior, Talbot would be. The foreman took an immediate step back, his eyes going flat with nervousness. Noah found cold pleasure in seeing the large man's reaction. "Screw that," said the foreman with a frown. "Grab it and get out of here."

Doc Broad leaned forward, no doubt curious about what Noah was doing. He had to know that the youth was not really visiting for the astronomy book. The spare, intelligent man watched Noah pick up the book next to the telescope with slow, deliberate motions. Doc bit his cigarette, probably trying to play it cool.

Noah walked over to Doc and tried to signal at him with blinks. *You're being too obvious!* he screamed mentally. *Just act normal!* Out loud he asked, "Did you really mean what you said about the stars? That they are all misaligned?" Before Doc could answer, he mouthed the words, *Give me the orb.*

Doc Broad didn't even hesitate to push the orb into his hand, which Noah then put into the center of the book as he folded it as best he could. Doc sucked hard on his cigarette and gazed into the night sky like something was really interesting up there. It took all Noah could do not to groan. Doc was a great guy, and super smart, but he was a really crappy actor. He kept holding his breath too and probably didn't release the smoke in his lungs until he couldn't hold it anymore.

When Noah came out on the other side of the cabin, Talbot glared, probably checking for the astronomy book. Noah was terrified of being caught, but he didn't fight it. He let the fear take over, putting on a show for the first foreman of the Red Chain. The young man kept his eyes glued to the ground as he passed by Talbot. Walking past the man was one of the most nerve-wracking few minutes of his life. He then passed by several members of the Red Chain and even Redford himself, who was still lecturing some of the raiders on the nature of pain again.

It wasn't until Noah finally got past the perimeter that the Red Chain controlled that his situation became truly real to him. He was alone now—completely alone. He quickly palmed the orb from inside the astronomy book and slipped it into his pocket, riding the familiar wave of static that rippled through his body. He didn't have time to enjoy the rush of sounds that came with the feeling, the clarity of the world singing in his ears. No, now was his chance. With no second thoughts, orb in hand, Noah broke for the deep forest.

He knew it wouldn't take long for the Red Chain to realize he had stolen the orb. Noah sprinted through the woods, certain he had saved Doc's life. All the blame would be on Noah. After the Shift, his entire life had just been a movie he watched while stuck in his own head. He had been watching through that lens, willing to allow the world to direct him, like he watched himself through Doc's telescope. But now he was thinking about someone else, and his body just seemed to keep acting on its own.

The fear was still there, lingering like a foul cloud overhead, but Noah had confronted it, *used* it. He knew he was going to die, but he couldn't stand living life as Worm anymore. No more letting others use fear as a weapon. Nothing could protect him from the realities of the world post-Shift, but if he couldn't control how he died, at least he could control how he lived. *If you're going to die*, he confirmed to himself, *you might as well die as Noah.*

The desperate youth held the purple orb like it was the only thing keeping him alive—in a way, it was.

On a practical level, the orb helped him navigate the forest as he ran as fast as he could with his weak, malnourished legs. He headed towards areas where sound traveled freely, where his frail body wouldn't have to fight to push through underbrush. He had learned to stay away from pockets of dampened sound, an indicator of areas heavy with vegetation or ditches.

Even with the help of the orb, his hands and face got scraped bloody by twigs and bushes as he barreled through the forest. Although his body was weak, Noah's grip on the orb was steel-like. Over the past few months, he'd wondered why he had been able to heal faster the more he used the orb. He'd also marveled at how the orb responded to the tuneless song in his head, the music with no name. He hadn't heard music in years, but he could *feel* it through the orb, singing the rhythms back to him.

The orb's response to songs in his head had been one of the only things keeping him sane the last few months in the Red Chain. It had reminded him of his old life, one with music. Fear of being caught mixed with the elation of successfully stealing the orb, making his heart flutter. Noah savagely slapped himself–he needed to focus on his escape. "What should I do?" he breathlessly muttered to himself. "Ah, yes!" Then he focused on the tuneless song in his head, drowning out the overwhelming terror that had crippled him his entire life after the Shift.

The purple orb pulsed in his hand and then through his entire body, touching every cell with the reverberation of the song in his head. Energy rippled through him like a small town hit by a tsunami. Suddenly, Noah realized that his breath was becoming more even, less ragged. *No way*, he thought. His eyes widened in shock, but his pace didn't flag, in fact, he was able to speed up a little. This was really happening; the orb was healing him and giving him energy even while he ran.

Even as he fled through the forest, he couldn't help but experiment. The more space he gave his mind for doubts or fear, the less power the orb gave him. The more he thought about the nameless song, the better he felt. *The song*, Noah realized. It wasn't his focus on the orb that had made the object help him more before. It had been the song. He didn't understand any of it, but he needed to use every advantage now to survive. He wanted to live, and eventually die as Noah. Hopefully, the dying part wouldn't come any time soon.

In addition to helping Noah find his way through the forest, the mysterious sphere also fed him energy, letting him maintain a breakneck pace. The young man had an odd sensation that the orb could do much more, but this was all he could manage at the moment. Angry shouts from the Red Chain echoed behind him in the forest, audible to his enhanced hearing. He couldn't tell exactly how far they were because the sounds were so distant now.

Despite the energy the orb was giving him, Noah was resigned that he wouldn't be able to outrun the Red Chain forever. If the Red Chain didn't find him, some equally bad, or worse, group would. His body had become too weak after the Shift–heck, his body had been weak *before* the Shift. He could feel his legs beginning to tighten up despite the orb's aid.

In high school, Noah had fantasized about working out and lifting weights with all the jocks on the football team. *Tomorrow,* he had told himself. *Tomorrow, I'll start exercising.* Instead, Noah had focused on mathematics, gaming, and chess club - easy escapes for him. But even in chess club, he had been an outsider. He hadn't even been that good at chess. Instead, he'd just liked that including himself, only four people were in the club. Three other people were manageable. Three chess nerds couldn't hurt him.

The Shift hadn't changed Noah so much as it had revealed how frightened he was of other people. But more recently, he had feared something even more...himself. He hated how his weakness had allowed others to use him. He'd hated how weakness had prevented him from living.

The truth was that Noah had always regretted not doing sports in high school, the Shift had just forced him to admit it. He had never *pushed* himself. His spirit was willing now and he felt a certain sense of joy in having faced his fear, but his body was weak. Noah knew he was close to the end. If he faltered, the Chain would get him. That would be bad.

Noah wasn't so much afraid of the rank-and-file members of the Red Chain, or the foremen, not even Talbot. They were just like Noah had been as Worm, slaves to their own fears, focused on base survival. No, just like everyone else in the Red Chain, Noah was truly afraid of Redford. The man with the scarred upper lip seemed to find joy in giving pain and lecturing on it, *teaching* suffering. Noah had watched Redford hunting potential slaves countless times while the man had had a sick smile plastered across his face, twisting his features.

Redford had been a hunter before the Shift and was skilled at tracking. Unlike the other members of the Chain who all more or less carried crossbows, Red always used a sleek compound bow. Noah kept half expecting one of the man's deadly arrows to go zipping by. No matter how he focused on his mental song, some of the fear kept nagging at the corner of his mind. Every step he took, every branch he broke during his flight would tell Redford where he was going. The man was relentless.

Noah wasn't sure what to do, or if escape long-term would even be possible. Sobering reality had come crashing down on him. Thinking about it wasn't helping, so he just kept repeating the special song in this head and expanding his mind, accepting to the sounds of the forest. He heard everything; the night wind making leaves scratch against each other, the neighing of the raiders' horses behind him as they pursued, even the Red Chain members warning each other of traps in the area that they'd set. Between all those noises were pockets of flat sound, open areas. He wove through the forest, rushing through open areas ahead, sticking to clearings.

Suddenly, he blinked and thought, *Wait, what? Traps?* He

mentally focused on some of the raiders' shouted warning and stopped running. His knees shook from his non-stop sprinting, legs shaking in exhaustion. The orb could give him energy and heal him somewhat, but it could only do so much. Noah's weak body was definitely holding him back.

The Red Chain members behind him mentioned traps again, but they were still too far for Noah to really make out what they were saying. *What kind of traps do they have?* Now he wondered if he might land in a bear trap or something. The orb would not be able to warn him of traps like that, but—

Noah expanded his mind as much as he could and listened for the *absence* of sound, or where sound was dampened. Then he began running again, flying past trees, somehow hearing the dead wood inside some of their trunks. *Bigger silence*, Noah thought. *I need more dampened sound. There has to be one.* Even with the energy of the orb, Noah found himself getting more and more exhausted. His thin legs wouldn't take him very far.

His half-cocked plan was stupid, terrible, and would probably get him killed, but he didn't have any other choice. He needed to find it, needed to find that absence of sound. *There,* Noah thought, his breath giving out. Then he plummeted into a hole.

***

Chris stared at the night sky illuminated by stars, stars that were wrong. Even without his astronomy book, he could see the misalignments, especially with his telescope. He really hadn't known much about stars before the Shift, but he had learned a lot.

When Noah had brought him the purple orb and explained what it did, it had renewed a sense of vigor, of purpose inside Christopher. But now, not only was the orb gone, Noah had fled too.

It had been three days since the boy had escaped. Redford had doggedly given chase. The leader of the Red Chain had come back several times unannounced, sometimes dragging a younger member of his group he'd disciplined for Chris to heal. Red had still never hurt Chris—he was the only person with medical training who could clean up potential slaves for sale to the Iron Wolves. Chris had never lied to himself; he knew the slavers left him unmolested out of convenience. Red could probably find another medically trained person, but trust didn't come freely. The man didn't understand Chris at all, but he seemed to accept that his motivations were altruistic. Of course, all of this had ended once the Red Chain leader had found out about the orb. Any object that could give him an edge against other raiders, much less the Aelves, would be precious indeed. Chris had seen the fear flash in the leader of the Chain's eyes. There probably wasn't a single man in the world who wasn't afraid of Aelves...unless they were really stupid.

But now, it seemed that Redford had given up the chase, at least he hadn't, nor any other member of the Red Chain, been back in almost a day. Chris was cautiously hopeful that the boy had lived, but he was realistically probably dead somewhere out in the woods, his body in rigor mortis.

It's funny, Chris thought. *I'm more sad about Noah's death than losing what was probably a power source for all of humanity.* With the orb, Chris could have saved thousands, maybe millions, but he had always been more focused on the life in front of him than hypotheticals. To this day, he still wasn't sure if that was a character weakness or a strength.

No, the reality was far grimmer. Realistically, even if Chris had brought back electricity, it would have just gone straight into Redford's hands. He would have just delivered power to another madman in this mad world.

Chris heard footsteps behind him on the back porch. Without turning around, he huffed a puff of smoke, anger scratching his voice to a growl. "I haven't seen the boy at all. Come back to taunt me again, Redford?"

"No," spoke a younger, tired voice. "I came to return a book."

The cigarette fell from Chris' mouth, and he turned. The youth stood with hollow cheeks, so dehydrated his skin looked like parchment. His leather jacket had been torn almost past the point of recognition. The young man's eyes were dark with fatigue, and his hands shook like a leaf in a storm. *Noah,* Chris thought, trying to fight back the tears in his eyes.

The healer inside Chris instantly diagnosed the boy. *He's starting to show signs of vitamin C deficiency. He probably hasn't eaten since his escape. Needs fluids badly, maybe a bag of saline—wish I had the equipment for it. Minor and major abrasions. Lack of sleep. He's in bad shape.*

After the shock passed, Chris pulled out another cigarette and lit it. Despite his best effort, tears fell down his cheeks and his mouth split into a grin. "What the heck am I going to do with you?"

CHAPTER 6

Noah opened the sliding door of the hidden cubby inside Doc's lab, basically where he lived now. He looked back and sighed, deciding to straighten up his sleeping area later. It could wait; now was time to find his de facto landlord and protector.

As he closed the door to his living space, hiding it again, he glanced around and shook his head in amusement. The lab itself was just a small room through a secret door from the makeshift medical bay in the cabin. The lab had been where Doc Broad had spent time breaking apart old gaming consoles and electronics, trying to figure out how the Shift had really affected electricity. Doc Broad's grandfather had built the room, but then apparently had shown it to the entire world.

"Grandpa was incredibly paranoid," Doc had reminisced fondly to Noah, about a month after the younger man had started living at the cabin. "Everyone in the family thought he was crazy because most all of them already knew about the room. What's the point of a secret room if you don't keep the room secret? So, Grandpa kind of built the cubby as a last 'eff you' to them. I guess he got the last laugh. He figured that if people found the first hidden room, they wouldn't think to look for another hidden compartment on top of that! A secret within a secret! Honestly, it's worked for me. But I never thought I'd need to actually use it. Then you came along…"

The secret lab seemed destined to never be a secret. Not long after the Shift, when the Red Chain had first visited Chris Broad's cabin, Redford had somehow noticed the lab on the first day. Despite the threat of violence during the entire meeting, the then-gang leader, now raider leader hadn't touched the lab at all. He had even encouraged Doc to keep experimenting with electronics. However, Doc Broad had quickly given up on it. With nothing to show for his time but failure after failure and no glimmers of hope, he'd started to just use the lab for storage. But then Noah had come along, and with the orb, the clever man had been able to puzzle out a few more mysteries.

"For example, electricity isn't just gone," Doc had once explained to Noah after his discovery. "It is *inaccessible*. It's difficult to explain in layman's terms unless you're obsessed with the physics of how electricity actually works like I am."

Noah gave him a look to challenge that. It wasn't like he was an idiot. He knew a little—

"Do you know anything about wave functions?" Doc countered with a sly look before Noah could say anything. "Like, do you know what a galvanometer is?"

"Erm, no."

"Don't worry; most people wouldn't. As for how the electricity is behaving, I barely understand it myself," Doc conceded.

Sometime after that, Doc had confided some of his regrets from before the Shift. Sometimes the clean-shaven man fantasized about having pursued his passion in physics and energy in college instead of just doing what every other Broad in his family had done. He had just sort of bowed to tradition. Noah had related to the story on some level, and he'd felt bad for the other man, but also somewhat comforted. If even a man as smart as Christopher Broad could have regrets, maybe anyone could. Doc really was a genius, after all.

The energetic, smoking man had explained that by the age of eight, he'd been able to list every bone and muscle in the human body, along with their general function. At nine, his parents had taught him all of the most important medical stitches. In the beginning, his study had just been a fun competition between him and his siblings. Then after a few years of always winning, he'd grown bored, and had also realized that his parents had already picked his path in life out for him. He was supposed to be another doctor, of course.

Doc's ability had become a curse after the Shift. His

compulsion to help everyone had been borne in part because he had the skills to do so. He could never back down from helping others, even at the risk to his own life. Retreating to his family's cabin to survive the apocalypse had been as much about living remotely as it was for safety.

And today, months after showing up to the cabin and being allowed to live there, Noah finally located Doc and asked, "Any update today?" The question was probably getting old, but Noah still couldn't help asking every day. Out of habit, he used the cracked purple orb in his hand to expand his hearing, making sure no one was around except for the two of them. *So far it's safe*, he thought. *If anyone comes by, I'll just go back into the cubby.* Noah felt extremely jumpy these days. Ever since Redford had snuck up on him months before, he didn't take safety or privacy for granted and usually searched for sounds of others at least once per hour.

Doc shook his head as he walked past a pile of empty cigarette cartons. "I'm close," he answered. "Well, I—never mind, I don't want to show you anything until it's concrete. It's also not enough that only I understand what I'm doing. I need to make sure that if something happens to me, you could hand someone else my findings and they'd be able to understand my research.

That made sense to Noah, and he slowly nodded. The two of them walked to the back porch as Noah cradled the orb in his hand. They had come close to being caught a few times by members of the Chain that Redford had sent back to spy on Doc.

Chris Broad remained valuable enough that Red wouldn't kill him for no reason, not with the orb being "missing." Doc could still treat slaves. All that would change if the Chain ever discovered Noah there, though. So far, every time other people had come around, Noah had escaped into his hidden cubby. Luckily, the remote cabin didn't get many visitors.

Redford would never accept that Noah was dead - a fact that had been confirmed by Doc. The last time he'd spoken to the Red Chain leader, the man had stated as a fact that he'd get the orb back. Then he'd threatened Doc, telling him he'd better not move from the cabin or try to escape. Red still intended to bring him the orb for experiments after he managed to recover it. Noah shook his head at the memory of Doc's story. Then thinking about Red also reminded him of how he'd eluded the Chain.

The evening he'd finally made it back to the cabin, sure that he had eluded the Chain, he'd felt like death walking. Apparently, he'd looked like it too, because Doc's face had gotten white as a sheet when they'd met. Then the crying man had asked him how he'd survived.

Noah had asked for water first, then explained how he'd heard the Chain warning each other about traps in the woods. There hadn't been any real purpose for the traps, not made around the cabin, so Noah had reasoned the raiders had been practicing wilderness skills. They might have been hedging their bets to create early warning against ambushes, too. Most folks visiting

Doc took the trail, and the slight man had never mentioned anyone dying in the woods, so he probably hadn't known the surrounding forest had been trapped either.

The night of the escape, after Noah had heard about the traps, he'd started looking for a hole. Some crazy part of Noah's mind had told him that a trap might be one of the last places Redford would check for him...if the Chain even remembered where they'd placed them all in the first place. To this day, Noah couldn't tell if the thought had been his own, or if the orb had helped. At the time, he hadn't had any other plans and had jumped into a hole on purpose. Luckily, the sharpened stakes at the bottom had bent and rotted over time, and his boots had crushed one that he'd landed on. Then he'd covered the whole thing with dirt and sticks. The slight drizzle that had started soon after had made him huddle in the muddy hole, miserable, but he'd been glad the weather would help cover his tracks.

When he'd heard about Noah's escape, Doc had frowned and said, "That wasn't the brightest idea. How did you know it would work?"

"I didn't, but it was the only plan I had." Noah shrugged.

Doc Broad had nodded. "Sometimes, the most desperate plans seem to attract the most luck or misfortune." At the time, Noah could only agree with that and ask for more water.

Back in the present, the young man took his customary place leaning against the railing of the cabin porch. Since Doc wasn't ready to tell him about his research with the orb yet, he decided to revisit a well-worn subject between the two. He pointed up and asked, "Where is Ursa Major? I mean, I know where it's supposed to be, but it's impossible to see the third star." He squinted, his tongue between his teeth before pointing at a specific spot in the sky. "Right there. It's a little off from its normal location."

Doc pulled out a cigarette and offered it to Noah. The young man declined with a hand gesture, and the wiry older man lit his 'cancer stick,' as he affectionately called them. "You know, space is a lonely place. If you look at the stars, the sky seems bright. But if you pay attention to the space *between* the stars and realize how many light years there are of nothing out there, it can make you feel tiny, like you don't matter."

A moment of silence stretched between them as Noah absorbed the words and stared into the heavens. When he'd been younger, people had said he wasn't a good listener, but Doc had a way of speaking that drew him in. The wiry man would probably be a great teacher.

Finally, Doc continued his train of thought. "By tracing the invisible paths between the stars, we can make some sense of the universe. Constellations, imaginary connections. To many, especially now, those connections are the things that matter. In our world after the Shift, after electricity and gunpowder and every form of advanced technology failed, we lost everything that kept us together. Right now, we all might feel like a single star alone in our own quiet galaxy. The first step of understanding the importance of communication is appreciating the invisible connections between us, what holds our universes together."

Noah tried to ignore the philosophy in Doc's reply, but some of it was sticking. He had gotten used to Doc's musings but never really seemed to respond to them the way Doc wanted him to. Since the smoking man hadn't answered his question about Ursa Major, Noah figured he might be missing something, had not asked the right question, or would receive a longer, but more thorough answer later. He was fairly used to it now. Doc was just like that. Noah pursed his lips, thinking about where the conversation might be heading, and asked, "What do you think caused the Shift?"

Even as the question left his mouth, he stiffened. Probably every surviving person on Earth had uttered those words at some point. After the first year, people seemed to care less, though. Survivors had stopped speculating. People had become more concerned with either holding onto what was theirs or taking resources from others. Surviving the Shift had become drastically more important than figuring out why it had happened.

Doc inhaled deeply and blew out a large cloud of smoke. "The Aelves," he said with a tone of complete certainty.

Noah narrowed his eyes. He had heard of the elves constantly after the Shift, or at least within the last year. Even Redford and the Red Chain threw the word around like the boogie-man or the chupacabra.

It wasn't like Noah didn't understand the fear. He'd seen first-hand what the bastards were capable of. From a distance, he'd witnessed the smoking ruins of a small town, small fires still burning. Headless bodies had been stacked like cordwood.

Noah shuddered. "I've never actually seen them. Do you know about the elves? I still don't understand why fantasy people are supposedly attacking us."

Doc matched his gaze with a grave look. "Not e-l-v-e-s, A-e-l-v-e-s. That's what we're calling them at least; it might even be what they call themselves. After the Shift, there was a lack of communication, well, everywhere. Ironically enough, the most connected people now are the raider factions because they're the most mobile. It all kind of reminds me of how the post office used to deliver messages by horse. I guess one advantage of treating anyone that comes by my cabin is a decent access to word of mouth. Usually, news is hard to come by.

"As you know, since the madness after the first month or two of the Shift, everybody had been focused on protecting themselves and building new communities. At first, this made sense, but it also kind of presents better targets, like for the raider factions."

Noah made a face. "What does this have to do with the Aelves? From what I've been able to pick up, they weren't even really around during the Shift." This conversation didn't seem like one of Doc's philosophical musings. He wasn't sure what Doc would say. Noah still remembered the fear in Redford's voice when Doc had mentioned the Aelves months earlier.

Doc Broad shook his head. "I've actually heard reports of their activity from the beginning. The average person seemed to be aware of them about six months after the Shift, but I believe they were here since day one. The evidence is damning. I mean, what better way to prey on humans than wiping out our technology and letting us stew in madness for a couple years? We've done a pretty good job of making ourselves weak enough to attack." Doc tapped some ash and continued, "I'm fairly sure this is an invasion, and the main force of the Aelves are coming eventually."

"But what are they?" demanded Noah. He was surprised by the heat in his own voice, but the subject made the hair on the back of his neck rise. Things had gotten bad, really bad after the Shift, but the destroyed village had haunted him for some time now. People could be truly terrible to each other, but human violence was rarely that...organized.

The wiry man said, "From what I've gathered, they look mostly like us, but different in a way that is striking. They definitely aren't like pop culture elves. I have a number of what I believe to be legit reports that they've raided human fortresses. Only a few Aelves come at a time, but that's all that are needed— their power is overwhelming. Survivors are always absolutely terrified. Aelves are worse than raiders who just go after resources, even worse than slavers. See, they don't kill everyone. Instead, they eliminate and dismember a number of humans and kidnap the rest, then disappear to God knows where." Doc paused for a couple seconds and amended, "Well, I guess that makes them exactly like raiders and slavers except for the rumors that they eat their captives. Anyway, the craziest thing I've heard about them is that they use magic."

For what seemed like the first time in two years, Noah let out a belly laugh. "That doesn't make any sense," he said. But even as he spoke, he realized it actually did. He was literally holding proof of some form of magic in his hand. The orb had clearly cracked and was probably damaged, but it had given him strange abilities and new insights.

As difficult as it was for Noah to accept, the more he thought about it, the more the possibility sunk in. The whole world had gone upside down after the Shift. Electricity, gunpowder, engines, none of it worked anymore. Even people trying to harness solar or nuclear power had no luck. And now there were rumors of creatures kidnapping and eating people? All of it had to be connected. It was the *only* thing that made sense. *Magic.*

When Noah nodded, Doc Broad gave him an approving look. "I felt the same way at first," he said. "Although I had to work out all this stuff on my own. It just didn't make sense. Have you ever wondered why a flashlight won't work, but lightning still happens during storms and seems unaffected?" Doc took another puff on his cigarette and shook his head.

The orb pulsed heavily without warning in Noah's hand, something it never done before unless he hummed the mysterious tune in his head. Now it seemed to be reacting to Doc Broad's words. Any doubts Noah might have had before were immediately banished. He decided to keep the orb's reaction to himself. Instead, Noah asked, "What kind of magic do they have?"

"Elemental—foundation of creation. Fire. Ice. Stuff that you'd see in the old RPG games and fantasy movies. I've heard that not all the Aelves use it, but this kind of magic is taking out entire towns and fortresses. Magical WMDs, or at least artillery—it's heavy stuff. So anyway, they're making a b-line from the West Coast to the East Coast, but it's confusing. Why aren't they launching a full-scale war? If the Aelves are the ones responsible for taking out humanity's technology with the Shift, then why aren't they attacking the entire Earth at the same time? If they have this magic, then they could wipe us all out at once. I think we are seeing a scout force, and the main force is still coming. Maybe they are going to snuff us, but it'll just take time."

"That is…kind of terrifying."

"As an understatement." Doc closed his eyes tightly before meeting Noah's eyes again. "People can go nuts talking about this stuff. The unknown is scary, but the evidence just keeps stacking up. These Aelves are moving, just small groups right now, but driving survivors before them, and apparently destroying towns. And that's not the worst of it—I've heard that they're no longer just kidnapping people, or attacking little towns. There have been fortresses and cities—entire cities—taken down by just one or two dozen Aelves."

"What? How?" Noah asked, aghast.

Chris crushed his cigarette under a heel and stared at the night sky. He said, "If you think about it. We're nothing without our technology. Even in the fortresses, it's hard to keep people in line or informed. Without warnings about the Aelves' attacks, it's hard to prepare for that kind of thing, especially if nobody believes they even exist, to begin with. But on top of that, like I told you before, they have magic. They're also reported to be stronger, faster, and tougher than us.

The older man paused, cocking his head while he re-buttoned the top of his flannel shirt that always came undone. The older man tried to act nonchalant, but his tone changed slightly, and he didn't look directly at Noah. "Actually, now that I think about it, remember that place I mentioned before?"

The young man had caught the gleam in Doc's eye—the smoker was a horrible actor. "What do you mean?" he lied. He knew exactly what the other man meant. Doc had teased Noah before about his curiosity regarding Hammerfist after Doc had brought it up in the first place.

They'd discussed Camp Hammerfist several times over the last few months. Doc had pieced together rumors into an inspiring, almost unbelievable story. Camp Hammerfist was reportedly one of the only fortresses that had survived pretty much everything thrown at it, remaining unscathed. Ever since Noah had asked a few very normal, very innocent questions about what a certain woman might look like, Doc had never let it go. For such a brilliant man, he could be really irritating about this subject.

Chris Broad raised an eyebrow at Noah and gave him a wolfish smile. "You know, Hammerfist! The place with the beautiful leader, Zelda—the rumored warrior beauty on the other side of the God forsaken country. If I recall, you were very curious about Zelda, even asking if we had pictures of her, right? Come on, Noah; you remember Hammerfist! There's no shame, we both know what kind of girls you're into now." Doc grinned so hard, his cheeks must have hurt.

Noah looked away in irritation. He hadn't thought about any girls since Krystal Conolly, his high school crush…well, mostly. Besides, he was too busy these days just surviving, and maybe even trying to save the entire Human race to worry about silly stuff like dating.

Doc seemed to catch his mood because he sobered and said, "Hammerfist is rumored to be one of the only places to ever survive an attack by Aelves. I actually just got this information fairly recently in a letter. I don't have any details, and it's probably not true, but I thought it was interesting."

"And you never mentioned this before? Why is—" Suddenly the orb pulsed again in Noah's hand, elevating his hearing on its own. The sounds in the area increased in his mind, and he heard something out of place, a ragged breath and someone dragging their leg. Noah held up a hand and gave Doc an alert look. The wiry man immediately nodded and stood, preparing for a visitor. Meanwhile, Noah quietly skulked to the not-so-hidden lab and hid in his secret cubby, latching it behind him. He held the purple orb to his chest and listened to the person approaching the cabin.

***

From his hiding place, Noah listened to the stranger's arrival. Being the professional he was, Doc Broad hadn't acted any differently than usual and diagnosed the visitor the same as he would anyone else. He didn't even ask the man why he was alone. Flying solo was a dangerous risk in the post-Shift world. *Is he a member of the Red Chain?* Noah wondered. Some part of him worried, as usual, that the newcomer could be a test from Redford. Then he heard Doc Broad's diagnosis that the guy had really hurt his ankle, and felt a bit silly. He continued to listen in.

"You're all set, James," Doc said from two rooms away. Noah wasn't sure whether James was a member of the Red Chain. Learning each other's first names was never a priority for the raiders, or at least hadn't been for Worm. Doc Broad obviously felt differently—about everyone.

In the past, Noah had asked Doc why he fixed anybody that came by, never even asked where anyone come from. More pointedly, he'd asked why he was helping the Red Chain. Chris

Broad had responded that he must help anybody he could, regardless of the kind of person they were. He didn't always want to, but he felt obligated. The man felt he had the skills for it, so he had no excuses for *not* helping people. The down-to-earth man had seemed melancholy about the subject but had been perking up over time.

Noah knew where part of Doc's new excitement came from. With the orb and his experimentations with it, he felt he could provide a *different* kind of help for humanity. He could give electricity back to everyone again. Of course, this meant it could definitely never fall into Redford's hands. Doc had bluntly told Noah that he might just hand over a copy of all his research to the youth once he was done, so it had more chance of reaching the right people.

If such a thing happened, the brilliant man wanted Noah to travel to Smalltown, one of the three safe fortresses in Ohio around the Cleveland area. Noah had already been heading there before he'd been captured by the Red Chain. "From the sounds of it," Doc Broad had once explained to Noah, "the three major fortresses in the Cleveland area are led by three people who go by the names Ruby, Blue, and Yellow. They must know each other— I've heard the three fortresses are constantly trading and even support each other against raider attacks. The Cleveland area is one of the last safe places in America."

As Noah sat in the hidden cupboard, he half-listened to Doc

talk to the new patient. At first, he'd actually been paying attention, but nobody was saying anything particularly interesting, and the young man felt antsy while thinking about the last strongholds left in the US.

Not many people were left anymore. So many people had died the last two years… He hadn't realized he'd started crying until a single tear fell to his stained blue jeans. Some of the memories he had now…he had nightmares almost every night. Noah rubbed his face and settled his emotions, studying his clothing as he did so. Doc cleaned their belongings pretty often, but the last few months had not been kind to anything Noah owned or had acquired. These days, the survivors just made do with what they could. Sure, there were plenty of clothes in the cities, but supply runs to those predator-infested areas were practically suicide these days.

Finally, he heard the stranger leave. James, or whoever he was, had left the area in a different direction than he'd arrived. This was good. If he had left in the same direction he'd arrived, that would have been cause for concern, signifying a home base or a separate group. The lanky young man sighed in relief and stepped out of the hidden cubby to wait for his host in the lab. When the slim, clean-shaven man returned, Noah said, "That could have been a trap."

"I know," said Doc. "But anyone who comes here has my help. You know this. Besides, without the help of some of my visitors with food and water and such, we might have a problem with basic survival."

Noah looked away and kept his disagreement silent. He had voiced his concerns about Doc Broad's treatment policy several times already. Some of the people that came to the cabin were shifty, even scarier than the Red Chain. One day, one of them might snap and kill their wilderness doctor.

Silence rang for a few seconds. Noah fidgeted with the orb in his hand, and Doc Broad sighed. He said, "I really was going to wait to show this to you, but I guess the final stage doesn't truly need to be done yet." Noah turned back with a questioning look. Doc stretched his hand out, wordlessly asking for the orb. After a slight hesitation, the young man handed it over. Giving up the precious object was hard to do, but he really did trust Doc with his life. The older man was responsible for both of their lives every day, actually.

Noah followed Doc around the makeshift lab. The center of the room didn't look special, but underneath several piles of old, salvaged video game consoles, Doc had hidden a contraption he'd built for the orb. Noah recognized it, surprised as usual by how simple it looked. The whole thing was small enough to hold in his hands.

Doc Broad examined the sphere and chuckled. "You know, even after all this time, I can't use this thing at all. I don't understand it now, but maybe we will in time." Then the man put the orb inside the cradle he'd made for it, part of a modified mini generator. The blocky gizmo was wired to an old MP3 player, which was, in turn, hooked up to a speaker. Doc Broad flipped on a switch, and the light of the MP3 player flared, static echoing softly through the speaker.

Noah sucked in a breath, and he took a step back. After two years, the sound of static was alien, equal parts joyful and terrifying. "Holy shit," he whispered. "You just brought back electricity. Like, is this even real?"

Chris must have been trying to play it cool, because his poker face broke into a huge grin. "I'll admit that when I first discovered this, you were sleeping, and I had to sit down for a while. One of my first thoughts after that was that I wanted to make hardcopy schematics and send you to Smalltown with the orb. You should be okay these days, at least if you're careful. The orb can help you avoid a bunch of nasty stuff out there. I haven't had a chance to even get very far with the schematics so far, though. Normal physics and electrical understanding don't work with the orb. I figured all of this stuff out pretty much by accident and a lot of trial and error."

"Wow, Doc," Noah breathed. He kind of wanted to say something snarky, but the awe of the moment was just too great. This must have been how the first humans to discover fire had felt!

Doc Broad's words tumbled out as he explained, "With this, we'll be able to make communication relays between towns, and eventually, even other states! Of course, we'd have to use the orb to power batteries and generators for other towns. Well, at least I think that batteries charged by the orb will stay charged. It doesn't make a lot of sense, none of this does, but I'm figuring it out. That said, I can't supply an entire town separately, but we'll find a way. This is just the first step. There are other people who are more qualified than me to do this, but I knew that I would be able to figure something out with that orb if I had the time to play with it."

"Do the MP3 player and speaker work?" Noah asked.

"You bet," the thin man said, smiling. "In fact, I have one of my favorite songs from a video game queued up. It's only an instrumental. I—To be honest, I've been dreaming of this moment ever since the Shift. This may be my favorite song of all time—the song playing during the first time I ever cried from a video game. I wanted this to be the first thing I heard if I could ever make electronics work again. Since it's only an instrumental, there are no words. I feel kind of awkward, but…maybe I should sing it?

"Yeah, that's fine, Doc," Noah said, his voice full of wonder. The young man stared at the speaker like he expected it to do a magic trick. Maybe it would.

"I have a really bad voice."

"It's fine, Doc, just do whatever." Noah waved a hand. "This is all amazing!"

"Okay, uh, the song was originally by Hikaru Utada, um—"

The older man scratched his head and shifted from foot to foot.

"Seriously, Doc, just play it."

"Okay, here we go!" Doc Broad shrugged and hit a button. Almost immediately, the song began playing, an acoustic guitar and techno background mixing together seamlessly. The lab swelled with the melody from the lonely little speaker, played at low volume. Doc nodded along, his eyes noticeably getting wet.

Meanwhile, Noah's knees buckled. The music wasn't anything like the aimless notes he mentally hummed when connecting with the orb. This song had structure, *purpose*, unlike his own life. The music pulled at him with longing and hope.

And then, Doc Broad sang. His voice was sharp and scratchy. He really wasn't a talented singer, but the words brought tears to Noah's eyes. Something in him broke, he felt the cracks in his spirit widen, and the song filled them with light. The orb in his hand pulsed with the music.

The thin man with the smoker's voice sang of what lies beyond the morning, of warnings, the future not scaring him, and nothing being the same anymore. Those words landed in Noah's heart like a seed dug deep into the Earth. They would stay with him forever.

CHAPTER 7

Kahlek watched Moore of the Silver Clouds single-handedly destroy a group of nearly fifty humans with her magic. Fresh blood sprayed her pallid Unaleshi skin, a fine mist dusting her white hair braided in the warrior style–long and tight on the sides. Some of the humans screamed, and a few kept talking until Moore killed them, snuffing them out.

If Kahlek's translation had been correct, this group of humans had issued a challenge before eventually cowering, and had called their human tribe the Red Metal Rope. Kahlek's own knowledge of the primitive human language was lacking, not yet at the same level that his mage-master's had been. But Twenek, his old mentor, was now dead, and Kahlek had no one else to learn from.

Twenek, the greatest scholar of the Blue Mountain tribe, had been wise enough to learn the most prominent languages and cultures of the humans before the Unaleshi had begun their mission. Before his people had sent the energy suppressors ahead of their ship, Twenek had been deep in study. Luckily, Kahlek had been taught his master's techniques to absorb new languages and information quickly. Even without a goddess orb, Kahlek had been an outstanding student among the scholars of the Blue Mountains.

The young Unaleshi watched in sick fascination as the humans died one by one by Moore's gravity magic. Kahlek stood with the Silver Cloud warriors in Moore's command, his differing uniform and hairstyle setting him apart from his cousins. With a quick glance, he noted that some of the other Unaleshi shared his reaction to the carnage, the rest looking bored with various degrees of sincerity. Moore herself was focused, intent. The female mage crushed some of the human's legs as if they'd been pressed under immeasurable weight. Other humans were flipped screaming, high into the air, landing half a *noq* away. *No, mile*, Kahlek corrected himself, reminded of his master's lessons. *The closest human equivalent to noqs are miles.* Remaining members of this human tribe were ripped apart with surgical precision. This group had been armed, but it hadn't helped them.

Moore had been indulging lately, listening to the humans scream as she slowly ripped their skin away from muscle and sinew. The way she dissected the humans and floated their organs in the air, suspended in neat little rows for the survivors to see, gave Kahlek an unwanted insight into the human anatomy. Moore's recent obsession was distasteful. Kahlek understood her motivation, but it made him impatient. He deeply wished he could put a stop to her...dalliances, but Moore still did her duty. Human brains and hearts were removed from both living and dead victims, and delivered to Moore's assistant to store for transport back to the ship. Part of Kahlek's irritation was how differently they viewed the humans. To her, they were the enemy, but he saw them as sustenance, nothing more.

Moore's pride and her hatred for the humans were on full display as she slowly picked them apart. She could have used her gravity magic to destroy them all at once, but she took her time, made it personal. The opportunity was used to experiment, discover new ways to apply her magic to the human bodies. Kahlek found her efforts wasteful and inefficient.

Their differences could be traced back to their training. Moore was of the Silver Clouds, a tribe of proud warriors. Kahlek himself had learned the ways of the Blue Mountains, scholars and keepers of the Old Way. Unfortunately, his tribe was now the weakest. He should be pursuing his mission alone, or perhaps with a trusted ally or two, but instead, he had to endure the zeal of the Silver Clouds.

Kahlek's mission was simple, but important—he had to reclaim his master's orb for his own tribe. The young Unaleshi frowned and thought, *We need to hold what little power we have left or else the Silver Clouds will truly take control.* When his master, Twenek, had gone missing, Kahlek had been the first to volunteer to reclaim the orb. The importance of the task had been immediately obvious.

Since he had still only been an apprentice scholar, the Silver Clouds had demanded that a number of their own mage-warriors accompany him. The result was...this. His tribe's weakness had resulted in traveling with his cousins, who proceeded to insist on destroying population after population of humans instead of focusing on their mission. Kahlek sidestepped as blood sprayed in his direction. If his robes became stained to the point of ruin, he'd have to wait another Earth-month before the ship would grow the leaves necessary to replace it. The Silver Clouds had no such concerns, of course. Their slick uniforms doubled as armor, and were designed to repel bodily fluids. Kahlek found his war-like cousins excessive at times, but he appreciated their efficiency in matters of violence.

Usually.

Kahlek eyed Moore carefully, wondering if her rage against the humans would not spill over onto him. *She's still bitter about losing her husband,* he noted as fact. When Kahlek's tracking party had attacked a particularly well-defended human settlement, none of the Unaleshi had expected to face a nightmarish...*abomination.* The human female had somehow attuned with a goddess orb. Then the unthinkable had happened—the human female had managed to defeat Moore's husband, Poran, in combat.

None of it made sense, and the Unaleshi who knew about it were still reeling. The orb-wielding human had fought with the proficiency of an experienced mage-master. She had caught the Unaleshi so off balance that they'd been required to make a tactical retreat to continue their mission. The scouting party had not even had time to reclaim the fallen Poran's body. Kahlek was beginning to realize Moore had probably never forgiven him for suggesting they move on. Of course, there were other aspects to her rage as well.

The Silver Clouds were justifiably proud of their honed battle skills, but Moore had watched her husband be slaughtered by a primitive alien. Her reaction was proving bothersome, but its source was Unaleshi pride. *She is the epitome of that pride*, Kahlek noted with grudging approval. *Our tribes may be at each other's throats since leaving our world, but we will never lose our heart. It is the only thing holding us together.* The Silver Clouds were a focused warrior tribe, with discipline and a tight chain of command that had won their standing after the Unaleshi escaped the Goddess' clutches. The Blue Mountain scholars recognized the Silver Cloud's military might and respected it. Martial pursuits had unified their shattered people.

Kahlek gazed at the stars above as the humans screamed in terror. *We were once bright. Now we are nothing but remnants, a legacy, stardust drifing in a forgotten galaxy*, he mused.

Unlike the Silver Clouds, the Blue Mountains focused on spiritual paths. If Kahlek were a full mage, his voice would have weight during the current expedition. The reality was that while

Moore delayed their efforts, Kahlek could say nothing. He could not risk his life unnecessarily, either. He and the few remaining scholars were the last holders of the Old Way, passing on knowledge and stories to the next generation of the Unaleshi.

"Enough," he wanted to say to Moore. But he was only an apprentice; he couldn't say anything. Kahlek wished his mage-master were still alive. Twenek would not have tolerated this excess. The Blue Mountain leader had been both wise and strong. In many ways, his teacher had been the father Kahlek had wished he'd had. When his mage-master had gone missing on a standard scouting mission to collect human data, and the precious orb had never returned to the ship, Kahlek was the first to hear about it. The orb was meant for him, after all.

But the Silver Clouds had convinced the High Council to send their warriors with him—politics. Kahlek grew sick of politics. It was obvious to anyone with eyes that the Silver Clouds had sent representatives to find their own treasures, maybe even to take his. Kahlek had no choice but to recover the orb first and attune with it before any of his cousins had the chance. At least he did not need to worry about being murdered, which was a slight relief. If the others returned without him, the High Council would investigate. If foul play was involved, punishment would be swift. Killing another Unaleshi was the highest crime, unforgivable with so few of them left.

If they take it from me, Kahlek thought with frustration, *they would not even give it to one of their experienced warriors. They believe our Blue Mountain goddess orbs are not fit for a warrior. They would just casually gift it to an apprentice. The Silver Clouds do not truly want the orb's powers, just its secrets—my tribe's secrets.*

Kahlek shook his head with a slight smile. *They don't even know what it's capable of.* He had to make sure that, no matter what, the orb was claimed by nobody but himself. Once he had been attuned to it, his companions could no longer stop him from returning to the ship. Once he returned, he would suddenly have a voice, be a guide for his people. He could represent the Silver Clouds, and perhaps even receive a share of the human organs farmed from the planet.

This never would have been a problem if the Silver Clouds hadn't insisted on slowly, selectively farming the humans, he thought. *For all their warrior ethos, they lack the guts to take over the entire planet at once. It is baffling. We could just take control, help the humans, give them structure. Then in exchange for our magic and technology, they would give us enough of their people to eat until we learn how to reverse what the goddess did to us. Simple.*

If not for the memories of old technology stored in the Blue Mountain's orbs, the Unaleshi would not have had the means to locate other life forms on new worlds for sustenance. Over the past several hundred years, they had visited multiple planets that would sustain them for a time but had always needed to move on. Until Earth, the Unaleshi had never encountered such abundant resources. Kahlek never could have imagined that they'd find a world with a nearly endless supply of element X. What's more, Earth was a true colonization opportunity, a potential new home for his people.

His mage master had discussed terraforming the planet with the Council in preparation for the inevitable return of the goddess. Unfortunately, he had been laughed out of the chambers. "It has been several thousand years since we escaped her clutches," the others had scoffed. "Why would she chase us after all this time?"

But they were blind, their memories growing stale. Only the Blue Mountain tribe kept the Old Ways, history preserved through the orbs. Soon, when Kahlek claimed his orb, Twenek's old orb, he would gain the knowledge of his mage-master—his inheritance. Then he would finally know how his master had died and receive the remaining secrets of his people. Kahlek simply must find the precious object before the Silver Clouds could. The other tribe had helped sustain his people, and were important, but they really did have too much power now, too great a voice on the Council.

Moore's barked words interrupted Kahlek's thoughts. "I need you to translate," she ordered. Then without warning, she used gravity magic to levitate him forward. He hated when she did that. After he became attuned to his orb, she would ask permission first.

The final handful of humans in this human tribe, the Red

Metal Rope, were pinned to the ground except for one—Moore must have found their leader. The human man floated in the air, vainly fighting the pressure that Moore held him with. Kahlek felt surprised and even impressed that the human still had so much fight, resisting despite the overwhelming power he had been confronted with. The young Blue Mountain Unaleshi noted that all the humans in this group wore black, tanned animal hides. He assumed them to be some kind of crude uniform. Humans already looked so much alike; the matching clothing did not help.

The man managed to speak under the magical pressure. He forced out words between labored gasps. Kahlek listened and translated to Moore. "He said you destroyed his people, the Red Metal Rope. And he said something else which I believe is an expletive. He has also mistaken you for a prostitute."

"Order him to tell me where the orb is," Moore commanded, twisting her hand, tightening her magical hold on the human.

Kahlek watched the human man's struggle and tried to piece together the language lessons that his master had taught him. He turned his attention back to the prisoner, a bald man with a scarred upper lip and asked, "Where is the orb? A sphere object that has...power. Small and important. Your name is Redford, yes? You understand?"

The human's eyes widened. He grinned nastily, showing his teeth below a split lip, and the he gasped, "So that is what you want. If I tell you, will you let me live?"

Kahlek glanced at Moore and thought carefully. The Silver Cloud leader's hatred for humans had not abated at all. In fact, her bloodlust had grown, evolving into pleasure while killing. Kahlek knew with certainty that Moore would not spare the human leader, but the orb was close now. The logical course of action was to lie, so he did.

The Blue Mountain scholar nodded and said, "If you tell me where the orb is, I will make sure you will live." He tried his best not to show any excitement—it was difficult. After all this time, after so much travel, they had slowly honed in on the location of the missing orb. This was good timing–they were running out of tracking flowers. If Kahlek had not at least known which continent his mage master had vanished on, the search might have taken much, much longer.

The bald human glared with spite. "The only thing that tells me I'm alive is pain." Then he said a few more things that Kahlek didn't entirely understand—something about goats, which was probably meant to be vulgar. Moore must not have liked his tone because the bald man visibly spasmed in pain from head to toe before relaxing again. He coughed and said, "Fine. I understand. What you are probably looking for is that way." The human bobbed his head east towards the deeper forest in the distance. Then he continued, "If you keep going in that direction, you'll find a building, a cabin. That was the last place I saw the orb. One of my men betrayed me and ran away with it. I haven't been able to find him yet, but that cabin is where you might find some clues. Now let me go."

Kahlek nodded in thought. He carefully, mentally repeated what the human had said to make sure he'd understood. He thought about holding some of the details for himself, but lying to his own people did not sit right with him, and there was also no guarantee that Moore didn't have another Silver Cloud there who could understand this human language. He mentally shrugged and translated the location information for Moore.

She smiled.

The air around Redford rippled, and the human received no other warning. He didn't have time to scream. In less time than it took to blink, a squelch accompanied his body below the neck being magically crushed to the size of a melon. The human's torso had become nothing more than tightly compressed meat. When Moore decided to release her power, the compacted matter would expand back into the jumbled mess it had been reduced to. The doomed, human's head remained alive for a few seemingly endless seconds, mouth working without air. His eyes, full of fear and rage, tracked between Moore and Kahlek before fading in death.

Kahlek frowned at the use of magic. He did not approve of the Silver Clouds so carelessly using Goddess magics. Unfortunately, harnessing the power was a necessity of survival now. Reminders of the Goddess weighed heavily on his mind. *Master believed she is coming back. Those others on the Councils are blind fools! Just more reason I must imprint myself onto that orb!*

Moore's second-in-command took a step forward and raised his hand. His warrior's braids declared his rank, a high standing, but nowhere near Moore's level. He said, "Leader, I offer to go first." After his display of humility—or ambition—several other Silver Cloud scouts stepped forward to volunteer. Kahlek snarled at their blatant disrespect. For a moment, he forgot his apprentice rank.

He screamed, "That orb is not yours! That was my master's. It is *my* inheritance. I will not let you ruin the last remains of the Old Way. You may have forgotten the history of our people, but I will not let you destroy the last of who we are!"

Kahlek found himself flat on his back in an instant. His body felt incredibly heavy, gravity magic bearing down, pinning him to the ground. He knew better than to struggle, so he didn't. Moore stood above him, studying him, then smiled with no humor. She waved to the other Silver Cloud warriors and ordered, "Let him go first. If the humans have discovered again how to bond with a goddess orb, I would like to watch this arrogant Blue Mountain die for this simple speech orb. Any Unaleshi perishing is a travesty of course, but if a Blue Mountain wishes to commit suicide over such a useless object, that would be his choice, no? A speech orb!" She flicked two fingers dismissively. "They are weak, useless except for the histories. Even if this one attunes with it, what is he going to do, *talk* the humans to death?"

As the others laughed, the Silver Cloud leader released the pressure on Kahlek and he stood up without complaint. He had made a mistake, allowing his emotions to get the better of him. Despite his bruised pride, he knew he could have suffered worse. Moore's reaction had been unjust but characteristically direct. *No subtlety*, he mused as he brushed himself off.

After situating himself, Kahlek ignored the other Unaleshi and stared in the direction the human had pointed. He flexed his fingers, imagining his new station among his people in the future. He would definitely have some pointed words with Moore, then.

The orb was the key to his people's future and for his own. It was time to reclaim his inheritance.

CHAPTER 8

"Testing, testing," Noah whispered into the radio. He walked around the lab alone—a soundproof wall separated him from Doc in the medical area of the cabin. The signal from the radio had a little static, but sound came through just fine.

Noah got a, "Roger, roger," through his radio, a response from Doc.

The hair on Noah's neck rose in excitement. His hand touched the cracked orb on the counter next to Doc's experiments. As soon as he touched it, all the surrounding sound attained perfect clarity. *The only new noises are the static of the radios*, he thought. The last thing he wanted was for anyone to hear this experiment with the radios. He gently set the orb back on the counter. Noah used to feel anxiety in his stomach every time he parted with the orb, but not anymore. Even though its magic didn't work for Doc, Noah felt the orb belonged to Doc now too.

The door to the lab slid open, and Doc Broad ran in to exclaim, "It worked!" Then he gave Noah a hug. The young man twitched, fighting his instinct to push him away.

Doc seemed to notice and backed off immediately. He pulled out his radio and opened it up. Noah did the same with his, then they both took out their respective batteries, setting them next to Doc's contraption. Several other batteries that they had charged using Doc's makeshift generator already sat on the counter. Noah recognized some of the video game console parts that had been used to make Doc's machinery.

Nothing was really protected—wires stuck out everywhere, exposed. Doc had explained that cosmetics and housing would be the last things he'd work on after Noah left. Next to the generator were several copies of schematics in large plastic bags. The detailed drawings and notes illustrated how to create new generators to work with the orb, along with Doc's plans for communicating between forts, towns, and settlements. Noah agreed with Doc's plans to unify the country once more, and perhaps humanity after that.

"With these," the trim man said, pocketing one of the batteries, "we'll be able to connect people to each other again. Maybe by doing that, we can all find ourselves again."

Noah had grown fond of Doc's random philosophical musings. Somehow, the man's brilliant, insane mind had been able to recreate electricity with the orb. He thought a bit of soul-speak was a small price to pay. As he pondered philosophy, Noah gave the machinery another once-over and noticed a weird box underneath the generator. He had seen it several times but had never asked the Doc what it was. "What's in there?"

Doc's expression turned grave. "Those, my young friend, are C4 explosives. Redford dropped them off here a while ago in case I ever could make electricity work again. See, for the last two years, even pressure wouldn't work on this stuff, so people have just been using it to cook food. Luckily, we've never been able to use this stuff until now."

Noah studied the box warily. "Is that stuff going to explode?"

Doc laughed. "No, they need to have energy wired through as well as some kind of catalyst. Nothing works the same as it used to anymore. Even if these batteries were right next to them, they wouldn't set off the explosives, at least I don't think so. Let's hold off any experiments though, okay?" The man smiled.

Noah picked up his backpack and put the batteries inside, but left one on the table. He gave Doc an uncertain look. "You should keep at least one. Also, are you sure you don't want to come with me?"

Doc shrugged and scooped up the battery before shaking his head. "I'd love to. But I need to stay here for a least another week before I catch up with you. If Redford comes back, or one of his people notice I'm gone, then he could track me down and find you as well. It's better if we split up. The map I gave you should help you get to Smalltown. You should have enough batteries to make the journey easier, too. Along with the orb and a flashlight, you should be set. You can also take any of those MRE's the Chain brought for me before. They'll keep you going."

Noah frowned at the mention of the military "food." He frowned in doubt but shrugged. At least he could make sure he took all the candy with him. As he began going through the tan MRE bags, he realized that he and Doc hadn't really said their goodbyes yet. They'd actually spent the last few weeks avoiding the subject. Noah didn't want to drag it out, but he couldn't bring himself to leave it at a simple thank you, either.

Before the Shift, he had never been good at saying what he felt. Unsurprisingly, it hadn't magically gotten easier for him. Doc hadn't just saved his life, he'd given it purpose. He had granted Noah back his humanity. The least Noah could do now for Doc was to take his work to Smalltown and get the communication network running.

The young man grabbed the orb from the counter, inspecting its crack. *This thing brought me good luck, bad luck, and a new chance for a better life*, he mused. The words 'Thanks, Doc,' were on the way from his mind to his mouth when he felt a sudden, savage pulse through the orb. His hearing sharpened on its own accord like it had only a few times before, and he cocked his head. It took a moment for him to realize what he was hearing, but then his eyes widened in confusion. He whispered, "I just heard footsteps *land*. I didn't hear them approach at all. It's like they jumped here."

Doc Broad's jaw tightened, but he moved quickly, pulling magazines from a nearby, tattered stack. He calmly said, "Get inside the cubby while I close up the lab. I'm going to stand out in the medical area in case they force their way in to make it look like I was surprised. If the newcomers know about the lab, catching me with some old nudie mags might help distract from all the stuff in here."

Noah tried to smile at the joke, but something felt off about these newcomers. The air weighed heavily on his skin, like the world was holding its breath. Even with his enhanced hearing, it was hard for him to get many details about who was coming, and an odd distortion surrounded the cabin, putting him on edge. He hesitated for half a second, but shook his head. He trusted Doc— the man hadn't steered them wrong yet. Noah took a deep breath and scrambled into the cubby, his home for the last few months, and closed the door after himself.

Not long after he'd hidden, he'd begun earnestly listening again, but a thundercrack of sound tore through the cabin. The shattering noise, amplified by his special hearing was too much, and he reeled. Noah clamped his hands over his ears, trying to still his spinning brain. Even as he gritted his teeth in pain, he realized what the sound must mean. His eyes widened and in disbelief he thought, *the roof was ripped off!* Maybe the orb had helped him understand what he'd heard—was still hearing—but he knew for sure he was right. Noah could pick up the thousands of wood splinters crack and fall, spraying in every direction above him. Ruined nails clattered to the ground, ripped from walls. Noah's mouth went dry. *I can hear people breathing in the sky*, he thought. *They aren't speaking any language I recognize, though. Maybe...it's the Aelves.* A flash of terror filled the sandy-haired young man, and he tightened his arms around his knees.

Luckily, the roof over his hidden cubby still held, but he could sense that now, most of the cabin was just...gone. With his orb hearing, he noticed when a pair of feet landed in the middle of the lab. Noah's hair on the back of his neck stood straight up. *Has to be Aelves*, he thought. His fears were confirmed after he heard the inhuman voice. The Aelve sounded mostly like a man but had an odd, lilting voice. He spoke in choppy, accented English. "Human. Where is the orb? Do not attempt a lie. One of your kin told us of its whereabouts."

A lighter flicked, and Doc Broad sucked in hard before letting out an easy breath. Somehow when the Doc spoke, he still sounded calm, even friendly. "Welcome to my house. I'd appreciate it next time if you knocked. It's common courtesy for us Earthlings, and—urgh."

With his orb hearing, Noah heard the lighter clatter to the lab floor. Fear for Doc's safety made his hands move on their own, and he opened his hidden cubby door a crack to peer out. Through the slit, he saw Doc Broad lurching into the air, his body contorting. Noah's friend and mentor's hands clawed at his neck as the slim man desperately tried to breathe.

A woman floated in front of Doc, and she definitely was not human. Her pointed ears poked out of her hair, and her deep-set eyes stood a little too far apart. She wore a tight-fitting silver outfit. The Aelve woman's skin was pale, almost like an albino, but she also looked unhealthy, sickly. Her flaky, frayed white hair had been tied into braids. Behind the floating Aelve woman stood several other Aelves, all sporting gleaming, silver tunics with leaf patterns. The clothing looked thick, like armor, but still hung like clothing.

One of the Aelves stood closer and wore a different color than the others, blue–his outfit seemed softer, made of a different material, and was cut differently, less angular. The floating Aelve woman glared at Doc and spat a string of words. Her speech sounded almost like German mixed with Chinese.

The Aelve in blue floated up next to Doc, his posture stiff. He said, "Human, I like your manners, but we need the orb. *I* need it. You will tell me the location of the orb if you wish to live. If I, Kahlek of the Blue Mountains, take control of the orb, I give you my word that you will live."

Noah' eyes widened with concern and fear. He had no idea what would happen next, and could barely believe what he was witnessing with his own eyes. In the back of his mind, he was distantly surprised that the Aelves didn't look like the feral monsters he had imaged from Doc Broad's stories. Despite their magic and alien uniforms, they could almost pass for an extremely good cosplayer with good makeup skills. Then what the Aelve had actually just said landed on his conscious mind as his brain slowly caught up. A hope began to grow. The young man desperately hoped that Doc would claim ignorance and the Aelves would let him go. Noah held his breath, clenching his hands together so hard they began to hurt.

Doc managed to choke out, "I don't know what you're talking about. Do what you need to do. The future doesn't scare me at all."

The male Aelve in blue gave Doc an unreadable look before nodding coldly. "Fine. So be it." He turned to talk to his female companion in their own language.

Noah's heart lurched and in the space of a second, every failure, every cowardly moment he'd lived through over the last two years came crashing in. He felt all the self-loathing, all the guilt that he'd buried in his heart time and time again. Memories played themselves one after another. He wanted to turn away, but his conviction wouldn't let him. Yusef had died for him. Noah had aided in countless slaves captured by the Red Chain. He'd been beaten, and hurt himself, and had debased himself just to survive. But no, not this time. He refused to fail Doc Broad, to just stand by and watch his friend be murdered.

His heart beat wildly, but he otherwise felt calm, a deep sense of purpose setting on his shoulders. The sandy-haired young man didn't have a plan, but there was no time. Anything to prolong the life of his friend, his teacher, that was the goal. Noah burst out of the cubby, grunting as his backpack got caught on the door, shifting and pushing harder to stand. Doc gurgled, "Noah, no!"

All the eyes of the Aelves swiveled and locked on the newcomer, their eyes flicking to the orb in his hand. Noah balled a fist and stared at the male Aelve in blue. The inhuman man seemed unnaturally composed, his hand held behind his back. Noah pointed and hissed, "Kahlek, right? Your word, bastard. Say it again—swear it! Let him live, and I will give you the orb!"

Even under the struggle of the strange magic, Doc's conflicting emotions were plain. "Stupid kid," he managed to whisper with a smile. The female Aelve barked out more of her guttural language to the one named Kahlek. Her hand made a beckoning motion, and Doc slowly floated closer to her. Kahlek sounded angry, like the Aelves were having an argument.

**

Chris Broad felt crushing pressure on all sides. The terrifying situation was bizarre, surreal, but he knew it wasn't a dream—his body hurt too much. His life hung on a thread, but all he could think of was Noah, how the boy had managed to be both so heroic and so very stupid at the same time. Chris was frustrated, but had also never been so proud of Noah—the young man had finally set himself free! The floating man wished he'd have more time to see his young friend continue to grow, but reality was cruel. Chris knew he probably didn't have much longer to live–his vision had begun to turn red. With his body under such intense pressure, including his clothing, he felt the charged battery in his pants pocket digging into his thigh. *Gravity,* Chris' analytical mind assessed. *Gravity magic, or maybe some sort of air magic.*

Blood began to pool in his throat, but he managed a gargled laugh. *Magic—that's it! There's a reason they're afraid of electricity! Keeping a single battery, what a strange coincidence, what are the odds?* He tried to chuckle again but could only manage a wheeze.

***

Moore frowned at the human in disgust. The creature looked very much like every other of its kind, and this one smelled like smoke and narcotics. She believed it was a male, not notable for anything other than being small and thin. How had these pathetic creatures managed to destroy her powerful husband? Whatever the humans were saying to Kahlek, she didn't care. There would always be new humans to interrogate and kill. Besides, even if they never found the useless Blue Mountain orb, it would be no great loss.

The Silver Cloud mage tripled her gravity magic against the floating human, condensing it. She hadn't pulped a human in a while. Maybe this time she could make the head pop off higher than before.

As her magic flexed, a light flashed. The power had pushed

hard enough to merge with something forbidden, foreign, and the pressure had created feedback. Violent energies mixed, creating a feedback loop and time stuttered before the world erupted. Moore distantly registered her shoulder slamming into the ground below, and then everything went black.

***

Noah watched in horror as Doc Broad's body exploded near to the female Aelve, blasting her to the ground in a spray of blue energy, ash, and viscera. The other Aelves were all knocked down like bowling pins. Kahlek had been further away than the woman but still hit the ground hard, rolling. The other Aelves in silver got tossed around violently by the cracking energy, all of it moving that one direction. A few of them bounced off the remaining walls of the cabin, three landing in the lab itself.

Noah ran to what remained of Doc's body, not much more than a severed arm and some clothing. One of the pockets probably contained the last of the dead man's cigarettes. Noah's chest heaved, and the world became muted like everything was very far away. He felt his tongue get too large, and his spine crawled. His hand reached for the Doc's arm, but then pulled back. No, his friend was gone now. Gone.

This doesn't make sense. I'm supposed to leave for Smalltown. Doc was going to follow me. He was going to give up smoking since he was almost out of cigarettes anyway. Something burned his arm. He turned and noticed a wall had caught on fire, and some of the splinters from the cabin being destroyed were eagerly lighting up. Noah shook his head and turned back to Doc's remains. The chaos around him didn't feel real. Regret hit him like a sock full of rocks. He should have run. Now he knew his friend was dead, and it was all his fault, but he still wanted to make certain that Doc was really gone. It was a stupid thought; the remains were literally in front of him on the cabin floor. Noah just couldn't accept that the man who had done so much for him, almost been like a father to him in the past few months, was gone, murdered by these *monsters.*

"Aelves." The young man tasted the word, and it grew sour on his tongue. He breathed in the hot, poisonous air, and said the word again, his chest wracked with scarlet hate. In that moment, he realized he'd never understood true hate before, had never despised a single word so strongly. *Aelves.*

Noah blinked and realized the orb wasn't in his hand anymore. He must have dropped it during the explosion. The Aelve in blue that spoke English, Kahlek, bent to pick something up, and Noah caught the glint of the orb on the floor at the pale monster's feet.

***

Kahlek told himself he felt no excitement while reaching for the orb, the moment was an inevitability, after all. Once his fingers made contact, he began to force his will into the sphere. This was his moment to imprint his will, his *voice* onto the orb and reclaim his inheritance. The Unaleshi scholar recalled the Blue Mountains song in his heart, the tune his master had taught him. The song was one of the first of his people, predating the time the Goddess had corrupted them.

Something was wrong. His imprint stopped halfway through, the song ended. *It's...another's will is already here!* Kahlek realized in astonishment. *Another song. How? Two wills at once shouldn't be possible unless....* He carefully examined the orb and found a crack.

Kahlek spun to find the remaining human man. *The human tried to bond with the orb?* The Blue Mountains scholar clenched his teeth, examining the crack in the precious sphere again before collecting his calm. He was a scholar of his tribe, and he would compose himself as such. Now was the time to use knowledge, not passion. *The human was unable to fully imprint the orb because of the damage. This same damage allowed me to add my will to it as well.* He knew he had to be right, but that meant he only had one chance now. The human must be killed, or his will forced out.

He wasn't sure where the human was, and time was precious. He'd just force out the other will. The First Song of the Unaleshi would allow him to do so, now that he had partial control of the orb. As he began to concentrate, focusing on the melody, pain spiked in his back, and he tumbled forward. Kahlek spun around, anger and pain singing through his body. One of Moore's scouts had recovered, standing next to a Silver Clouds mage, Fohesh. The sneering mage pointed his hand at Kahlek, and it began to glow.

***

Noah knew if he had been smart, he would have run instead of hiding. He hadn't had any hope of grabbing the orb or even avenging Doc. But now, for some reason, the Aelves were attacking each other. If he was going to act, to do something, this would be the perfect time. He was hesitating, though. Even if he got the orb and escaped, the Aelves could probably easily track and kill him with their magic. *No more running away, Noah*, he thought. Redford, Talbot, or crazy floating aliens, none of it mattered. Nothing would make him change his mind now, Noah had decided who he wanted to be.

He glared at the only thing he hated more in this world than his past self, the Aelves. They had stolen away the person who had redeemed Noah. In light of that fact, everything became somewhat simple: Aelves—all of them—needed to die. He could smell his own burned hair, triggering the memory of the explosion that had killed Doc.

The batteries, Noah realized. *Doc put that battery in his pocket. The flying Aelve woman exploded when she was close and used her magic. Maybe...the batteries must disrupt their magic!* Noah snarled, his eyes blazing. A feeling he'd never really experienced before filled his entire body, giving him fiery strength. If it was his time to die, he might as well take the Aelves out with him. *They need to pay.*

He carefully scanned the area and watched the Aelves, his vision cold, blood hot, when he remembered something, realized his chance...if it worked. *The box. Inside the box are explosives.*

None of the distracted Aelves noticed as Noah rushed over and grabbed the box, ripping it open. He secured all the C4, which turned out to at least a few pounds of the stuff, about enough to fill a lunch box. He threw it all into his backpack with most of the batteries, saving a few in his pockets. One of the Aelves, the tallest who had attacked the one named Kahlek saw Noah. His glowing hands he'd been using to threaten the Aelve in blue swung to point at Noah.

With a growl, Noah threw his entire backpack at the group of Aelves. The improvised missile sailed through the air almost comically slowly, and the Aelves cocked their heads. The pack landed short, and Noah's growl turned to frustration, but the bundle slid just a bit closer. The world went sideways as white and red light exploded in Noah's vision. Through the distortion, he witnessed the Aelve with the glowing hands erupt into fire, burning alive. The inhuman monster screamed in agony as the white magic began lancing out from his hands, running wild, knocking down his comrades. Some of them screamed as the magic removed their limbs.

***

Moore finally stood, her ears ringing, her entire body barely responding. She'd somehow survived the magical explosion, but a shaky inspection revealed most of her hair was gone. One of her eyes refused to work anymore, and an arm was unresponsive. With a great deal of effort, she was able to correct the remains of the magical feedback in her head, but a lesser mage would have probably just died or lost control. Her senses were still in disarray from the gravity magic feedback and the resulting explosion. *The human.* This had to be the human's fault. The creature had somehow figured out a way to hurt her people with their own magic.

The Unaleshi mage shook her head. She wouldn't rest until every human was dead or caged. The only human she could actually see now to vent her hatred on was the fragile looking male, standing and gaping at a group of dead, dying, or unresponsive Silver Clouds...and a fallen Kahlek. Moore's lip raised in disdain at the sight of her incompetent subordinates, especially Fohesh, his magic out of control as the mage-warrior burned. *I should purge the weak Blue Mountain boy*, she thought, glaring at Kahlek. All of this was that weakling's fault, and at this point, the Council and their rules were not a concern.

With all the energy she could muster, Moore summoned the deepest gravity anomaly that she had ever pulled. The weight of it almost crushed her, but she thought of her beautiful husband. She stewed on the human female that had beat her husband's face into the ground, and tears swelled in her eyes.

***

Kahlek's fuzzy, stunned mind immediately understood what was going on after he felt growing, crushing weight and noticed Moore standing on unsteady feet, her hands held outwards. *She is going to take us all with her!* he realized in horror. *No! I was so close!* Suddenly, his nostrils flared, and he began crawling, each movement more difficult than the last. *If I bond with the orb, it can save me.* His vision blurred in the distortion, but he could still see the orb. He used the last of his strength to leap for it.

***

The explosives hadn't worked, but the batteries had done their thing. Noah had never seen C4 explode before, but he knew the Aelves wouldn't still be around anymore to groan and roll around, or flail around on fire if it had. On the ground ahead, he could actually see the crack in the orb now, like it'd gotten bigger. Noah wondered what would happen if something could set the C4 off. Maybe throwing it hadn't been such a good idea. Doc had mentioned electricity and pressure before. Maybe it needed both now?

When Noah felt a crushing weight, he scanned the inside of the destroyed cabin and noticed Doc's killer showing her teeth, her eyes wild. Noah understood that the murderous Aelve was attacking. The orb rolled a little bit, coming closer. Noah was beginning to have trouble moving, but he took a couple batteries out of his pockets and threw them as best he could at the group of downed Aelves from before, and the monster woman holding her hands out. The weight grew greater, like he was at the bottom of the ocean, and Noah knew he wouldn't be able to stand much longer. The world around him began to distort as his eyes were pushed into his head. The young man desperately leapt forward, reaching for the orb. As his fingers brushed it, he saw the Aelve, Kahlek, touch it at the same time.

Noise assaulted him so loudly his mind split, and two different notes became one. God seemed to shake the entire world, and everything around him flashed white. Reality cycled through every color of the rainbow before fading to nothing.

CHAPTER 9

Noah watched the plain white space around him break into a thousand lesser lights, each fragment a new reality. The fragments shattered into dust, and the dust reformed into new lights, repeating the process over again.

He shifted and discovered that he existed between all the specks, as if he didn't belong with any of them. *Am I dead?* Noah wondered, a little underwhelmed. In life, he had never known what to expect after death, but this couldn't be right, not this confusing mess. Some part of him had wanted to believe that the afterlife would solve all of his problems. Death should have made everyone equal.

Instead, now Noah was an observer as worlds were grown and sundered.

One universe, in particular, held his attention, pulling him closer. He never thought he'd find himself so amused while dead after such a wasteful life. *I had only actually begun living right before dying,* he thought. In life, he had let others push him around. He'd bent himself to their will.

Noah's essence, his soul, pulsed with disgust. *At least I don't have to be burdened anymore,* he thought. *Even my last act wasn't heroic. It was just retaliation. I couldn't save Doc. All I managed to do was destroy the only thing that could have been the last hope for humanity against those monsters.*

The Aelves.

He tried pushing down his growing hatred for the alien monsters, understanding that any further vengeance was no longer possible with no body. Still, the emotion kept him focused. Suddenly, Noah found himself, whatever his existence was now, hovering somewhere new, witnessing the history of a foreign planet.

The world was strange and green, populated by beautiful, humanoid people. They seemed familiar—two legs, two arms, ten fingers—the same shape as humans, but with key differences. Their flawless skin held a silver sheen, and their eyes were the color of a full moon. These people were at peace with themselves and with the world around them.

Noah's spirit surged with joy, delighted by the lives of the strangers on the foreign planet. He watched thousands of the silver-skinned people as they went about their business. He learned their names as they lived and forgot them after they died. None of them left a lasting impression, a lingering memory—he couldn't seem to remember any of them. The strangers' lives flowed through him like history in water.

Whether he watched events from the past or the future was unclear. For thousands of years, the silver-skinned people had lived in balance with their world, growing more sophisticated, but remaining unchanged. They were travelers, sailors of the stars, exchanging their peace and plant-based technology with other worlds. The people called themselves the Yuna, spending their time recording history in songs. Noah had never heard anything like it on Earth. Every aspect of their songs emphasized harmony.

Suddenly, something changed–a discordance had come to the planet. A new presence had arrived.

She descended on their world as a calamity. Stained with decay, matte and sick, the newcomer's skin had an unhealthy sheen, an aura of decay. Billions of souls from scattered worlds were woven into her hair, worlds she had turned and broken. Even as he watched, Noah felt an alarming intuition that he should carefully witness the unhappy tableau before him. His essence trembled, as if at any moment he could break.

"Why has she done all this?" the Yuna asked. The newcomer didn't answer them with words, only a cruel smile. Whether because of his alien background or his perspective as he watched, Noah sensed she was driven merely by whim, amusement. They were her playthings.

Noah's spirit recoiled as the newcomer twisted the Yuna's beautiful songs, their histories, and even the building block of their proud bodies. Within one hundred years, she had full control of the world. The vegetation that the silver-skinned people had used for food and had crafted their starships with decayed at the discordant being's direction. She didn't even sing.

Her will was a single note, a disruption to all harmonies.

At first, the population dropped by hundreds, then by millions. Noah watched in horror as the Yuna's numbers dwindled; his heart broke for them. He knew what it was like to have no power. To the disruptive force, the newcomer, the Yuna were toys to be bent and shaped as she pleased, to be discarded when they were no longer of interest. Eventually, the once-proud people broke.

The silver-skinned people were no longer silver. Instead, becoming pallid and pale like the newcomer, the goddess. Noah pulsed with fear for them, knowing how this would end. His entire life had filled with an endless cycle of unhealthy relationships. Doc Broad had broken the cycle, now Noah wished he could break the Yuna's cycle.

He related and wanted to intervene, to warn them to not feed from the hand that choked them. But like so many times before, he didn't have the power and had trouble finding his voice.

After more time passed, Noah knew the people were doomed forever. A few thousand of the Yuna organized to escape the goddess, becoming wise to her, blooming their last ship-seed to travel to the stars and escape her clutches. They had even managed to steal some of her secrets, but it was too late.

She spoke a single word, and they were forever changed. Now to sustain their life, they could only eat sick meat, specific flesh so rare and scattered among the stars that they would die anyway. After casting her curse upon the entire Yuna world, the destructive goddess left her broken toys behind.

Noah ached for the broken world and the broken people but followed the Yuna people's hope.

The few thousand who had escaped on their final ship with stolen power were also cursed. Their situation was dire, but at least they still lived. No more Yuna existed on their home planet. The survivors sped off to distant worlds, doing their best to survive.

What was that thing, that goddess, the creature that broke the Yuna? Noah wondered. Even thinking of her made his spirit want to scream into the void. He tried to hold on to the memories that slipped past. It was so difficult to keep them without a body, without a mind to store them in.

Who was she? Noah asked himself one more time, desperate to hold on to the memories. Something inside of him warned to stay away from that secret knowledge, to just let it go. But the stubbornness he had gained at the end of his life, drove him, emboldened him. With great effort, he managed to keep some of the memories, but only as images. The hardest thing to hold onto, beyond anything else, was a single word, one name.

Xantha.

When he repeated the name, tendrils of fear snaked through his essence, a terror so great that he wanted to let go of the name, to throw it away. It was too terrible a truth, too titanic for his limited existence to keep—heavy beyond belief. The name was a cosmic force that lanced into Noah's spirit, attempting to rend him apart.

As the pain exploded, Noah felt a part of himself wanting to give up, to let the name overwhelm him to the point of breaking. He knew instinctively that if he did so, he wouldn't have to think anymore. But a smaller part of him–a spark of flame–whispered to not only endure but to *fight.*

Submission was the old way, the old Noah. That Noah had given in passively, had allowed others to control his destiny. When he was given the name Worm, he hadn't suddenly transformed into that spineless creature. He'd always been Worm deep inside, Redford had just named it.

Then he'd met Doc Broad. His friend had called him Noah, reminding him that redemption was difficult, but not impossible. Everyone had a choice, even if the choice was unpleasant.

The spark inside Noah grew, devouring the alien darkness growing inside him, banishing that false promise of relief. Doc had shown Noah how to fight back against doubt by simply willing himself to be more, to act, not to pity himself so much. The new, remembered name was out to destroy him, but so had everything else in his life—the Shift, bandits, survival, Talbot, Redford…himself.

Worm would have given in. But Noah, the Noah that Doc Broad saw and pulled out, that Noah pushed back against the force, struggled against it with everything he had.

To his surprise, by refusing to let it take over, Noah felt the name stop gaining power against him. His inner spark turned into a roaring flame, and he let that flame devour the pain.

Pain. The word brought with it terrible memories of his beatings from Talbot and Redford. The leader of the Red Chain had said so many times, "When all else fails, pain is the only discipline left. It is the reminder we are still alive." When Noah had been alive, the mantra had been like a sick joke.

But the mantra that had been used to beat Noah into submission actually became relevant now. *I'm not dead,* Noah realized. Redford was a monster, but the leader of the Red Chain's dark philosophy was actually helping Noah turn the tide against the power trying to tear him apart. *I'm alive,* Noah told himself. He was in pain, so this was real…whatever this was. It didn't matter where he was. He was alive.

That knowledge brought another fear to Noah. If he kept fighting back against the name, what would happen? Uncertainty of the future began to bloom in his spirit. Would he have to struggle forever?

At least he'd be fighting back, not just allowing things to

happen to him.

Once the thought filled him, he knew he'd made his choice. *Fight.* He had spent his entire life trying to avoid pain, which had only resulted in more suffering. Now he understood the truth— pain was inevitable. It had been a part of his life.

Instead of making him weak, Noah could use struggle, conflict, to grow stronger. Rather than continue to fight back against the pain using only his inner flame, he mixed pain into the fire, feeding it with what sought to destroy him. The spark had been borne from Doc Broad's kindness, then it had been a fire, and now, it was ablaze. Now the pain assaulting him belonged to Noah, becoming his weapon.

The heat of his convictions morphed into something hot and bright, like pure light. It lanced through the creeping memory he held, the dreaded name. After a titanic struggle, he felt his will shatter the force that had threatened to end him, banishing it.

Noah blazed like a star. He was alive, existing in the between- place of everything. While he'd lived, he'd let everything affect him, being influenced by anything and everything that had sought to control him. No more. His spirit—his new self—had discovered his truth. Suddenly, Noah felt tired, almost like he was drifting off. He didn't know what was happening but felt certain that any new conflict he might encounter, he would fight.

Fight to live. Never give up. Fight to stay free.

CHAPTER 10

The first thing he heard was a familiar song.

Except for the melody, all other sounds were murmurs to him, indecipherable mumbles that echoed around strangely. The confusing noises came from blurry giants. Beneath the chaos of the noise, lights that burned his eyes even through his eyelids, and large hands poking his sensitive body, the song calmed him like a buoy in a storm. But this time, unlike before, the melody wasn't inside his mind. Instead, it was sung by someone else.

The singer was a woman, he was sure of that. Why was the song so familiar? He had lost track of time, actually even the concept of time. He focused on the seconds ticking by, then minutes, and pondered the song. As he continued to listen, his world became clearer.

Time passed. Each time the woman sang, something inside him responded, until one day, thought began to be clearer, and with it, memory. *Noah. My name is Noah*, he recalled. *I died. The end of the world...Doc...the explosion.* Even though he'd only been able to catch the tip of his memories, they overwhelmed him.

Remembering his death generated massive spikes of raw emotion. Fear. Panic. Noah wailed, flailing, unable to cope with the rush of memories and his confused senses. Someone patted his back, and he burped in response. *That feels better*, Noah thought as the woman with soft hands turn him over onto his back.

Soon after, everything grew turbulent and confusing again. Enduring storms of emotion proved worse than overwhelming physical sensations and overall difficulty with thinking. Every new feeling spiraled out of his control, causing his body to react in ways he couldn't predict. His limbs were weak, awkward. Everything felt wrong.

The woman's voice helped, calming him. The song brought peace. Noah began to focus on the wordless tune even when the woman wasn't singing. Something in his body seemed to appreciate the focus.

More time passed as he tamed his emotions—days, months, years? He began to remember everything. Noah's entire life came back to him like the first dawn on a new world, and his mind sharpened with increasing clarity.

Sitting in his playpen, Noah began to panic again as the trickle of memories from his old life became a flood. Emotion began to well, threatening to make his body lose control again, but he pushed the confusion and negativity down with the mysterious song.

What is going on? he wondered. *Am I dead for real this time?* Something about the bright primary colors and plastic toys of the playpen seemed familiar. He remembered his life before death with perfect clarity, but his experiences after that were just vague images of silver-skinned people, decay, and a figure cloaked in malice and horrific indifference. *Then after that,* he thought, his mind becoming less muddled, *there was some sort of struggle followed by light.*

He stood up with shaky legs and immediately lost balance, falling on his butt. Pain. Pain meant he was alive. Redford's scarred upper lip flashed in his mind, the grim memory of his former leader leaving a sour taste in his mouth. *I'm not dead,* he realized. After another second's thought, a concept returned to him, and it echoed in his head. *Reincarnation.* He couldn't remember much about the idea except for vague theories and lessons on religion from his History class in high school.

At first, a sense of elation burst through him, and he giggled. This made him throw up, but he just rolled over and ignored it. *I have a new life!* When he tried to stop gurgling so he could collect his thoughts, he found himself unable to. Then reality set in about his situation. *I'm a baby.* The giggles evaporated. *Babies are just sacks of hormones, reacting to everything. This sucks. I need to get ahold of myself.*

Thinking was still hard. It took a long time to process any kind of actual thoughts, but he kept at it, focusing on logic and on the comforting song. It slowly dawned on him that the music he'd been channeling for so long was actually the little hum his mother had sung wordlessly to him when he'd been an infant. The melody had been somehow burned into his subconscious for his entire life. *I can't believe I had a song stuck in my head my whole life. Thanks, Mom.*

It was difficult to focus, but after studying the room and the house around him, he realized that he was in his old, childhood home. *So, I'm reincarnated in my previous life,* he concluded. Noah didn't know how to feel about that. All of his memories couldn't have been a dream. He felt pain. If there was anything Redford had taught him which had stuck with Noah, it was that pain was a reminder he was still alive. His emotions were less turbulent since he'd started consciously focusing on the song in the back of his mind.

Further evidence that he wasn't crazy or imagining things…was the fact he was currently a baby. Having an existential crisis pre-toddler was probably a good sign that something extraordinary was happening.

Noah opened his mouth to speak, but only gurgles came out. His tongue felt awkward and huge between his small teeth. Spit trailed out the corner of his mouth.

Even with most of his old, past memories, he was still working with his baby's body and mind. Frustration threatened to overwhelm him, but he focused on the wandering song and felt the familiar pulse of the orb echo through him. Noah looked around but couldn't find the orb. The pulse had come from within him.

What in the world? he thought furiously, working his tiny, undeveloped brain as fast as he could. *Time for an experiment.*

Eyes closed, Noah focused on all the sounds around him. Mom and Dad were in the other room, talking about what they were going to have for dinner. *Mom. Dad.* He held his breath at the sound of their voices, keeping down the flutter of emotion that could turn into a storm. The television cycled news in the other room. As his focus wavered, the noises became less clear.

Noah opened his eyes in shock. The orb was somehow with him. It wasn't physically there, but he still had its powers. Unlike when he had touched it before, the sounds hadn't come automatically. Now he had to focus on the ability.

One more test, he thought. Noah blinked and willed the blue, transparent screen into existence. He giggled triumphantly. *Are my only reactions now seriously only crying, only giggling?* Just like before he'd died, the words to the floating screen were still fuzzed out.

Suddenly, another screen opened, and Noah tumbled back in surprise. This screen's words were crystal clear. *It's in English,* Noah thought. *Why is this thing in English?*

His jaw dropped, and he wiped his mouth with a soft sleeve, grateful that he could still read.

Anomaly detected. Modifier has been reset after double bonding during anomaly event. Memories intact. Soul intact, but unstable. Require assistance from Modifier to stabilize soul.

Noah didn't know what to make of that. He could read the words, but none of it made sense to him. In fact, the words confused him even more. He was sure the Aelves hadn't created magical orbs for humans. *The orb must be responding to my mind*, Noah reasoned.

He began breathing heavily. The reality of his situation began to sink in—a real opportunity to live his life again. It was exactly what he had always wanted, a chance to correct his mistakes. How many times had he fantasized about asking Krystal Connolly on a date, or telling his parents that he loved them, or trying out for a sports team? *Living my life to the fullest instead of cowering in fear, a slave to my own failures.* He pushed down the sudden weight in his chest, his heart. His baby body was confused and wanted to let out the tension with a good cry, but Noah focused.

This is my chance.

Then his elation faded as another thought crept up his consciousness like heavy vines. He might need to be careful. Living his life differently could change things in ways he couldn't predict, and not just his life, but everything else too. Noah didn't know much about physics, or time, or the butterfly effect, but he suddenly worried that he might screw everything up for the worse. Each of his choices could cause the death of someone he loved earlier than when they died before. The sudden fear of failure, a familiar feeling, made him want to crawl in a hole.

What if I can't change anything? What if this is my punishment from my previous life? He didn't believe in hell, but he was beginning to understand he could just be replaying his entire life over again. *I might have to relive everything – my crippling social anxiety, the fear during the Shift, the death of my parents, surviving on my own, Yusef, the Red Chain, Doc–I might just have to watch and endure all over again.* Noah's heart began to race, but he tried to find peace with his mother's song. Even with the calming tune, Noah still felt a wave of panic beginning to take over.

But then something sharper, hotter than the song descended— he thought about the Aelves. Jagged hatred focused his turbulent emotions into a blade. Without the aliens preying on humanity, without them causing the Shift, none of the worst pain in his past would have happened. Everything prior to the Shift was Noah's fault. He could accept that. But the Shift? No one deserved to live in a world like that. The Aelves had brought the whole world to its knees, exposed the worst that humanity had to offer, and gave it a place to grow. Noah had given into despair, like so many others.

Except for people like Doc, Noah thought with a smile. Doc Broad planted a seed of hope in him, and Noah knew it was still there. Doc would have chuckled at Noah's fear of his very existence causing more harm. Noah's only friend after the Shift had given him a gift that still endured. The ability to move forward.

He knew what Doc would say to him right now. *The guy would just pull out a cigarette, blow it in my face, and tell me to stop being silly.* Doc's signature calm and raised eyebrow flashed through Noah's mind.

Even if I have no control and have to relive everything all over again, I'm not going to do it while being afraid. If there's anything I can control, it's myself.

Noah mentally went through a laundry list of past regrets. He had never tried out for any sport in school because he'd been a bit smaller, weak, and uncoordinated. His height hadn't been a real excuse, he knew that, but his attitude at the time had been a symptom of a much deeper issue. The realization hit with less force than it might have before he'd died, but being an infant, he still had to hold back tears.

I'm afraid of failing, Noah thought bitterly. *Or, at least I was.*

He recalled all the ways he'd grown before dying, and how Doc Broad being killed had changed everything. All the uncertainty and fear he'd built up over the course of his life had boiled into rage against the Aelves. *They put us back to the Dark Ages, killed us, and...killed Doc.*

But the Aelves had just been the breaking point, the focus for all of his anger. Maybe the anger had always been there, but he'd just aimed it at himself. He never wanted to relive his old life again, at least not as he'd lived it before. That would truly be hell.

But with this new life, despite the weirdness, he had options. He briefly wondered what a pissed off baby looked like and felt ridiculous. His new existence was exciting, but would also take some getting used to.

Okay, he thought. *Risky or not, I need to take action. Even with my short life before, having my memories gives me a huge advantage. I have to use it.*

He flexed his chubby little fingers and frowned. The floor of his crib felt unsteady as he tried to get up on both feet. His baby body felt awkward, his limbs unused to the new commands. *My head feels heavier than my body*, Noah thought as waved his hands to right himself. The physical issues, emotional issues, and mental issues would be difficult to deal with, but at least he knew his situation was temporary. The song helped, and so did the hate in his belly.

Noah briefly struck a martial arts pose, balling his soft hands into fists, but then rolled his eyes at himself. With his chubby face and cartoon jammies, he couldn't even take himself seriously. He sighed and laid back down.

Control. Noah repeated the word over and over. *I need control over my body, over myself. If I have control, I can do anything.* With great effort, he got up again and forced his unsteady legs to move him across the playpen. Walking normally felt like balancing on a rope, and he had to keep his arms out to steady himself. His body was completely unused to the movement, resisting his commands with every step. It took a few attempts, but eventually, Noah found himself making awkward but more confident strides across the playpen.

Tired, he sat back down, leaning against his stuffed teddy bear, Mr. Cuddles. *I didn't think I'd see you again.* Noah smiled at the toy. He held out a hand to rest on the bear and sadly shook his head. *My relationship with you will definitely be different than when I was a kid. That kind of makes me sad. Maybe not everything will be better with my old memories.*

That thought led to his memories themselves, how they were not the only thing he'd brought back with him. He still had the powers of the orb. Eyes closed, Noah focused on the sounds around him once more. Unlike before when he had simply touched the orb to get perfect clarity, now Noah could sense he needed to focus. With a few tries, he verified that he'd been correct. The more effort he put into listening, the clearer the sounds became.

I wonder... He turned his attention inward as he soundlessly sang his mother's song. A familiar pulse came from inside him, a rhythm separate from his own heartbeat. Even if he could speak, Noah wouldn't have been able to explain the sensation in words. It was a feeling unlike any other he had ever experienced.

After a moment, Noah opened his eyes and discovered that his fatigue from walking around the playpen was mostly gone. He tried to laugh, but it came out as a giggle. Then he opened the blue screens again. The first one was still fuzzy, but Noah pushed his will into it, trying to force the words to become clear.

A sharp pain spiked through his head, rocking him back into Mr. Cuddles. A screen opened in his vision.

Soul intact, but unstable. Require assistance from Modifier's to stabilize soul.

The sheer number of discoveries he'd made finally overwhelmed his limited emotional control. Noah found himself crying. He lost himself for a while, reverting to just a normal baby again, but when he came back to himself, he was still crying. The door to his room suddenly opened, and through his tears, he saw his parents, Lana and Clark, walk in. The sight of them caused Noah to lose his breath.

The last time he'd seen them, they'd been beaten and bloodied by a wandering raider gang, busy distracting the raiders for Noah to escape. His mother's jet black hair had gone grey soon after the Shift. His father's proud back had bent, his face wrinkled. *They look so young*, Noah thought. He found himself crying even harder, but not with pain or sadness. *I'm just so damn happy to see them.*

Noah's mother, Lana Henson, had been the most loving, caring mom Noah could have ever asked for. In his previous life, she'd spent most of Noah's early childhood at home to care for him. Looking back on those times, he wondered if his mother had been too soft on him, never challenging him enough. His father, Clark, was an accountant. He worked the standard nine to five and didn't know a thing about sports. Still, he hosted a Super Bowl game every year just because he liked having friends over. On the surface, Noah had had an ideal childhood.

Seeing his parents again made a new rush of memories wash over Noah, and he cried louder. His mother tsked and rushed forward, scooping him up. Noah's baby brain was calmed by this, but his rational mind examined all of the memories flooding his consciousness. In his former life, when he'd reached middle school and had taken state aptitude tests, the way his parents treated him had changed. Noah had scored ridiculously high, and his parents had praised him a lot, probably only wanting the best for him.

They'd used phrases like, "You have so much potential." But his parents hadn't really pushed him in any way. Instead, they'd let him drift, perhaps believing that he would find his own way. Then when he'd stagnated, he'd felt like his parents had hung an imaginary blade above him, judging him, the unspoken reality being that he could be better than he was, do better. To Noah, "You have so much potential," had eventually translated to, "You aren't good enough."

After that, his grades had dropped. He'd drifted away from his childhood friends. Any talk of his future had made him want to shut down. Shame had filled him. He'd watched people who had been given so much less, who had far worse families still do better than him in just about everything. Noah had been afraid that any choice he made wouldn't be good enough, that it could lead to failure, to broken expectations. In his previous life, he had never been able to put any of this into words, hadn't even been able to admit how deeply he'd been depressed. But with all his past memories now, after enduring the Shift and seeing his parents again like this, he understood.

They only wanted the best for me, he realized. He'd never really blamed them in the past, he'd known that he was a failure, and it hadn't been his parents' fault. But one thing was for certain: In this new life, Noah wanted to give his parents a reason to be proud of him. They'd always been supportive, even when he'd been useless as a teenager. They'd sacrificed themselves to save his life.

He would never forget.

After his mother checked him over, she set him back down. Noah had stopped crying. His parents began leaving the room when Noah made a loud gurgling sound, his attempt to say something, anything. When they both stopped, Noah propped himself off Mr. Cuddles to look at them better.

"Oh," his mom exclaimed happily. "Testing out your legs, huh?"

Noah was about to stand up, to show them how he could walk now, or even spell out something using his toy blocks, but he hesitated. He wasn't even entirely sure how old he was, so it might be too unusual, maybe even terrifying if he revealed himself to his parents now. He settled down, waiting for his parents to leave the room, and after they did, Noah gingerly folded his baby arms and frowned. He had some thinking to do.

**

After a lot of thought, Noah decided to keep most of his walking and…thinking secret, at least for the time being. A freakishly brilliant toddler would be easier for most people to stomach than a talking baby, even for his parents. That gave him some time to kill for about a year at least though. Noah realized he needed to come up with a plan, not only for the next year but for the next twenty.

At least the terrible pain in his head had gone, leaving behind a lesson in the price of messing with the screens. Noah didn't know what a Modifier was, and wondering about it in circles wouldn't do much good—he needed more information. In the meantime, Noah could reason his way through a few other problems. The last few hours had definitely proven an important fact. *I changed things.* It was clear to him now that this wasn't some cruel hell where he had to relive all his previous failures over again.

This gave him a huge sense of relief. He had a definite chance to do things right this second time around. Noah's oversized head began bobbing in excitement. *With the orb magic combined with my life experience, who knows what I can accomplish? I could become rich!*

His excitement was cut short by echoes of anger inside of him. The violent memory of Doc's death came to mind, banishing any fantasies of living a fun life on the beach.

Never again, he thought. He needed to prepare for the Shift. More importantly, he needed to prepare others, too. He knew he'd sound crazy if he tried to tell people what was going to happen, even after he was older. Who would believe him that in seventeen years, most technology would stop working and alien Aelves would hunt humanity down for food? No, he couldn't save the world, but he could at least protect his family. Noah didn't know how he was going to do it, but he had some time. His heart began to beat faster at the thought. *I can actually change things.*

Ideas slowly whirred through his developing mind. *Maybe I can at least try to spread word of…the possibility of something like the Shift happening*, Noah thought. Even as that idea crossed his mind, he knew it would be a long shot. Other options he considered were to try becoming internet famous or make a blog, leaking information slowly. The whole notion sounded ridiculous, but armed with the powerful knowledge that he could change history, he was ready to shoot high.

He would need resources first - and would need to do it quietly. Maybe he could save money and prepare at night after going to school during the day. He would definitely need to plan how best to get his family to a fortress as soon as possible after the shift, maybe even before it happened. *Money should come easy by playing the stock markets, at least to begin with. In general, I already know which companies will tank or rise. After the Shift, dollars and cents will have zero value, so I can spend all of it before it becomes useless. I'll need to figure out how to get a little money to play with first, though. That may not be easy.*

As Noah kept thinking about the coming apocalypse, he wondered, *Maybe I can take my parents close to Camp Hammerfist after the Shift. It was the only place that had been able to resist the Aelves.*

Time was on his side—for the moment. The time to act would come quickly, though. Having a solid plan was critical, and it wasn't like Noah could do much else right now while he was stuck as an infant, so he laid down, stared at the ceiling, and thought. He thought harder than he ever had before in his life, fighting the sluggish speed he could currently think, but over time, a plan began to come together.

CHAPTER 11

For Noah, time flew by in a blur. His thoughts notably grew faster, and his body grew physically. Noah also snuck onto his parents' computers when they weren't looking to keep abreast of world events and even brush up on his knowledge.

He considered his second life a precious gift and cherished spending time with his parents, even if he had to hide his true intellect. At times he even felt guilty, especially when he intentionally knocked things off of tables after reviewing standard toddler behavior.

In addition to the work he spent on the present, he also reflected on the past. He reviewed past mistakes and triumphs. His prior knowledge was critical for planning the best way to prepare his family for the coming Shift.

The memory from his first life of his mother's broken, bloody smile as she screamed for him to get away from the raiders hounded Noah like a rabid dog at his heels, motivating him to find a way to keep his parents safe. The greatest immediate hurdle he identified was funding. As an infant, he couldn't exactly run out and get a job.

Noah planned to capitalize on his knowledge of future stocks and financials to make money as quickly as possible, and most importantly, spend that money wisely before the Shift came again. It was a longshot, but at first, Noah created several email accounts for himself and sent his father investment ideas, but Clark must have either passed it off as spam or thought it was creepy. Either way, Noah decided to stop, but his parents had already definitely noticed he wasn't a normal child.

Noah took advantage of the fact that all parents think their children are gifted, and he simply began showing more gifted behavior that he had read about online. After confirming his father and mothers' biases, they had him tested, and he easily passed the tests. After that, he could allow himself to start speaking more freely, and he'd already accomplished some of what he'd set out to do.

His parents were proud of him.

Soon after he'd been confirmed a "genius", he'd started showing an interest in his father's work, and in "current" events on the news. Over time, his parents eventually noticed his curiosity.

Noah began asking questions about finances, remembering to

keep his language simple. Luckily, this touched on his father's passions, and Clark immediately engaged with him about business and accounting, even at three years old. Noah was worried that he might be pushing it a little too far too fast, but he had underestimated his father's passion for finances.

Although Clark looked like a strict dad on the surface, he was pretty easy going except for where numbers and money concerned. In Noah's previous life, it had been a running joke to poke fun at his dad's thriftiness. Clark had always been too cheap to spend money on corrective eye surgery instead wearing his inexpensive, ridiculous looking glasses. Noah's father had always been far too conservative with his money to do something like invest in young, upstart ventures as well—they were too risky for him.

Noah and his father talking about accounting or finances became almost a nightly occurrence at the Henson house.

Granted, Noah still had to stunt his vocabulary, use incorrect tenses, and speak more slowly, but for the most part, neither of his parents treated him like a normal child of his age anymore.

When he had almost turned four, it had dawned on a frustrated Noah that he hadn't connected with his mother intellectually yet the way he had with his father. His mother Lana was a severely underpaid elementary school teacher. He couldn't remember a time she didn't have a side job to help pay for extra Christmas presents or family trips. Between the two Henson parents, Lana always acted as the trailblazer, willing to try something new. Slower to try new things, Clark's skepticism to anything new would usually break down in the face of Lana's enthusiasm. Her adventurous streak was what finally got her husband to try a weekly session of yoga, or to incorporate Brussel sprouts into some of the meals that she cooked.

Noah remembered that his mother had always wanted to travel, and held a fascination with Japan and Japanese culture. Since Noah knew of a startup in Japan that would absolutely explode soon, becoming the world's leader in solar power, he decided he could use his mother's interest to kill two birds with one stone.

At first, he just asked his mother about other countries. Then he focused on Japan. This led to deeper conversations with his mother about Japanese history and even industry, so Noah made a big production of studying Japan on his own, which absolutely delighted Lana. This allowed him to start gently nudging his mother about the business he'd "found" that was very impressive, and that he believed his parents should invest in.

It took Noah asking for the favor as a 4th birthday present, but he finally got his mom to talk to his dad about the Japanese solar power company, Kanazawa Corporation. After a family meeting where his father argued two on one, he finally invested in the company. Clark did not hide the fact that he was planning to use the investment as a teaching moment for Noah, fully expecting that the money would be lost. However, Noah soon overheard a few excited conversations between his parents about the Kanazawa Corporation, and that as one of the first investors in the company, Clark was being offered first pick of a new round of stock options. With another nudge from Lana, Clark did a very un-Clark thing and invested a large sum of money. Not long after that, Noah noticed his mom had stopped picking up weekend hours as a waitress at Lucy's Diner. She stayed home more to help raise her son. On top of that, his dad did something on his own that Noah never would have never imagined Clark doing in a million years— he bought a new car.

The car itself even surprised Noah. It wasn't the typical Henson family car with fifty replacement parts and a sputtering exhaust, but a brand new, right off the lot sporty SUV. This had shocked the four-year-old Noah more than his own rebirth.

That day, Noah had said to himself, "If there's anything that proves I can change the future, it's this. I bet dad still spent three days haggling with the dealership for the best deal possible, though. Next time I need to draw blood from a rock, I'll ask him for help."

In addition to the investments that Clark had made in Kanazawa, Noah also suspected that his father used his background to vote as a shareholder.

Other than the new car and his mother being home more often, Noah's family didn't have many other signs of their improved financial situation due to dad's spendthrift values. But that didn't stop Noah from secretly logging into his parents' accounts to check on their stock portfolios. He had known about the concept of compound interest, but the numbers shocked him. If Kanazawa Corporation kept growing, which Noah knew it would, his parents would be able to retire comfortably in another few years.

"I got my parents some financial stability and proved investing into Kanazawa Corp worked," Noah muttered to himself. "But now it's my turn to raise my own money."

He had a few ideas of how to do it. As long as he could get a few hundred dollars, Noah knew he could grow that into a staggering amount of money by the time he reached high school. Betting on sports wouldn't be necessary...which was good since he hadn't paid all that much attention to sports in his past life. Kanazawa Corporation was just one of the companies he knew would do well in the years to come. *The real trick is how I can do this without my parents suspecting.* After plenty of time to think and plan, Noah had thought of several ways to make it happen.

One day he absently swung on a swing set, somewhat amused that as a child, nobody paid him any mind for swinging, whereas people had given him weird looks as a teen for doing the same thing. He'd enjoy the judgement-free time he had left. His parents were currently a stone's throw away, talking to another couple, and Noah used his rare downtime to let his mind wander. *I spent a year going back and forth about coming out as a genius baby, and trying to get some celebrity status to convince a few people about the Aelve invasion,* he mused, then frowned. *I'm glad I didn't go forward with that idea. Even if a lot of people thought I was special, I wouldn't have resulted in anything more than a quick internet headline. The article probably would have read something like, "Genius Baby or Crazy Baby? Click Here To Find Out!"*

He suddenly felt pain behind his eyes and put his hand to his forehead, but as the feeling started to fade, he quickly dropped his arm so nobody would notice. There was no reason to worry his parents, but his headaches had been getting worse. For the time being, he would continue to bear the concern alone. The headaches had gotten to the point they could incapacitate him for an hour. The pain wasn't terrible, just constant, preventing him from focusing on anything. They were sort of like having a painful itch he couldn't scratch, distracting him from all other thoughts.

More time passed, Noah constantly working, learning, and planning. At almost five years old, he stood in the family kitchen, staring at a completed aptitude test on the table. His mother and father had voiced their disappointment that Noah wanted to skip elementary school. The school was an expensive academy for gifted students, and Noah knew his parents probably worried about him becoming socially stunted if he didn't spend time around kids his age. Wilshire Academy also offered some really fantastic programs for gifted children. Noah could accept all that, and knew that his parents were being logical—there was no way they could know he had been reincarnated and didn't need to learn how to socialize all over again. However, while gently arguing, his parents had begun saying some of the same things they had said in his previous life, like, "But you have so much potential!" Something bruised and hurt, an old wound that had been healing but still existed flared, lighting up memories of old pain. Noah suppressed his extremely negative emotional reaction but knew it was time to speak about it. Luckily, he had rehearsed what he was about to say over two lifetimes. It was time to be honest with his parents.

"You may not know what's best for me," he said flatly, carefully holding back a lifetime's worth of anger from his voice. Noah knew the moment of blunt honesty was crucial to how his family would view him from that point onward. "Let's be honest. You're the best Mom and Dad anyone could hope for, but no parent really knows what they're doing, much less with someone like me. I'm not normal, and that is not your fault—there isn't a manual for dealing with a situation like this–I know, I looked. However, it's kind of messed up that you guys are telling me I could do so much more. Okay, more what? I just proved through testing that I'm already at college levels on every subject. You're not being specific because you don't know. What's worse, this all makes me feel like I'm not good enough for you right now. I know you mean well, but the way you phrase this stuff doesn't give me a goal, it won't ever let me feel like I've accomplished anything." Noah held back tears and tried to keep his expression neutral, even as his parents recoiled with a number of emotions.

It wasn't like Noah didn't know he was being a little unfair. His parents had no way to know how badly their good intentions had hurt him in his past life. However, he knew from experience that if he didn't nip this in the bud, he'd hate himself for another lifetime.

In the moment of silence, while his mother and father just stared at him, Noah winced, already regretting what he'd said. Luckily, his parents really were better than he'd ever deserved, and they asked him why he didn't want to go to school. What's even better, they actually listened.

Noah didn't like the idea of lying to his family, but he had to get rather creative with the truth. Luckily, he had prepared a little bit for this moment and was able to cite studies about the psychology of genius children, and how they were impacted by various peer groups. The conversation was incredibly meta, a fact Noah was aware of and tried not to think about too much. He needed to focus on logic that his parents would believe, so his main points to his family were that he might be bullied, he already got lots of socialization, school was an unnecessary expense for the family, and he was already learning through self-study—he didn't need teachers, much less to teach him how to read.

Ultimately, after a lot of talking and his mother finally breaking down in tears, the Hensons decided to trust him, agreeing with his plan to be homeschooled with his mom until at least junior high school. This was a huge win. Noah would have died of boredom in a kindergarten class, and despite taking another lifetime to do so, he had finally been able to say what he'd wanted to tell his parents in his previous life.

That night, he reflected on all the real reasons he had forced the issue, avoiding elementary school, and talking his parents out of private schools in general.

He already had far beyond an elementary education and didn't need to socialize with children. Also, all the information he needed for research was on the internet. Most importantly, he needed freedom to act on his own. Going to school, especially at a strict private school, would demand a good chunk of his time through mandated sports and extracurricular activities. By putting off his schooling and going to a public school in the future meant he could hopefully keep a better schedule.

At this point in his life, anything that took much time away from preparing for the Shift would be a waste.

***

Faster than he would have imagined possible, Noah's fifth birthday came and went. The next night he headed to bed after writing a report for his mother, as usual, but suddenly found himself standing in front of a mirror, looking at his own reflection. It didn't take long for Noah to realize he was in a dream. *That's weird,* he thought. He'd had lucid dreams before, especially after being reincarnated, but this one felt different.

A blue screen suddenly appeared before of him, showing a beautiful young woman with long, curly red hair that bounced when she moved. Her eyes constantly shifted between hazel and deep forest green, depending on the light. Noah recognized the girl, and the image encased in the translucent screen made him cringe inside even as he grinned.

He was suddenly reminded of his argument with his parents several months before about school. *That's right*, he thought. *I hadn't even admitted to myself back then that another reason I can't go to a private school is that private schools won't have Krystal Connolly.*

"Mom and Dad actually listened to me. I was never that good at arguing before," he commented to himself. "I wonder if that has anything to do with the orb powers."

His words echoed outward as if he were in a cave. He blinked and studied the darkness surrounding him, his thoughts growing clearer by the moment. Noah couldn't place it, but something felt off about the dream, different. *This isn't just a lucid dream*, he realized, caught off guard. *Why does it feel more real than usual?*

Since his lucid dreams had begun years ago, about the same time he'd started getting his headaches, Noah had learned a trick to get out of them. No matter where he was in the dream, as long as he envisioned himself a door that led to the waking world, he would wake up. Noah closed his eyes and envisioned a simple wooden door with a loose doorknob.

When he opened his eyes, he blinked in surprise. Instead of a door, another blue, translucent screen had appeared before him. It multiplied several times, the copies circling around him like sentinels, preventing his escape. *Don't panic, Noah. It's probably something from the orb.* He reached out with his hand and touched the blank, blue screen. Upon contact, the object absorbed all of the other screens in the area and grew five stories high. Words appeared on the screen.

Meeting With Modifier:

Should the wielder not meet with the designated Modifier, the wielder's soul will continue to become less stable. Soul-death may occur due to instability. Meeting with the Modifier may induce soul-death depending on the result of the Trial of the Archetype.

"My soul is unstable? What does...Wait a second," he muttered to himself. "I remember seeing something like this before." He quickly realized that his headaches might be related. Since he'd never experienced the headaches in his previous life, he'd already reasoned that they had to be because of something different in this life.

Noah reread the words on the screen over and over until it made more sense. *If I decide not to meet with this Modifier, then I would have to live the rest of my life with the headaches, all while they probably get worse. And I don't like the sound of soul-death.* At five years old, the headaches were manageable right now, but what about when he turned eighteen, and the Shift happened again? For all he knew, they might get so bad that he'd just be a drooling mess, unable to keep his promise to protect his family.

However, he didn't like the idea of possible soul-death if he met with the Modifier, whatever that was. Noah had already experienced death, and it wasn't fun—he had a feeling the next time around wouldn't be, either. On top of that, soul-death sounded a million times worse than normal death. On the other hand, it sounded like not meeting with the Modifier might actually be riskier.

Seriously, what the heck is a Modifier? He looked into the blackness and wondered if it was staring back, but he wasn't afraid. Although this exact scenario wasn't something he could have calculated, Noah had expected to have more orb-related weirdness eventually.

He flexed his fingers, determined that he would face whatever happened next with a calm mind. *Should I touch it?* he wondered, eyeballing the screen. Finally, he mumbled, "Here goes nothing." Noah spread his arms wide and yelled, "I accept meeting with the Modifier!"

He warily looked around, expecting some hulking tentacle-faced monster to rush out of nowhere to devour him. Instead, the screen condensed into an orb the height of two people, its color morphing from translucent blue to a misty purple. The ball took the shape of a dog, then a cow. It rapidly transformed into a hundred other shapes before slowing down, each shape becoming more recognizable again to Noah. They were just silhouettes, but he was sure he knew them – a tree he used to lean on to study after school. Krystal Connolly. Johnny Dormund. Noah's childhood home. His parents.

Is it using my memories? he wondered, his knees bent in case the morphing mist attacked him.

Finally, the shifting colors settled on a single shape - one Noah could instantly recognize. It was the shape of a man, tall and wiry, leaning casually on his back foot the way a professor might while lecturing an engaged student. "Doc," Noah whispered.

At first, the mist just solidified into Doc Broad's silhouette, but then it quickly filled out to look and act exactly as Noah's friend had, sad smile and all. Although Noah was happy to see the shape of his friend, he knew it wasn't him. Something in Noah's gut warned him to be careful. The false-Doc slowly pulled out a cigarette from a pack of smokes. Then with no match, he lit it with a snap of his fingers.

The apparition eyed Noah through the unnaturally thick smoke coming out the end of his cigarette and spoke in Doc's chain-smoker voice, "I chose a form that would make you most comfortable. Usually, orb-wielders tend to favor their parents, a lover, or a mentor. In this case, it's the latter. I am the Modifier."

Noah's thoughts ran wild, a thousand questions piling up in his head. He suddenly felt strange and looked down at his hands, realizing he was no longer a five-year-old child. His body had somehow taken his twenty-year-old form after the Shift. After collecting himself, he tried to keep his voice steady and confident, saying, "Do you have a name I should call you?"

The Modifier raised an eyebrow, puffing out a thin line of smoke that transformed into the shape of a star before disappearing into the darkness. Noah swore he saw a ghost of a grin cross the Modifier's face. "I've been around for a very long time, and I've never been asked that by a wielder. You humans are...*funny*. I don't have an answer for you."

Without thinking, Noah replied, a little anger caught in his throat, "I'm not going to call you Doc because you're definitely not Doc. Instead, let's go with Mod, short for Modifier. Is that cool?"

Mod blinked before giving him Doc's easy smile. The Modifier leaned on a cabin wall that appeared out of nowhere. "Whatever you say, kid. Now, you have some questions?"

"I have plenty," Noah said, getting straight to the point. There wasn't any need for banter. He found himself putting his weight on another cabin pillar that had appeared out of nowhere. Now they stood on a fully formed cabin porch surrounded by inky darkness. "I need you to tell me about the orb, why I can't access the screens when I'm awake, why my soul is unstable, what the Shift is and how I can stop it, what the Aelves are and how I can stop them, and —"

Mod made a swiping motion with his hand, cutting Noah off.

"There's a lot I can't say," the Modifier said evenly.

Already exasperated, Noah rolled his eyes. "What's the point in asking questions, then?"

Doc tilted his head to Noah as if he had just scored a point in a tennis match. "I can answer a few of your questions. You're asking me to tell you about the orb. It's like asking me to explain reality. It would take forever, and then some. Even if I tried to explain, you wouldn't understand most of it, and the rest wouldn't be useful to you. Just know I'm an impartial party with a single purpose. As the Modifier, I'm supposed to guide your spirit through the Trial of the Archetype."

Noah frowned, his senses tingling. *He's baiting me to ask about what an Archetype is. I have a feeling if I do ask about it, I'll never get answers to my other questions.* He ignored the lure. "What about the screen with the fuzzed-out words?"

Mod ashed his cigarette onto the imaginary porch floor, something Doc never would have done. The real Doc would have used a tray. "Since you received the orb cracked but still functioning—which I didn't think was possible until recent events proved to me otherwise—you'll have a difficult time accessing it, even though you're imprinted."

Again, Noah thought. *He's baiting me to ask about what an imprint is. Fine, I'll bite on this one.*" What's an imprint?" he asked.

Mod gave a wolfish smile. "Good call, kid. *You* are an imprint, your soul. Each orb is different in how you imprint onto it. This one happens to like music. It liked your song and then, *bam*. The orb and the abilities it could impart while it was cracked were yours."

Noah reflexively looked up to gaze at the night sky, to see the stars, but found only more nothing. He shook his head, looking back at Mod, who seemed to be enjoying playing with Noah's head. *I could ask about what it means that my soul is unstable, but I have a feeling that is not the correct path to take.* Noah couldn't tell if Mod had a friendly tone merely because of Doc's form, or because it was genuinely trying to make him relax. He hadn't forgotten the screen's warning of a possible soul-death just by interacting with the Modifier.

Cautiously, he asked. "What about the Aelves and how they caused the Shift? Can you tell me about that?"

Mod tilted his head as if trying to make out what Noah had said. After a moment, he nodded in understanding. "Ah. That's what you call them. Unfortunately, I don't have access to that either. Even if your Trial works out and you make it to the point your time anomaly realigns itself, I don't think I'll be able to access those secret histories by myself. Plus, there's...another factor."

Noah slammed his fist on the railing, and the ethereal wood vanished into smoke. "So, you're useless."

Mod frowned, the cigarette burning up in a sudden flash of heat, disintegrating into ash between his lips. His voice was still Doc's when he spoke, but the tone and words came out much darker. "Kid, I've been around longer than your species has existed.

I hold ancient and secret knowledge from distant stars. I've watched galaxies be ripped apart by upper dimensional beings. Don't blame me. You just aren't very good at asking the right questions."

Vague memories—only images—flashed through Noah's mind of his time between his two lives. He nodded. "I've seen worlds shattered too, universes, even."

Mod opened his mouth and closed it, his eyes searching, probably through Noah's memories. "Huh. Maybe you have. I don't know how your soul survived that ordeal."

It was now Noah's turn to frown. *Did Mod purposefully land on the subject of my soul?* The being that stood before him had just admitted he was older than the Earth. *I can't underestimate how much this thing is manipulating me. I have to be purposeful in how I talk to him.* Noah had already reasoned that his unstable soul was probably the reason for his headaches that were growing worse every year. The headaches were becoming a problem. "Tell me why my soul is unstable and how I can fix it."

Mod eased back into his Doc persona, pulling out another cigarette and lighting it with a snap of his fingers. "Cancer sticks." He chuckled. "Your friend had a good sense of humor. Anyway, I can't tell you about the instability of your soul because you've tucked that away somewhere deep. Right now, I just tried accessing that memory, but whatever happened, your mind is doing a damn good job of hiding that information. It was probably pretty traumatic. In regards to fixing it..."

He puffed out smoke that morphed into an exclamation mark. "You'll have to enter the Trial of the Archetype."

A trial, Noah thought. *This must be the thing that will threaten my life.* "And what happens if I don't stabilize it?"

The Modifier shrugged. "You'll live as you already were, but with your soul becoming less stable over time. You might even experience soul-death before the time anomaly resolves itself. What that means is your body would still live, but you'd just be a vegetable."

Noah gulped. "Time anomaly. You mean my rebirth."

"Sure, if that's what you want to call it," Mod replied with a dismissive wave of his cigarette. "Those who have gone through the Trial of the Archetype may experience soul-death. Everyone's Trial is different, even if they had the same orb, giving them the slight variations for their archetype. Some fight a monster and get eaten. Others traverse through a maze, never waking from their dreams."

"So," Noah said, exhaling slowly, trying to grasp all the information being thrown at him. "If I don't take this Trial, I'll have blistering headaches until I become a walking vegetable. But if I do take this trial, I *might* still experience soul-death, but if it works out, I won't have headaches anymore? Sounds like an easy choice. What's the catch?"

Mod smiled joylessly. "Well, you're quick to make a decision, aren't you? The catch is—"

The Modifier stopped and looked around warily, as if hearing something in the distance. For a quick moment, even though Mod wore Doc's face, Noah saw his eyes shift to something darker than black. The apparition sniffed the air and frowned before his attention focused back to Noah. "Do you accept the Trial or not? Choose now or leave forever."

The whole point of this new life is to protect my family, Noah confirmed to himself. *I can't do that if I'm incapacitated from the headaches. Who cares what the catch is as long as I can stabilize my soul and not die permanently?* "Fine. I accept the Trial."

The Modifier wasn't smiling anymore. He licked the cigarette and swallowed it. "Confirmed." Mod snapped his fingers. "If it's any comfort, I hope you survive your trial."

Nothing happened. Noah looked around at the nothingness surrounding him expectantly. He made a face, and his eyes went to Mod for a reaction, but the Modifier seemed equally confused. Not-Doc frowned deeply, looking out into the ether.

Mod muttered, "Interesting," but he didn't sound interested— he sounded shocked.

"Is this my trial?" Noah asked, still unsure of what was happening.

The Modifier's gaze shifted back to Noah, studying him, and the ancient being's confused expression turned into curiosity. "That other factor I mentioned, before? That was another imprint.

It looks like that imprint has accepted the Trial as well."

Imprint? Noah wondered. *Who would have imprinted—what?* No one who had touched the orb had been able to use it. Doc and Redford hadn't been able to. He had often wondered about Yusef, but the man had died while giving the orb to Noah. Then his eyes widened as he realized what might have happened. Kahlek, the Aelve, had touched the orb.

"Is it Kahlek?" Noah asked. "The Aelve?"

The thing with Doc's face seemed to suppress a grin. "I cannot confirm or deny that. Impartial party, remember? But it doesn't matter. You still have the Trial of the Archetype. The only difference is that both of you are taking the Trial, changing it in a way that affects you both equally and fairly. We've never had mutations like this before. This is a first, I think, to have happened in the Trial, so I don't think the system knows what to do about it."

Noah flexed his hands cautiously. "What does that mean for me?"

Mod tapped his finger on his lower lip in thought. "Just hold your horses, kid. Ah. There we go. Here is your trial. It looks like you two are splitting it, dichotomous-like. Alright, your trial starts now."

Noah braced himself. Would he have to fight monsters? He hoped not. Maybe it was a series of death traps. Either way, he instinctively understood that the Trial—whatever it was—had to be possible for they were created for whoever was imprinted on an orb. At least, that's what Mod had implied. The situation gave Noah a sense of familiarity. Stories about young heroes facing down the personified versions of their fears and defeating them with cunning or a magic sword came to mind. Noah thought about all his fears, which were many, and how he would confront them.

Mod dropped the Doc persona and turned into an amorphous blob once more, growing several stories taller than before. He, or it, morphed into the head of a beautiful woman, the body of a lion, the wings of an eagle, and a snake for a tail.

"I have to fight a sphinx?" Noah exclaimed. He readied himself for the sphinx's attack, prepared to dodge or roll out of the way. The snake tail waved and flexed behind the body of the lion, snapping its viper-jaws.

However, instead of attacking, the sphinx lazily sat and spoke in a high soprano, cold and almost mechanical, chilling Noah's spine. "For this mutated Archetype, your Trials have been decided. Depending on your responses, you will be accepting all responsibilities of your dichotomous Archetype. If you fail to respond, you will be devoured."

Noah gulped. He didn't completely understand but put effort into collecting himself. *This is my mind, despite the trial. I can make anything I want here.* He blinked, and a dozen tanks appeared around him, pointing their weapons at what had been Mod.

The sphinx gave Noah an impassive look, ignoring the tanks.

"Your trial is now. Answer me, is it better to hear or to be heard?"

The surrounding tanks disappeared into puffs of smoke as Noah's jaw dropped. "What?" he asked, caught off guard. *My trial is a question?*

The sphinx said, "The question will not be repeated. Answer or be devoured."

Noah opened his mouth to give the obvious answer: to be heard. He had spent an entire lifetime wishing he could just speak out against the cruelties of the world after the Shift, to rail against his parents' expectations, and most of all, against his own inaction and weakness. If only he had had a powerful voice, he could have done the right things. He wouldn't have ever become Worm.

But he stopped himself. *Was that what I wanted all along, to have a voice?* Noah asked himself. *Didn't I always have a voice...but just didn't use it?*

Memories of his first life flowed through him. His parent's expectations had been the root anxiety that led to other fears later in his life, but hadn't that been his choice to react that way, to let his fears fester? What would have happened if he had only spoken out about the matter? *Nothing really would have changed*, he said to himself honestly. *I would have just said what I wanted to say and would have still acted the same way.*

I blamed everyone else, Noah thought. *They were all trying to help me, even Redford in his own messed up way. What would have my life have been like if I had listened to my parents and the advice of my friends and mentors before the Shift? It would have been a tougher road, but I could have come out stronger. I was just afraid of a potential future. Fear of failure was the problem, not my voice.*

The first time he had *really* listened to someone had been after the Shift. It took months of short conversations, but Noah had found himself fascinated with Doc Broad's perspective, his easy enthusiasm for hope, his endless curiosity, and his compulsion to involve himself in the lives of others. Noah had changed because he had simply listened to Doc.

After that realization, Noah didn't hesitate any further. He smiled and declared. "It is better to hear."

The sphinx nodded in confirmation and closed its eyes. When it opened them again, white light poured out and enveloped the surrounding area, cascading over Noah. A lightning sensation rushed through him, and the song he had sung countless times in his mind echoed from his heart out into the distant darkness.

He knew then that nothing would ever be the same. His conviction to protect his family hadn't just strengthened, it had suddenly grown, becoming more. Spending his new life to prepare his family for the Shift and the coming of the Aelves wasn't enough anymore. Strength flowed through him like a mighty river.

I have power now, maybe even enough to change things. Noah thought of Doc Broad's dream to connect humanity after the Shift, how if the people of America had united, much less the world, more people would have survived, and they might have had a chance against the Aelves and their terrible magic. *Maybe I don't have to send my parents to a fort. I can build one here in this town.* The thought was powerful, profound, and Noah felt a confidence within himself he'd never truly experienced before.

Then suddenly, the light and strength faded as Noah was surrounded once more by darkness and silence.

Mod stood in front of him in Doc's form again, looking a little tired. "Okay. This means you're the Listener Archetype now. Huh. That's a new one," he mused. Then he spoke like a pharmacy tech rattling off the side effects for a prescription drug. "You two are the first dichotomy of an orb. Limited abilities will be afforded to you due to two factors, the first being the other imprint. Second, the orb has been damaged. Once the time dilation realigns, you will have access to more of your abilities. In this timeline, this moment should be close to what you refer to as the Shift. The nascent energies of the suppressors should help with that. You have now accepted all responsibilities of your Archetype."

Noah's eyes widened. He had so many questions and blurted out the first that came to mind. "What about Kahlek? What is an Archetype?"

The Modifier with Doc's face smiled sadly. "The Trial is done. The time for questions is over. Goodbye."

With that, the darkness faded away, and Noah opened his eyes.

CHAPTER 12

Noah woke up from the not-a-dream, examining all the glow-in-the-dark star stickers littered across his bedroom ceiling as he collected himself. He had wondered several times why the stars had changed after the Shift, and his research online had not yet yielded results. The alarm clock on his nightstand displayed the date, March 5th, 2025. It was two in the morning.

I can't believe a couple hours passed in that dream. It felt like the whole thing lasted only twenty minutes! I hope I can meet Modifier again to get more answers. There's too much I don't know about the Aelves that would help my family if I were to get answers, Noah mused.

Now that he was getting his wits back, Noah's heart began to race a little. He had passed the mysterious Trial of the Archetype, giving him new abilities. He sat up in his bed and rifled his fingers through his hair, eager to see his reward for passing the Trial. It didn't take a lot of intuition to figure the screens would be involved, and he hadn't been wrong.

Three screens appeared in his vision. The first two screens read:

The Listener

The wielder is now the Listener Archetype. By accepting the role of the Listener, the wielder has inherited the responsibilities and abilities of this Archetype.

Listener Stats

Agility: 1

Dexterity: 1

Defense: 1

Magic Defense: 1

Spirit: 2

Spirit Defense: 2

Magic: 0

Charisma: 3

Noah's eyes widened, taking in all the new information. He reread the words several times before he finally set his gaze on the third screen. The last display wasn't like the first two, which simply showed words and numbers. Instead, it held the image of a six-string acoustic guitar with only one string attached between the pegs. His hand went through the instrument when he tried to grab it, as if it were a hologram.

The guitar itself didn't look ornate or have any distinct

features, but when Noah's hand passed through the frets, the string vibrated as if it were just strummed. Another screen appeared.

Listener Skills:

[Listening] (Passive): Maxed

[Stumble] (Passive): Level 1

[Harmony] (Passive): Level 1

[Jack of All] (Passive): Level 1

He sucked a sharp breath. "They're abilities—it's just like a game! Does magic display itself like this to the Aelves or is this because of me?" he wondered aloud.

There was no way for him to explore that question, but he felt like he might be on to something. When he had first seen English letters on the screens, he had assumed the orb had used whatever language he had felt comfortable with. After the Trial of the Archetype, it was no longer just a tool but had become a part of him. In his dream, Mod had even admitted to using the form of Doc Broad from Noah's memories to make communication easier.

After his flash of excitement passed, Noah cracked his neck and let out a slow breath. "Okay. Let's see what we have here. First, stats."

He blinked away everything but his skills. Acting on his will, more screens appeared, each giving him descriptions of a single stat.

Agility was pretty straightforward, describing was how fast he was. Dexterity was simple as well, explaining how much control he had over his own body. This would help with things that required coordination.

Defense was how hard a hit he could take. Magic Defense was the same thing but with magic attacks. After reviewing this stat, Noah paused, realizing it proved he would have to face magic in the future. It had really been common sense, it was inevitable with the coming of the Aelves, but now it seemed more real to him.

He didn't know how he was going to raise the level of Magic Defense, let alone any of his stats, but it was definitely going to be something he'd invest in as soon as he could. Noah had seen the power of the Aelves, and Magic Defense would be a key stat to help protect himself against, to survive.

The Spirit stat was vague. 'Spiritual essence' was its only description. Noah wondered if the skill tree held abilities he would need spiritual power for, drawing on his own soul as an energy source separate from magic. Ultimately, this was just another question he didn't have answers to.

Next he moved on to Spirit Defense. The description for this state was a bit more concrete, pretty much in line with Defense and Magic Defense. *Maybe reincarnating and fixing my unstable soul has something to do with my higher Spirit and Spirit Defense stats.*

Noah frowned at his Magic stat. To his disappointment, it held a big fat zero. Some part of him wanted to be able to cast fireballs or use magic to fly and impress a bunch of cute girls...or maybe just one very pretty redhead.

His last stat, Charisma, was the most alarming, three times higher than his physical stats and even higher than his Spirit stat. The description for Charisma read that it was a unique stat specifically for his Archetype.

"Each Archetype must have its own unique stat," Noah concluded and nodded his head. "Figuring out an Aelve's Archetype and what makes them special will give us an edge nobody had in the last Shift."

A thought began to grow steadily when he remembered the screen with the guitar. His special Archetype stat was Charisma, so the guitar probably wasn't just for show. Like the English on his screens, the guitar must be another way the orb was using Noah's memories. Noah carefully thought back to his trial, and his conversation with the sphinx. A thought slowly dawned on him, and he thought, *No way, it couldn't be, right?* However, the more he thought about it, the more he realized he might be right.

Finally, he couldn't help but let out a muffled laugh, burying his face into his pillow, not wanting to wake up his parents. It was too ridiculous to not be true. "I'm a bard. The guitar. My Charisma stat. The fact I always wanted to learn to play the guitar. I'm a friggin' bard!"

Of all the magical abilities he could have gained—fire magic, teleportation, invisibility—Noah had received the least combative set of skills. At first, a bitter taste of disappointment crawled onto his tongue, but he quickly swallowed it when he remembered his true goal. *Protecting my family isn't enough. I need to build a Fort, and prepare as much of humanity as I can for the Shift.*

He laid down fully again, staring at the glow-in-the-dark stars above. If he had gained combative abilities, he probably could have shown his power to the world. Maybe he could have convinced everyone about the Shift and the Aelves. If that had happened, Noah would have absolutely changed things so much by revealing his abilities, he would have found himself in a future he couldn't predict.

"If there are Aelves on Earth before the Shift, the sight of a human kid shooting laser beams out of his armpits would have attracted their attention pretty quickly. No. Being a bard is good. I can't fight all the Aelves on my own. They're stronger than us in every way, and that's probably not even counting their own orbs."

Uniting humanity and preparing them for the horrors to come was his priority. Since the days of old tabletop games, long before the virtual reality video games Noah had grown up with, bards were a class of character that usually acted as support for other types of characters. Their role was simply to strengthen the people they fought with. Bards made others stronger.

"What if I had told the sphinx that it was better to be heard instead?" he wondered. Noah pushed the thought aside. It was useless to think about paths he could have taken but didn't. Besides, maybe if he had chosen that route, he would have died.

Oddly enough, a wave of relief washed over him. He knew his role now and had a better idea of how he was going to accomplish the giant task ahead of him. *If someone had asked me how I was going to help save the world against the Aelves, I definitely would have never guessed any of this. But now, I know what my strengths are. Like a game, maybe my stats can be exploited. I'll need every advantage I can get.*

Noah's confidence rose. He knew his role, but he needed to get back to exploring his tools again. After willing away the Listener Stat screens, he replaced them with what he assumed was his skill tree.

The guitar was a six-string, or would be. The first time he had plucked the only string, a few other screens had appeared displaying different skills. *Each string must represent their own skills, like tiers. I bet if I get another string, I'll get more powerful skills. For now, let's see what these skills are and how they'll me help me.* He examined the main screen again.

Listener Skills:

[Listening] (Passive): Maxed

[Stumble] (Passive): Level 1

[Harmony] (Passive): Level 1

[Jack of All] (Passive): Level 1

Noah willed for descriptions to appear so he could have a better understanding of what any of this meant.

Currently unable to level up Archetype skills. Must have

dispensable skill points to distribute.

A little frustration welled up in his chest. "Well, that makes sense. I probably need to level up, but I don't have any display showing me how to do it, or any requirements or anything. I don't even have a level for my Archetype!"

If a game designer had actually constructed his abilities, that designer would have been fired in the real world. This was ridiculous. The screens were too vague and only hinted at greater powers. Noah sighed and thought, *It's like I've been thrust into a game without any tutorial. But hey, that's pretty much life.*

The displays continued to change, showing more specific descriptions.

[Listening] (Passive): Maxed

Wielder may hear sounds with heightened clarity within a two hundred yard range.

Noah raised an eyebrow at the description. "I can't believe I never bothered to test the actual limits on my hearing," he muttered.

[Stumble] (Passive): Level 1

10% chance to automatically stumble to avoid immediate danger.

He made a face at this awkward skill. "It's like a goofy version of a spider sense or something. I need to test what will even qualify as danger. Gosh, this might even cause issues if I don't have control over it." So far, his new abilities hadn't exactly wowed him. He moved on.

[Harmony] (Passive): Level 1

By playing music, the wielder may assign people to each note, helping the wielder create strategies or find balance for each person.

"This should be renamed backseat driver," Noah noted with a frown. "I don't know how I'll implement it yet, but maybe if I combine it with my high Charisma stat, I can find some use for it." He moved on to the last skill.

[Jack of All] (Passive): Level 1

Wielder can learn every non-Archetype skill with greater ease, depending on the skill. Alignment with the wielder's Listener Archetype will determine the strength of Jack of All. Maxed level of learned skills is five (5) per level of Jack of All.

"Whoa," Noah breathed. "I could learn Kung Fu."

Of all his new abilities, Jack of All had Noah the most excited. His dream of using his new life to learn new abilities that would help him survive in the Shift, like basic survival, navigation, and a myriad of other things seemed much more attainable now. Before, even with all the knowledge of his previous life, Noah had been having a difficult time juggling all his responsibilities and focuses. Building his relationship with his parents, scouring the internet for more information, and just simply enjoying his time with his family while he had it...all took time. He knew from prior study that if he had completely devoted his life to work, it might not have been the most efficient way to actually get things done either.

Even if he'd had time to learn new skills, actually practicing would be necessary to make them useable. Then trying to avoid unwanted attention would be difficult on top of all the time constraints. Learning several new languages would have taken just as much time in his new life as it would have his old one, but his new skill might change all of that!

"With Jack of All," Noah said, "maybe I can learn whatever I want!"

Languages, archery, weapons crafting, town building, and a hundred other skills would have eaten up most of Noah's time before. *I can't just make myself strong*, he thought. *I need connections, people to invest in long before the Shift occurs. Charisma and maybe [Harmony] will help with that. I'll figure out the details later.*

Noah hoped that now, with time, he could be both an encyclopedia of knowledge *and* be at the top of his game physically. His plan had already been to learn the basics of most martial arts, medieval weaponry, and gymnastics. But maybe now, in effect, he could be the closest thing to the ultimate human specimen.

He frowned. "Even then, it won't be enough."

Noah needed money and resources. His knowledge of the future would take care of his finances. He'd already made headway with tricking his father into unexpected wealth. Maybe with Jack of All, he might be able to explore more...discreet avenues to make money. As a child, he'd have a difficult time investing any money at all, even if he had it to spend. But if Noah learned how to make another identity for himself, he could potentially become a billionaire in ten years.

The money itself didn't excite him, like he'd already reasoned before, it would be useless when the Shift came. No, he'd need those resources to spend on things to help prepare the world for what was to come. It wouldn't matter how strong or smart he would be when the Aelves came. A single person couldn't stop them alone.

Noah willed away the screens, a little overwhelmed by the information. He let his eyes trace the space between the stars on the ceiling, just like how Doc had taught him. Before the dream and the Trial, the empty space on his bedroom ceiling had only reminded Noah of how nearly impossible it seemed to unite so many people against a threat they didn't even know existed. He'd honestly felt a little lost.

But now as his eyes traced the constellations he had learned on Doc's porch, a new screen appeared in his view on its own.

You have learned the mundane skill [Navigation by Stars]. Level one.

Under the stars, the wielder cannot get lost, able to plot a course (based on skill level).

Noah smiled as he was filled with a sudden, savage joy. He closed his eyes and couldn't wait to wake up in a few hours. The world had changed for him—again.

CHAPTER 13

Ten-year-old Noah and his parents sat at the table, each flicking through their own tablet. Lana rifled through local news, a slight frown on her face. Clark's eyes darted between different graphs while his forefinger tapped on the table, a sign he was calculating numbers in his head.

The tip of Noah's fork burst the center of his egg, letting the yolk bleed into his hash browns. Next to his plate, his own tablet sat on the breakfast table, the screen split into two windows. The first window showed a top-down perspective of a figure, a man clad in white robes, face covered with a scarf. He held twin scimitars as he walked carefully through a forest. Letters floated above the figure's head, showing the name of the player controlling the avatar, "Shiek Freak", the most famous streamer for the decade-old online game, Adventures on Corinthia.

He's in the Forests of Dumadull, Noah noted to himself.

Hopefully, Johnny's party doesn't have to face him anytime soon. Shiek Freak is a loner, and likes exploring more than fighting, but they still haven't lost a single battle.

Noah exited out of the game stream window, letting the other side take over the full screen. The larger picture contained several complicated graphs of different stocks and a little window with international news. He took a bite of his hash browns as he absorbed the information. Several familiar companies appeared on the screen, numbers changing every second – Kanazawa Corp, Muller Green and Sons, and Bender Steel.

Some part of him wanted to find the pattern between the numbers and use that information to boost his investments. A blue, translucent screen only he could see appeared in his field of view.

[Harmony]

Wielder may assign each company their own note.

Noah hid a smile and willed the prompt away. With his Archetype skill, [Harmony], he could have assigned each company their own musical note. Then if he played a guitar with those notes and tried to make different songs out of them, the skill would allow him to understand patterns through the music. He didn't need to waste time doing any of that, though–his knowledge of the future had already been enough to make him a multi-millionaire by nine years old. Of course, most of that money had been made through an alternate identity, one kept secret from his parents.

"What are you smiling about there, champ?" his father asked from the across the table. "Did you see something in the numbers that caught your attention?"

The numbers. That was how his father referred to the companies they had invested in based on Noah's suggestions. When he'd been five, it had taken a lot of effort and patience to convince his father to invest. But by the time he had been seven, the companies had done better than anything Clark had ever dreamed of. In fact, Kanazawa Corp's success was at least ten times larger now than in Noah's previous life at this point.

He was certain his father had played a small role in the international solar company's unexpected growth with his voting rights. To Clark, it didn't matter how much money you made. The passionate accountant cared most about cost efficiency. He must have voted as a shareholder after crunching numbers.

Noah shrugged and answered his father's question. "I was just thinking that Kanazawa Corp's control over Asia isn't enough. With the right contacts, they might be able to find footing in America."

Clark adjusted his cheap, owlish glasses and hummed with curiosity. He leaned forward a little over the table and gave his son a fierce grin. Noah recognized the gesture–his father was preparing for battle. Their daily spars about international business usually began with a simple comment like this. Before Noah could make a proposal, influencing his dad to act and maybe even create a few thousand American jobs, Lana Henson cleared her throat.

"Boys," she warned sweetly without looking up from her tablet.

Lana didn't say anything more than that because she didn't have to. Noah's mother had a way of saying a lot in one word. Her inflection had told them two things. First, her husband had a limit on how much business could be discussed at breakfast. Second, there was no way her son was going to continue a conversation with food still in his mouth.

Noah swallowed.

Clark may wear the pants in the house, but it was Lana who told him when he could wear them and how. Noah's mom was the nicest person he had ever known, but she could be frightening sometimes.

Suddenly, Noah's tablet buzzed, and a small hologram of a chubby-faced blond boy hovered above the screen - his best friend, Johnny Dormund. "Hey, trash monkey, we're fighting against Anonymoose in thirty minutes. Make sure you get your butt over here."

Johnny was talking about their weekly video game session for Adventures on Corinthia. His friend had a party of four adventurers who had been playing together for a year before Noah had started watching their games. After acting on Noah's small suggestions while he played his guitar, their group, Dragonx42, had rocketed through the international rankings. Even though

Noah didn't even have an avatar in the game, Dargonx42's success was a direct result of his meddling. He'd been getting great practice with [Harmony].

"Trash monkey?" Lana asked, raising an eyebrow.

Johnny's hologram widened its eyes, head turning around slowly. "Uh," Johnny stammered. "Hey there, Mrs. Henson. Just gamer talk. Right, yeah. You look great today!"

Noah's mother tried frowning, but he noticed a hint of a playful smile at the edge of her lips. She said, "Tell your mom I'll see her at yoga later tonight."

"Will do, Mrs. H!" Johnny's hologram turned to face Noah again and gave him a nervous look. "Seriously, bro. These guys are second in the world, just under Shiek Freak. We need you for this."

Noah nodded but looked a question at his mom. Even though it was summertime, Noah was homeschooled and still had homework every day. Lately, his mom had been giving him assignments that would have made a college level student tear his hair out. To anyone else, the tasks would have been too challenging, but with Noah's skill [Jack of All], he was luckily able to accomplish them with relative ease.

In fact, he loved that his mom kept trying new ways to teach and challenge his way of thinking. Not only did it bring them closer together, always giving them something to discuss at the dinner table, but it also helped Noah gain new mundane skills with

[Jack of All]. Over the years through homeschooling, he had acquired a few levels in [Geography], [Astronomy], and a hundred other subjects that his orb abilities had qualified as skills.

Lana tapped a finger on her arm and finally gave a soft smile. She said, "Even geniuses need a break. Go ahead and play with Johnny. Just tell him to watch his mouth. I know how you two can get when you're gaming."

Johnny's hologram head bounced up and down, giddy and nervous. He grinned and said, "See you in thirty, Navi. Don't be late, Brains."

With that, the hologram vanished, and Noah's tablet screen went black. This would be another opportunity to enjoy his childhood, to create a memory he could hold on to for after the Shift. He was legitimately excited to see his friend, even if their maturity levels were different, it was intellectual. Having a child's body still allowed Noah to enjoy spending time with other children.

But helping Johnny's group fight against Anonymoose held real benefits for Noah's plan to help humanity. Some part of him felt a little guilty for not telling Johnny his real purpose for hanging out, but the face of the Aelves and their horrifying power held sway in Noah's thoughts, reminding him that guilt wouldn't save anyone's life.

Noah noticed his mother continuing to frown while scrolling through the local news. Eventually, she let out a frustrated sigh and folded the tablet. Noah's mind connected the dots quickly, and he had a good idea what was worrying his mom. Before he spoke, his Charisma stat tickled the back of his mind, telling him it was probably better to ask his mom what was happening instead of just stating it as a fact.

"What's wrong?" he asked.

Lana stood up and began to collect everyone's plates for the sink. "You know all those potholes downtown?"

Noah nodded. Michigan's famously harsh winters always did a number on the roads. The city was constantly working on them during the non-winter seasons, at least, they were supposed to. "Yeah, what about them?"

"The mayor is what's wrong," she complained. "I know several other people who have made complaints to city hall about the potholes on Main Street getting fixed, but nothing happens. It's actually getting borderline dangerous in some areas, I think. You should have seen Mrs. Colmeyer's car last week. She needed a new tire and a new rim. It's not like she has the money to replace that willy-nilly."

"According to her finances," Clark rebutted mildly, "she can."

Lana shot him a look, and her husband shrank inside his oversized suit like an owl being faced down by a hawk. She pleasantly warned, "Honey, it's been so long since you've been to yoga."

Clark quietly sipped his coffee, hiding behind his mug.

Meanwhile, Noah made a mental note to do some hacking later that day. Levelling that particular skill had definitely come in handy. With it, he planned to discreetly use one of his shell companies to send a congratulatory email, and a fat check to Mrs. Colmeyer for winning a contest that she'd definitely never remember entering.

"And how is it the mayor's fault?" Noah asked.

His mom squinted at him, suspicion marring her face. "You're doing it again."

"Doing what?" Noah replied innocently.

She gave him a knowing look, "You're asking questions which you already have the answers to. I've been going on for weeks about how the new mayor is probably corrupt and tied in with the east coast mob. You've heard why I think he's incentivized to keep the downtown area riddled with potholes."

"Yeah, so his cousins who own several auto repair shops in that area can profit," Noah said with a nod. He added with a joking tone, "It's most likely to launder money."

It was definitely to launder money, he thought. Over the years, Noah's mundane skill [Hacking] had grown to level three. Apparently, that had been enough to get into the repair shops' digital records remotely from his own computer. He'd found that the shops really did have connections with the new, charismatic mayor. He hadn't known what to do with the information, but speaking with his mother gave him a fun idea.

He stood up, "Well, I gotta head over to Johnny's. Why don't you and Azar do a peaceful demonstration?"

His mom's eyebrows shot up. "Like, with signs that say, 'Say a Prayer for a New Mayor'?"

"Yah, just like students at college campuses do."

"That might—" his mom pondered. "What's your angle? I don't see nice old Azar doing something so radical."

"I wouldn't be so sure about that." Noah thought of old lady Azar, a family friend who had grown considerably closer to his mom in this new lifetime. A screen appeared in Noah's view.

[Community] (Mundane) Level 2

Azar (last name unknown)

Age: 80+ years old

Race: Human

Notes:

-Persian immigrant

-Won several international feminism awards in the early 2020s

-Family died in the Great Korean War during a trip to Seoul

-Hates lying

-Loves pie

-Makes frequent attempts to set wielder up with her niece

-Possibly follows Zoroastrianism but most likely Atheist. Celebrates Christmas as a holiday

-Dislikes formalities

-**Hates corrupt governments and politicians**

It was the last item Noah focused on. Out of all the [Listener] skills he had gained after the Trial of the Archetype, Noah had relied most on [Jack of All]. It had not only allowed him to learn mundane skills with nearly superhuman ease, but had also organized information he'd learned in ways that proved to be more useful than he could have ever imagined.

The mundane skill [Community] had allowed Noah to gather and compile important information about every person he had ever met. With his high Charisma, this had allowed him to create strong bonds with everyone in the community, spreading his influence among them over the years. Of course, he also had the mundane skill [Memory Palace], but it was limited compared to [Community]. Even at level five, [Memory Palace] only afforded him five very small rooms worth of information.

He hummed two notes silently in his head, assigning his mother and Azar to each. *Normally, I'd need my guitar for this,* Noah thought. *But it's just two notes.*

Harmony

Wielder may assign each entity their own note.

The notes played around in his head, and Noah received a better understanding of how the new interaction between his mom and her friend Azar would turn out. If his mom followed through, the corrupt mayor and his cousins were probably going to have a bad day soon. Noah suppressed a smile and walked to the door.

"I'll be back later tonight. I have my phone on vibrate if you need to get a hold of me. I think Azar might be able to help you get through to the mayor."

Noah made sure to grab his acoustic guitar leaning against the wall in the hallway, checking to make sure it was in tune before stepping outside. The instrument was necessary if Johnny's team was going to have a shot at taking down the powerful gamer group, Anonymoose.

The grinning young man didn't need to see his mother's expression as he closed the door behind him–he knew she would take his advice. Even at ten years old, it was difficult for him to wrap his head around how overpowered his high Charisma felt. Sometimes at night, he felt haunted, wondering if he was merely manipulating his parents like puppets. He had to constantly remind himself that his skills were a part of him, like his limbs.

Charisma may have given him advantages others didn't have, but others didn't need to prepare humanity for the end of the world and fend off an invasion of Aelves. *I'll take every advantage I can get.*

The lanky boy let his mind wander as he made his way through his quiet suburban neighborhood. The summer sun climbed the stark blue sky, brightening Noah's mood. He took it all in, savoring this moment like others that he could revisit after the Shift occurred.

Suddenly, his thought process about his skills and stats

reminded him of Mod. The memory of the Trial of the Archetype years ago left a bitter taste in his mouth. He hadn't seen the Modifier in his dreams again since his test. *I probably have to meet certain conditions for it to show up again, just like my abilities.*

When he had turned seven, it had become increasingly clear to Noah that although he had levels for his abilities like most role-playing games, they didn't work the same way. Whether it was a [Listener] skill or a mundane skill, he wasn't exactly granted any kind of measurable experience to judge how far he was in growing a specific ability.

If he could figure out how the system worked, maybe he could figure out a way to exploit the system, levelling up all his skills and stats to their maximum.

Noah hadn't been a huge gamer in his previous life, which was one reason spending time with Johnny was proving educational. Besides being a fun goofball, Johnny Dormund loved playing games. Since Noah's abilities had manifested through screens that resembled video games, Noah had reasoned that learning gamer culture would prove beneficial to figuring out his new abilities–online research hadn't been enough. Plus, it was nice to have a best friend, something he never had in his previous life.

Hanging around Johnny and his online gamer friends had led Noah to realize that there were other ways to level up in some video games. Noah had watched the other boys play games that required certain quests to be fulfilled before achieving new abilities or powers, or unlocking new things. This had led him to believe that levelling his [Listener] stats like Charisma didn't require experience, but perhaps completing certain tasks.

Maybe he was wrong, but it was the best guess he currently had.

Except, Noah thought, a little irritated, *I don't know what the darn conditions are. It could be, "collect five raspberries for your mom by the end of the day and you'll be rewarded a new [Listener] stat point."* So far, none of his experiments had helped at all.

Noah made a face, scuffing a foot on the ground. Now he was only a few blocks away from the Dormunds' bright yellow, two-story house. He'd be arriving five minutes before Johnny's group fought against Anonymoose for the coveted number one spot in their online game. Noah used this last bit of time to block away his thoughts and focus on his oldest and most reliable skill, [Listen].

With his sharpened focus, all the sounds within a two hundred yard radius around Noah came to him with perfect clarity. His ability helped isolate each sound and note where they were. The skill wasn't perfect - it didn't usually allow him to hear every conversation within homes. Walls still muffled sounds. But he could pick up conversations between neighbors, strained arguments between young couples, and dogs barking at each other. If he strained, he could hear farther, but with less clarity.

All of the information got filed away into his increasingly useful skill, [Community]. He didn't know when the information would be useful, but it might be good to have it. After surviving the Shift for a while, he understood the value of being prepared.

After reaching his destination, Noah cut off his [Listen] skill, letting the world fade into background noise again as he opened the fence to Johnny Dormund's house. He smiled and strummed his guitar, playing a perfect e major chord.

**

"Navi!" Johnny shouted over his shoulder to Noah. The chubby blond boy sat cross-legged on a flat pillow, his body tilted as he mashed buttons on his game control. Before him, the holographic display showed eight game characters duking it out in fantastical forest. Magical beam attacks shot in every direction.

Noah heard his friend but was busy looking at his phone screen. His thumb swiped through a few real estate listings in Colorado, all houses within the same neighborhood. With a few presses, the houses were earmarked to be purchased under one of his manufactured identities—this one created when he'd been seven. His alias was also named Noah Henson but was old enough to legally spend the ridiculous sums of money he had accrued over the years. Noah set the phone down and picked up his guitar, his attention back on the hologram screen.

"Navi!" Johnny screamed in frustration, his eyes glued to his character, a paladin, currently taking the brunt of Anonymoose's long-range attacks. "Dude, any tips?"

Noah breathed out and strummed an open c major chord on

his guitar.

[Harmony]

Wielder may assign each person their own note.

Johnny's group, Dragonx42, had four players and characters—his own paladin, a spellsword, a blood barbarian, and a body witch. Even though they had only been fighting Anonymoose's players for a few minutes, Dragonx42 was getting destroyed. The nervous voices of Johnny's team came through his coms.

"Friggin' Christ! How am I on my last potion?"

"How the heck are their skills combining like that?"

"No, no, no, no, no. I'm almost out of MP!"

"They're definitely cheating, using aimbots or something. I call HAX!"

"Naviiii," Johnny repeated to Noah nervously, wearing out the buttons on his controller. "We could really use your help right about now."

Four avatars for Johnny's team. Noah assigned each of them a note. A major chord would do nicely. More voices came through the stereo, the other team trash talking. Their voices were filtered, altered to disguise their identities.

"How did these punks get to third place?"

"Don't know, bro. I give it another two mins before we sack their corpses."

"I almost feel bad for 'em."

"You heard them say Navi, right?"

Noah smiled and gave the four opposing players of Anonymoose their own notes on his guitar, all in a minor chord, then he played.

His eyes stayed glued to the hologram as his fingers danced on the guitar strings. At first, the notes were arranged simply, the minor chords overpowering the major chords. But through [Harmony], Noah pushed for a song where the major chords overtook the minor.

It took some tricky finger positions and picking, but he was able to make a song that sounded like victory.

The song took about half a minute to create. The music burst through the small, second story bedroom lined with football and video game posters. Although everyone on his team was down to only half health, Johnny looked over his shoulder and matched Noah's grin.

The chubby, friendly boy let out an imitation of an evil villain's laugh. "You guys are in for it now. Navi, talk to me."

Noah played the song through his guitar with perfect clarity and spoke with calm authority, "Cut to only team chat." Johnny pressed a button, and the hologram flared purple for half a second followed by several frustrated exclamations from Johnny's online teammates.

"Finally!"

"Marry me, Navi."

"We need a miracle."

A chord echoed through the room. Noah said, "Listen! Blood barbarian, when I tell you to, begin your mid-range twin attack, but cancel it halfway through. Then drop your last potion while moving to your three o'clock. Spellsword, pick up the dropped potion and then use your area of effect on their dragonkin."

"But he's fire resistant!" a voice countered.

"Shut up!" Johnny ordered. "It's Navi; you know this."

Noah continued. "Body witch, drop a curse spell on their mirror knight when your blood barbarian starts the attack I signal, and jump back immediately. That jump is important. Paladin, pour every ounce of faith magic into healing your party."

Johnny gave Noah a double-take. "All of it?"

Noah played the same chord again to make sure—it rang true. "All of it."

"Alright, pal," Johnny agreed nervously.

Noah breathed in and kept playing the song. "Okay, execute in three. You can go back to main chat if you want."

The enemy voices came back through the stereo.

"Who's that other voice?"

"I think it's the one we're talking about."

"The kid?"

"Yeah, maybe this won't be so boring anymore."

Anonymoose's responses made Noah's heart flutter. All the hard work he had poured into helping Johnny's team grow in the rankings would be worth it. Noah shouted. "Two. One!"

Dragonx42's blood barbarian feinted a mid-level double-axe swipe, fell back, and dropped something that looked suspiciously like a potion. The raven-haired spellsword's avatar floated over the potion, causing her to erupt in a blue aura. She swiped her giant, rune-covered sword at the four enemy avatars.

"Ha!" the dragonkin said. "Noob move! Fire can't—"

Noah stopped playing the guitar to enjoy the next moment. The body witch's ritualistic incantation had finally finished, unleashing her most powerful curse, containing every negative status ailment she'd wrapped into it. Normally, the curse would affect only one target, but since it fell on the enemy mirror knight, it bounced off the avatar's magical armor and spread to an area twenty yards around, hitting all of his teammates.

One of the enemy voices managed an, "Uh oh," before the hologram forest filled with black smoke, immediately followed by the spellsword's red flames. Johnny's fingers pressed a complex series of buttons to execute his special healing move, pouring all of his faith and magic into the skill.

The screen went white.

No one spoke, all the players probably engrossed with the startling turn of events. Soon, the blinding white light disappeared. The hologram finally cleared to show four avatars standing above the crispy corpses of Anonymoose. The view suddenly transitioned to a fireworks display as the rankings replaced Anonymoose with Dragonx42 as the second best team in Adventures on Corinthia.

"No way."

"W-we did it. Does this mean Shiek Freak is next?"

"So like, all the DOTs were multipliers for the fire, and we all almost died, but they got hit harder? We came out on top? That's wild!"

"Navi, I meant it. Marry me."

"Noah," Johnny turned to his friend with wide-eyed disbelief. "Bro."

Noah gave him an annoyed look for using his real name, but it didn't matter now. Helping Dragonx42 defeat the second-ranked team in the game hadn't been his main goal. Their enemy's reaction was what he'd been looking forward to for a year. He bit his lip, waiting for their reply.

Surprisingly, the voice that came through the speakers wasn't mad. A young man's voice, oddly calm and commanding said, "Navi, you there?"

Johnny gave Noah a look as if asking him if it was okay. Noah nodded, and his friend pressed a button, allowing Anonymoose to hear him speak. Cautiously, trying to hide the excitement in his voice he said, "I'm here."

A pause, then, "Noah Henson, you have our attention. We'll be in touch."

The line cut to static and the hologram shut off. Johnny fumbled over to Noah and gave him a giant, sweaty hug. "Dude! We did it! Heck, you did it! We can take Shiek Freak on now!"

Noah pushed his enthusiastic friend away. Johnny always sweated when his character had an intense fight. "I don't think even I can help you take him down. There's a reason the number one team is made of just a single player. The guy is undefeated. Even Anonymoose got manhandled by Shiek Freak a few months back when they accidentally ran into him."

The excitement in his Johnny's face faltered, but was quickly replaced again by excitement. "Pshh. That's okay. This means our gaming streams are gonna rake in some hard cash. I might be able to buy that bike in the window at Racks on Racks on Racks."

The image of a garish, ugly, overpriced, bright red mountain bike flashed through Noah's mind. With the money he had just spent on his phone buying houses, Noah could have bought the entire bike shop and the neighboring five blocks. He wanted to be honest with his friend about how stupid the bike looked, but Johnny's infectious goofy grin proved too much for Noah.

All he could manage was, "Yeah, man. You do you."

Johnny stepped back and rubbed the back of his head awkwardly. "Sorry about saying your real name there. I got a little carried away."

Noah held a smile for his friend but felt his stomach stir. He didn't mention the fact that Johnny had only said Noah's first name, and that Anonymoose had said both Noah's first and last name through the game. It was exactly what he expected. "Don't worry. It'll all work out."

***

Noah sat in his computer chair as light from the full moon spilled through his room. The bright holographic screen of his computer showed letters being typed, but his fingers were not on the keyboard. The message read: "Noah Henson. Ten years old. Hacked the White House at age nine. Created a secret identity that even we can't completely trace. Why did you spend all that time helping your friends just to fight us?"

To gamers of the world, Anonymoose was known as four of the best players in Adventures on Corinthia. But in the darker side of the internet, to those who broke systems and securities to plant, destroy, or obtain information, they weren't just famous—they were infamous. Anonymoose were whispered to be the most elite, freelance hacker group. Their gaming activities were thought to be a way of flaunting their status, mocking the system around them.

Noah's [Listener] skill, [Jack of All], had allowed him to learn the mundane ability [Hacking] ages ago. He hadn't even levelled it to five yet, but was still proficient enough to hack some of the world's securest networks. With [Hacking], Noah had scoured the internet for any information he could find on the Aelves, the coming Shift, and Chris Broad. Even with his considerable ability, he had gotten nothing but false leads and dead ends.

He needed more skilled contacts; people could get him into places he couldn't reach yet. Anyonmoose could help him with that. He had already laid a strong support foundation in his small

Michigan town, people he could trust. This would grow deeper and larger in the years to come thanks to his Charisma stat and [Community] skill.

To prepare for the coming Shift, Noah had created separate digital identities to make an astronomical amount of money. His plans were starting to come to fruition. The only thing he didn't have yet was a reliable information network, people he could trust. It had taken some effort to prove himself, but maybe he'd changed that now.

Noah let out a sigh and stretched his fingers out onto his keyboard. He typed.

CHAPTER 14

Fourteen-year-old Noah had already hit the end of the hallway by the time the clock chimed for the top of the hour. He'd gotten done with the computer lab right about the same time that most of the athletes were about to head home too.

"Henson!"

Noah pushed hurriedly through the front school doors ahead of the strong voice calling his name. He smirked and let the doors shut before running forward, aiming toward the steep stairs.

"Wait up, man!"

Noah ignored the voice and hopped onto the railing by the front stairs, the snow pushing against his boots. His black wristwatch read, December 14th, 2034, 3:45pm. "She's gonna kill me," he muttered as he slid effortlessly down the long rail. Several students pointed to him, giving him props for the cool move.

When he landed at the bottom of the stairs, Noah risked a

glance over his shoulder. A tall, dark-skinned young man with dreads tied back in a neat bun burst through the school doors, his eyes searching the crowd of departing athletes lingering in front of the building. He wore an open US Marines uniform top that was too big for him over the rest of his clothes. Feet flashing, the young man flew down the steps, taking huge leaps and only keeping his balance through sheer athleticism and a little bit of luck. He waved and pointed at Noah, yelling, "Hold on, Henson!"

Noah realized that this would be a perfect time to get some more training in. He'd accepted in the past that he couldn't avoid going to school in some capacity, and getting out of the house helped him meet lots of new people and grow his skills. However, he still liked to train whenever he could, and the current situation was ideal for some practical exercise.

Noah booked it down the street toward Steelton's downtown shopping plaza. Even with the students blocking the sidewalks, he knew he could outrun Jamal Hendricks. With [Listen], Noah was able to pick up a few awed murmurs from several students as he rocketed past.

"Whoa, is that Noah Henson?"

"That freshman is *fast*."

"Why is Jamal chasing—wait, Noah's faster than Jamal? Didn't Jamal break a track record or something last year?"

Noah felt slightly guilty. Part of him knew he should be hiding his abilities–standing out too much created its own problems, but a slight grin tugged the edge of his lips. For years, Noah had spent time each day pushing his body to its limits. Magic abilities or not, getting an athletic physique required hard work. He enjoyed the results. In his first life, he'd gotten winded going up a single flight of stairs. This time around was different.

With [Listen], he caught Jamal's frustrated voice at the edge of his skill's range. "Darn. When did he get so fast?"

Apparently, some of the watching students had decided to help Jamal, because Noah was suddenly attacked. A few snowballs whizzed by his ear, and he reflexively took a [Stumble] forward, barely catching himself in a skidding crouch on the icy sidewalk. A couple snowballs sailed harmlessly over his head, and he almost immediately began running again.

In another dozen lunging steps, he sensed another barrage coming, and decided to be proactive. Luckily, he had picked up several acrobatics and gymnast abilities with [Jack of All] over the years. After hopping over a concrete barrier to a ledge, he leapt over a street below to another ledge, ending his momentum in a forward flip. He landed perfectly and took off running again. Behind him, a few members of the swim team simultaneously yelled and laughed, looking down at the drop. One of the brave ones lowered himself to fall a person's height to the ground below, but Noah was already long gone.

As soon as Washington High School was out of sight, Noah

slowed his pace to what he considered an easy jog, his boots crunching against the Michigan snow. Within ten minutes, he'd reached Steelton's downtown plaza. Christmas music echoed over the neighborly chatter in the town square. Tomorrow would be the final day before winter break, ending his freshman high school semester with the winter talent show. After that, his family would be heading to Colorado.

Noah couldn't help but grin as he took in the cheery atmosphere. His [Community] skill flared to life, and he found his vision crowded with screens next to each familiar face he passed. Each box held various information and reminders for Noah that he had accrued over the years. He'd used this knowledge and his high [Charisma] stat to further build relationships with the people of Steelton. Noah carefully made his way through groups of friendly faces, greeting people by name or being greeted in turn. The light dusting of snow tumbled lazily around him but wasn't uncomfortable. Everyone stayed warm in their winter coats. Luckily, Noah had kept his physical exertion before to just below the point he would start sweating and become uncomfortable.

In the years since he had gained his powers, Noah hadn't been able to level up his Listener skills–his core class skills. It was disappointing, but he had plenty of other concerns on his mind too, spending every waking hour on preparing humanity for the Shift.

Noah had broken his titanic goal into different tasks: Growing a powerful financial empire, acquiring necessary resources to build forts across the world, stocking weapons and gear to outfit his people, learning about survival without electricity, and creating a reliable network to spread his preparations and exchange information across the world.

The city of Steelton had its own category because he had planned on building his first fort here after the Shift had occurred. He'd been making headway in every aspect of his plan so far, including spending considerable time and effort using his high Charisma to create a stronger community.

Steelton's downtown plaza had never been this active during the holidays in Noah's previous life. The bright sound of friendly banter mixed with the scent of pine, proving how powerful Noah's [Charisma] stat really was. The city had an average population of just over thirty thousand people, but by the time Noah had reached high school, the community had changed. He'd helped make the place feel like a small town where everyone knew each other by first name.

This had been an important part of his plan.

When the Shift comes, Noah reminded himself, *Steelton can act as the perfect example of what humanity can look like when they band together. Hopefully, this will create a ripple effect. People will flock to Steelton and travelers will tell others about it, spreading word of what a fort is supposed to act like. At least, that's my hope.*

Of course, his plan had other facets, but he had around four more years until the Shift came. This wasn't a lot of time, but Noah felt confident he could give humanity the edge it needed to eventually unite against the invading Aelves.

He glanced around, always aware of his surroundings, and noted that he was getting close to his destination. Lucy's Diner was a go-to hub for most of the high schoolers and young adults of Steelton. The restaurant had the best milkshakes and tastiest burgers in the entire state of Michigan, at least Noah suspected so. He pulled out his phone and unfolded it, turning on the holo display, updating himself on some crucial information while he had the time to do so.

At fourteen years of age, Noah Henson was a billionaire. With the help of the Anonymoose hackers, he had largely kept his alternate digital accounts completely secret and isolated from his real, younger identity. If the government had found out that one of the richest people in the world secretly bought buildings all over the world, filling them with food and weapons, it's safe to say they would have had some questions. This was the kind of attention Noah had hoped to avoid.

In fact, this was why he tried not to flaunt his abilities, wealth, or too many skills. Being exceptional helped him make friends and build his community, and allowed him to help everyone have a better life. But being too exceptional would make others see him as too alien, and would cause problems—at least he believed so.

Noah had no desire to be a face on talk shows. He was trying to save his family and friends, not have 15 minutes of fame.

After checking the status of some recent land purchases across a dozen countries, he smiled, pride swelling his chest. Besides his financial resources, he had also checked Steelton's local statistics and how they had changed over the past nine years. Noah folded his phone back into his pocket.

As of this year, Steelton has the lowest crime rate of any city in America. School and college graduation numbers have skyrocketed. If the Shift were to never occur, Steelton's growing economy would be on track to compete with a major city within ten years.

He had never said any of this out loud, savoring the secret like candy that never went stale. For some reason, it made him feel a little embarrassed whenever he thought about his subtle interventions over the years, jump-starting Steelton's massive growth. Noah had changed things for the better, he was sure of it. He had personally funded all of the local schools and colleges, even the preschools. The money had steadily come into the community through anonymous donors who had claimed to be alumni. Noah had the means and had known what strings to attach to his gifts.

Steelton had even recently attracted the attention of state universities, sending some of their sociology and economics students to study the sudden positive growth of the city.

Noah picked up the scent of fried food, and he felt his stomach rumble. His destination was only two blocks away. He checked his watch again before waving a car to a stop, then jogging across the road and into the restaurant.

Lucy's Diner was bright and packed. Rowdy high school kids filled booths and tables. Adults sat at the counter, shooting gossip with Lucy herself, sipping hot coffee to cut the sweetness of her famous pies. The place's owner was tall and broad-shouldered, her black hair in a pixie cut. She had a bodybuilder's frame and wasn't afraid to get physical if someone proved too rowdy, although no one had in years. Lucy had a way of listening to customers as if they might be stretching the truth a little, skepticism freezing a raised eyebrow. She'd listen before doling out her harsh worldly wisdom.

The whole diner had been decorated to look like something from the 1960s. After so much effort, the place looked like it'd been plunked down by a time machine. The wallpaper, seats, and swivel-stool cushions shined a plastic baby blue. Chrome tables reflected the soft light, making Noah feel like he had escaped Michigan's winter and stepped into a period movie set in spring. Every woman working at the diner was tattooed up to their wrists. They wore matching baby blue polos and skirts with white ascots. Around town, it was an open secret that Lucy usually only hired tough chicks who could drink most of the town under the table.

Noah recognized everyone in the diner, and they recognized him right back. Each of them had their own screens appear as [Community] kicked in. With [Listen], Noah gathered gossip and conversations, updating the notes on their screens. This action was reflexive these days, something he didn't really need to think about, so most of his attention stayed forward as he pushed his way through the crowded diner.

He spotted Johnny Dormund sitting with his buddies from the martial arts club. The chubby blond gamer-kid had sprouted into a gigantic athlete, easily the biggest student at Washington High. Johnny's dad had once joked that all Dormunds were fifty percent muscle and sixty percent heart. From that brilliant math alone, Noah had a good idea of why none of the Dormunds were known for their academic prowess. They were good people, though— some of the best.

Noah rubbed the top of his own head self-consciously. In his new life, he had actually gained a few inches of height compared to his previous body. It could have been the orb's magic or the fact his body was at peak human capability, fueled with dozens of skills he'd picked up over the years with [Jack of All]. Maybe it was both. He'd also studied nutrition and hadn't existed on junk food this time around.

Up ahead, Lucy's mousy daughter, Danielle Perkins, studied a newspaper. Noah knew she would become the class valedictorian. With her nose always glued to a book, it seemed inevitable.

Unlike most other Steelton residents, not much had changed between Danielle Perkins' current life and how Noah had remembered her. However, she'd somehow begun a friendly, one-sided rivalry with Noah starting in middle school, when she caught him purposefully leaving two questions unanswered on their math test. She'd gotten the highest score but must have thought she hadn't really earned the win. Since then, it seemed she had been working twice as hard since she knew she technically wasn't really the smartest student in the school. Noah had nothing against her, but he did feel good when his mere presence deflated her a bit. She had always seemed a bit smug.

Everything around him seemed very normal, happy, and it filled Noah with joy. There was an anomaly, though. One person didn't have their own screen for [Community]. This only happened when Noah first met someone he hadn't encountered before. Right now, it was odd because he had met all the relatives and friends who came into Steelton for the holidays over the years. Strangers rarely found themselves at Lucy's. The unfamiliar person was a man in a sharp black suit and tie. He had grey eyes, trim silver hair, and the thick neck of a veteran boxer. *Probably a new relative visiting for the holidays*, Noah mused.

He mentally dismissed the stranger and scanned the room, then spotted who he was looking for, the only redhead in the diner. Noah took off his coat and rushed over, plopping into the seat opposite to her. He looked into her green eyes and smiled. "You are late, Kay," he accused, pretending it was he who had been waiting on her.

Krystal Connolly's thin, ginger eyebrows knotted together for a half a second before they shot up. She didn't buy it and pushed back. "If you were another minute late, I'd have left. I have to watch Sam tonight." Her smooth, alto voice seemed entirely flat and serious.

Sam was Krystal's eight-year-old brother, who Noah had quickly learned liked to materialize whenever Noah and Krystal were at her house. The kid seemed to believe that Noah was after his sister. While Noah had admittedly held a crush on Krystal in his first life, and while he still thought she was very pretty, there were several reasons preventing things going any further than friendship.

For one, Noah wasn't sure he should date at all until he was an adult, and even that seemed a little unlikely. While he didn't feel any older than his current fourteen years, and sometimes forgot that he was technically older than most of his friends, he couldn't ignore reality. Every time something happened that triggered a memory of his parents dying, or receiving beatings as Worm, Noah's resolve to prepare for the Shift strengthened. Whenever his past traumas surfaced, he felt distant from everyone around him for a while.

He hadn't had much experience with girls prior to the Shift either, and while his Charisma stat helped him make friends and connect with people easily now, it would probably make him second guess any initial romantic possibilities for the rest of his life. He'd wonder if people liked him for him, or for his stats.

Noah kind of thought Krystal might like him, but he wasn't

entirely certain, and he wasn't sure what to do with that information if there was any concrete way to find out. Even if it would be okay for him to date someone his age while he could remember his previous life, he wasn't sure he had time for it. If he dated someone, they'd probably want to walk around the track at school holding hands, or go to festivals, or whatever else people do who go on dates–Noah wasn't an expert. What he did know, was that right now, he probably wouldn't be much of a boyfriend.

Krystal was special—interesting, funny, witty, and very wise for her age. She deserved someone better than a secretive guy relying on a Charisma stat and past memories to build an empire, preparing for an apocalypse that may or may not still even happen. Unfortunately, whenever Noah was at her house, her brother Sam would often make fake, sloppy kissing sounds before running away, leaving a startled Krystal and pained Noah behind.

Noah blinked, focusing on the present, and throwing his coat on the seat beside him. "Nothing is stopping you now. I won't hold it against you if you leave. Really, all I can do is apologize. I tried coming as fast as I could after using the computer lab. In fact, I even did a cool flip when some of the athletes leaving school tried using me for target practice."

Krystal's eyes twinkled, and she made a long, dramatic sigh before taking a sip of her milkshake. "I guess I'll let it slide this time, but we have a class project to plan."

"Uh huh."

The girl's head shot up, and a suspicious look crossed her face. "You already did it again, didn't you?"

With a sheepish look, Noah said, "I only did my parts—well, maybe a little extra. There's an outline and pointers on research that should help you out, though."

"Noah! This is getting ridiculous. Everyone is going to think I just want to partner up with you for class projects because you do everything!"

In the next booth, Melissa Dayle said in a stage whisper, "Uhh, I don't think anyone will think that's the only reason—"

Krystal hissed at her friend, looking embarrassed, and Melissa's table all laughed. To let Krystal save face, Noah pretended not to notice and raised a hand to get one of the waitress' attention. [Community] reminded him the approaching server's name was Becky, and luckily, she already held a platter bearing a chocolate milkshake. With a click, she set the tray down on the table, and Noah said, "Bless you, Becky." He grabbed the shake and started pushing his straw out of its paper.

Meanwhile, Becky ignored him and gave Krystal a wink. In a throaty voice, she said, "You better hold on tight to this one, sugar. He's probably a wild one." Then she walked off.

Noah blinked, watching Becky leave and mentally shook his head. Why did older people always do that? It's like they teased teens constantly about relationships and dating, but then if teens actually dated or had relationships, they'd get freaked out—then it suddenly wasn't funny or cute anymore. Adults seemed to only tease about that stuff to get some kind of glee about everyone being embarrassed.

A lightbulb went off in Noah's head, and he suddenly had insight into how to deal with nosy adults commenting on his love life…or lack thereof. He smiled broadly as he turned around. Krystal's eyes met his and her cheeks colored before she bent to her own drink. She said, "Maybe you can help me with my part of the project at my house again. I won't even get mad if you're glued to your phone the whole time."

A shadow fell on Noah, and a low voice said, "Does this mean you two are dating?"

Jamal, Noah thought, irritated. *I thought I lost him.* He rolled his eyes at Krystal as if to say, "See what I have to deal with?" and turned around to face Jamal, the six-foot-eight, star basketball player of the Washington High School Cheetahs. Up close, Jamal's freckles were visible on his dark skin. Some snow had fallen on his dreds and hadn't melted yet. The young man really was insanely athletic. He'd probably run here just like Noah had.

Noah sighed and said, "We're just friends, Jamal. Now, what can I do for you?"

The basketball player shrugged his broad shoulders, making the thick jacket he wore open, flashing the military top that he usually used as a light coat. "Can we talk, Henson?"

Krystal's eyes narrowed, and she not-so-subtly turned her

glass, grinding it against the table. Noah felt tired. This wasn't the first time he wished he'd found a way to level his Charisma stat over the past nine years. Maybe if he had, Jamal would have left him alone since football season. The guy was stubborn. Noah pointed at Krystal. "We're talking," he said neutrally.

"Alone," Jamal insisted.

Krystal objected, "Your team is good enough, Jamal. Can't you guys win a championship without Noah? Didn't he do enough for you when you played quarterback?"

The tall young black man frowned, pushing a finger down onto the table as he spoke. "We lost at state by a touchdown. One touchdown."

Noah made a face and took a sip of his milkshake, enjoying the thick, malty goodness. "Not my fault, man. Your halfback didn't listen to me and veered off script."

Jamal leaned forward and stared Noah down. "I don't know how you do what you do, Henson, but it's a gift. Dad always said you can't keep gifts to yourself; they belong to the world. This is my last year, man. I need a sports scholarship to get into college and so do a bunch of other guys. The money Mom gets from the military after Pop was gone isn't cutting it. Help a brother out. Also, look, you might as well join the team. Just a few minutes ago, you proved to a heck of a lot of people how fast you are."

Noah sighed. Jamal's financial situation wasn't news to him. *I am planning to pay for his college anonymously already, sheesh.* His

Charisma stat helped warn him to keep his approach subtle since Jamal was clearly on edge, but Noah had had enough of the cat and mouse. He said, "The scholarship you are talking about go out to students in junior year. If you were going to win that one, it would have been then, not now. Something will still probably come up, though. You're one of the best players in the state."

Before Jamal could say another word, a large hand gripped the senior's shoulder. Noah followed the hand up to its owner's face and nodded to Johnny, his best friend. Despite only being a freshman, Johnny was the only guy both taller and wider than Jamal in their entire high school. He pulled the basketball player a step back from Noah's table as easily as opening a door.

"There a problem, buddy?" the big freshman asked Noah with a pleasant tone, maintaining his grip on Jamal's shoulder.

Noah sipped his milkshake some more, waving at Johnny that everything was fine. The truth was he was beginning to strongly regret having used [Harmony] to help the football team. He said, "Jamal here wants me to help out with basketball team plays and do my chess pieces thing even though I told him I was done after the football season."

Jamal rolled his eyes, shrugging Johnny's hand off. "Why be like this, Henson? I mean, you can help, and it doesn't hurt anyone. You'd be helping your school and your friends. Instead, you're doing what? Hanging out with your totally-not-a-girlfriend and messing with group projects you're probably already finished?

Is this fun for you, casually showing off how fast you are and then refusing to do sports?"

Ouch, Noah thought. *That kind of hit close to home.* He carefully did not look at Krystal. Things were already awkward enough. Noah's Charisma helped him think of a couple counterarguments to Jamal's statement. If he'd really wanted to, he probably could have used the full force of his stats to be aggressive and attack the other guy's pride too, which would be devastating, but would make him an enemy and might even start a fight. Jamal had been being pushy and annoying lately, but Noah couldn't hold the concerns about his team or his future against him. This was also partially Noah's own fault for helping out before using [Harmony] without thinking through the consequences.

There were two paths he could take here. Jamal was not a bad guy, he was actually one of the most popular guys in school for a reason, so venting any frustration was off the table. Instead, Noah decided to just level with the big athlete. They weren't close friends, but he and Jamal had always respected each other.

Honey over vinegar, Noah, he reminded himself. His Charisma was best used with a subtle hand, too. "Dude. Let's be real. You've been stalking me for two weeks, and I've made it very clear I want to be left alone. I've got nothing against you or the team. In fact, helping out in the fall should have made that clear. But now you're acting like I owe you something, not even just the team, but you personally."

Jamal's chest rose, his hands tightening. Johnny looked concerned, but Noah slightly shook his head. He ruefully thought, *I guess I led with vinegar after all.* Noah knew that the words had probably stung. Jamal was extremely proud, and proud of his father. His dad had served as a Marine and had died overseas, but had always made it very clear how proud of his son he was. Jamal had a fiercely independent streak and a strong core of decency that Noah planned to exploit.

Time for the honey. It was time to just be honest. In a softer tone, Noah said, "I like you, Jamal. Heck, I even look up to you, and not just 'cause you're a few inches taller than me. You work hard like no one I know—"

A small hand with blue nail polish pushed Noah's shoulder. "Ahem."

"Besides Krystal who is really good at helping me with my homework and is very pretty," he added quickly. "But seriously, because of you, I feel like if I work hard enough, I can make anything happen. Michigan was stupid to not give you that scholarship, but that's not my fault, and it's not my job to fix it. This is my life, and the only person I have to answer to is me. Let's stop the nagging, please.*"

Jamal's anger visibly deflated, the bravado he'd built up gone.

Noah pressed, "You're a leader, both naturally and because you work your butt off. People need you." He let the compliment hang in the air before he delivered the sucker punch he'd been working towards. "If you don't get a scholarship, why don't you join the military?"

Of course Noah already knew that Jamal would get a scholarship, courtesy of one of Noah's many shell companies—and he really did deserve one. Jamal worked hard at everything, and kept very respectable grades while still playing practically every sport he could, still somehow keeping a social life on top of that. Noah was betting that reminding the proud young man that not getting a scholarship was not the end of the world would put their conflict to rest. Jamal had even told Noah before that he'd wanted to be a Marine like his father before he'd gotten into sports in middle school.

Hopefully, if Noah had hit the right buttons, the conflict would end. He also hoped that if everyone knew even Jamal couldn't convince him to plan sports strategies anymore, they'd all leave him alone.

The basketball player opened his mouth like he'd say something, but shut it. He studied Noah as if looking at a stranger for the first time. The tall young man paused before shaking his head. He evenly said, "You're an interesting guy, Henson," before turning to walk away. His posture was different now, and he stood like he normally did—back straight and proud. Jamal really was a natural leader, unlike Noah.

The surrounding tables started their chatter again, but Krystal, Johnny, and Noah watched Jamal walk out of the diner in silence.

With [Listen], Noah could hear the high school senior's breath catch outside, as if the guy had something caught in his throat. Jamal muttered under his breath at first, but then clearly said, "Oorah, Pops. I guess it's Semper Fi for me. Mom is not gonna be happy." He chuckled.

Noah turned off [Listen], suddenly feeling like he was intruding,

Back in the diner, silenced passed between Noah and his friends for a few moments before Johnny raised an eyebrow and lifted his palms up, backing away like Noah was cursed. "You're a drama magnet, bro."

Noah put a hand to his chest like he'd been wounded. "Is that why you hang around me so much, then?"

His friend ignored the jibe. "Wanna watch us do some holo gaming later? Adventures on Corinthia got a new expansion pack. My paladin just upgraded his armor. We're still top hundred, but it's more fun now that Dragonx42 doesn't focus on rankings anymore. I think Shiek Freak had it right to just explore and do cool quests. That game is huge."

Noah shook his head. "Can't. Gotta prep for the talent show tomorrow."

Johnny set his legs wide in a v-stance and rocked out to an air guitar. "Later, brains."

"Later, brawns."

Noah turned to grab his milkshake and absently took another

sip. He mentally sighed in relief that he could stop dodging Jamal at school now. Then he pulled out his phone and opened his favorite real estate app. "There you go again," sighed Krystal. "Are you going to check out now?"

Noah lifted his eyes and thought furiously. He was normally completely focused and devoted on his mission, to prepare humanity for the Shift, but he also knew he needed to allow himself breaks or he'd burn out. Not only that, but maintaining relationships and building new ones was part of his mission. Of course, these were all great ways to rationalize the fact that he really just wanted to hang out with his friends for a little while.

"Nah, it can wait," he said and put the phone away. "Want to order something? It's been a while since we got burgers here. I'll buy."

Krystal grinned. "I thought you'd never ask."

CHAPTER 15

Dinner for the Henson family was Chinese take-out, a weekly family tradition. Noah and Clark busily attacked their food while Lana worked on her tablet. Noah's mom pressed the end-conversation button and raised her eyebrow at her son as he slurped up the broth of his wonton soup. Her look said, 'I know you're about to say that slurping in China is considered polite, but this is my house and you play by my rules.'

Noah set down the bowl. "Sorry."

"Thank you," said Lana. "So, I just got pinged by Eileen Connolly, confirming she just accepted her new position as the mayor. Exciting news."

Something in his mom's overly friendly tone tickled Noah's sixth sense. "Uh huh," he replied cautiously.

Lana continued, her voice picking up more artificial sweetness that confirmed Noah's suspicion. He had a good idea of what was coming and reminded himself to act accordingly. She said, "Well, she also had some even more exciting news! You can imagine my surprise when she said you and Krystal were seen together at Lucy's earlier today *with your own booth*."

With a luminous smile, Lana let the implication hang in the air of the dining room. Noah's father stopped eating his General Tso's chicken and set the bowl down next to his plate of white rice. He adjusted his cheap, owlish glasses and leaned over his dinner, barely noticing when Lana helpfully pulled his tie to the side, out of his food.

His face grave, Clark spoke with the most serious tone his son had ever heard, "Spill."

Noah set aside his own chopstick and thought carefully about his response. In his first life, he had never had to face his parents getting involved with his social life for one simple fact, he'd never had one. The most difficult challenge he faced in his new life had been staying consistent with how someone his age would actually react to things. Being smart and wise for his age was okay, but going too extreme would be creepy. Even with his Charisma stat, Noah had failed a few times in his early attempts to sound like a normal teenager.

Sometimes he came across too cartoony, other times too reserved. It had been a difficult balancing act, one he had to refine and tread carefully over time. Ironically, just being himself had seemed to help a lot. Sometimes he had to remind himself that everyone is a little weird, and other teens were all over the place as people. Being "a teen" would never work, because teens were all different.

As for his parents, he just didn't want to hurt their feelings. *If there is anything I've learned about my parents in my new life it's that they love finding ways to embarrass me. They must get a lot out of it. Unfortunately for them, I don't get embarrassed easily.*

Noah recalled the books on adolescent psychology and his own previous life. His Charisma stat tickled the back of his head, reminding him of another important factor. *Before, I probably robbed them of moments like this. Mom and Dad seem to really enjoy teasing me.* This realization led him to the best option, to acknowledge what was happening but deflect a little.

"Uh," he said, trying his best to sound caught off guard. He blurted, "It's not a big deal."

"Honey?" Clark asked his wife, trying his best to look genuinely confused, Noah noticed the faint smile.

Oh, you rotten scoundrel, Noah thought. *He does enjoy this. You suck, Dad!* Despite his irritation with his parents that at their core, they seemed to be such goofballs, he was happy that he'd chosen this path. Noah didn't always have opportunities to share moments like this one with them, and he'd never forget how they'd sacrificed themselves, selling their lives for him in his past life. He could put up with their terrible sense of humor and corny personalities—he knew of the loyalty that lay beneath it, even when he'd been a depressed, antisocial misfit.

Clark continued, "Does Noah sound like he's spilling right now? Or maybe he already spilled, and our son is so smart that he learned how to speak with his mouth closed."

Noah figured the most melodramatic thing he could do in that moment was to let his face fall into his hands, hiding behind them sheepishly. He peeked through his fingers and watched in fake-horror as his mom played along, her expression innocent, chin resting on the knuckles of her hand. Even though he was hamming it up, his mother's smug grin still made Noah feel a little nervous.

"No, dear," she replied. "He sure didn't explain to us why he was sitting alone with a pretty girl. A very pretty girl. In fact, it sounds like Noah is ashamed to tell his wonderful parents who clothe and feed him that he might be interested in someone. I mean, this is Krystal Connolly. They've been spending a lot of time together." Then Lana threw head back dramatically, her face pained, "Think about what all our friends will say when they hear how this son of mine shows his thanks to us! You told me to give up on him, but I, his mother, believed in him! Our little genius has feelings just like every other kid out there—"

Noah did his best to suppress a smile. He was starting to get a kick out of watching how corny and lame his parents could sink. Apparently there was no end in sight. He had to be careful not to break his act. *I don't think I can hold my frown anymore.* Noah pushed his chair back from the table, stood up abruptly, and announced defiantly, "I'm going to my room!" He set the chair down, pushed it in, and walked to the stairs without another word.

His parents booed playfully at his response.

Noah was halfway up the stairs when [Listen] picked up his mom and dad whispering merrily, "Noah and Krystal sitting in a tree. K-I-S-S-I-N-G," before quietly laughing.

Oh my God. Seriously. I'm actually getting embarrassed for them now. "Gosh! Grow up!" he yelled down the stairs with as much indignity as possible, but couldn't keep the smile out of his voice. *That was a good touch*, he thought approvingly, then mentally muttered, *Dorks*.

***

Hours later in his room, Noah turned on his computer and punched a fifty-letter password into his keyboard, recalled easily with his level five [Memory Palace]. The skill had limited usefulness since he only had one room in his mind per level. This complex password had taken one of the mundane skill's rooms, but with a lot of space to spare. Although he couldn't hold a lot of information with [Memory Palace], it synergized perfectly with [Hacking], allowing Noah to store and perfectly recall important related information. After a few more clicks with his mouse, followed by peak-level typing speed, Noah stared at an encrypted message. A few more minutes passed before he was able to decrypt it with his [Cipher] skill. The message was in French, one of the many languages he was completely fluent in.

He translated, *"They're on to us. Get out."*

A chill ran through Noah's spine, blood draining from his face. The message had come from the small, but powerful group of hacker friends, Anonymoose. His own [Hacking] ability was level five, and he couldn't raise it anymore. Functionally, this meant he was great, but would never be amazing, and the group of talented hackers could simply do things he couldn't.

After establishing contact with them through the video game Adventures on Corinthia, it still hadn't been easy to gain their trust. [Charisma] didn't affect people over the internet. He had to be in person with someone in order for it to take full effect.

They probably only trusted me because they recognized I'm just as, if not more, paranoid than all of them combined.

Upon joining the group, even the notoriously reclusive and private members of Anonymoose had obviously thought Noah was a little strange. He had created overly redundant security measures to prevent any of his activities from being leaked. Still, he suspected that if any of the other hackers in the group had really wanted to, they could have penetrated Noah's systems.

Anonymoose had been a fantastic resource for Noah over the years. They had even raked several international databases for Noah to search for specific information. Noah had asked them to look for anything on Doc Broad, his list of future fort names, the fort leaders' names he could still remember, and raider faction names. To his surprise, they had done it without asking him why he'd asked. Noah had a hunch they were trying to figure out his angle or motivation, and he wished them luck. If they could discover he was preparing for the end of the world, they were welcome to the crippling anxiety that came with it.

Seeing the message reminded Noah that he'd been hoping to have a lead on tracking down Zelda from Camp Hammerfist by now, the only fort thought to have survived an Aelve attack. Nothing had come up for Doc either, which was more than mildly concerning. The only thing they'd found was a single article about the disappearance of Chris Broad the day of Noah's birth in 2020. It was like Doc had vanished off the face of the Earth. That information had rocked Noah to the core, leading him to the theory that the magical blast that had killed Noah was both the reason for his rebirth, and possibly the cause of Doc's disappearance.

The hackers of Anonymoose were experienced, careful, and talented. They were good, probably the best in the world. It had never seemed real to Noah that Anonymoose could be found or caught.

This new message had come from the hacker who went by the moniker Dressrosa, Noah's French contact. This alone was enough to worry him. Dressrosa was the leader of the small hacker group. If *he* was giving Noah a warning that they'd been compromised, it was even more alarming.

Noah tapped his desk nervously. *Who is on to us? The Russians?*

Another thought came to him. *Aelves. I don't think they'd use human technology, but there's too much I don't know about them to rule anything out.* The last thing Noah had asked the hacker group to look into was the U.S. government's databases for any hints of the Aelves or things other than EMPs that could wipe out an entire nation's technology, affecting both electricity and pressure.

They had actually said they thought he was crazier than they were, which for them, was a compliment. *What if one of the members had actually found something on the Aelves?* The memory of Noah's Trial of the Archetype came to mind, reminding him that Kahlek had probably been reborn as well. What if the Aelves had found a way to track Noah and his online friend's down? He couldn't think of how the Aelves would have managed it, but since he still knew so little about them, anything was possible.

Noah summoned several mundane skills to calm his mind.

The shock of seeing Dressrosa's message slowly faded as his skills helped him focus. He knew the Aelves would always be a problem, but they would be arriving after the Shift, that was obvious. Doc had always theorized that the Shift had prepared the way for the Aelves. Electricity didn't work. Explosives never went off. Airguns didn't shoot. Engines didn't work. In essence, humanity had been ripe for the picking.

What if they could appear before the Shift? Did they arrive on Earth before it? he wondered. Terrifying stuff. From what

Anonymoose had been able to find by scouring several international space databases, there had been no sightings of anything that even looked remotely like spaceships heading toward Earth. It hadn't entirely surprised Noah that several governments around the world had teams to watch the stars for alien attackers. Of course, this begged the question of how nobody had known about the Aelves before, but Noah had no more answers.

Even with all his calculated preparations, there was too much crucial information out of his grasp. If Kahlek had been reborn, the Aelve might have received similar powers to Noah. If Kahlek had been reborn like Noah, then the Aelve might have also been aware that Noah had taken the Trial of the Archetype. *Meh, thinking about this too much is a waste of time. All I can do is prepare the best that I can.*

He pressed a few commands on his keyboard, opening a folder labelled 'The Shift.' Inside the folder was contact information for all of the several thousands of storage houses he had secretly purchased with his vast wealth over the years. Detailed instructions were ready to be sent to all of the people occupying his properties all over the world. Of course, he had letters printed on-site, too, but in case anyone got into one, he'd been intentionally vague with instructions in them, wording them to make sense if the power went out. The instructions he could send in email form right before the Shift were much, much more detailed and specific.

Other communications were ready to go, too. All it would take was a simple series of codes and commands on his computer to send them along to some of the most influential people in the world. The tireless young man had also prepared emails to send to various political authorities should he die before the Shift. If he didn't input a code into his systems every six months, the emails would automatically send—a failsafe in case he somehow died before the end of the world. The warehouses held food, weapons, instructions on how to build forts, and a hundred other resources to help humanity survive and unite against the coming of the Aelves. The resources were far too precious to go to waste if something were to happen to Noah. Of course, he had his personnel stationed at all the warehouses too, but they'd need help.

He shook his head and got back to the subject at hand. *It's okay. Kahlek only had my face and name to go off.* Noah stared at the message in French from Dressrosa. Someone had caught them. Did the Aelves even know how to use computers? They obviously had technology that was far superior to Earth's. *Computers might be children's toys to them.*

Noah slammed his fist on the table. He punched in a few sequences into this keyboard, and the computer shut off. *I shouldn't go online for a while, keep my digital footprint to a minimum. I'll lay low for a few days, and then try reaching out to Dressrosa, Fickle, Unkle, and Wash.*

But I still don't know about the Aelves. Should I pack up my parents and leave Michigan for my safehouses in Colorado? That would mess with all my plans to turn Steelton into the central fort, but I'd be closer to where Camp Hammerfist will grow, and my family would be safe.

As he argued with himself, Noah did a quick check of his weapons. He'd decided years before not to keep any guns, mainly because his parents weren't weapons people, and the pros were far outweighed by the cons. He was too young to purchase firearms legally, and if he got caught with them, it could be a serious pain. Stealth had been his best defense so far, but he still kept a brace of quality throwing knives, a powerful pistol crossbow, and a machete in his room. He checked the edge on his machete before putting it away under his bed again.

"Krystal is going to be pissed if I just take off without an explanation," he mused out loud. Noah let out a sigh, weighing his options, staring at the snowfall out his window.

"No," he muttered. "I'll stay here. Even if I bought some safety for my parents, the Aelves would still wipe everyone off the map eventually. If we all get arrested, I can afford the best lawyers and probably still prepare. Life will get way more complicated, but I only have a few more years until everything goes sideways. If the Aelves come for me, I'll think about it then. I should at least be able to lead them away from my family." A big ball of stress twisted Noah's back until he had a hard time breathing. For over a decade, he'd been keeping this secret, bearing this burden. The open questions were not making things easier. There were just too many unknowns about the Aelves.

Noah was paranoid, but that didn't mean he needed to abandon all his plans at the first sign of real trouble, not yet. Maybe Anonymoose got in over their heads about something unrelated to Noah's challenge. *I should still exercise caution*, he thought, typing in a few more keys. He double checked his fail safes, double checked his secure cloud storage, protected by top-of-the-line encryption, the servers in a secure location he owned, and hit a complex number of keys. Then Noah folded his computer, set it on the floor, and crushed it beneath his feet. It was useless now. He'd just triple wiped his drives and fried all the components using a special dead man's switch he'd had installed on every computer he ever used. Later that day, he'd need to grab one of his spares from a nearby storage area. *I need to lay low until I hear from Dressrosa again. It could be the Aelves, but it also might not be.*

For the time being, he would stick to his original plan. It would suck to die again, or get locked in prison, but if humanity survived due to his preparations, then it'd be worth it. If he died without ever having his first kiss—again—he could be sure the universe was playing a cruel joke on him, but he was still at peace about it. Noah walked over to his bed and stared at stars on the ceiling, and named the various constellations until he fell asleep.

***

The next morning, Noah walked to school with his guitar case strapped to his back, Dressrosa's message lingered on his mind.

I just need to focus on what I can control instead of worrying about things I can't, he tried assuring himself. The Shift was going to come, with or without him. He'd been busy, not only trying to prepare humanity, but working on himself too. Noah had spent nearly every day mastering his body, pushing himself past his limits. The skills he had learned through [Jack of All] had only made acquiring martial skills, combat knowledge, survival skills, and gymnastics easier—cutting the time required to get better at them. It had saved him time, but not effort.

If anything, Noah worked ten times harder because he was afraid to rely on magic. His drive wasn't just about having a body to survive the Shift, Noah wanted to push his mind—his identity—past who he had used to be as far as he could.

All of his efforts had produced a strange side effect. These days, whether through his effort, or magic, or being the Listener, he had gained several inches of height. *Maybe it's my diet,* Noah joked to himself. Then he realized he had had almost this exact same conversation with himself the day before and rolled his shoulder, calming himself with an effort. Despite trying to suppress his nerves, he was still jumpy as a fox in a culvert.

Noah realized he'd be late to school while he was only a few blocks away from his house. Luckily, he felt confident his teachers would give him a pass. This would be a good day, yes. He tried to think about school, but his more serious worries kept surfacing. He warred internally with himself, part of him wanting to work through the issues with Anonymoose, but another part just wanting to enjoy his walk to high school. *There won't be many moments like this after the Shift,* Noah mused. *Even with all my effort, peace will be rarer than Doc's cancer sticks. Actually, how the heck had he had so many anyway?* Now that was an interesting thought. Noah couldn't believe he'd never wondered about that before.

Walking to Washington High from his house only took about half an hour. Noah had enough money to buy a car, actually any car that he wanted, but was legally still too young to drive. Besides, he loved the walk, one of the few times of the day he gave himself to just enjoy the present. Peace and quiet also helped him think sometimes.

Suddenly, he caught an odd, static sound with [Listen], the noise coming from two joggers a few blocks down the street.

I don't recognize them and [Community] isn't picking anything up, he realized. Hoods covered their faces. *Why would they do be dressed like that, both of them? They could just wear knitted hats.* Noah closed his eyes and focused on [Listen], amplifying the clarity around him. Everything was normal. The joggers' breaths were easy and relaxed. They clearly weren't trying to push themselves.

What in the world is that sound? Noah wondered. With additional scrutiny, he realized that next to the joggers' breath was some kind of fuzzy sound. Noah focused on the static while walking down the street, doing his best to look as if he was just a normal fourteen-year-old running late to school. The static opened up and noise came through, a stutter of short and long beeps.

The noise didn't make sense to Noah at first, but he began picking up a pattern. *It's Morse Code,* he realized grimly. Normally, he'd force himself to stay calm, but instead, he let his heart race. *I might need some adrenaline here in a minute,* Noah warned himself.

He let the joggers pass him on the street.

His [Morse Code] was level three. Among the different kind of skills Noah had picked up over the years, levelling up his languages had been the easiest for him, and the highest priority. The beeps translated to: "Do you have your sights on him?"

One of the joggers was a woman. She huffed in a breath, held it, and responded in Russian, "Just checked over my shoulder, sir. Doesn't suspect a thing."

Beeps came through the static again. "Keep your eyes on him."

The woman spoke in Russian, but the Morse Code responded in English? *That's odd.* Noah's nerves were on edge. The joggers were clearly here for him. *The person on the radio told the woman to keep an eye on me. What for? Russian and Morse Code are two completely different languages, well, three, sort of. Would the Aelves use two languages when they could just use their own?*

Noah slowly tightened the straps on his guitar case so they held fast to his shoulders. He suddenly deeply wished he had a weapon, and started searching for a stick or broom handle, or even a rock. Carrying weapons to school had obviously never been an option, but he wished he'd planted caches of useful things along the route to and from school. He planned to fix that mistake as soon as he could. His mind raced about the joggers, *Maybe Aelves wouldn't want to be caught speaking in their own language. If Kahlek got sent back to the past, he might know that I did the Trial of the Archetype too. He might have been searching for me this entire time to take me out. The Aelves were looking for the orb before. It was pretty obvious why they'd want it. If I die, will the orb appear again for them to pick up from my corpse?*

He didn't know. As usual, he just had more questions, never any new answers. Noah hadn't seen the Modifier again to get more information, but he was pretty sure that being reborn, going back in time or whatever he'd done had not been a normal thing for orb-wielders. His had probably been a special case. Maybe.

The lean young man gritted his teeth. If they were Aelves, they probably had magic to disguise their appearances, and Kahlek had shown that they could speak a human language. With [Listen], Noah discovered that the two "joggers'" breathing was closer than before. They were circling around. What did they want? If they were the Aelves, wouldn't they just use magic to scoop him into the air like they had done with Doc? Noah knew they were definitely capable of it. According to Doc, sightings of the Aelves had only come after the Shift, and Noah had learned their secret, and the reason they were afraid of human technology. Electricity had a devastating effect on their magical capabilities, disrupting whatever forces they summoned. *Maybe that's why they aren't shooting fireballs at me right now,* he realized. *Not only would it attract unwanted attention, but they might not be able to use their magic at all.*

But the Aelves hadn't seemed to have a lot of restraint before. It was far more likely that the fake joggers were human, but if so...who were they with?

Either way, Noah had a problem. He could go throughout his day as if nothing was different, using [Listen] to learn more about his stalkers–there was no way they could know that he had heard and understood them. But the more he thought about that idea, the more it sickened him. Noah had made a promise to himself that in his new life, he would never let others dictate how he was going to act or live. He would play by his own rules, be his own person.

Washington High School was a straight shot on the street, twenty more minutes and he'd be there. Noah reached the end of the block and took a left, opening one of the five rooms of his [Memory Palace], the map room. It held several locations, and he instantly recalled the satellite image of his neighborhood. Even without [Memory Palace], he knew the entire neighborhood like the back of his hand, but the map helped him predict where the stalkers were. The method wasn't perfectly accurate, but it'd help.

"Crap," he heard the woman curse in Russian.

"What?" the other hoodie asked, also in Russian, a man's voice.

"The kid took a detour," the woman said. Noah heard them picking up the pace, but gradually, probably not to cause him alarm. "Boss said the kid was going to school and just to keep an eye on him. What the heck is he doing?"

Boss, huh? Noah mused, already thinking of his next part of the plan.

The man spoke up a few seconds later as Noah hooked back toward his house. "M says she has eyes on the kid from her vantage point. He's heading back to the house. Maybe he forgot something."

"Or not," the woman replied. "Maybe he's on to us."

"He's a fourteen-year-old," the man said, skepticism in his voice.

The woman muttered, "Boss said—"

So, there's another one that can see me walking on the street. Noah couldn't hear any other joggers in the area, or even anything out of the ordinary. Wherever this 'M' was, she could keep an eye on him outside the range of [Listen]. Either that, or she might be inside a building where his ability was muffled.

There was no way he was going to let these hoodie watchers control the situation. He refused to play their game. Maybe it was time to get his weapons after all. After another second, Noah dismissed that idea. It was more important right now to escape, and move toward his 'Vette. Legal or not, he kept a car he sort of technically owned near his house. If his mom ever found about that, she would kill him, but these people speaking Russian might try to take him out for real.

Time to change the rules. Noah spotted his house, checked the balance of his guitar case on his back, and sprinted.

"The kid is running back to his house," the woman said with alarm in her voice. Both of the joggers' breathing quickened, their footsteps hitting harder on the winter street. Morse code beeped through the static: "We need multiple eyes on him. We don't know what he is capable of."

Is it my abilities they're worried about? Noah leaped over his front yard fence with grace. *No, I can't lead them back to my house. If they've been watching me for a while, they probably know the layout of the place. Luckily, one of my safe houses I prepared for the Shift is nearby.* He grimaced. *I am definitely putting weapons freaking everywhere if I get out of this.*

Noah ran toward his back fence, scaled it in one jump, and flipped into his neighbor's backyard.

[Front Flip] is now level four.

As he blinked the screen away, Noah heard the man mutter, "M says he just front flipped over his back fence like an Olympic gymnast. Who the heck is this kid?"

Morse code beeped through the radio: "Just keep your eyes on the prize."

Noah scaled another fence and ran through the next yard,

taking a sharp left. *They're blocking the path to the car. Alright, fine. All I need to do is make it to the next block, take a right, and I'm only a block away from the safe house. Even if they follow me inside, they'll never find me if I get there first.* He had ordered some interior modifications to the house as soon as he purchased it through one of his several shell companies.

His map from the [Memory Palace] combined with [Listen] informed him that the joggers were rounding the corner to catch up quickly. They were fast, but Noah's speed was superior. Even the day before, he'd hidden some of his ability. There were faster people in the world than him, but probably not many.

Noah banked a hard right around a corner and almost collided into a woman walking her dog, a German Shepard. Instantly, Noah's senses and skills flared with warning. The woman had medium-length blonde hair, and her face was sharp and angular, probably from a Nordic descent. She wore typical Michigan upper-class clothing—leggings, Ugg boots, pink pea coat, and earrings, but Noah sensed she wasn't a local.

The woman shouted, "Oh, sorry!"

Filled with adrenaline and freaked out by so many skills and instincts firing off at once, Noah hissed, "M!"

The woman's eyes widened, confirming his slip of the tongue.

Realizing what he had done, Noah lifted his hands as if apologizing to a neighbor. The world turned grey, and Noah wondered if he would have to kill a person for the first time. He kept a wary eye on M, noting different ways he could attack if she pulled a gun or some other weapon. He didn't have any weapons except for a ballpoint pen, but that would have to be enough. If the woman was actually an Aelve, Noah prepared to endure a wave of magic and launch himself at her. Tense as a coiled spring, he ran around her without a word, but suddenly felt himself [Stumble]. Heart beating, adrenaline spiking, Noah forced himself to contort midair with the assistance of [Acrobatics], glancing at the woman who'd just attacked him, but it hadn't been her. Her dog had snapped its jaws at Noah. He normally wouldn't assume that a dog was trying to hurt him with a snap or a growl, but his abilities had recognized danger.

Midair, everything in Noah's view slowed to a crawl. He threw his legs sideways in a scissor kick like he'd entered a real-life Kung Fu movie. In the clarity of the moment, Noah had a clear view of the woman's shocked face and winter clothes. *Her coat still has the tag on. The boots aren't weathered enough. Her cheeks are tanned and not wind burnt. She isn't from here,* Noah assessed quickly. *The German Shepard is the real issue, muscles bunched to rush. Don't know why the dog is attacking but this is bad news. Not much time.*

Time sped up again as his right foot planted in the snow. His left boot collided into the German Shepard's muzzle, and the dog collapsed instantly in the sidewalk. Noah narrowed his eyes, contemplating going for the woman's throat, but decided against it. He still didn't know who these people were or their motives.

Instead, he pivoted and burst down the block. [Listen] informed him the dog was softly whining and not chasing after him. Noah could hear the blonde woman, M, speak in panicked French, "Sir, I think he's hacked our channel. He called me M and…I don't know why, but Bruiser lunged, then the target put him down. All of it happened so fast I couldn't react. He's moving now—northbound. He's fast, boss, real fast. Seems to have some kind of formal training. I can't believe this."

Noah didn't hear any Morse code reply. In a few breaths and several more bouncing, sprinting strides, he arrived at the purchased house. Noah paid groundskeepers to keep the exterior of all his purchased properties maintained, so this house blended in with the rest of the neighborhood. Leaping over the four stairs to the front porch, his shoulder collided with the door as he turned the knob, forcing it open. It hadn't been locked. Thank God for the small-town atmosphere.

Every second counted.

The home was fully furnished, as if people had been living there for years. He ran into the kitchen, pulled the chef knife from the knife block and reversed his grip on it. Noah still wasn't eager to use lethal force, but at least now he had a weapon. *I can hear three people running toward me. Their breathing is harsh.*

He pulled on a pan hanging from overhead and something clicked in the kitchen, a sound only Noah could hear. He ran to a hidden partition in the wall that had suddenly swung open next to the fridge, climbed inside, and closed the wall behind him. The hidden door made a sucking sound when it shut.

Noah stood up in the hidden room behind the kitchen, only a thin wall between him and his pursuers. He heard five pairs of footsteps. *No,* he corrected himself. *Three bipeds and one limping quadruped - the people and the dog.* The dog's nails gave it away as plain as day now.

He held his breath. *If the dog is here, it may be able to hear me.*

"Where the heck did he go?" the hoodie man asked in hushed English, a slight bit of Brooklyn in his speech. "Boss would have been able to see him if he came out the back. He said the kid might come here."

A woman quietly spoke, Noah recognized her voice as the other jogger. "M, search upstairs with Bruiser. Stunners ready."

"Stunners? Really?"

"He ran. That's enough cause. Plus, I got a funny feeling. I think we need to move the op to level four."

Noah tracked their footsteps, [Listen] picking up their general location. Sweat dripped down his temple. *They knew about my purchase of the house?* Noah thought. *How? Well, at least it doesn't sound like they're Aelves or out to kill me.*

As soon as he heard the dog's footsteps above, Noah plodded quietly backward deeper into the secret room, entering a narrow hallway. He could still hear the pursuers speaking in English and updating whoever their Boss was in Russian and French, but they were muffled now. Soon, Noah found himself walking down a dark corridor, but light wasn't really necessary down here. This way led to the house next door, and there was only one way he could go.

Noah felt a sudden smile as an odd thought came to him. *Dressrosa thought I was being too paranoid by buying two houses next to each other and connecting them,* Noah remembered. *If we ever talk again, I'm going to rub this in his face.* Of course, the hacker hadn't had any way to know that Noah didn't really get tired these days, and the work had leveled his [Dig] skill. After shuffling forward some more, his outstretched fingers touched the exit. He groped for a latch.

The sound seemed incredibly loud as Noah pushed the sliding door to the side, then stepped through and closed it behind him. He stood in the dining room of the adjacent house. This house wasn't set up to be normal; the walls were lined with non-perishable foods, survival gear, and various other things Noah had packed away in case of emergency. The entire house and basement had been filled to the brim with things needed to survive the fall of civilization. Steelton was riddled with similarly stocked buildings, most of them outside of town.

The cagey young man consciously used some of his mundane mental skills like [Calm] and [Meditative Breathing], helping clear his head while he walked into the kitchen. There was something wrong about his pursuers, well, something he couldn't quite put his finger on. They had been speaking in several languages. *Why would they do that? Did Anonymoose hack the Russians and get caught? The only reason I can think of is that they are afraid of people hacking their line of communication.*

Noah shook his head as he considered what to do next. This house had actual weapons, but they were in the basement, and he wasn't willing to risk the squeaky steps to get down there. Not only that, since the hoodie people seemed more interested in catching than killing him, his new focus was on escaping.

What should I do?

He had two choices - hide or fight. The problem was he didn't have enough information. Were these people acting alone? Did they have air support? If they were plugged in with local law enforcement, maybe Noah should just give himself up. He was friends with all the police officers in town, after all. Whatever these people arrested him for, he had money for the very best legal team money could buy.

Of course, the possibility still remained that the pursuers could be affiliated with the Aelves, but Noah didn't think that was the case anymore. It just didn't fit, and he trusted his gut.

As Noah got his breathing fully back under control, he remembered the blonde, M, probably in her late twenties. Her face hadn't been covered. *That woman was definitely human,* Noah thought. He drowned out all other sounds with [Listen] to focus on the voices next door. It took a lot of concentration, but they were close enough that he could barely make out what they were saying. They were pretty much freaking out.

"The prints just end in the kitchen!" said the man. "What is he, a magician Olympic-level athlete and elite hacker?"

"It doesn't make sense," said M.

Noah closed his eyes, sacrificing his sight to focus on hearing as he slowly moved towards the back door of the house. *One thing's for certain*, Noah realized. *[Listen] isn't a perfect skill. I wasn't completely alert to that woman with the dog until I saw her. If my focus is too much in one place, I can lose track—*

Noah opened his eyes and spread [Listen] evenly to all the sounds around him. He couldn't ping it on any one thing, but he got the feeling that something was wrong. As he rounded a corner to the room before the door, he dropped his kitchen knife in shock, but [Reflex] activated, allowing him to nimbly grab it in midair. Noah stared at the man in the crisp black suit from Lucy's Diner he had seen the day before.

The stranger's broad shoulders and military high-and-tight silver hair contrasted well with the smart outfit. Although he was shorter than Noah, the man's thick neck made him seem a much more threatening figure. He lips were pressed in an even line that betrayed no emotion.

"Good catch, Noah," he complimented in a rich baritone. He spoke to Noah as if they were relatives catching up. "Please do me a favor and drop the knife, you're not in any danger. Also, stop trying to be clever—now is not the time. We both know this is checkmate. My name is Burgess Goodrich. I'd like it very much if you would come with me for a few hours. I'm afraid I must insist, too. We'd rather not use force, but we will if we have to."

This new man, Burgess, didn't have any weapons out, but Noah believed him. He swallowed.

CHAPTER 16

Noah sat patiently inside the small room of an abandoned office and did his best to look how he would probably be expected to act, like he was too good to be there. Shoulders hunched, lower lip extruded a little in a pout, he kept his gaze suspicious. *This is a good combination,* he thought. *One part moody, two parts rebellious, and one part arrogant. Blended together, you get a "genius hacker teen who likes to rebel against any authority."*

A large, dark mirror occupied the opposite wall next to the door leading outside, and the room had only a table and two chairs. The mirror was probably a one-way with Burgess watching on the other side. Noah propped his boots on the office table and teetered his chair on the back two legs.

M, the maybe-pretty blonde woman with sharp features, leaned her back against the darkened mirror. She currently gave off a sour mood like old food leaking from a plastic bag. Her pinched face seemed set in a scowl, and she kept one arm crossed across her body. Noah had a feeling she'd be crossing both arms except she probably was trained to keep one hand free to draw a weapon. She tapped a finger impatiently against her bicep, clearly communicating annoyance.

Thankfully, the ride in the van had only been a couple silent minutes before reaching the office building at the edge of Steelton. Burgess Goodrich had assured his team before arrival that Noah was coming with them voluntarily, and that answers would be exchanged on friendly terms. The fake joggers had agreed politely - the way employees did when responding to orders from a manager. However, "M," who seemed to be the youngest of the trio who had chased Noah, had glared at him the whole ride, stroking her dog's forehead.

At first, Noah had wanted to apologize, but he held his tongue. He wasn't exactly thrilled that he'd kicked the dog, but the animal had lunged at him. The Shift had proven how dangerous dogs could be after packs of them had roamed around, growing more feral. Noah loved dogs, but he'd seen the aftermath of serious bites…and deaths.

That whole situation had been strange, though. Logic suggested that the dog was highly trained, which aligned with how surprised 'M' had been. Ultimately, something had spooked the dog, and if Noah hadn't defended himself, he might be getting stitches right now—or worse. So Noah didn't speak at all, he just used the ride and as many of his skills as he could think of to get a read on his mysterious stalkers. By the time he'd been wordlessly led to the room inside the abandoned building, he'd had a strong idea of who the people were and what they might want with him.

If I was in real trouble, I'd be in handcuffs, he reasoned. *If they wanted to kill me, they would have used guns with actual bullets instead of stunners. Heck, they could have just sniped me.* On top of the fact he was still breathing, Noah had even noticed Burgess' subtle disapproval to the others for having pulled the stunners earlier.

Their origins were still unclear. He thought, *These people obviously work for the government. This probably has something to do with Anonymoose. If one of them got caught, Burgess and his team will have a lot of information on me. The fact that I'm not in a jail cell or a police station means they have other intentions than pinning me as a criminal. At least, not at first.* Noah shook his head, realizing the longer he thought about it, the more questions he had—this seemed to be the story of his life now. The only thing he knew for sure about these people was that they must want something from him.

He had decided that it would be important how he portrayed himself. This would have to be a more nuanced act than with his parents—these people were more sophisticated, and the stakes were higher. He would need his wits about him if he was going to talk his way out of digital crime. *If I act too naïve, then Burgess might see through me. That guy seems smart as a whip. But if I'm too withdrawn or unwilling to talk, then they might pressure me with threats, and I'd rather not deal with that.*

Noah decided that his goal, whenever they began interrogating him, would be to stay consistent with a plausible, consistent persona. If Noah played his cards right, then he might even come across as charming or earn his de facto captors' pity.

His first task would be to find out exactly what information they had on him. They would be observing him. Actually, they probably had been this whole time. Whatever they were after, they'd probably be deciding if he was dangerous—the fact he'd met Burgess with a knife in hand might not have been a good first impression, come to think of it. So while they would be trying to get information out of him, Noah was going to have to do the same to them—and try doing so without letting them know. Luckily, he had years of experience with this, using his Charisma on his parents and the entire community of Steelton.

He grimaced and thought, *I'm still walking a very tight wire. This isn't a game; they're pros...I think.*

Noah watched 'M' carefully. Despite how she tried to hide it, her annoyance wasn't difficult to spot. Who she was annoyed with wasn't a difficult guess. He had no idea what kind of person she was, but he wanted to test her reaction. Maybe he could learn something more about the people he was dealing with.

"I'm not going to apologize for your dog," Noah challenged,

leaning forward on the table to make his point.

He thought she was going to respond, but instead she turned her attention to the large dark mirror impatiently. She wasn't talking to him, but [Listen] picked up her muttering under her breath, "Little piece of–"

"M is like a codename, is it?" Noah stated, filling his voice with cocky confidence. From the way she froze perfectly still, he knew he was on the money. Of course, it wouldn't take a rocket scientist to figure that out, so maybe she was just restraining herself.

Noah paused and activated [Community]. It displayed several notes he had input during the ride to the office building. These people definitely had their own dossier on him, but they had probably never expected him to make one as well! [Listen] really was a handy skill, and a decade of constant study didn't hurt either. He read his notes, trying to sound as if he was coming up with the words on the spot, like a genius would. "Your name is Emily, isn't it? Your accent is too Parisian to have learned it second hand. Probably lived there most of your life."

Her eyes grew wide as saucers, but Noah kept saying, "You worked hard to get your English to sound as American as possible, but it has too much of that stereotypical Brooklyn in it that people like to imitate in movies. Maybe you like gangster films? You swagger like you do. This means you most likely aren't FBI— you're too international, not uptight enough. Plus, none of you identified yourselves as the feds during pursuit. In fact, none of you identified yourselves at all."

Noah rattled off the notes without any question in his voice. Then he blinked away [Community] and waited for her reaction. If his suspicions were accurate about these people, it would pay off to act the way he did.

The woman's head snapped to Noah, her blonde hair whipping around, her crystal blue eyes smoldering with a mixture of anger and horror. "How-"

The door opened and Burgess Goodrich, the man with the snappy black suit, seeming comfortable in his mid-fifties, stepped into the small room. He had a few manila folders in one hand. "That's enough, Em," he said good-naturedly. "Bruiser's fine. You're dismissed."

The woman stomped out of the room, but before she closed the door, Noah's mind raced, and he affected a closed posture before blurting defensively, "The kick was self-defense!"

Burgess raised a curious eyebrow before slowly closing the door. As he watched him, the tall young man reviewed everything he knew about the older man so far—how he moved, his cadence when he spoke—but none of his mundane skills or knowledge gave him anything to work with. He didn't have anything to commit to add to [Community] about the man yet, and that was concerning at this point.

The older man was intimidating. The strength of his presence wasn't all from his thick neck, or athletic build, or that he seemed to be twice as old as the others—he just gave off an air of absolute authority. He walked like he had all the time in the world, as if people would not continue what they were doing without his permission. The feeling did not put Noah at ease, but it did help him refine his suspicions.

"So," Burgess began, sitting in the opposite chair as if they were catching up on old times. "You like to assert control in unpredictable situations by trying to look clever."

Noah had been ready for this, glad to have his performance already paying off. He sat up quickly; his chin raised a little in defiance. This would be the beginning of a well-crafted act on his part, but he still felt legitimately intimidated. "I'm pretty sure I got most of that right," he countered.

Burgess raised his finger in a chiding motion and set the manila folders on the table. "I never said you weren't clever, only that you were trying to look clever. If anything, Noah Henson, born on September 24th, 2020, you proved my point just now."

Good, Noah thought. He felt the familiar tickle of Charisma helping him with his performance. *The foundation is there now; I just need to guide him along. Now it's time for some reverse psychology.* He crossed his arms and broke eye contact with Burgess. "You don't know anything about me."

The thick-necked man watched Noah brood for a few seconds, as if weighing his options, then chuckled. "I beg to differ, young man." He opened one of the folders and began reading off a dossier, enunciating his words crisply. "You purchased two adjacent houses on Avalon Drive back in 2030 through shell companies created with the assistance of your online friends under the false identity, Caleb McMahon-Eagan. I won't go over the obvious renovations and non-perishable foods you stocked the house with. See, there is a problem, Noah—none of this makes sense. Who do you think is out to get you?"

The young man threw his hands up in the air, rolling his eyes and giving the whole room a meaningful glance, but Burgess shook his head saying, "No, if it were us, or someone like us you were worried about, it would not have been so easy to bring you in."

That hurt. This time when Noah narrowed his eyes, it wasn't an act.

The calm, stocky man continued, "The fact you were buying real estate isn't all that interesting, especially since you weren't renting them, or letting them deteriorate, or doing anything illegal with them. The fact you've made millions with the false identity via the stock market, a few smart investments, and a handful of startups isn't notable in itself either, well, not for the kind of person you obviously are. No, what's noteworthy and confusing is the sheer number of properties you've bought, and how varied their locations are all are across the country. There doesn't seem to be a pattern."

The way Burgess revealed his information made it seem like

'Caleb' was the only fake identity they'd uncovered. *That's a relief,* Noah thought. *It'd be a lot harder to talk my way out of this if they knew about more of my shell personas, much less if they knew I'm actually a billionaire,* He thought. *Maybe he'll slip and reveal more about who he is and why they want me to talk.* He considered interjecting something, a line or two to lead the conversation, but Charisma told him to stay silent. Burgess seemed to be taking pains to show off the information that his group held. The man probably wanted to humble Noah and make him feel like he had no way out. After thinking about it some more, Noah decided to trust his Charisma stat. He kept his mouth shut and shot a penetrating look at the closed door.

"I bet you're trying to be clever again," Burgess said, gesturing to the door. He shook his head. "Please don't. Just be honest. You've done a good job of hiding whatever it is you're doing–a very good job–but that ends here. You must know this. From what we've gathered, this whole pattern of accruing vast monetary resources began when you were ten or eleven. See, at first we investigated your parents, made sure they weren't involved in money laundering or organized crime, but we finally pinned everything to you—well, another agency did. Anyway, maybe when you were ten was when you truly understood you weren't like the other kids and got bored, using hacking as an outlet for that energy. Am I getting warm here?"

The intimidating man's words made Noah pause–he'd never

considered that his actions might get his parents into trouble. In hindsight, that had been a rather obvious oversight. Noah had two lifetimes of experience now, and the [Jack of All] skill, but he could still definitely make mistakes. He mentally shook himself and focused on the conversations again. *I've been keeping my eye contact away from him for a bit, seems like a good time to establish it again.*

Noah gave Burgess Goodrich a hesitant look, and he noticed a ghost of a fatherly grin. Apparently, the glance had been enough to keep him talking. "I've seen a lot of things, but this is quite alarming. There are plenty of millionaires with your level of wealth, but not many who are in the early stages of puberty."

He said the word 'alarming', Noah noted. *That's usually not a good word.* At this point, he was fairly certain he was safe. Other than the hacking, he hadn't done anything illegal, just unusual, and his more…adventurous adventures online shouldn't be traceable. Anonymoose could probably give officials a lot of really strange information about him, but unless they were Aelves, none of it would probably make any sense. Noah stayed quiet for a moment, then when he calculated it was time, he averted his eyes for a moment and said, "I'm not a child."

Burgess' eyebrows raised and nodded appreciatively. He held up a hand and said, "You're right. I'm sorry. I was only speaking in legal terms."

Legalities being mentioned, Noah wondered if he should

demand a lawyer, but decided not to. He still wasn't entirely sure who he was dealing with, but they probably weren't cops or feds, and probably weren't trying to incriminate him. Those were a lot of assumptions, but Noah reasoned that they already had a manila file on him, and he didn't want to escalate the situation—he'd keep up his act instead. Noah gave Goodrich a dubious look, squinting his eyes. "Right. What else do you have on me?"

The older man smiled and said, "I was hoping you could tell me. There are a few fuzzy things that we hope you might help us with."

"I'm no rat," Noah jumped in quickly. He wanted to establish that he was loyal to Anonymoose, to his friends.

"I know. I know," Goodrich nodded reassuringly. He read another report and seemed impressed with what he saw. "Apparently, there was an incident where a teacher of yours was exposed selling illegal drugs to faculty and students. A video of her selling the drugs on school grounds mysteriously popped up at local new stations. You wouldn't happen to know anything about that, right?"

Now he's expecting me to give a little more, Noah realized. *I'm making headway. If I reveal some information to him, he might give me more too...but I still need to do this in a defiant way.*

Noah decided to borrow a trick from his mom's book and raised an eyebrow at the man that said, 'really?' He followed it up with the most charming smirk.

Burgess smiled, "Alright. You're smart and don't want to incriminate yourself or give me much at all, that's probably to be expected. So moving along, we're also pretty sure you were the catalyst for inciting a small riot in the town square. It began with a peaceful demonstration about the potholes in the downtown area. Within a week, a woman known as Azar gave a few speeches that led to a riot, and the old, corrupt mayor ended up exposed and ousted. We found traces of hacking at local businesses that were charged for money laundering after that whole situation."

Oh yeah, I forgot about that one, Noah thought, remembering his conversation with his mom a few years earlier. He had told her to speak with Azar, which inevitably had created a domino effect. Azar had a record of turning peaceful demonstrations into riots. She never seemed to do it on purpose, it just happened. When he'd heard about it on the news, and realized his mother could have gotten hurt at one point, Noah had made a promise not act out on every little tickle Charisma gave him anymore.

Noah had a feeling that the riot incident was probably the furthest back Goodrich's data went. *Good. At least I know how far back they went in on my history,* he concluded. *This implies one of the members of Anonymoose was probably compromised. They were the only ones I told about any of that.* He didn't buy that Burgess and his friends had actually found any traces of his hacks. The rinky-dink systems he'd penetrated back then were about as well protected as a soda can, and even back then, his intrusions had been pretty good.

Burgess pushed another manila folder forward and gestured for Noah to open it. He leaned back, watching Noah's reactions like a hawk.

Noah looked down, seeing more information in bullet point format. "Your hacker moniker is Doc, and you are the leader of the hacker group, Anonymoose."

Noah shook his head, genuinely confused. "The leader? Those guys could blow me out of the water with their skill and experience."

The man in the black suit looked a little shocked at Noah's direct response. He paused and said, "What you probably already know is Dressrosa was the leader of the small group of internet friends who happened to be very skilled hackers. They were all originally rivals, competing to see who could crack the most challenging system. Like you, they were probably just bored geniuses. Soon, they joined forces, pooling together their own information and skills. They had been on our radar, but we considered their hacks mostly harmless.

I should probably defend Anonymoose some more, Noah realized. "I wouldn't call them harmless, old man."

Burgess hummed to himself. "You're loyal. That's good. If it's any consolation, some people in my circles saw your friends as benevolent hackers. They were known for harassing corrupt politicians and CEOs. Even if we had spent the effort to catch your group, it would have been difficult with their aimless hacks. Before you, they had no funds and no pattern to their behavior."

What? Noah thought. Had Anonymoose really just been a bunch of random, aimless hackers before Noah had stepped in as Doc? He had funded some of their operations through the Caleb McMahon-Eagan identity, true, spending money on gifts for bribes, motivating the hackers to work on special projects. *Burgess Goodrich and whoever he represents don't know everything, but okay, I'll admit they seem to know a lot. I'll bet my bottom dollar one of the members of Anonymoose spilled the beans.* He mentally considered the top members, Dressrosa, Fickle, Unkle, and Wash, trying to decide who could have ratted them out. They all seemed so loyal to each other, though, and to him. It didn't make sense.

Noah's original aim had been to figure out what these people wanted, and then talk his way out of it. However, Goodrich seemed more relaxed now, less authoritative. *That's interesting,* Noah thought. The man's change in demeanor triggered Charisma to tickle the back of his mind. *Maybe this situation can be turned into an opportunity. If I feel this out right, maybe I can incorporate all of...this into my plans,* Noah mused. *I'd never considered being involved in the government before, but maybe it could be helpful to make contacts this way.*

Goodrich said, "After contact with you, Anonymoose's efforts had grown exponentially, seeking out classified information, particularly on specific keywords like Chris Broad, Doc, Aelve,

Aliens, Interstellar, Shift, E.M.P. technology, EOTWAWKI, SHTF, prepping, doomsday cults— For a while, there was even an investigation into your little band of misfits being involved in a cult, or an extremist survivalist group."

Apparently, Noah had been lost in thought because Goodrich leaned forward and snapped his finger. "Focus, kid. I get it, I'm a boring adult, but we have problems right now that I can't let slide without some clarification from you."

Noah thought about where Goodrich had been going with the questions before and had a hunch he'd figured out where everything was going. It might be time to play hardball, or at least up the intensity a bit. One thing was sure - these folks were definitely involved in the government, whose, he wasn't sure yet. He said, "You're concerned about the online searches and hacking activity, thinking we're maybe a little too interested in weapons of mass destruction for comfort, eh?" His finger tapped on the table a few times.

Burgess looked at the fingers and gave Noah the first real reaction he had seen since meeting the man—a frown. He said, "You're telling me you want your lawyer in Morse Code. You speak other languages as well. From your correspondences with your hacker group, you speak at least all the romantic languages, both Cantonese and Mandarin in various dialects, Japanese, a handful of islander languages, and most European languages— maybe more. From the intelligence you've shown us, definitely more. This is all very impressive." The man's words seemed genuine, it wasn't an act, and Noah suddenly got excited about a new plan that had popped into his head. At the moment, he was just a brilliant hacker kid who had been caught somewhat red-handed. They were trying to get more information out of him, and the fact he was still a minor had probably helped a lot. He had done his best to steer the conversation where he wanted it to go.

But now, he had an opportunity to take it to a new level.

Noah stopped tapping his finger. Whoever this man represented, they had vast resources and intel. They could be a powerful ally in preparing for the Shift, well, depending on who they were. *I still don't know enough about them*, he thought. *What do they want with me? This guy said earlier that I was bored.*

Charisma tickled him again, and he rolled with his instincts. Noah kept the smirk on his face and rolled his eyes like he was talking to the most boring person in the world. He said, "So you don't like how smart I am. Maybe this puts you or whoever you work for on edge because of international contacts, money, and an independent network. You don't think I'm a genius, no, you're concerned that I was trained, that I'm some kind of super spy planted and funded by a foreign government."

Goodrich closed his eyes and let out a sigh. "That's what they think."

Perfect. His bosses think I'm a spy, but Burgess probably thinks I'm just a misguided kid. I can use that. Noah toned down the arrogance in his voice and replaced it with discontent, adding just a hint of worry. "I'm not. It's just—"

"Yes?"

"It's just my class, you know? This town!" He gave a dramatic wave around the room and rolled his eyes again, letting out an exasperated sigh. "There's nothing to do here, man." He crossed his arms and huffed. A moment of silence passed and Noah saw genuine concern pass across Burgess' face. Earlier, the man's grey hair had made him look distinguished in his crisp black suit. But now, his posture and expression made him look like a father trying to connect with a son.

Burgess spoke softly, "Noah. I don't think you're a bad kid. I think you're just bored."

Noah locked eyes with Burgess and asked, "How would you know?"

"You're smarter than everyone in your class. I've seen your records. You're always ranked in the top ten for your academics, but you never push to be the best. I get it. Why bother doing your best if your effort just goes into something you don't care about?" Goodrich replied. "Thankfully I have an idea. Wait here." The man stood up from his chair.

Goodrich stepped out of the room for a few minutes before coming back with yet another manila folder thick with papers. He handed a pen to Noah and pushed the manila folder across the table. The man nodded to him and said, "You're bored and need an outlet. School isn't cutting it for you, is it?"

Noah's heart raced with excitement, looking at the content of the papers. It was everything he'd hoped for. *I wasn't completely confident it would work. Gosh, I love you, Charisma.* Not wanting to show his glee, Noah let his head roll back and said, "You have no idea, old man."

Burgess smirked. "I do, kid, trust me. Listen, you don't want to go to jail. You don't want your house searched, your parents detained, or your friends questioned. I don't want to fill out all the paperwork on you, because it would already be a ton, and I think we might just be scratching the surface. I hate paperwork—hate it. Luckily, I have found an elegant solution to both of our problems."

On the table in front of Noah were forms full of questions and multiple choice answers, and a handful of pencils. The young man forced out a sigh. "You tell me I'm too good for tests, but you give me another one? And I'm supposed to believe that if I pass this test, you won't send me to jail?"

Goodrich held up two fingers. "Two tests, in fact. I have a feeling you'll handle this one well. Please, just humor me."

If Noah had truly been worried, there would have been no way he'd continue . Instead, he'd be keeping his mouth shut, demanding a lawyer, and sending out coded messages as soon as possible to begin hiding asset and moving money around. Instead, Noah shot Burgess a sideways look, staying in character. "Fine, old man. I'll do it. But your word better be good."

"It always is," the man replied. Burgess opened the door, then before he closed it behind himself, he said, "This first test is a standardized test given to new Interpol agents. If you'd like to get back to school before noon and not be arrested for breaking several international laws, I suggest you start right away."

Interpol huh? thought Noah. His mind began racing as he touched his pencil to the paper before him.

***

Ten minutes later, Noah tapped on the two-way mirror in Morse Code, saying, "I'm finished."

Instead of Goodrich, the man with the hoodie walked in. Noah hadn't gotten a good look at the joggers' faces or builds earlier that day. It turned out Mr. Hoodie Runner was shorter than Noah by a few inches, black, and had cropped hair. His eyes sparkled with either wit or humor, and he walked into the room with an athletic confidence.

"Damn. You really are smart," he said to Noah, looking at the thick stack of papers in disbelief. "Emily is blaming you for her dog being spooked, and her training being called into question. I convinced her not to trash your guitar in response. She can be a bit protective of Bruiser, but she's okay most of the time."

Noah felt eased by the man's relaxed demeanor. He'd thought it through, every angle that might be used to deceive him, but had decided that Goodrich and his people really were trying to recruit him for Interpol. Noah still wanted to be cautious just in case they decided he was more dangerous than useful.

He sighed appreciatively and tried to sound as casual as possible. "At least one of you seems normal around here. My name's Noah."

The man looked the papers over quickly, then backed into the open door. Before closing it, he said, "I know. Sorry, brother. We aren't allowed to touch you. But from this test, it looks like I can tell you my name. I'm Kareem."

Something about the way Kareem had spoken led Noah to believe he was speaking the truth. The door closed and Noah sat back down, tilting the chair back with his legs kicked up on the desk. He closed his eyes to think and weigh his options. *They obviously remember how I got away from the dog. If they're smart, and it seems they are, they probably know I could have hurt M really bad. Holy cow. I'm glad it didn't go down that way.*

His thoughts drifted to the test he'd just taken. While filling out the forms, moving quickly but confidently through them, he had gained an even greater appreciation for how his mother had pushed him to do his best. *Maybe that's really what was wrong with my past life, perspective. I always saw the way my parents kept reminding me about my potential to say that I wasn't good enough. But I guess they just wanted me to work hard and constantly grow. I guess it's one thing to know this intellectually, but another to feel it in my heart.*

Suddenly, Goodrich stepped back into the room. It could have been an act, but the man seemed even more relaxed, as if he'd received good news.

I must have passed with flying colors, Noah thought. The solid older man dropped another folder on to the table, five times thicker than the previous one. He said, "This is your final test. Sorry about the time. Depending on how you do, we can either have a more casual conversation, or a more pointed one."

What does "casual" mean? Noah wondered. He made a face, then without a word, opened the test and began reading.

***

Three hours later, a dejected and nervous-looking Noah tapped the chewed end of his pencil against the mirror. The woman in the hoodie walked in. Ms. Hoodie Runner was cute in a severe way, her hair buzzed completely off, moving with the bravado and grace of a fighter. Her light olive skin glowed with the health of someone seriously into fitness.

The woman snatched the test out of Noah's hand and shut the door behind her when she left—no conversation. Noah didn't even bother testing to see if the door was unlocked. He wasn't trying to escape, and it if looked like he was, he'd be treated differently.

That test was targeted, Noah thought as he sat back down, exhausted. *The first part was probably standard Interpol like Burgess said. The second part was to see if I had any military training. I did okay on that one but only did a bit better than a normal kid my age would who was into military television shows. Spending three hours looking nervous and distraught is harder than I thought it'd be. Gosh, I'm hungry.*

Most of the questions on the second test had been about military tactics and geopolitical conflict. Luckily, Noah had had a little bit of fun crafting his answers to seem like someone making everything up, winging it, but doing a fairly good job.

Unfortunately, during the last three hours, Noah had come to realize how stupid he'd been for meekly coming with these people to this warehouse. It had all worked out, but what if they had been with the Aelves? *I'd been pretending to be arrogant and narrowminded this whole time, but maybe that's not too far from the truth.* Either way, for good or ill, he'd chosen his path and would see it through to the bitter end.

He could have quit the test early, or asked for guidance, or any number of other things, but he'd continue to stay in character. Noah needed to come across as a bored genius who needed guidance, very loyal, and too stubborn to quit. If they were going to hire him, or keep him around to watch, he'd probably need to be someone who would not easily give up.

Fulfilling Noah's expectations, Burgess walked back into the room only five minutes later, a sly grin on his face. He dropped the test back on the table, face down. Noah noticed the grey-haired man didn't sit down and instead stood in the open doorway. The Interpol agent crossed his arms, as if weighing his options, but Noah knew the man had already made a decision. He said, "It's easier to collar a tiger than to cage it, you know. Maybe more dangerous, but easier."

Noah breathed a genuine sigh of relief, but Goodrich continued, pointing to the exam which Noah flipped over. The test was riddled with red marks. It was technically his first failed test in his new life, and he had to suppress a laugh.

Burgess cracked his thick neck. "Luckily, I've got quite the collar for you. No cage, no jail."

Noah's eyebrows shot up. *This is good. He's pointing out my mistakes on the test like a teacher would.*

The older man stood up and motioned for the cautious young man to follow him into the hallway of the abandoned office building. Silently, he led Noah to a set of stairs that led downward, where he was allowed into a nearby restroom for a much-needed break before continuing.

When the two of them reached the bottom of the stairs, two stories down, Burgess opened a door. A long hallway lit with bright, artificial light led forward, the walls scrubbed clean. When the gravity of the situation settled, excitement ran through Noah. He had already accomplished a great deal of his plan to prepare humanity for the Shift. He'd generated a great deal of money to spend acquiring information and stocking up on everything his community and network would need. He'd even pushed his body and mind beyond anything he had ever dreamed possible, but he had identified a gap in his plans.

It didn't matter if he littered the entire world with stockpiles of resources if the right people didn't find them. After all, most all of it had already existed in his first life and hadn't significantly helped anyone. He had a folder on his cloud computer server with instructions, all ready to send to a distribution list via email, but while he'd identified powerful people to receive this information, powerful didn't mean trustworthy. He needed people he could trust to follow his overall vision, not just forts that catered to greed and broke down over time. From experience, he knew that toxic communities didn't protect anyone, they just eventually made everything worse.

These days, Noah lived under the daily, crushing pressure of responsibility. He sometimes had terrible nightmares of Redford finding all of the resources that had been prepared. The man might still be out there, Noah still couldn't track him down. If the scarred-lipped sadist had found a supply warehouse in Noah's past like the young man was building in the present, the Red Chain would have evolved from a wandering raider group to a small, terrifying nation unto themselves. King Redford had a ring to it that made Noah break into a cold sweat even after all these years.

Noah needed the right people who would not only trust his words, but also trust *in* him. He realized that this would be a long shot while he was still fourteen years old. Even the smartest, most logical teens were usually ignored. Realistically, the best he could do would to lay a very strong, social foundation and keep networking.

It was beginning to look like he'd played his cards right in the current situation. Dressrosa had always told him stories of hackers who were caught by the government and recruited to work for them. *If I'm right, I can use this to establish more contacts across the world, people I can trust to carry out my plans after the Shift occurs. There are still people I need to find who have specialized skills.*

Noah's concentration sharpened, noticing interesting security measures and metal doors with sturdy locks. Noah could only imagine that this office building was some sort of Interpol safehouse or cache. After he followed Burgess to the end of the hallway, the older man led him inside. Noah sat in a chair facing a metallic table, and the man in the black suit sat opposite. Burgess steepled his fingers and leaned his elbows on the metal table. Noah decided to start the conversation on a friendly note. "Your second test can eat it."

Burgess smiled appreciatively. "Not used to not getting things your way?"

"What was the point of those questions?" Noah replied. He knew the answer but had to act as if he found the test pointless, adding an offended tone.

Burgess leaned back comfortably in his chair. "The first measured quick thinking and adaptability with a tactical mindset. You passed."

"Cool." Noah smirked. He didn't have to pretend here; it

actually felt nice to show off his prowess and get complimented on it for once. His mom was supportive, but she never praised him all that much, probably because she was afraid of feeding his ego. He had to admit, sometimes it just felt good to impress people.

Before he could say anything else, Burgess said, "The second test I gave you was to see if you had any military training. It's clear that you don't. Even if you tried to flunk it on purpose, I would have known. You really are doing everything on your own, aren't you?"

Burgess' large frame leaning back in the chair reminded Noah of scenes in movies where a rebellious kid is given a chance to tell the truth. Noah found himself liking the man. He replied, "I just got a head start on everybody. The stuff I've been doing seemed fun and I learn fast. What about Anonymoose?"

Burgess frowned. "Like I implied earlier, it was easy to lay a trap for your friends when we knew what specific phrases they were cracking databases to search for. Unfortunately, we were only able to apprehend some of their machines, some of which had data, but it still led us to you."

Good. That means none of Anonymoose was a rat. I'm glad they got away. Noah considered the angles. *It looks like the offer is about to come. Time to push a little in that direction.* "What do you guys want? You think I'll rat on my friends?"

Goodrich let out a tired sigh. The man said, "Noah, you're smart. I bet everyone says that. But like I said before, you're bored,

270

aren't you? I'm a man of my word. You passed both tests, so no jail. You can walk out of here right now. Of course, we're still going to monitor what you do within our jurisdiction. If you pursue any more criminal activity, I might not be there to save you again."

"I can just walk out of here?"

"Yes. But..."

"But what? Why did you bring me all the way down here? We just traded one uncomfortable little room for another."

The older man belly laughed and took a second to get his mirth under control. He pointed at the filing cabinets, scanner, and copy machine in the corner. "This room is set up to handle paperwork," he said. "I have a proposal." Burgess paused for a moment then said evenly, "Why don't you come work for us? You've proven you have the skills. We can give you training. Working for us will help your legitimacy if your character is ever called into question again, and more importantly, it will give you purpose."

This is it, Noah realized. Charisma tingled at the back of Noah's mind, telling him to resist Goodrich a little. He said, "I'm fourteen."

Burgess shrugged. "A minor detail. Emily has already met with your parents to explain you had a misunderstanding with the law. She'd gotten their consent for you to work. Of course, if you decide not to work with us, we will be forced to tell your parents the true nature of your crimes and activities instead of merely securing their consent for you to work. Based on our research, they don't seem to know you own multiple homes."

Noah squinted his eyes at him. "Is that a threat?"

He nodded. "Yes, it is, and I don't enjoy it–that's why I have Emily do it for me. But if I didn't take serious situations seriously, I wouldn't be sitting where I am."

"I do fine on my own," Noah said without looking the man in the eye. "Why would I work for you guys? What would I even do?"

Burgess chuckled. "I'll lay it out for you plainly. Like I said, you're smart. We won't ask anything about Anonymoose that you won't provide voluntarily. If you work with us, you won't go to jail, and that should be incentive enough. Anything you do under us will be considered legal. Other than that, you can think of us like the international law enforcement version of ROTC. You will be required to take a few more tests in the future. To be frank, this is an unpaid position for someone like you, but you should agree."

"Why?"

"Because you have nothing to lose and everything to gain."

"I thought I could walk away free?"

Burgess smiled. "There are different levels of freedom after you've been identified as a cyber-criminal."

Perfect, Noah thought. *He needs to believe that he is gradually winning me over.*

The smartly dressed man glanced behind Noah, nodding at a camera on the ceiling. He said, "You aren't the first problem-teen we've hired and turned into a career analyst, you're just the oddest. It's not like you need money, but we still don't understand why you do what you do. At this point, I'm not sure you do either."

Noah squinted his eyes and said, "It's my money."

Burgess nodded. "Besides the fake Caleb identity, you earned it fair and square, unlike most of the stock traders I've met. I doubt your parents know you're worth more than they are, though."

Noah paused before replying. "So, you're basically saying I gotta work for you guys or you lock me in the slammer, and pass manila files to my family. How long is this gig for, anyway?"

"Four years minimum. Once you graduate high school, we can send you to London to train as a full agent. But keep in mind we will be keeping an eye on you the entire time. Trust will have to be built. You think you're up for it?" Burgess phrased the words as a challenge, like he had given this pitch before.

Noah wondered if Kareem and Emily had been in similar situations before. Now he knew they were Interpol, but that was about the extent of it. He asked, "What do you guys really do anyway? Why are you in town here?"

Burgess adjusted his tie and said seriously, "We are in town because of you. As for what we do, we prevent problems, Noah. I'd rather deal with a fire when it's still just a spark than after it's turned into a disaster."

Noah's feeling of being in control wavered a little bit, but he settled himself. One way or another, he'd made his choice.

CHAPTER 17

Noah tried to appear nonchalant as the bus rumbled forward. Other than a couple goons in suits and M, he was the only person on the bus. The effect was eerie, and while the gifted young man had pretended to be in over his head before, this time he really was not in control.

M, or Emily, still definitely did not like him, and pointedly kept to herself during the ride. The Interpol-Merriweather agent might never warm to him, and that was fine. Then again, it could be she was grouchy because she didn't have her dog. Weren't law enforcement animal trainers really tightly bonded with their animals? Noah made a note to look it up when he got a chance.

The Merriweather division was still a bit of a mystery to him, but Burgess had said that their group's name was a somewhat common word for a reason. As to why they seemed to be operating with impunity on US soil, it had something to do with American budget cuts and international law enforcement agreements.

Noah's thoughts were drifted, trying to distract himself from the enormous pain he'd somehow landed himself in.

A summer camp for at-risk geniuses, really? he thought. Of course, the camp had been pitched to his parents as a special learning environment, but Noah knew better, not least because Burgess had told him to keep his mouth shut.

Ultimately, playing along was a price Noah was willing to pay to avoid getting harassed anymore by the government, any government, and ten days out in the mountains wouldn't tank everything he'd been working on—but was still a little frustrating. His only choice was to try getting some benefit out of the situation, since he couldn't change it.

He frowned at the bags at his feet before staring glumly out the windows of the bus. Rolling hills full of trees, lots of trees, blurred by.

From a practical standpoint, maybe being out in the wilderness at a summer camp would give Noah the opportunity to brush up on some wilderness skills. He focused on that thought, another glimmer of light in the situation. One of his greatest enemies was wasted time. Still, as long as he could improve himself or otherwise prepare for the Shift, a week of bad food and forced singing shouldn't be too hard to handle.

Noah felt his glum expression lighten a bit and he forced a smile at one of the agents in suits, a big, pale-skinned man with a crew cut. The big man looked away. *Friendly, huh?* Noah thought.

It felt like he'd been traveling forever before the bus turned off the main highway onto a dirt road, and crept forward for what felt like another hour. Even though he'd been traveling for hours, Noah felt a little lucky. Burgess had said that some of the other campers he'd meet had been flown in from other countries.

Lucky! Hah. His sour mood tried to return, and Noah vowed to find a bow the first chance he got to make sure the next week and a half wouldn't be a complete waste of time. Right now, it was hard not to think about desirable real estate that might come up for sale while he was stuck out in the boonies. Roasting marshmallows was not going to save anyone from the Aelves.

Finally, the bus stopped, and Noah grabbed his bags before cautiously exiting, scanning the area.

The layout of the camp seemed fairly normal. A large mess hall stood next to the small office building with a sign labelled "Administration." Next to the mess hall stood a giant open field of grass, wide enough to house two soccer goals and a small basketball court. Near the tree lines were wooden cabins of various sizes, each with their own sign–fun names and unique mascot animals like, "Goat Cabin," whose mascot was, of course, a goat. The basketball court was littered with balls of various sizes, multi-colored jump ropes, scoreboards, and everything a kid might use to have good, clean, active fun.

As he stood there, the bus rumbled away–the goons in suits

had stayed put, and so had M. Noah figured the military presence he'd passed on the way must serve as enough security for all the shady geniuses he'd apparently be surrounded by.

A cheery looking counselor, or who Noah assumed to be a counselor because of the T-shirt, burst out of the office building and rushed towards him, waving wildly. Noah frowned and thought, *Well, this is weird, but maybe it won't be so bad.*

***

Two days later inside the mess hall, Noah glumly rested his head in his hands. *This is miserable*, he thought. He'd never been so bored since he'd been born in this lifetime. He hadn't truly known what to expect at Camp Firestarter, but some part of him had wanted some sort of challenge. Maybe gritty competitions between the campers.

Instead, Noah had been forced to clap along to cheesy songs by the campfire and play circle games. There had been no strenuous obstacles to overcome, no battle of wits. On the first day, Noah had thought it all a necessary farce, fooling the geniuses' parents that Firestarter was a camp for special kids—not a paramilitary training ground.

By lunch of the second day, the dread that had been steadily building in Noah's body had made itself a comfortable home in the pit of his stomach. The reality of his situation actually made him feel ill. He had things to do, and none of them involved s'mores and singing kumbaya by the fireside. *I could be purchasing more warehouses, or doing R&D, procuring rice and beans, buying farms, or re-establishing contact with Anonymoose. Heck, I could be doing practically anything else instead of wasting my time here.*

Plastic strings of boondoggle sat unwoven in his hand as he fumed about his situation. Forced to wear a cheery camp T-shirt, he sat on a wooden bench with a group of children–not other teens—children. Out of the twenty-three geniuses at Camp Firestarter, Noah had been the oldest among them by at least two years. He was pretty sure the oldest in the group besides him was Pietro, a twelve-year-old from Russia.

Everyone but Noah happily weaved one plastic string over and under each other in simple, repeating patterns, creating lanyards which they could give their parents. The counselors, mostly in their early twenties, quietly shared stories from college or flirted with each other. Noah watched all of them, both the counselors and the campers, in stupefied disbelief.

Were these children actually the geniuses Burgess told me to watch out for? Noah wondered. Nothing about them gave him the indication they were even smarter than average, much less exceptional. They gossiped, giggled, and picked fights with each other like every other kid in the world. Even with [Listen], he hadn't picked up whispers between the other campers that might have hinted at any secret motives or plans.

At this point, he didn't care anymore. Noah wanted something, anything, to do besides weave lanyards to give away that would be thrown out a week later. Luckily, something new seemed to be happening. One of government goons who drifted through camp from time to time had entered the building, briefcase in hand. Each step the Interpol agent took quieted the voices in the hall a little more. When he reached the front, the room had fallen silent.

A few of the counselors went to the windows, drawing the blinds to stop the midday light from entering. The Interpol agent was a tall, severe-looking blonde woman, probably originally FBI or CIA and re-tasked to technically be Interpol. Noah was still a bit unsure of how the Merriweather organization was actually structured or funded, but he'd made an effort to keep his cyber snooping to a minimum lately. He'd probably be in the dark for a while about his new employers, a fact that didn't sit really well with him. Some of his sources had confirmed that Merriweather was legit, they just couldn't exactly explain how.

The blonde agent set the briefcase on a nearby table, opened it, and pivoted it around. Noah saw the familiar green light of a hologram computer spilling from the briefcase. The light expanded filling the entire wall it was adjacent to, displaying a screen.

One of the counselors, a petite, normally-bubbly young woman wearing a pink watch came to the front of the room, a serious expression on her face. Noah was suddenly reminded that all of the camp counselors were probably highly trained in their own right, a fact that had been easy to forget over the last couple days of boredom. The counselor—Noah thought her name might be Tiffany—said, "Hey, everyone, we're going to have a little change of pace. We know that some of you need an outlet once in a while, and this might be a good bonding experience, so we are going to have a little game!"

The screen on the wall flashed, and lines of text appeared:

Scenario: Each of you has been assigned a country. On your papers you will find the various metrics and statistics for your country over the past ten years, including current budget and economic standard in comparison with other countries. Based on these metrics alone, you are tasked to prepare your country for war, and either repel invaders, or become an aggressor. First place gets extra material for s'mores. You will have two hours.

Tiffany, the counselor, said, "Okay, guys, get ready! We'll be handing out VR rigs, and your login credentials should be the same as your username and password for the online Merriweather portal. I would give you instructions on how to retrieve a lost password, but I know in this group, that won't be an issue." She smiled, and some of the campers in the room smiled back, but Noah just watched curiously, his face neutral.

A few other counselors began handing out VR headsets and hand controllers. The battery-powered rigs were a little old, already out of date, but seemed to be in good working order. Noah put his on, and after logging in, using his hands to type, he found himself automatically loaded to the game.

He was in luck. The game seemed to be based off a popular strategy game he'd played for ages. Noah couldn't start yet, but he quickly opened menus to check out what kind of information he'd be able to use in the game, a smile spreading across his face. *Yes! I used to play stuff like this with Johnny and even Anonymoose! This will be a piece of cake!*

In the upper left corner of his field of view, a screen showed the counselor at the front of the room, a camera slaved to his VR unit. She was giving out basic instructions for how to play the game and use the equipment, but Noah tuned her out. In the other corner of his vision, he could see an extended version of the game's rules. He quickly scanned them, then began planning strategies. Suddenly, the rules blinked red, and the campers in the room immediately became icons in the game. Noah could invest in skills within the game to tell if any of the other leaders were talking, but he hadn't bought any skills at all yet, so the other leaders just drifted as icons. Some of them flashed, noting activity. Noah assumed they were already chatting with each other, discussing trade agreements or forming diplomatic ties. A few of the campers pinged him, getting his attention to text, but Noah ignored them all.

His eyes widened as he opened his menu to see what country he'd been assigned. He'd been handed the United States of America. It couldn't get better than this for him—one of the most powerful countries in the world that he was already intimately familiar with. He'd been thrown a soft ball, set up for a home run—it almost wasn't fair. *They couldn't have given me a better test to stand out in,* Noah thought before grinning confidently. He had been preparing the world for the Shift for years. No one in the room would be able to touch him; he could effortlessly roflstomp all of them. The kids wouldn't know what hit them.

Noah cracked his neck and calmed himself before suddenly breaking out into a series of gestures and finger movements, rapidly opening menus and investing resources. This was going to be a massacre.

***

The moonlight was Noah's only company in the mess hall as he sat staring at the green hologram screen against the wall. The rest of the day had passed in a blur, and after eating hot dogs by the fire, he'd somehow made his way back here. The names of all the other campers, the children–no, the geniuses—burned in his mind. He would never forget their names.

His eyes traced each line one by one, he had lost count how many times he had done so. The situation hadn't made sense at first. Hours earlier, the children he had spent nearly three days with had been happy to play kickball and call each other silly names, just like every other normal kid he had seen. But when the game started, they had completely changed—creating alliances, forming economic unions, and establishing trade embargos. A few of them had created military strategies the likes that Noah had never seen before. It had been like they'd been completely different people.

Noah had been stupid to ignore reality staring him in the face at first, so focused on winning. Of course, by the time he had made aggressive moves on Canada and somehow over half of his country had been occupied, it had been too late. He shook his head as his eyes finally trailed down to the final name on the list—his. Noah Henson. Last place.

He wondered for what felt like the hundredth time if there had been something wrong with the game, but he knew in his heart that this was not the case. Earlier, when he'd first come back to the mess hall, one of the counselors had tried to bring him back to the cabin to get ready for campfire songs, but a goon in a suit had stopped her, leaving Noah to figure out how he had gotten last place.

I know that I've been preparing the world for something Interpol could never imagine, but what I've been doing should have directly translated to skill in the game. In fact, I've even played a less realistic version online of the game we actually played before and did well! What the heck? When he had seen his name at the bottom of the list, a seed of doubt had been planted in his heart. Before that moment, he'd had complete confidence that he was on the right track for his mission to save the world.

He still believed that he was moving in the right direction, but his faith had been shaken. Thankfully, it would take a lot more than a VR game loss to ever revert to a pitiful version of his past self, like Worm. Noah had just been surprised, and the results had hurt his pride.

This was his first real failure in his new life with something he had really tried at. Things had come easily to him this time around because of his core skills like [Jack of All], and his past experience. Of course, this didn't mean that he hadn't worked hard to get to where he was. In fact, he had worked his butt off to get away from his lowest point, moving as far away from Worm as possible. He'd pushed his limits to create a new and better version of himself.

But sitting alone in the mess hall, staring at the screen made him want to reevaluate if not his plan, then definitely himself. *Is there something wrong with me?*

Lost in thought, it took him a second longer with [Listen] to realize that someone had stepped into the mess hall. The steps were small but deliberate. A young girl's voice echoed in the room, "Carlo from the Philippines said you were still in here, sulking. I came to see if he was just being crazy again or if you really are as emo as everyone else thinks you are."

Noah turned around to see Yoko Terada, the twelve-year-old girl from Japan, standing in the center of the mess hall with her arms crossed. Beneath her camp T-shirt, she wore jean shorts with flowers embroidered on the pockets. Her jet-black hair had been cut in a bob, and her bangs fell down to her thin eyebrows, one of which was raised. Noah was certain that he was being judged.

"I'm not sulking," he replied, and immediately regretted sounding so defensive.

Yoko chuckled, her tone strange for her age. "Not just Carlo, Pietro too. Pietro says he's been watching you since you came. He's been through worse than any of us here, so if he says you're being emo, you are."

Noah let out a sigh. "What do you want?"

"I just wanted to talk to the boy who's had Interpol running around like chickens with their heads cut off, or so I hear."

"And?"

Yoko uncrossed her arms and tapped her lower lip, eyes locked on his. "I'm disappointed."

Noah nodded at the rankings on the wall. "You and everyone else. I'm older than everyone here, and I still got last place. I guess I really am surrounded by geniuses."

A faint frown twitched Yoko's lips. She said, "You know, genius is a title, or a measure. I am more than any title anyone ever gives me, so are you." Then she made a subtle gesture at the cameras in the mess hall. The young girl briskly walked to Noah and stretched to whisper, overcoming their difference in height. "I'm not disappointed by your intelligence. We know all about you, Noah Henson. In fact, we know more than Interpol."

Noah froze and decided to be cautious. "Like what."

She spoke even more quietly, "Like how Caleb McMahon-Eagan isn't your only fake identity. Or how all of your identities combined make you one of the wealthiest people in the world and the youngest billionaire in history. Or how Carlo, Pietro, and I managed to find out you've been making some very interesting purchases for several years. Interpol and other feds don't know the half of it. You own patents!"

Noah's jaw clenched, and he felt all of his blood drain to his feet. He could sense that a denial would be pointless, and he really didn't want Yoko to drop any more verbal bombs. "How did you know?"

She stepped back and tilted her head. "Did you think your Anonymoose pals were the best hackers in the world, or even top tier? The smartest people in the world hide their skills, Noah. When you know you're the best, you don't need to boast."

Noah's Charisma helped him gain some ground. After feeling the familiar tickle, he countered, "You don't look so hiding-in-the-shadows to me."

Yoko screwed up her face like she'd bitten into a lemon and looked away. Her tone bitter, she whispered, "Even so-called prodigies make mistakes."

In that moment, he really understood who he was dealing with, what Yoko really was—a real genius. This girl, and probably the rest of the camp, were not like him, just someone powered with stolen magical abilities and impossible knowledge...no, these were truly special people. This girl standing before him talked like he did, differently to others his age, but her mind worked on another level than his. *She's only twelve,* he reminded himself. *I can't believe how much control over her emotions she has at her age. In my first life, I would have just stomped off after saying a mean name.*

The girl took in a deep breath and gave Noah a cool look. She said, "So anyway, after actually meeting you, I've been disappointed. This isn't because of some stupid, arbitrary test though–you hadn't tried to talk to any of us the past thirty-six hours. We gave you an entire day to introduce yourself to us, but you didn't. Even during the test we just took, you didn't try to make connections with any of us, and that was practically the point of the game. Any way you look at it, that was just stupid. Heck, you've been bunkmates with Pietro since you arrived and you haven't exchanged a word with him...in any language. Everyone here is a polyglot. You've acted like all the adults, treating us like we were just children. This is not only narrow-minded, it's dumb. I expected better of you."

Noah closed his eyes and felt guilt creep up his spine. He said out loud, to himself, "I wonder what Doc would say?"

Yoko's eyebrows shot up in surprise, but she quickly reined them back in to form her cool mask. "Your most common handle." She studied him for a long moment, perhaps wondering why he'd said what he'd said. Noah mentally smiled sadly—she'd have a tough time finding any ulterior motive—there hadn't been one. Finally, she said, "We won't tell Interpol your secrets, Noah. My point is if there is anyone here who can understand you, it's us. No need to get emo about it. If they succeeded in anything by bringing us all together, it's proof that none of us are special. You aren't special. Me, Pietro, not even Carlo." She blushed and tried to hide a smile. "Maybe Carlo. He's weird."

The extreme irony of the situation actually made Noah start to feel better. He was getting a pep talk from a young girl about how he wasn't special, and now he really did understand that he wasn't. Oh, he might be trying to save the world, sure...but what if one of these kids at Camp Firestarter had gotten his magic, his skills, or his memory? While this was a good realization for perspective, Noah decided not to dwell on it.

The Japanese girl must have interpreted his silence for resistance. "This is probably one of the best chances you will ever get in your life to meet people you can relate to. From a Machiavellian perspective, it's probably a networking dream, too."

Noah let his smile show, all tension in his body relaxing. "So, you're saying us geniuses have to stick together?"

Yoko nodded. "Yeah. Who else can understand what it's like to run an international business at my age, or doesn't run away when Carlo babbles on about weapon schematics or tech that is useless in peacetime? Yes, we stick together not only because we are thought leaders in our respective fields, but because we're friends."

She's not saying it out loud, at least not spelling it out, Noah realized. Something inside of Noah fluttered a little, and the truth breezed over him like an uncomfortable chill. He had been lonely. Being focused on preparing the world for the Shift alone hadn't left a lot of time for other things, even though he'd tried disciplining himself to also have a social life. Maybe solitude was a price of being a genius, even a fake one like Noah.

But now, a young girl had just reached out to him, told him that she and at least a few other campers knew what he was doing, if not what for…and they didn't care. *Yoko didn't ask me what I was doing with everything I was buying*, thought Noah. There had been no judgment, just a simple statement of fact.

Yoko glanced him over once more before pivoting, dismissing the conversation and walking to the door. Noah called out to her, "You're wrong."

The girl stopped but didn't turn around. "Oh yeah?"

"You said none of us are special," Noah replied. "But what if everyone is? What if everyone is worthy of a second chance, or a helping hand?"

Yoko shook her head before opening the door to the mess hall and stepping through. She must have noticed that Noah hadn't actually contradicted her. If everyone is special, then nobody is. But if it's one thing Noah had learned, it was that the same fact can be looked at in two different ways that can both change a person's worldview.

He stared at the exam score one more time. Then he got up slowly, walked to the briefcase, and shut it.

***

An hour later, using [Listen], Noah picked up the easy breathing of the other campers inside the small cabin. Noah lay on the bottom bunk, unable to sleep. His mind wasn't the usual kind of restless–buzzing with plans of the future. Instead, he was thinking about the past.

For some reason, he thought how the cigarettes that Doc had been slowly killing himself with had always bounced up whenever he grinned. Noah had experienced plenty of fun moments since his new life with his friends and family, but until an hour earlier, he didn't know that he had been missing something. Granted, he'd been depressed and alone in his first life, so he'd thought he had everything this time around. Noah genuinely loved the new memories he'd created, but playing games with Johnny and being goofy with his parents felt...lesser compared to surviving the Shift and his lessons he'd received from Doc.

His new memories weren't truly spontaneous, didn't feel as genuine. They felt manufactured with his Charisma - like staged photographs. Even though he had genuinely had a great time with his loved ones, the moments had always been plagued by the dark undercurrent of the coming Shift. Because of that, he had never really felt like he truly belonged, had always felt different.

Until today, Noah thought, *I didn't realize I kept a distance between me and everyone else. I never even tried telling anyone any of my secrets, just assumed everyone would think I was nuts. Nobody—I never gave anyone a chance.*

He narrowed his eyes and decided he refused to brood without action—that would be an old Noah thing to do. Instead, he got up from his bunk bed and stepped outside. [Listen] alerted him to movement in the nearby tree line–one of the Interpol agents. Noah wasn't going anywhere; they could watch him all they liked. He sat on the stairs of the front porch and stared at the night sky, tracing the invisible lines between the stars like Doc had taught him.

Someone opened the door behind him, and Pietro from Russia sat next to Noah without looking at him. The boy's messy black hair fell down to the top of his eyes, making him looking like a shaggy dog. Noah cleared his throat, held out his hand, and said, "Hi, Pietro. My name is Noah."

Pietro looked at Noah's hand but didn't take it. He nodded and spoke English in a perfect North American accent, "So, Yoko got to you?"

Noah let out a defeated sigh. "Yeah, and she was right. I've been kind of a jerk." Not one to repeat the same mistake, Noah talked to Pietro like an equal.

The Russian boy hugged his knees under his chin and looked up at the stars. He didn't acknowledge Noah's words and continued to stare at the sky. Noah's Charisma stat wasn't necessary to stay silent. He didn't need his abilities to remind him what it was like to be fourteen.

After several minutes of silence, Noah turned his head and saw something wet glisten Pietro's eyes. The Russian boy seemed to be filled with wonder, like he couldn't believe where he was. He whispered, "It's so quiet here."

Pietro had been fidgeting, trying to hide his hands, but Noah had seen the burn scars, small little dark spots across the tips of his fingers. He frowned and to his own surprise, found himself saying, "Not for me. I can still hear things."

Pietro finally broke his gaze from the stars and read Noah's face carefully. After a moment, the boy nodded solemnly. "You too, huh? Me? I see things. Can't unsee them. They tell me sometimes that I'm lucky to be alive. I think they're lucky to be ignorant."

The boy paused, his eyes moving back to the sky. Pietro's voice was strong but brittle as he asked, "In such a peaceful place, what do you have to be afraid of, Noah?"

Silence passed between them before Noah's hands stretched back behind him, his weight leaning on his palms just like Doc used to. Somehow, the gesture gave him comfort. Ever since he'd been reborn, his mind had been working non-stop. For the first time since hanging out with Doc on the back porch of his cabin, Noah stopped thinking and allowed himself to feel without any restraint.

Somehow, he felt a kindred spirit in the Russian boy sitting beside him, something Pietro must have felt too. Finally, Noah decided to be entirely honest and said, "I've seen people I care for die horrific deaths. I saw monsters, both human and not, do things no one should witness. Everything I do, every second of my waking life, is to make sure that never happens again. No matter how much I prepare, I'm afraid I can't stop it. No matter how much I push myself, I'm afraid I'm not enough."

Noah didn't feel sorrow as he spoke the words. Instead, he felt lighter, less removed from his own humanity. It was an odd feeling, to give away such a terrible secret and get back comfort in return. *It's been so long since I've talked to anyone like this*, Noah realized.

Pietro let out a stuttered breath, his voice hesitant. "I'm afraid all the atmosphere in the world will be sucked up into the vacuum of space where no one can hear me. I'm afraid to wake up in a vegetative state where my mind still works but I can't move my tongue."

Then the younger boy silently cried, hands buried under his legs. Noah eyed him, but respected his space and didn't acknowledge the tears. Suddenly, he didn't see Pietro the boy genius from Russia. Instead, he saw himself a lifetime ago. Noah knew Pietro's fear because he could relate. *When life, the very foundation of everyone's existence, seemed so rocky, what do we have to anchor us? If we don't already have them, we need to create those ties.*

Noah slowly stood, stretched, and gave Pietro his best Doc Broad smile. "So you're afraid you will have no voice, that no one will hear you. But I will, Pietro. I'm a good Listener. In fact, I'm listening right now."

The words had been spoken without any double meaning. In a way, Noah had been speaking to his past self. Pietro eyed him for a moment, his shoulders hunched forward, and Noah could see the strength in the boy, cracked by old wounds. It was a surreal moment, like staring into a mirror crossing time and space, and somehow, Pietro must have picked up on it too. The boy's searching look ended, and he nodded.

Something warmed in Noah's chest as he held out his hand to the Russian boy. Pietro stared at the hand before nodding again and grasping it tightly, as if it were a lifeline in a storm. Noah helped him up, and they went wordlessly back into the cabin to their bunks. The connection, the friendship had been made and didn't need to be rushed.

As Noah stared upwards before sleep, he wondered if the Merriweather division had planned on the other kids at Camp Firestarter being younger, and Noah older. It couldn't be. *Government agencies are never that efficient...are they?*

The thought was the last Noah had before drifting off to sleep.

CHAPTER 18

Seven days later, Noah sat in the back of a bus full of noisy campers, sandwiched between Pietro and Carlo. Yoko sat in front of Carlo, tying a boondoggle lanyard she had made around his wrist. When she finished, every camper on the bus would have a blue and white plastic lanyard.

Carlo leaned over Noah to show Pietro a video on his phone. It wasn't the typical 3d hologram video, but a normal one from in the early days of the internet. Noah caught the logo and recognized that it was an old YouTube video. Carlo was fascinated with old world technology, and could spend hours watching videos of people building huts out of mud. This video was about weapons, with someone fashioning a crude bow out of PVC pipe.

Pietro watched the video suspiciously, shaking his head. "It doesn't make sense to me why you watch these old crafting videos. These weapons are ineffective in war."

Carlo rolled his eyes and said, "Says you. But you are missing the point. They have stabby parts and things that go zoom. They're cool. You must have that word in Russia, right? I mean, your country is full of ice and snow, how can you not understand what cool means? Besides, not every weapon has to blow up."

"They should," Pietro countered quickly, raising his chin a little. "Explosives are the science of physics, and a mere engineer like you wouldn't understand the complexity."

Carlo's eyes went dull, and his voice dripped sarcasm. "Things go boom. Wow. So complex. My butt goes boom every time I fart. Does that make your precious physics–"

"Boys," Yoko said impatiently, adjusting her lanyard. "Noah has the next stop. Also, Carlo, really?"

The Filipino boy blushed and quieted as Pietro pretended he hadn't been involved. After the two boys stopped arguing, Noah nodded appreciatively to Yoko for cutting their conversation early. Although friends, once Pietro and Carlo got going, a shouting match between the two geniuses usually followed. Noah said, "I was actually interested in the video. Carlo, could you send me a few links?"

The genius from the Philippines nodded excitedly. At thirteen years old, he already had a graduate degree in Metallurgical Engineering and a few other degrees as well, on top of speaking at least ten languages that Noah knew of. He said, "Oh, man, just you wait till you get—"

Yoko placed her hand on Carlo's wrist, and he pulled back reflexively, squinting his eyes at the Japanese girl. Pietro made a face and said, "I understand what you two are doing is parting of adolescent courtship, but I still think it's weird."

The bus began to slow down in front of a familiar abandoned office building. Standing outside the building were three Interpol agents and a man in a crisp black suit with silver hair. The Japanese girl sighed and let go of Carlo's hand, his lanyard tied. To Noah, she said, "I'm glad we met you."

Noah got up and fist bumped Pietro, Jed, and Yoko. "Me too." Noah had never felt like a big brother before, but had discovered that it fit fairly well.

"See ya, dude," Carlo said.

Pietro gave Noah a slight smile. "Goodbye. Don't forget to stay in touch."

"I won't," Noah replied.

He walked down the aisle, bumping fists with all the campers. As he stepped off the bus, he noticed that one of the Interpol agents had already unloaded his bags from the bus. Noah watched the vehicle drive off with his new friends. He assumed they'd be heading to the airport.

Burgess raised an eyebrow. "You were last in all your scenario tests."

Noah shrugged. "Don't pretend that's the reason you sent me there in the first place."

"Oh, really?"

"Yah. Camp Firestarter isn't a training ground or a test facility."

"Then, what is it?"

"I had enough time to figure it out," Noah replied. "It's just a normal camp. The tests were there to distract the campers and give them stimulus so they wouldn't get bored. They were more just for fun, and less annoying than exams that could teach us anything important."

Burgess chuckled. "I would keep your opinion to yourself and make sure none of the higher-ups hear that. It would wound their pride. But now you've only told me what the camp wasn't, not what it was."

Noah picked up his bags, and Burgess turned around, leading him inside the building which housed the current secret location for Merriweather Division operations. Noah thought before speaking. "Like I said, it's just a normal camp for at-risk geniuses. Whoever designed that camp made it to address the at-risk part more than the genius part. The program is for weird kids to interact and not feel so alone."

Burgess hummed as he held the door open for Noah. "That's an astute observation. But why wouldn't Interpol just send them to therapy? It would be much more efficient."

Noah gave him a look. "Efficient but not effective. Kids hate psychologists."

Burgess nodded as they reached the bottom floor door, leading to the real offices of the Merriweather Division. "Children can smell clinical testing a mile away. I've found that if you give a troubled child a safe environment to just be a child–not whatever the world wants them to be–some problems can kind of sort themselves out."

That gave Noah pause. "Then what was my problem?"

Burgess opened the door and smiled. "Welcome to the Merriweather Division again, Noah. I hope you have your workout gear. We have some training to do."

***

"That looked painful!" The unfamiliar voice drifted from the small group of people on one side of the room.

"We can go again whenever you're ready," said Louis from the opposite side of the wrestling mat.

It took Noah another second to catch his breath. For some reason, he couldn't make out the name of the constellations he was seeing. *Oh. Wrong stars.*

He groaned as he got back up for at least the hundredth time, stretching his back. The other members of the Merriweather Division surrounded the wrestling match, passing money around every time Noah got up. He sighed and said, "This is technically child abuse. I'm fourteen."

"I didn't take you as one to make excuses," said Louis. Noah wondered what that meant since they'd basically met for the first time that day. After being introduced, Noah had changed into athletic clothes and begun getting dismantled in front of an audience.

Obviously another Merriweather agent, Louis oozed self-confidence. The big, bald black man stood a couple inches shorter than Noah, but must have outweighed him by fifty pounds. Probably in his early thirties, every inch of the muscular man screamed ex-military. The fact he was easily manhandling Noah in hand to hand combatives was somehow made even more frustrating by the man's unflappable, French-accented drawl.

Noah pulled up his [Listener] menus and quickly glanced at all the martial, mundane skills he had acquired over the years. All of them were at least level three. He frowned at screens and thought, *I know I have a level five limit with mundane skills, but I didn't realize exactly what that meant until recently.* He mentally sighed.

The black French man crouched in front of him and grinned. Even without knowing that the man was a friend of Emily's, the smile would have made him uncomfortable.

Noah blinked the screens away. Burgess had originally told him to last only five minutes against Louis. When he'd passed that test, the older man had shrugged and challenged him to last as long as he could. Noah had felt a flash of irritation that seemed to have activated his core of stubbornness that had been growing during the course of his new life.

After that, word had apparently spread around the

Merriweather building that the new kid, the Michigan genius, was getting his butt kicked by Louis in the training room.

That had been two hours ago. Since then, Louis had beaten Noah more than nine times out of ten, all while somehow avoiding seriously hurting or bruising him too badly. They'd boxed, they'd wrestled, they'd done floor exercises, and Louis had even beaten him at fencing! Noah's pride was still delicate after his experiences at Camp Firestarter, which made everything worse. It was one thing to get beat up - he'd endured plenty of that in his past life - but it was entirely different to be out-skilled at martial arts—something he'd felt confident in—over and over again in front of an audience. Emily, in particular, had seemed to enjoy watching Noah be thrown around like a rag doll.

While [Listen] had picked up some of the Merriweathers marveling that Noah had won at all, and that he'd lasted so long, the young man had taken no comfort in it. The world post-Shift would be a dangerous place, and he was training to fight more dangerous foes than people—the Aelves. The memory of how Doc had died, and the overwhelming power of the Aelves he'd faced, made him grit his teeth and just try harder.

To his surprise, the painful and incredibly embarrassing experience had allowed him to level up several of his martial art skills. Still, even when he combined all his physical mundane skills together, he'd been unable to beat Louis any better than a fluke here and there. A few martial skills had even leveled to the maximum of five points, but regardless, he had been unable to level any of them past that.

After flexing his hands in his padded gloves, Noah feinted and shuffled to the side, testing Louis' defenses. They were sparring with mixed martial arts now, technically using a point system, but it kind of didn't matter since Noah kept being incapacitated or thrown.

His only advantage was a slightly longer reach, and the occasional stroke of luck—the French fighter was on a different level. The man seemed to always know what Noah was going to do, have a counter, and have better timing too. Louis even had better endurance! Noah had been tempted to use [Harmony] while humming a tune. He wasn't sure it would work for a fight, but had decided against it either way. Cheating wouldn't help him get better.

Noah concentrated on minding his distance and throwing exploratory jabs. He'd tried playing defense before, but if he did, he'd just lose faster—probably because Louis got bored. Instead, he was focusing on looking for openings, using as many martial arts skills as he could, levelling the ones that needed it. Noah kept a watchful eye on his opponent, knowing that Louis seemed equally good at striking and grappling. Luckily, the man hadn't been following through on his strikes, just batting Noah around.

After a couple exploratory kicks, Noah calmed himself. Frustration had started welling in his stomach, but he suppressed it as best he could. While sparring like this, impatience would be a terrible enemy. Louis stood like an impassive wall, deftly blocking or evading everything Noah threw, letting him tire himself out. Noah had a strange feeling that Louis was using this opportunity to train too, but in a different way.

Suddenly, Noah thought he saw an opening and took advantage. As Louis lazily punched at Noah's face, the teen lowered his center of gravity and met the fist with his forehead before parrying the hand to the side, stutter-stepping to add to the misdirection. He darted in, aiming a left jab to his opponent's ribs and a cross to his face. The plan had been to follow that combo with a nasty elbow, something he normally wouldn't do while sparring because it could really hurt someone, and maybe snap kick away to create some room again.

Instead, Noah felt strong hands firmly take hold of his arm and waist before the world went upside down. His back hit the mat with all his weight behind it, his lungs explosively exhaling. He closed his eyes and lay there a moment, questioning his life choices, his sanity, and getting his breath back.

What did Louis just do? Now that Noah had been beaten, he knew that he'd been baited, but not exactly how he'd been thrown. If this had been a real fight, his opponent could have fallen with him to the ground, and that would have been bad. Granted Noah wasn't playing for keeps right now, but he knew Louis wasn't either. The thought of fighting the other man in a dark alley with knives was actually terrifying. The combination of being skilled in martial arts in this life, and having seen the deadly consequences of real violence in his past life, made the reality of this current skill gap very, very real.

Noah could still last a bit longer, but he'd just gotten back from camp that day, and he'd been at the current Merriweather office location for a while now. Burgess' motivation for immediately introducing Noah to Louis seemed strange, too. At least the time spent hadn't been a waste, his skills had leveled, but it was time to throw in the towel. The young man painfully climbed to his feet.

"I've had enough. I need to go home and see my parents," Noah said. He sighed and put his hands up in surrender. *This is my weakness*, Noah realized. *I had been relying on [Jack of All] so much that I only saw its benefits, not its limitations. I still haven't able to level my core Listener archetype, so all my mundane skills are limited to max of level five.*

The truth was bitter. *Even if I maxed all my mundane skills to five, getting better than that would probably require a lot of time and energy spent, like normal people. [Jack of All] is a shortcut but has that skill cap limitation. In fact, maybe being maxed out might even mean I start to learn skills more slowly than other people, or it might even actively resist me!* That was a wild thought. Either way, he definitely needed to figure out how to level up his [Listener] status, class, archetype, whatever.

He watched as Louis grabbed a towel and was handed a fat wad of bills from the other employees. The man accepted the money and nodded at Noah, his expression unreadable. *Louis is incredibly talented at martial arts. With my current level of skills, I'll never be able to beat him consistently.*

Burgess Goodrich stepped onto the mat and waved everyone away. "That's enough, everyone. Back to work; playtime is over." The man in the black suit stepped over to Noah and patted him on the back. He said, "We all have our limits, Noah. That's why we work together."

Noah breathed in and let out a long sigh. Burgess' idea of ramming home a point seemed a little overkill at this point, but he couldn't deny the lessons he'd learned over the past couple weeks. An idea suddenly came to mind. He smiled. "You're right, Boss."

***

Hours later, Noah opened up his new laptop with ten times more encryption than his previous computer had had. After having Chinese food with his parents and catching them up on his very fun and very normal Camp Firestarter experience, Noah went to his room and immediately employed the new encryption techniques taught to him by Yoko. A lot of it didn't make sense to him, but he followed the instructions to the letter, using one of his five rooms of his [Memory Palace] to store the steps.

Soon, he was back online without having to worry about Burgess or Interpol tracking his activity. A few minutes later, he found himself on a forum with twenty-three other members. He opened up a new thread to send a message to the other campers from Camp Firestarter, but he paused before typing.

He thought about his own limitations, and not just with [Jack of All], but how his main source of strength had ended up being a weakness when meeting people who were actually better than him. He'd been closed off, isolated...and he didn't have to be. *These people are the best at what they do. Yoko has hacking. Carlo...I don't even know all Carlo knows. Pietro knows physics and psychology. The other kids are all incredibly talented too.*

The Aelves were bound to have exceptional people, plus the orb-wielders. If Noah couldn't beat a bunch of kid-geniuses, then he would have a much more difficult road against technologically advanced aliens wielding magic.

But, Noah thought, *what if our geniuses are on my side?*

He remembered his time on the front porch of the cabin with Pietro, and how it had felt when he told the Russian boy a little bit of his secrets. He also remembered how Yoko had convinced him that if anyone could understand what Noah was going through, it would be the members of camp Firestarter.

Noah's fingers moved, and he began typing.

Hey, guys, I want to let you in on something. Maybe in time, I might feel comfortable telling you the whole story, but we're not there yet. As it is, you will probably think I am a "doomsday prepper" or something.

The fact is, I believe the world as we know it is going to drastically change within the next—

Noah thought for a while, wondering how specific to actually get with his information. Some of the Firestarter kids would assume he believed in the possibility of a future economic collapse, or war, or a shift of the planet's axis or something. He decided to remain vague to gauge his audience's reaction first. He was opening up, but it was still premature to spill everything.

–ten years or so. Imagine a world with no more electricity, where pressure only builds to a certain point, where the fundamental laws of physics have been warped. Humor me.

Let's have a thought exercise.

Noah wrote, and edited, then deleted almost everything he'd written before writing some more. Finally, he had an email that he didn't hate too much and hit send with a shaky finger. Now that he'd actually done it, he immediately felt ten times lighter.

Only time would tell if he was making the right choice. Now he understood that even with all of his memories and a new life, he couldn't do everything by himself. At some point, he would need to take some risks, to start trusting people. He'd just planted some seeds. Butterflies in his stomach made him jittery, feeling a weird combination of relief, hope, anxiety, and embarrassment.

Baby steps, he thought, and wondered what Doc Broad would say.

CHAPTER 19

Noah really liked driving, so of course, between turning sixteen years old and the arrival of Shift, he knew that he would have less than three years to enjoy it. It was just his luck.

In his past life, he'd been stuck with a crappy, beat-up old station wagon that he'd saved up to buy at the end of his junior year in high school. In this life, he'd bought exactly what he'd wanted after he'd gotten his driver's license–an armored pickup truck.

Unofficially probably the richest teen in the world, and officially a millionaire, Noah could have just about any flashy car he desired. But instead of a crazy sports car, or something that would turn heads, he'd gone a different direction. His heavy truck would be too expensive to purchase and run for the average person, but was still practical for his life. He didn't have a bodyguard–it wasn't necessary since most people didn't even know he was rich.

But the closer the Shift came, the more Noah acknowledged how silly it would be to die from some freak accident after working so hard and so long to save everyone.

Maybe he was his parents' son after all. Through Noah's interference, Clark and Lana Henson had acquired quite a bit of wealth of their own now, but they still lived in the same house that Noah had grown up in. He'd asked them about it before, and they'd looked at him like he'd grown another head. Noah had a suspicion that they'd already had everything they'd really needed before, and they continued to grow their wealth now as more of a game than anything. Both of them still worked the same jobs that they'd had in Noah's past life.

Noah smiled while thinking about his parents. Dorks, he thought fondly. He was nearing his destination, and turned onto a side road on the outskirts of town, winding further away from Steelton before approaching a guard shack. The guard on duty recognized him, but he still went through the motions of checking his ID and credentials. Good. Noah didn't want the guards to get lazy.

The thick gate opened, swinging ponderously upward, and Noah drove forward into a sprawling industrial complex. This area hadn't existed, hadn't been built in his previous life, but Steelton had been growing at an incredible rate. The influx of money and jobs into town had justified the construction of quite a few new developed areas over the years. At the very rear of this location, a few lines of warehouses stood, the last of them butting up against the base of a series of large, rocky hills.

Noah owned all of them. In fact, he owned this entire industrial park.

He turned his truck in between a couple warehouses and began making his way to his destination. Finally, he arrived and pulled up to the side of a warehouse before getting out. As usual, he reflexively [Listen]ed to notice if anything was out of the ordinary, but the coast was clear. Out the corner of his eye, Noah spotted one of the site's security guards, employed by his own security company, Log Cabin Security Inc. He nodded to the guard.

Remembering the name of his security company made him think of Doc as he walked around to a side entrance of the warehouse. A year earlier, his private investigators had confirmed that Christopher Broad had indeed disappeared around the same time that Noah had been born.

History had changed. Doc's family didn't even own the cabin where Doc had been living and where Noah had learned about the stars. The building didn't even exist until a couple years ago, and while Noah assumed that the Broads must have bought it soon after it'd been built in his past life, in this life, some other family owned it.

Waiting until he'd been older to seriously look for Doc had been a mistake. Noah's logic had admittedly made sense. Ten years ago, Doc would be too young to connect with, and probably not interested in talking to a kid. But now, less than three years from the Shift, a million things going on, and zero leads on what had happened to Doc, Noah didn't even know what to do about his missing mentor.

He absently checked his phone to see if his investigators had sent him any updates about Doc...nothing. Noah sighed. If his people couldn't find anything, then he probably wouldn't be able to either.

Mysteries upon mysteries.

Noah stepped up to the door and used a series of complex combinations to open the lock. None of his warehouses depended on electricity to function at a basic level. If everything he'd built over the last dozen years had used electronic locks, it would have been tragically ironic.

The door opened, and Noah stepped through to a richly appointed lobby. Jamal Hendricks looked up from the report he was writing, a Log Cabin Security hat on his head and his Log Cabin Security jacket open in the front. "Hey, what's up, Noah? You here to do some more secret hush-hush stuff?"

"Something like that," said Noah with a grin.

Jamal grinned back and held out a clipboard. "Rules are rules. You should know, you made them for this place."

Noah nodded as he accepted the clipboard and wrote his name and the time. Then he handed the clipboard back with a copy of his ID. Jamal compared his name on the sheet to the one on the

ID, then looked up Noah's name and a picture in the hardcopy notebook of approved personnel. As someone preparing for the Shift, being friends with some of the most talented hackers in the world, and being a hacker himself, Noah didn't trust digital records, at least not for something as important as this.

Finally, Jamal nodded and handed Noah back his ID. "You're good to go, like always."

"Thanks, Jamal. How is the baby?"

"Jamal Junior is screaming a lot, but me and Kiera get breaks because her mom is helping out. You know, you're invited over to meet him if you have a chance."

Noah held up a hand and pulled out his phone, making a note of it. "I will see if I can find time," he said and meant it. Jamal had turned out to be a surprisingly important new addition to what he was beginning to think of his Steelton crew.

Over a year earlier, when Noah had been fifteen, he'd run into Jamal at Lucy's Diner, and the tall young man had really cut a striking figure, having filled out some. It wasn't like Jamal had been small before, but he'd somehow gotten even more athletic-looking. On top of that, his hair had been buzzed, and he'd been wearing a Marines backpack.

It turned out that Jamal had gone to college on his mysterious scholarship, but had decided he didn't know what to major in and wanted a break from school. As a result, instead of wasting his scholarship money, Jamal had joined the Marines reserves. When

Noah had bumped into him, Jamal had been back from boot camp, and about to start looking for a job. The new Marine had been planning to marry Kiera, his high school sweetheart.

In his past life, Noah vaguely remembered that Jamal had died protecting strangers from bandits, or at least that was what he'd heard a year after the Shift. As recommendations for character go, it didn't get much better than that. Noah had been in the process of growing his new security company anyway and had pulled Jamal aside before telling him about Log Cabin. Noah had said that he could just email the hiring manager, which had been true.

Since then, Jamal had proven himself invaluable and had quickly become a sergeant in Log Cabin Security. It would be a shame when Jamal eventually got promoted to a high-level leadership role, because then he wouldn't be assigned to just one location anymore. Noah really liked when the people he trusted most in Log Cabin were assigned to his most sensitive locations–like this one.

The tall, muscular black man stretched, and Noah caught sight of his rifle propped against the wall. He chuckled and said, "Still waiting for a revolver?"

"Yeah. It's kind of ridiculous that they give me a machine gun in the Marines, but civilian-side, I can't carry a pistol yet because I'm not 21. Lugging this thing around is a pain," he said, jerking his thumb at the rifle.

"Yeah, well, at least your company gave you one of those Ruger nine-millimeter carbines that break down, right? Don't you have a case for it?" asked Noah. Jamal knew that Noah owned the warehouses, but didn't know he owned Log Cabin. Noah never lied to any of his Steelton crew, but creative truth really helped avoid awkward issues sometimes.

"Yes, but with the new baby and all, Kiera's been freaking out. I think she'll calm down eventually, but right now she wants it locked up when I'm not at work, and it costs a lot less for a pistol safe than a rifle safe. Money's tight after the delivery, so it's been a pain."

"Oh, I see." Noah really did understand. He knew Kiera from high school, but back then she'd been Kiera White. A natural charmer and smart as a whip, she'd also been known for extreme emotional reactions to things that eventually blew over like nothing had ever happened. On top of that, the pregnancy had been difficult, and Kiera had been turning into a bit of a helicopter parent, hopefully not for too long. Actually, Noah amended, after the Shift, she won't have a choice but to drop it.

Out loud he said, "I can tell the folks at Log Cabin to hook you up with a bonus for a safe or something. You've been a huge help here."

"Oh, that's really nice of you, man, but you don't need to worry about it."

"Nah, it's fine." Noah played with his phone. "I'm sending a message now." He sent an email to the Log Cabin central office that read,

Call Jamal Hendricks and organize the delivery of a company-bought rifle safe. Price doesn't matter. Should not take more than a week. -N

That taken care of, Noah nodded and began heading past the desk. Suddenly, Jamal said, "You know, you're always doing that."

"Doing what?"

"Solving problems."

Noah fully turned to face the guard–Charisma had tickled the back of his mind, telling him that the man had something to say. He waited patiently until Jamal said, "You know, the last time I was at Marines drill, I tried to tell Gunny about you. He flat out didn't believe me." The tall man paused, seeming to gather his thoughts. "A sixteen-year-old kid who owns multiple companies, at least that I know of and maybe a few I don't, who is good enough to play college sports after high school, but just quit every sport at school after one season, and who I hear girls at school and around town constantly talking about...but doesn't date."

Despite trying to suppress it, Noah could feel an awkward flush starting at the base of his neck. He schooled his expression, but Jamal wasn't done yet. He continued, "On top of that you are a genius, and only go to school for fun. Your parents let you do whatever you want, and even teachers at school leave you alone. Almost everyone in town seems to know you, or know of you. I've seen you using gear or wearing stuff that half a year later comes out from some new company out of nowhere with a patent."

"I know a lot of people–" Noah began, but Jamal just kept talking.

"When Log Cabin did special training for all employees a few months ago, and you came along, you outshot the instructors, with rifles and pistols. Then you threw knives. Who even does that?

"You can probably play every instrument I could actually name, and you sing, but again, I hear you dropped out of all the art classes at Washington High after a single year at most. Half the time, nobody knows where you are, but grown people, like, older people, sometimes seek you out looking for guidance or orders. Your phone buzzes pretty much non-stop.

"Henson, you are probably the strangest person I will meet my entire life. No wonder Gunny didn't believe me about you. Something he said after telling me I was crazy was true. He said if someone like you really existed, they'd be on every talk show in the world, and be at least as famous as movie stars, maybe even in movies already. Yet while practically everyone in Steelton knows you, nobody else knows you exist. It doesn't make sense."

Noah just blinked. He didn't know what to say. With everything laid out like that, it did all sound pretty fantastic, and also made him feel a little guilty. At least he had made the decision a long time ago not to use his second life selfishly, or the guilt would be a lot worse. Becoming world famous had never been an option, though–not when the Aelves might be looking for him.

Jamal's tone grew introspective. "When I first heard about you during my senior year of high school, people were saying that over the summer, you fought three or four guys from Sidmore High and Creola Middle School who were picking on a kid in a wheelchair. I didn't believe it at first, in fact I didn't believe anything about you. I thought you were just a showboating glory hound with great hype. But then you did that thing with your guitar, and I saw those guys glaring at you from the other bleachers during the Sidmore game. I also heard you broke up a fight at a dance with practically no effort at all.

"I didn't used to like you, Henson. The more I found out everything about you was true, the more I thought you were just an arrogant, rich kid showoff. I could never figure you out.

"But being a Marine now has given me a different perspective, and I can spot leadership easier now. I'll never forget what you told me years ago at the diner. That was a bitter pill to swallow, but I grew up a little that day, and I grew up a lot at boot camp. I've also known some seriously deadly people now, and here's the weird thing, I think you're one of them.

"You are probably one of the most dangerous, most powerful people in Steelton, maybe even the state.

"I was just able–"

"You're a weird guy, Henson. I don't know what you're trying to do. Like, warehouses full of water purifiers, with armed security? Weird combination locks? The company, Log Cabin had us do that crossbow training before too, and you also came along for that. I would bet money you were involved somehow."

Noah raised his eyebrows and tried to steady his beating heart.

Jamal shook his head. "I guess what I'm trying to say is that nothing about you makes sense, but what people do means a lot more than what they say. You are obviously loaded and connected enough that you could just travel around and do whatever you wanted all year long, but for some reason, you drive around Steelton...solving problems and filling warehouses with canned goods, employing weird people. And I may not be a genius, but I'm not blind. I have my suspicions about the mystery scholarship I got for college, and my mom's miraculous approval for her home loan last year. It would be rude to ask questions about it, but whoever that was, I am very grateful, just like I'm grateful if a gun safe magically turns up at my house soon."

Noah was losing the battle against his flush. "Whatever breaks you caught, I'm sure you earned them," he said.

"Darn right," said Jamal, pride in his voice. "But that isn't how the real world works, is it? Fairness doesn't seem to have much to do with it, or my mom wouldn't have been stuck raising two kids, working herself to death, and still barely making it even with food stamps. I earned everything I've gotten, but I still might not have ever gotten anything it if someone hadn't been watching out.

"Thing is, I'm not sure I'm the only example in Steelton. I've seen the news reports. This city is doing great, and nobody seems to understand why. I'll bet if some folks started investigating a certain sixteen-year-old kid driving around an armored pickup truck, who constantly practices archery in warehouses he owns and learns new languages for fun, they might find some leads."

"Uhhh," Noah said intelligently.

Jamal shrugged and said, "My dad taught us to fight, to stand up for what we believe in. I see that in you too, Henson. While I don't know what your motivation is, I know you're fighting for something. You're a weird dude, but I've decided to believe in you. For everything I've seen you do for the community, and for everything I might not know about, thank you."

In Noah's entire second life, he'd only been completely at a loss for words a handful of times, and this was one of them. He felt deeply embarrassed, and Charisma wasn't helping out at all, staying completely silent. "I don't know what to say. That was...a lot."

"You don't have to say anything. Kiera kind of put me up to this, but she was right that I should say something. I'm a Marine now. Part of having honor, courage, and commitment is recognizing it in others."

Noah shook his head ruefully. "You know, of all the accidental friendships I've made, I think I got really lucky with you. I won't confirm or deny anything, but thanks a lot, man. I think I know what you're trying to say, but I don't do stuff for recognition."

"I know, and that's why people follow you."

"People follow you too, Jamal. I work really hard, and some people notice that, but you are a natural born leader," said Noah, and now it was the guard's turn to look uncomfortable. Noah laughed and waved, "I'll let you get back to work. Venu is waiting for me."

As he turned to head deeper into the warehouse, [Listen] picked up Jamal muttering, "Venu. Yeah. Have fun with that guy. God, this job is weird sometimes."

CHAPTER 20

Past the front office of this warehouse, where the Log Cabin security sergeant–currently Jamal–oversaw the entire industrial park, the warehouse was just a warehouse. Noah had set it up to have a long, winding hallway that switched back and forth with rows and rows of shelves on either side. When he'd first had the warehouses built, he'd opted for a simpler format, with a walkway down the center and multiple rooms built into both sides. However, the rooms had been difficult to check, and Noah had forgotten what he'd had at times without using [Memory Palace].

Now with a winding path, Noah could see everything he had in the warehouse, all neatly labeled. When he visited his warehouses, like this occupied command unit, they helped him plan on any additions or changes to what he had stocked.

Each warehouse he owned around the world had a variety of items, so even if only one survived in an area he'd seeded, they would still benefit the community in a serious way after the Shift. Over time, Noah had refined his communications plans. His post-Shift planning had been made easier now that he'd been delegating for the last two years. He had contingencies upon contingencies, and Log Cabin Security Company had come in handy too.

At night sometimes, when he was thinking and being honest with himself, Noah had admitted that he was kind of building a private army. Sometimes he felt weird about it, but he couldn't deny that it made sense to do. In another year, he might even start training a quick reaction force in Steelton.

The artificial hallway wound through the warehouse, and Noah briefly scanned each section of storage. As in every other warehouse, the first area was full of honey, rice, and beans. To preserve the rice and beans, Noah had bought industrial freezers in Detroit and had created a process set up for distribution in the US. The dry rice and beans were frozen to kill any weevils or eggs, then they were all placed in special buckets, so the air could be vacuumed out. This made each bucket shelf-stable for a very long time.

Honey never went bad, so he just had it shipped directly to his warehouses in buckets from honey farms.

Noah kept walking, slowly scanning his storage. He noted boxes of knives, crates full of candles, racks of water purifiers of various sizes and types, extra filters, iodine tablets, and pest control products. Rats had gotten really bad in some cities, but Noah couldn't remember which, so adding rat poison became a standard item to stock. He remembered the dog problem that some place had suffered too. Rat poison, while inhumane, could be used to kill dogs.

Noah hated thinking about stuff like that.

He noted hundreds of mini sewing kits, bottles of antibiotics…"Hmm," he muttered. Each warehouse he'd stocked around the world had at least a few thousand pounds of salt, but maybe he should add to that. He made a mental note of it and moved on.

As he walked, he read the labels of boxes that contained thousands of lighters, thousands of ferro rods for starting fires, first aid kits, lanterns, lantern fuel, alcohol stoves, thousands of gallons of rubbing alcohol, hunting gear—including snares, supplies for tanning leather, basic fishing gear, crates of nails and screws, and plenty of other things to help people survive after the power went out.

Steelton would be much better off than any other town after the Shift in Noah's first life, as would every other location he'd seeded with warehouses and safe houses. Actually, plenty of cities would have been able to survive on their own in his first life if people had cooperated with each other, but panic, disorganization, and greed had doomed millions of people.

Realistically, Noah couldn't save the country, much less the world, just by filling warehouses, but he could give a core group of leaders a massive advantage. Tools to help people learn how to survive would be literally worth more than gold.

Further to the rear of the warehouse, Noah read even more labels, crates of wool blankets, plastic containers full of heirloom seeds for farming, barrels of cooking oil, bottles of bleach, spools of duct tape, and containers full of paracord.

There were some quality of life goods too, meant to be given out sparingly, like soap, basic spices for cooking, toothpaste, and sugar. Shelves of books, both fiction and nonfiction, lined the path, and boxes of Shift survival guides that had been written by Noah, printed and bound as spiral notebooks waited, ready to be passed out.

Quite a bit of each warehouse was devoted to storing alcohol. Whiskey, tequila, vodka, rum, and brandy, rows of bottles represented great wealth after the Shift. In fact, booze would become so valuable, Noah had actually filled several safe houses with alcohol, and had hidden distillery equipment in multiple places around the country.

At the rear of the warehouse, Noah paused before a solid steel box bolted to the concrete floor, anchored to ten feet of rebar deep in the ground. The box was secured with complicated combination locks, built into the steel itself, even more robust than on the warehouse door. Next to the box stood a large set of thick, steel doors with their own combination locks. Noah knew that the metal wall of the warehouse and the doors were surrounded by solid rock.

The young man grinned and thought, *Let's see people try to get into these things with no power and nothing but a hand tool!* He quickly opened the box to check what was inside.

Every warehouse across the world that had been built or bought to prepare for the Shift had a steel box like this one. Noah called them his jam boxes. Every jam box contained two changes of clothes, a pair of shoes, a jacket, and a pair of boots–all sized for Noah.

Half of each box was devoted to bottles of water, and several kinds of non-perishable foods, including military MREs. A quality hiking pack full of camping and survival gear sat next to a belt knife, a machete, and a thick, canvas bag full of multiple steel weapons, oiled for storage. Last but not least, Noah checked the plastic case that held a compound bow, and a quiver of carbon arrows. He nodded, closed the box, and locked it back up again.

One of Noah's only selfish acts had been to create the jam boxes for his use in case he was ever in a jam and needed to resupply.

Once the jam box had been secured, he unlocked and opened the massive steel doors in the wall, and entered one of the secret underground lairs he'd had built as armories. To prevent future raiders or enemies from getting ahold of any serious weapons he hoarded, Noah had ordered a number of secret, secure locations built. Not even Jamal or the other Log Cabin guards had access to this area. Jamal knew that Noah had someone working back here, but had never actually seen it.

Noah walked slowly through the tunnel, awed as always that such a thing existed and that he'd had it built. A single work crew, silenced by a non-disclosure agreement, had traveled all over the United States building these types of hidden, fortified locations for him. After the Shift, the number of people who got the combinations to open the doors would be limited.

In Steelton, Jamal was actually one of them–so were Noah's parents.

At the end of the hallway stood another set of doors - normal wooden double doors. Noah heard the sound of buzzing from the other side and smiled. Venu must be working. He pushed through the doors, and his smile turned to a grin.

One side of the enormous, subterranean warehouse functioned as an armory. Racks of crossbows and sleek, compound bows lined an entire wall, hanging next to laminated recurve bows. A few of the compound bows had modern sights–Noah had chosen the toughest set available on the market. But he knew after the Shift, most modern bows had lost their sights, or they'd broken. As a result, most modern bows Noah stocked were designed to be shot like the recurves, using fingers instead of a mechanical release, and by archers trained to aim instinctively.

Past several boxes full of replacement parts for the compound bows, Noah had stacked ammunition. Arrows to feed the bows and bolts to feed the crossbows filled barrels, buckets, and crates. Ultimately, compound bows had to be sized for each archer, were difficult to repair, and needed special arrows, but they more powerful and easier to use than recurves. Ten years or more after the Shift, all of humanity would probably use recurves or longbows, but Noah wanted each area he'd invested in to have the initial advantage of the modern bows, even if they all eventually broke and became useless several years later.

Boxes full of oiled chainmail–several types and sizes–occupied boxes stacked the ceiling. Noah had commissioned thousands of sets of chainmail from Pakistan, giving several factories years of work. The two main types he'd began stocking were riveted aluminum hauberks for children or adults who needed lighter protection and welded steel sets.

Most modern, reenactment chainmail used butted links, where the ends of each small ring were just pressed together, but Noah knew from his past experiences that butted construction was next to useless against modern bows and crossbows. They required constant maintenance, too.

In addition to the complete chainmail armor, all of his hidden armories also held a number of loose steel rings ready for riveted construction, where both ends of each tiny ring were flattened and secured with a peened piece of metal. This process took a long time and was difficult to do, but created strong armor. After the

Shift, the strongest, welded chainmail Noah had been stocking would no longer be possible to produce.

Sometimes, the fact he was in effect creating modern-day Mithril seemed really strange. Defenders of Noah's settlements and forts would have the finest armor in the world.

A special box in this warehouse held unique armor, chainmail made with thick, welded steel rings, and solid titanium rings. The rings were thicker than normal, but the titanium kept the weight down. The result was a hauberk that weighed the same as standard steel chainmail but was twice as strong. Noah thought of this hybrid armor as Dragon Mithril.

He had spent years in elementary school researching armor, exploring ways to make the best protection possible for his people. Ultimately, he'd accepted the truth that people in the distant past had really known what they were doing. The best armor he could actually order produced in large quantity were ancient designs made with strong, modern materials.

Chainmail was not the only type of armor that Noah stocked, though, especially in Steelton. Brigandines, leather or canvas coats with steel plates sewn inside, hung from pegs above boxes full of gambesons, fluffy, stuffed coats that could stop a blade.

Containers of hardware and large free-standing parts waited, ready to build catapults, or ballistas, the giant siege bows that could launch arrows the size of spears.

Hundreds of swords and thousands of machetes lay neatly

stacked in plastic containers, covered in oil and wrapped in wax paper. Kydex and nylon sheaths, tough and weather resistant, had been crammed into separate containers.

Racks of spears stood ready to be wielded, and crates full of greased spearheads waited for handles. Bucklers and various types of shields hung in specially-built racks. The entire warehouse had been filled with armor and weapons of war, as well as serious hunting tools. Racks of wrist-mounted slingshots and boxes full of rubber to replace slingshot bands had been Noah's newest additions to the arsenal.

On the other side of the enormous, custom-built room was a workshop. A man who'd been working on wood with a power sander turned with a smile. "Hi, Noah. I was not expecting you today."

"Hello, Venu." Noah noted the thick layer of sawdust covering the Indian man's apron. It read "Kiss the Cook." Standing a bit shorter than Noah had in his previous life, Venu had become another of his luckiest additions to the Steelton crew.

Almost two years ago, when Noah had decided to start experimenting with new weapons after covering the basics, he'd put out an ad in the Steelton paper for someone interested in ancient weapons, with a basic understanding of engineering, and some woodworking skill. Venu Anand had recently been laid off from an IT job and worried about his Visa to stay in the United States. He'd answered the ad and after a series of admittedly bizarre interviews, had agreed to work for Noah if the youth could fix his Visa problem.

Even back then, this hadn't been a problem, so Venu had become Noah's weapon development research scientist. Their working relationship had started off surprisingly well, with Venu excited, actually getting a chance to be paid for his passion—ancient weapons. The man's flexible mind and adaptability had helped. Most people would not be okay with signing non-disclosure agreements, working for a teen, or going to work in a secret, underground lair every day.

The brilliant man had just turned twenty-eight a few months earlier, and as far as Noah knew, he still told his family that he worked as a programmer.

Noah paid Venu three times what he'd made in IT. The only rules he'd signed to follow were that he couldn't tell others about his work with muscle-powered weapons and that he had to fly home to India a couple weeks before the shift, so in less than three more years. To Venu, the date given was just an arbitrary day and a really strange request. However, Noah had given him an agreement in writing stating that he'd be paid three years wages before he left, and be eligible to return to work with Noah after only six months.

The minor deception bothered Noah a little, but he wanted his friend to be with his family when things got hard. If Venu didn't make it back to India before the Shift, he might never see his family again.

"So what do you have for me today?" asked Noah. He absently picked up a compound bow from a nearby table, fitted an arrow through the whisker biscuit arrow rest, drew, and released—all in one smooth motion. The arrow solidly thunked into a target set up on the other side of the chamber.

Noah's [Instinctive Archery] skill had been level five for years now, but he'd never gotten tired of shooting a bow.

Venu took off his gloves and gestured, another smile on his dusky, smooth-shaven face. "I'm done with the newest prototype."

"Oh, you mean the revolver?" Noah lifted his eyebrows.

"Exactly. Those videos you showed me with Joerg Sprave have helped a lot. That man is like the Leonardo da Vinci of slingshots. I would have never thought of using rubber the way he does."

Noah nodded, immediately knowing what Venu was talking about. Two years ago, when he'd been at Camp Firestarter, Carlo had showed him old videos from the earlier days of this internet. This had reminded Noah about YouTube. Since then, he'd compared notes with the kooky Filipino genius, eventually discovering Joerg Sprave and the Slingshot Channel.

Joerg Sprave, a German man with an infectious laugh, had made videos featuring his unique, rubber-powered inventions for years, and Noah had been floored. This discovery had been the catalyst that had made Noah start thinking differently about weapons. In fact, the first few projects Noah had started Venu working on had originally been inventions of Joerg's.

While Venu fetched his newest prototype, Noah examined some of the other weapons on the nearby tables. There were a few magazine-fed compound bows, notable because they allowed an archer to shoot four arrows in only a couple seconds. Noah picked up a sniper rifle made of plywood and slingshot bands, complete with a scope. The device could launch a standard, billiards-style dart accurately at forty paces.

Off to the side stood the massive, rubber-powered ballista that Venu had been working on. The contraption would allow anyone to load it, even a child. The device was powered by dozens of stretched rubber bands, creating incredible force, but each band could be tensioned individually and attached using a winch.

On another table, a repeating, rubber-powered crossbow that fired pencils had been a fun experiment. A cho-ko-nu, an ancient Chinese repeating crossbow design, had been modified to be powered by rubber. This invention and the dart sniper rifle had both been winners and were being mass produced in overseas factories. The first shipment of finished weapons would be ready in a few months.

Stocking thousands of throwing darts as ammunition would be easy, and take up far less room than arrows.

More strange devices sat on the table too, plastic shells in bright primary colors that Noah had asked Venu to modify. Standard foam blasters that children had played with for decades had been outfitted with stronger springs, tougher internal hardware, and the safe, foam darts replaced with shorter foam, tipped with razor blades.

The new weapons would probably horrify people today, especially if they were used to arm children, but those people hadn't experienced the Shift yet, hadn't seen the terrible things that could be done to children. Noah shuddered at the memory, and his old anger came back, filling with him fire.

Even kids should get a chance to fight back.

Raiders, slavers, murderers, or the Aelves, Noah was committed to giving good, every day people the tools to survive. He'd sworn it to himself.

Finally, Venu came back holding a strange device. "What is that?" Noah asked.

"This is what I came up with to solve the ambush problem you gave me."

Noah nodded. He hadn't told Venu the whole truth about the Shift, but had told the man that he sincerely believed the world as they knew it would come to an end. He didn't think Venu really believed him, but the man was creative and loved medieval history. Every time Noah gave him a scenario, real things that would happen after the Shift, Venu had been happy to build tools that would apply. Whether the man thought Noah was brilliant, an eccentric rich kid, or a kooky survivalist, Noah didn't care as long as he kept creating excellent weapons.

Noah's old memories of his time as Worm burned, and he could never forget how that felt. He wished he'd paid better attention to the weapons and fighting around him at the time, but it couldn't be helped now. Luckily, he did remember some things, like surviving ambushes among Redford's Red Chain, and his experiences before that as he survived post-Shift America.

Ambushes had always been a problem.

"This is a repeating slingshot crossbow," said Venu. "It runs on rubber. Basically, there is a wooden octagon inside that you can remove from the stock like this." The swarthy man demonstrated, hitting a few latches and opening a door in the side of the contraption. Noah immediately began to understand how the device would function.

"These blocks basically function like magazines. They hold seven shots each."

"Why seven? There are eight sides, right?" asked Noah.

"Yes, but I had to put each ammo slot in at an angle or it wouldn't work. However, because of this, it's really easy to load the thing properly. You just align the blank side like this, see?" Venu placed the chunky block back into the weapon and closed the door. Then he opened the door again and removed it.

Venu continued, "The magazine holds seven modified crossbow bolts of my design, but they're really easy to make. Each ammo slot can be loaded by multiple individual rubber bands, just like the prototype rubber-powered ballista," he said and pointed to the siege weapon in the corner."

Noah nodded. "Uh huh. But wouldn't those blocks be slow to load?"

"Yes, but once loaded, several could be kept on hand per person, especially with a wagon or while riding a horse. Plus, even a child or a handicapped person could use one effectively. The trigger is simple, and the weapon indexes itself, just like a real revolver."

Noah soundlessly whistled. "So what you're saying is that with two reloads, this thing could fire twenty-one bolts in, how long?"

"If someone was trained with the weapon? Maybe fifteen seconds. Probably less if they were good."

"Wow." Noah was impressed. The best defense for an ambush was not to be ambushed. But if someone was unfortunate enough to be surprised, running away was not usually an option. Standing to fight, and bringing every weapon possible to bear was usually the best option. The problem was that with bows and even with melee weapons, an enemy would have a massive advantage. Maybe this weapon would help, especially if a caravan had several of them.

"Did you come up with a name for this thing yet?" asked the excited teen.

"I think dazzler is a good name," said Venu, puffing his chest out.

"No, it's really not." Noah sighed. "Okay, what else can you tell me about dazzlers?"

"Everything else I could tell you, you probably already know. This thing solves the problem of repeating crossbows like a cho-ko-nu, that they need to be relatively weak to work correctly. Our standard bows with built-in magazines for arrows don't always work right, and only hold a few arrows."

"I can see that," said Noah. "What about aiming and power?"

"Since the bolts are simple, accuracy isn't amazing. Maybe we could add a tube or something to function as a sight of sorts. Power is better than a standard pistol crossbow, but still not anything like a full-sized bow. If an attacker was wearing decent armor, it would not be effective, but in the scenario you gave me, most attackers would not be armored."

Noah rubbed his chin. "True, but can you rig up a batch of bolts that have long, thin, needle-like bodkin points? Since we know that the bolts won't ever penetrate serious armor, maybe we can still set it up to punch through thick clothing, or chainmail links."

Venu nodded slowly. "I think so. The bolts will be shorter then, but maybe we could have an equal number of both types of bolts in each magazine."

"Does a," Noah started and squeezed his eyes shut before continuing, "dazzler have to be wood, or do you think we could make parts out of plastic?"

"The stock could probably be made out of plastic to keep the weight down, and the magazine probably could be too, but magazines are easy to make out of wood and would probably wear out quickly anyway. If you theoretically wanted to build a lot of these, it would be best to have the stocks made of plastic, but make the magazines locally. The trigger parts could all be made out of aluminum, and I could probably mass produce them or give it to you to...do whatever it is you do."

Noah made a face. These dazzlers had lots of potential–as Venu had said before, he could already see the benefits of weapons like this. He wanted to see a real-world demonstration, though.

Dazzlers would never take the place of a good crossbow or bow, but they could be devastating against most bandits, even if the weapons were wielded by average people. And if bad guys wised up and began attacking while protected with shields, or hiding behind trees, that would slow them down and give defenders a chance.

Preventing or ending an initial rush had been the problem Noah had given Venu, and he'd solved it. "What would I do without you?" asked Noah with a smile.

"Well for starters, you would probably be wasting a lot less money filling warehouses with enough obsolete weapons to conquer fourteenth century Europe," quipped Venu.

Noah laughed, but his heart raced. Something dark stirred inside him, where the scars from his past life existed. All the people he'd seen hurt after the Shift, everything he'd allowed himself to just stand and watch as Worm, none of that was acceptable anymore, not in this new world.

This time, all predators—humans or Aelves—would not find such easy prey. Noah grinned savagely and impulsively grabbed the nearby dart rifle to play with. Venu, used to this sort of thing, patiently waited while Noah stared at the weapon in thought.

Finally, Noah snapped out of his contemplation and turned. "Please start focusing on this...dazzler, Venu," asked Noah. "Next time I stop by, I'd like to have a firing demonstration."

"Got it, boss. But seriously, you really do waste a lot of money."

CHAPTER 21

At seventeen years old, Noah was actually beginning to miss school. During his first life, he'd practically slept through classes, caught in an endless cycle of depression. He'd never really felt like he was actually there. In this new life, it seemed he was literally never there.

"I hate flying," he muttered. He glanced around his private plane and sighed before getting up to fetch a bottle of water and some chips. He'd realized that he would need to buy or charter a plane almost a year ago. This close to the Shift, it wasn't enough to get reports from employees or take virtual tours of his properties. Some would need to be visited in person.

Flying filled Noah with anxiety, but not for the all same reasons most people might feel uncomfortable on planes. Even as good as internet connections could be in the air these days, they still didn't compare to being on the ground. The loss of productivity was a normal concern, but not the memories he carried. He could remember the Shift, when everything that ran on gas, or compression, or electricity had stopped working. Every vehicle in the world that ran with an engine or electricity had suddenly stopped, including airplanes.

A lot of the fires that had started the day of the Shift had been because of fallen airplanes.

The first year after the Shift, when Noah had traveled most, he'd occasionally come across the wreckage of a plane. Each instance had given him a chill, as he'd imagined actually being on one as it plummeted from the sky. Most planes in the world had probably gone down over water too, which had been an even scarier thought.

And somehow, now, Noah regularly found himself in airplanes. Even knowing that the Shift was still a year away didn't help his nerves. His skin crawled while he thought about how close the Shift was now. Luckily, distraction came in the form of a phone call. Noah checked his cell–Johnny was calling.

"Hey, what's up?"

"Wow. I'm surprised you picked up," came Johnny's voice on the other end of the line. "I know you said you'd be busy for the next few days, but I wanted to make sure we are still gonna go hunting next week."

"Yeah, I think so. Let me check," muttered Noah. He pulled up his calendar using his phone, flashing a hologram to the side.

"Yes. We are good to go." Noah had never hunted before the Shift in his past life. His parents were not exactly hunting or outdoorsy people...at all. Neither of them had ever shot a bow or a gun before. Noah's parents had flat out rejected all of his attempts to learn to shoot a bow. He'd tried to get everyone close to him to spend more time in the woods, to get away from civilization and learn a few new skills. Noah knew what was coming.

Speaking of skills, he checked his mundane skills and verified that [Skinning: Small Animals] was at level four. Next week if he and Johnny got a few squirrels in the mountains, he might level it to five.

The last year or so, Noah had really begun wondering about his mundane skills. His [Listener] skills, what he thought of as his core, class skills hadn't changed, but he still picked up at least one new mundane skill every other week. It was strange that [Mathematics] existed all by itself as a skill, but skills like skinning were divided into sub skills, like [Skinning: Small Animals].

Other examples were sports and martial arts. He didn't have a skill for just [Sports], instead they were broken into skills like, [Sports: Wrestling], or [Sports: Football]. There were obviously different types of wrestling, just like there were different types of Karate, so [Hand to Hand: Karate] seemed strange, too broad. Skills like [Singing] were even stranger, even broader.

There were obviously multiple disciplines of singing, but maybe Noah couldn't access them until his [Listener] level was raised. He had a sinking feeling that until he could level up and gain access to higher tier skills, some of his advancement in the more general skills might just note knowledge of how broad they were.

Noah's mind snapped back to his conversation when Johnny spoke again–there had been a pause. His best friend said, "That's cool, but, um, can I be honest?"

"Of course. Always."

"You've been gone even more than usual, man. People are starting to worry about you. Krystal asked me about you the other day, in fact."

Noah frowned. "Krystal Connolly? I see her all the time! In fact, I think I have something planned with her and someone else next week–I'd have to check my calendar. She could just text or call me if she wants to know what's up."

"That's the thing, man, like, you're not approachable at all anymore. We've been best friends for so long that you're like my brother, but other people feel weird about bothering you. Like, you're doing seriously important stuff, and even employ other people, right? I mean, the fact we don't even know for sure what you do makes it even harder to bother you. How could someone call to ask about movie plans when you might be in France doing a business deal or something?"

"Wait, it's not like that–" Noah began to say.

Johnny interrupted, "The problem is that nobody knows what

it's like, we just know you're always busy and always gone. People like you, and they notice that you make an effort to spend time with them, but you're a mysterious sort of dude now, you know?"

"So what do you want me to do about it?" Noah tried to control his irritation. These days, he practically got no free time, had to keep working, and even had to fly sometimes to visit special sites in person. Of course, he knew that Johnny and his other friends had no way to really know that. Noah had been more upfront with the people he relied on lately that he trusted, but still hadn't told anyone the whole truth– all he did, or why.

Johnny sounded hesitant. "Just letting people know that you're okay would be a start, like checking in, especially with your parents. They've asked me about you before. Sometimes they worry. I think if you hadn't been willing to take a urinalysis test last year, and your father hadn't been watching the companies that you own grow, they might not have been as hands-off over the last couple years."

"That bad, huh?"

"Yeah. Dude, you're still in high school. You're still a kid, but you get no sleep and you're always working. When you are at school, everyone wants to say hi, but half the time you have bags under your eyes and just brush everyone off. You didn't use to be like that."

"Okay, man. I hear you. I'll think about it."

"Alright. Sorry to be a wet blanket. I'll see you next week," said Johnny.

"Bye."

"Bye."

Noah hung up and closed his eyes, letting his head roll back. He'd been under a lot of stress. The Shift kept getting closer, and he kept wishing he had another ten years to prepare. Ultimately though, all of his work with the community would suffer if he got too distracted from Steelton. Everything he did felt like a huge balancing act.

His emotions roiled, but he finally decided that this was yet another thing he needed help with. It was one thing to be busy, but it was unacceptable to be seen as unfriendly.

He quickly typed out an email on his phone to his administrative assistant, Veronica. The message asked her to start helping with his social engagement planning, and increase his time spent at school by at least ten percent. He also asked her to hire another logistics manager, and a buying agent to deal with more of the gear, fuel, and weapons he kept stocking.

That done, Noah leaned back and thought deeply for a long time. He remembered everyone who had helped him, both in his past life and in this one. To this day, he still didn't know if he'd killed Yusef or not, and the memory haunted him. In some ways, he realized he'd been trying to protect his friends and family in multiple ways, even from his knowledge.

Telling people willy-nilly about the Shift and the Aelves would still be unwise, but this close to the Shift, maybe it was time to level with someone.

The more Noah thought, the more he realized that his best friend and his greatest ally in this life had always been Johnny. Befriending the chubby kid who'd turned into a huge, honest young man had really been a huge stroke of good luck. Noah's friendship with Johnny had also convinced him to reach out to the community more, too.

A decision was hard to come to, and even harder to swallow after keeping secrets for so long, but next week, during his hunting trip with his best friend, he decided to tell Johnny about the Aelves. His big friend probably wouldn't believe him, but whether he did or not, he wouldn't judge and would keep the secret to himself. Noah trusted his friend with his life, something he had never experienced before he'd died, and something he found precious.

He'd been doing Johnny a disservice.

Forcing his friends and family to watch him as he tore himself apart with stress and work wasn't keeping them safe, it was causing them harm. Sharing his burden was difficult, but in this new life, Noah had vowed to never turn away from unpleasant truths, and to never be passive again.

His nerves a bit frayed, the tired youth turned on his tablet and began scrolling through financial spreadsheets for the companies he owned, both as himself, and through intermediaries or phantom identities.

The idea of telling anyone about the Aelves was still a bit terrifying, but Noah felt lighter now too. It was time to accept that he wasn't alone anymore.

***

After Noah's plane touched down, he thanked his pilot, Steve Gregory, and caught a ride to his destination in a Log Cabin security truck. Colorado was beautiful this time of the year, and Noah took the opportunity to watch the passing scenery, even as he kept thinking about all the things he needed to do. When he thought of something new, he briefly made notes in his phone's calendar.

Noah had placed safe houses, warehouses, and stashes all over the world. On top of that, he had also built a small number of special locations to act as bases, hidden forts. Noah didn't know exactly where people had rallied in Colorado during his first life, but had heard too many rumors about Colorado to not establish a stronghold there.

The truck pulled into the site he'd picked, nestled in the hills away from civilization, but close enough to several towns and cities to make it a good, strategic rally point. Noah had thought about buying old military installations a few years ago, but had rejected the idea. Military installations were usually known locations, which defeated the point of a secret base.

This particular place had been blown out of solid rock, the base bored into the side of a cliff, and extended deep into the ground. The work crew that Noah had originally hired to build his secret warehouses had made the initial dig and construction. They'd proven so valuable, he'd actually created his own company to hire them through, and paid them several times the salary they could get anywhere else. After years of working for him, they had experience and knowledge he didn't want to lose. Of course, the situation posed a security hazard, but this close to the Shift, Noah couldn't afford to be too picky anymore.

Efficiency and speed were starting to matter more than sneakiness.

This location, what Noah called the Fallback Den, had been built as a secret command facility, and the ultimate safe house. The building's main entrance was at the base of several hills, at the end of a long valley. The only visible part of the base was almost like the side of a castle built into the hill. Assaulting the location would be practically impossible. The walls were so thick, and part of the hill itself–they'd laugh at siege weapons.

Over a thousand people could live at this location. Enough food was stocked up for almost two years. Living underground for years wouldn't be pleasant, but would be possible. The location was stocked with weapons, ammo, and basic necessities.

An underground spring had been tapped deep on the bottom level.

The idea behind the Fallback Den and the two other similar

locations that Noah had built in the US were to be impossible for human attackers to defeat, and hidden so nobody would know they were there in the first place. This would hopefully protect them from the Aelves, too.

Due to the remote location, Noah had been using Fallback Den to test larger, more destructive weapons. He had pieces shipped out from Michigan and other places to assemble here. After the Shift, since the Den was high in the mountains, all the assembled siege weapons could be brought down to the surrounding areas if there were ever needed; it was all downhill.

Noah drove past acres of farm in the valley, all maintained by people he paid to run the place, allowed to live in their own houses that Noah owned, rent-free. People who wanted to spend a year in the mountains, being paid to work on a peaceful farm in front of a mansion had been surprisingly easy to find.

Of course, they didn't know that the Den was a fortress, they could only see the outside. Houses for the helpers had only been built after the main structure had been finished. All the work on siege weapons were chalked up by the workers as Noah's "employer" being a medieval reenactor. Still obviously a teenager, Noah had realized that acting like he was an assistant to another older person who owned the land would raise fewer questions.

Noah had come to the Fallback Den for a few reasons, and one was to inspect some of Venu's new inventions. The parts had been shipped to this location and assembled by interns. After the truck stopped, Noah got out and continued on foot. He passed a row of rabbit hutches before ducking under a huge pavilion that had been set up to build and test post-Shift weapons.

He briefly studied the ballista built with modern cams to function more like a huge compound bow before continuing. The design had potential, but not with spears or arrows. Shock from the giant bow being fired was too great for wooden shafts, even with reinforced ends, so his engineers had been working to convert it to fire steel balls instead.

Weapons designed to throw Molotov cocktails full of napalm stood in a row and were particularly nasty. They would be one way to keep a valley like this safe if it were ever attacked.

He approached the end of the pavilion where some railroad tracks had been set up. A box on wheels sat on the tracks, and another similar one stood behind it, resting on thick rubber tires. Noah pulled out his cell and dialed Venu's number. When the quirky inventor answered, Noah switched to a video call, and his phone displayed a hologram image of Venu at his workstation. He wore a honey badger hat with a snake in its mouth.

"What is going on, boss?"

Noah turned the phone around to show Venu what he was looking at, then turned the phone back. "Okay, I'm here. What are these things?"

"You know, if you would come by my workstation more often, maybe you would not need to fly all the way to other states just to see my inventions. As a reminder, my workstation is in Steelton...where you live."

"Yeah, yeah," Noah said, ignoring the man's gibes. Venu had gotten married a few months before and was still settling into married life. He'd been a little more testy than usual lately. The stress from a new marriage, moving to a new home, being back in the US from India, and his parents finding out he didn't work in IT anymore had obviously been adding up. Noah said, "I remember some of this stuff from the last time I dropped by the armory, but walk me through it. If you remember, I told you to ship this stuff out here because with my schedule, I would be able to actually see it faster this way."

"Of course, of course." Venu absently scratched at his cheek with the eraser end of a pencil, looking up at the ceiling in thought. "What you are looking at are the prototypes I created for the travel scenario you gave me. As usual, the scenario involved a post-apocalypse America with no electricity and arbitrary limits on pressure. Because steam power and solar were out of the question, the most obvious choices were horses and muscle power.

"Included in your scenario were combat capabilities, defenses, and robust construction. The two vehicles you see before you are basically the same, but configured to either follow railroad tracks, or be pulled by horses."

"Oh, I see." Now that Noah's memory had been jogged, he could see how the two boxes might move, and the differences in the wheels. At times like this, it was frustrating that his [Memory Palace] skill had so many limitations. "I can see how the one with rubber tires would be pulled, but what about the rail one?"

"The version to ride on railroad tracks uses a modified mechanical system like an old handcar, the kind with levers that people push up and down with a pumping motion. This one has two pumps, so it can be crewed by two to eight people. The pumping mechanisms run using ceramic bearings so efficiency is very high. All the pumps also have gears, so once the vehicle gets momentum, the pumpers can change gears to go faster."

"Huh." Noah walked forward and opened one of the doors to the vehicle on railroad tracks. Sure enough, there were two sets of pillars with perpendicular bars attached to pump with. He was reminded of old black and white movies with the weird railway cars; handcars, Venu had called them. "What about steering?"

"Okay, that is one way that these two are different. Only the horse-drawn version needs to be turned. The railway version needs to stay as light as possible. These armored railroad cars are really best suited to transport people, and maybe light cargo. Humans are just not strong enough for heavy loads on railroad tracks. If more people are added to pump, the car would need to be larger, and it would weigh more. There is a point of diminishing returns."

"Okay, I can see that."

Venu said, "So again, there is no driver for the railroad version, just someone on top who has a stationary bike. The bike has a chain going all the way down to the driving mechanism to help add power."

Noah nodded, noting a tube coming down the center of the car, probably with the chain inside. He said, "Go on."

"Okay, please climb the ladder and look up top."

Noah could see the top of the bike and something else up there. He nodded and climbed the obvious ladder, then his eyebrows went up. "Oh, I see."

"Yes, the person on the bike has a brake. The people inside would have brakes too, but the person on the top also has two hard point weapon mounts, maybe four if you want to get real crazy. The mounts right now are on the sides, but if you want one front and back, the driver would need to actually get up to use them or they would not be able to point down. If they were pointing up, then they could be mounted closer...like if they were shooting at a dragon or something. You didn't mention dragons in your fantasy scenario, though."

Noah rolled his eyes. "Okay, so they could put some heavy weapons up here. Got it."

"You can go down now to check out the inside." Noah climbed down while Venu kept talking. "There are sliding windows on every side of the car, and also sliding panels for murder holes, in case someone wanted to use dazzlers or another defensive weapon from the inside." Noah rolled his eyes again. Most of Venu's inventions got cool names, but for some reason the man would not change his mind about dazzlers.

Noah said, "That makes sense. So if it's hot outside they can keep the windows open, but if it's cold or they're under attack, they can close them up."

"Exactly. Also, the walls are mostly made of decently strong aluminum panels with steel framing to keep the weight down. For armor, I added one of my inventions from earlier this year - the corrugated steel net."

"Oh yeah, I can see it now." Noah poked his head in the car and looked around, noting how the strong, thin mesh had been anchored at the top and sides of each wall, but not the bottom. "This stuff catches arrows, right?"

"Correct. The diameter of the holes will stop any arrow tip, and since the netting flexes, it actually absorbs a lot of the kinetic energy. It would be useless against bullets, but works great on arrows. In testing, the combination of the walls and the net stopped anything I shot short of siege weapons. Well, some of the modern crossbows penetrated, but I could just add an extra net and they'd be stopped too. It all comes down to weight."

"I understand. Okay, this makes a lot of sense now."

"Yes, well, it's still just a prototype. If you give the go-ahead to use up more funding, I can improve on the design."

Noah pursed his lips. He liked what he saw so far but wasn't entirely sold yet. "Okay, what about the carriage version."

"The carriage version is still light, but more heavily armored, with three mesh net layers inside. There are no hand pumps, and as you can see, it was easy to remove them. "

"Go on."

Venu said, "This design is practical because the box part can be used for both applications. The carriage version has a driver's section up front that is easy to bolt on. Other than that, the axles and wheels are a simple switch out. In fact, the main bodies could even be drilled for both applications to make the change even faster."

Now that Noah was up close, he could see what Venu was talking about. He asked, "So there are still hard points for weapons up top?"

"Correct, and since horses are much stronger than people, you could easily put heavier weapons up there."

Now that everything had been explained to him, Noah crossed his arms and carefully examined both vehicles before putting Venu on hold, climbing into the driver's portion of the horse-powered variation.

As usual, the IT Programmer-turned-engineer had really created something special. The fact that the vehicles could be repurposed would definitely come in handy. Noah couldn't remember people using railways after the Shift in his first life, but he was sure they had.

Over the last few years, he had looked up tactics used in wars that involved trains. An obvious weakness of anything on rails was that an enemy could mess up the tracks. Noah liked that the armored pump car could be stopped and reversed. This meant it could stop and run away from an ambush, or torn up tracks. What's more, if an enemy destroyed all the rails, the vehicles could just be converted to be pulled by horses.

Noah smiled, his mind made up. "These are good. Let's build at least a couple dozen of them to start with. I'll figure out where they all go later. You have my permission to modify them as you see fit."

"Understood."

Noah asked, "Is there any other stuff at this location for me to see, or was that all you had shipped and built here?"

"Yes, boss, that is all. I will not take any more of your time, so now you can go back to doing all the other strange things you do. I would wish you a good day, but you are probably determined to keep trying to give yourself an ulcer."

"You have a good day too, Venu," chuckled Noah. His inspection of the weapons finished, he turned and began walking to the Den itself. There was something else he wanted to check on inside the fortress.

The teen's cargo pants rustled as he walked, and he absently pulled a harmonica from his front pocket to play while he thought. He wasn't using [Harmony] or even playing for anyone else. Sometimes it was just good to get lost in music.

After walking past several courtyards, all designed to make the building even more defensible, Noah entered the lobby, barely noticing the robust but attractive architecture. Instead, he looped around, heading for the garage and the first set of underground warehouses. A hand-operated lift would allow anything stored in the Den to be transported to the surface.

Once his destination had been reached, Noah surveyed rows and rows of bicycles. Most were fairly standard, twenty-one-speed mountain bikes, but several rows were sturdier, military bicycles, meant to support a great deal of weight. The last row included a handful of experimental bicycles that Venu and his team had invented. They were rigged for tandem riders. The forward rider steered, and the rear rider faced the opposite direction, with a large, bicycle-mounted crossbow. The weapon could be cocked quickly because of how it was attached to the bike, and had a magazine for bolts on top. If Noah remembered correctly, it could hold five. Since each shot had to be cocked, it was not as fast a weapon as a dazzler, or one of the newer, similar weapons that Venu had developed. However, the 150-pound draw weight crossbow was plenty powerful and easy to aim with the offset scope.

Noah could think of multiple ways that bikes like this could come in handy. Each new tool or weapon that had been developed to prepare for the Shift couldn't solve every problem, but the more, the better.

Problems, he thought, and moved to the next area he wanted to inspect.

The next warehouse he eventually located was filled with heavy duty shelves full of steel parts, and strange looking pipes. To the average person, nothing in this room would be that impressive, but Noah smiled. All the parts and pieces could be assembled to make large, powerful manual pumps. Water shortages had been a huge problem in post-Shift America. Noah had several solutions in mind for this problem, but for this solution, he wasn't freely sharing with the world.

Whoever had water would have power, which was one reason why locations by waterways had fared well at first, until the predators had come.

Noah planned to use the pumps as trade, and they would be precious enough that he kept the majority of them in hardened locations like this one. He slowly walked among the shelves, gingerly touching the cold metal, and imagining what the world would have been like in his first life if more communities had had pumps like these.

The decision not to store pump parts in the standard warehouses had been a difficult one, but like his armories, the harm the pumps could cause in the wrong hands was just too great to risk.

"Okay, that's that," said Noah. Nobody was around to hear. He realized that his Log Cabin escort hadn't entered the building. Noah chuckled a bit–he hadn't asked them to stay behind, but entering this place seemed to quickly becoming taboo among everyone who visited the site.

Noah left the warehouses, knowing what the rest of them held. He had one more place to visit here in the Fallback Den.

Deep down, several floors lower, past the living sections, Noah found the sensitive area of the complex, where guards would be posted and average vault dwellers would not be allowed. Past the security point, he reached the office set aside for himself, behind a thick steel door and locks. He wasn't there to see his office site, though. Noah turned down a short hallway and yet another steel door, this one even thicker, like a bank vault. *Well,* Noah amended, *it was a bank vault a few years ago.*

He opened the door, and witnessed the most important room in the entire Den.

The library was stacked from floor to ceiling with books, full of thousands of years of human knowledge and history, all in print. This room of the Den had been designed to stay dry, and could be pumped with air if necessary.

Books on animal husbandry, carpentry, medicine...Noah had tried to plan for everything. He slowly walked around the edges of the large room, touching the solid shelving. His heart practically burst with pride. If all his other preparations failed, this room could still help humanity survive the Shift.

In the rear of the room, another solid door stood closed. Noah opened it, and explored the Den's printing room for the first time in person. This room was huge, almost the size of a warehouse. It had an alternate entrance on the other side of the room leading to the barracks, so in the future, if workers were using the dozen printing presses, they would not need to come through the library.

Shelving stood ready to aid in the printing process, and Noah knew that tons of vacuum-wrapped paper sat in the warehouses.

If the den's library was the brain of Noah's future plans, this printing room could be its heart. Noah had several similar setups throughout the US. They'd all been difficult and expensive to create, not to mention potentially even more dangerous than his secret armories.

Noah took out his harmonica again, playing a thoughtful song to break the almost sacred stillness of the room. He didn't think of himself as special and didn't take a lot of pride in his life's work, it had just needed to be done. The libraries and printing rooms he'd set up were exceptions. His chest swelled–if he died today, his life had made a difference.

He wondered what Doc would think of the place as he let his eyes roam, the harmonica music bouncing off cold concrete. Right now the room was lit with electric lights, but one day, it would be filled with the yellow light of lanterns.

With that thought, Noah left and locked up, heading back towards the entrance. As he passed his office, he opened the door on a whim and checked inside. A huge desk for his use stood at the other end of the room, and shelves had been built into the walls, exactly how he would want them situated.

Noah had drawn up the plans for the entire building, after all.

On one wall hung a number of instruments, including a guitar, bongo drums, a flute, and even cymbals. After the Shift, Noah remembered how music had all but vanished, only existing if people could create their own music. Maybe with the skills he'd learned in this new life, and the help of instruments, he could help make the world a happier, warmer place.

Noah softly closed and locked the door to his future office, humbled that several rooms exactly like it existed in other places in the world, too. He really had been working hard. This building hadn't been easy, nor cheap to build.

His harmonica seemed to switch music on its own, playing a sad melody as Noah thought about all the people who would die in the first few weeks of the Shift. He couldn't stop all of it, not on his own, but hopefully he could save the people he loved, maybe even bringing them to special places like the Den. By the time Noah had finished playing, he was outside again.

With one last wistful look through the open doors of the Fallback Den, he locked the door and gestured to the nearest Log Cabin guard. Bella, an average height, overweight, reliable, and utterly trustworthy woman, jogged over. She had her brunette hair piled up under a Log Cabin hat. Her uniform bulged a bit over her body armor, and Noah knew she was an expert with the FN Five-seven on her hip.

[Community] information that displayed in Noah's vision reminded him that Bella had served in the US Army and had worked as a police officer before being employed by Log Cabin.

"Bella, please let Steve at the airport know that we're heading back. Tell him that since we're already in Colorado, I want to visit the horse farm. He'll know what I mean."

"Understood." The guard turned, pressing an earbud with her fingers as she whispered into her mic. Noah took a few steps out of the pavilion, letting the sun hit his face and breathing in the fresh mountain air. He wanted to enjoy the sensation of his feet being on solid ground since he'd be flying again in about an hour.

The day was not finished yet, not even close.

CHAPTER 22

Krystal Connolly's curly red hair bounced in the springtime wind as she walked with Noah, the intermittent trees throughout her neighborhood cast friendly shadows. Noah had lost count how many times they had strolled wordlessly like this together, simply enjoying each other's company. As usual, he was lost in thought.

New ways he'd recently realized that he hadn't prepared for the Shift spun through his head, as well as worries about long-term projects he'd put into motion years before. The lab he'd hired to develop a way to produce insulin for diabetics without the use of electricity was nearing completion. Even though he didn't have a physical orb anymore, or Doc's strange machine to generate post-Shift power, Noah had still recently stocked up batteries just in case.

Of course, all of his current pondering was so he could distract himself from the moment at hand. *We're eighteen now*, he reminded himself. Equal parts excitement and nervousness warred in his chest.

In his previous life, he never could have imagined growing this close with his high school crush. Now, he and Krystal had become close friends, complete with inside jokes. When they were younger, Noah had noticed her fascination with him when he'd entered Washington High School. Up until then, he had just been homeschooled, his mother had continued to push his academics far beyond what a normal kid his age would have been able to handle.

The way Noah saw it, to Krystal, he had been the mysterious homeschooled kid her friends sometimes saw around town. When she had introduced herself, welcoming him to the school, Noah had been a little shy, but had forced himself to talk to her. Unexpectedly, as that first semester went by, he found himself spending more time Krystal.

He knew his former self would have killed to be in his position, but the mental age gap between them forced Noah to distance himself from her, even as they got closer. Noah never felt older than his physical age, but he agonized over the ethics of his situation, and deep down, wondered if Krystal deserved better than a guy who still woke every other night with Shift-related nightmares. For four years he had learned everything about her, but refused to ever seriously consider asking her out on a legitimate date. They had always hung out as friends.

But now, they were both eighteen years old. The Shift would

happen in less than a year and they were both young adults—it was now or never. He couldn't imagine completely failing at relationships and enduring the Shift without ever experiencing his first kiss...again.

Noah had never really talked to girls much at all in his first life, but in this life, he had made some great female friends. Krystal in particular, in addition to being enchanting, was a truly wonderful person. Over the four years they had known each other, Noah witnessed the naïve crush he had once harbored for her be replaced with real friendship and respect.

Time had always been his enemy, but things had changed.

Even though he still stressed about Shift preparations, there actually wasn't much left for him to personally handle. Most of his new plans and projects were delegated, now. *In another thirty days, I'll be sending out messages to Log Cabin Security offices to do another training module on uncommon disasters. I also left those envelopes with instructions with Log Cabin folks to give to the Firestarter geniuses.* Noah thought that move had been smart. He still planned to mail letters to all of his gifted friends with snail mail before the Shift, but he liked layers of redundancy just in case.

The more Noah thought about it, the more he knew there really wasn't much more for him to directly oversee anymore. Anyone who tried to prey on the communities he'd planted seeds in—whether raider or Aelves—would get a nasty surprise...hopefully. After over a decade, all the pieces were in place; all his planning had paid off.

Noah had barely taken any time for himself, had hardly spent any money on selfish things. In fact, his entire fortune would be gone in just a few months. Once Noah's plans went into action, Steelton would be the safest place in the world. His family and friends would be protected in the first fort after the Shift.

Krystal will be here too, and I'll be able to protect her.

Everything else was done, but there was one last thing Noah wanted to do before the world collapsed into chaos.

The redhead at his side kicked a pile of leaves on the sidewalk and said, "It looks like I'm going to OSU for biology."

Noah gave her an admonishing look. "A Michigan-born girl working for the enemy, eh?"

Krystal laughed. She flicked at a piece of dry leaf that had blown onto her shoulder. Noah took a deep breath, screwing up his courage and stopped walking. It took Krystal a few seconds to realize that she was walking alone. She turned around with a cocked eyebrow. "What?"

Noah moved forward until he stood only a few inches away, towering over her. "Krystal, we've been friends for four years," he said, his voice steady.

"Yeah," she agreed. "It feels like we've been hanging out since we were kids."

She tilted her head as if she were confused, and Noah saw her lip tremble, betraying a hidden emotion. *She has feelings for me too,*

Noah thought, his heart swelling. Over the years, it had pained him to be so close but force himself to keep a healthy distance from her. If Noah was going to have anything more than friendship now, he wanted to do it right.

His heart began to race as the words came out. There wasn't any need to drag it out any longer. "Things are going to change in a couple of months, Kay, and not just for you and me, but for everyone."

"Yeah, everyone's going to college," she added soberly.

"That's not what I mean. " Noah shook his head. A pressure had built inside him, ready to burst. "But that doesn't matter right now. Krystal, before anything major happens, I thought I should tell you something important."

"Noah—"

"I have feelings for you," he said plainly. The words finally spoken, a weight lifted that he hadn't known was there. His shoulders relaxed, and all could think was how good it felt to speak the truth after all this time.

Krystal closed her eyes and inched forward. Their chests were so close that even without [Listen] he could hear her breath. Her hair smelled like lavender. She opened her eyes...and stepped away. Everything about the way she stood had changed, and Noah could sense something was wrong. Her hands tightened into fists, and she looked angry, hurt.

"Are you kidding me, Noah Henson?"

"What?" Noah blinked.

"This? Now?" Krystal seethed. "For four years I dropped every hint I could. Even an idiot like you should have picked up on it, and now you're telling me you have feelings for me? I can't believe this. You friend-zoned me from the beginning. I cried for you, Noah. Do you know how pathetic that made me feel?

"My friends said I should move on. Every time I was about to actually do that, you'd come sweeping into town again, talking to everyone, and take me to a movie—as friends—and I would die inside all over again. It was a like a force of nature—you were like a force of nature. Like a hurricane. And every time, I'd get caught up in it, happy with what we had, and afraid to ruin everything or completely let go.

"See, deep down, I realized a long time ago that you were never going to return my feelings, but I couldn't give up hope. Then I wondered if there was something wrong with me." Krystal's voice wavered, about to turn into a sob, but firmed again. "You were never anything but sweet to me, and sometimes even saved time for me instead of your family. I couldn't be mad at you, but I...I just couldn't. I cried so, so many times." The words came out in a rush, and Krystal's face began to turn red, her voice growing louder.

"It was only a few months ago that I really, finally moved on, or so I thought. I decided that college would be a fresh start. Do you know the really crappy thing too? Even as a friend, you treated me so well, my parents kept asking when we were going to date. They. Love. You. Noah. Do you know how much harder that made it for me to give up on how I felt? But now, after I spent an embarrassing amount of time agonizing over all of this, and finally moved on, you spring this on me? On a walk? Oh no, buster. No way, Jose."

Noah's heart slowed so much, he thought it almost stopped. His throat went dry. *No*, he thought, confused. *This isn't how it's supposed to go.* Lamely, even to his own ears, he managed to get out, "It's the truth. I–I do have feelings for you."

Krystal straightened her back and raised her chin. "I waited, Noah. I waited a long, long time."

He recognized the tone in her voice, and it cut him like a katana. He could still hear the frustration and resentment in her words, but below all of that, the deep hurt. Noah had kept a measured distance from Krystal throughout their friendship, resolved to never cross the platonic line until they were adults.

But he never thought about how it must have been for her. He'd never even considered that she might have real feelings for him. Even with his Charisma stat, and all his other advantages, the possibility just hadn't been real to him. One of the most important people in his life had been hurting, he'd been to blame, and he'd been oblivious.

Unlike Noah, Krystal didn't have a mission to save the world. She'd had a reason to hold back. Now Noah was struck with the clarity of hindsight. Moments they had spent together were given new meaning now.

Noah thought about all the things he'd brushed off as coincidence or wishful thinking on his part—her hand "accidentally" brushing against his, her insistence to study on the smaller couch so they sat closer together, or asking him to a movie with friends, only for others to bail and end up going alone with her. *I always just thought she saw me as kooky and weird–the smart, new kid.* Noah needed to wrap his head around the machine gun lightning bolts of clarity. *She had real feelings. She cares for me. What was I thinking?*

He grimaced, realizing how he'd tortured someone he cared about. The weight that lifted from him earlier came back, tripled, having absorbed crushing guilt. Stunned, he could only manage to whisper, "I'm sorry."

Krystal studied him sadly, silent for a while. She finally said, "I know. As usual, you're a decent guy, and I can't truly hold anything against you. I could have said something before too, but you had your own stuff going on. It wasn't like I was blind, I've always known how busy you were. Like, what was a crush compared to all the people you employ? But we're eighteen now, Noah. You had your chance."

She's right, Noah thought. *If I were her, I would have given up on me ages ago. She deserves someone who can be there for her all the time and not when it's convenient.* Noah swallowed. *I'm an idiot.*

Before he could say anything more, or wrap his mind around the situation, to stomach his disappointment, Krystal added, "We can still be friends."

Noah winced, and even as he reacted, he could tell that Krystal knew she's said the wrong thing too.

They'd already been friends.

Krystal crossed her arms and bit her lip. "Noah?"

He shook his head, still shocked by...everything. It had all happened so fast. He'd planned this day for years, fantasizing about being finished with his preparation for the Shift, to live a normal life for at least a few months. Everything had gone wrong. Guilt, disappointment, frustration, and sorrow pulled different directions on his heart. He haltingly said, "I think I need some time alone right now. I'm not...I'm not mad. If anything, I feel really stupid. I actually understand. I just want some time to process, if that's okay."

Big, silent tears began to descend down Krystal's cheeks and her lip trembled, making it harder for Noah to keep his composure. His eyes tickled.

It took Krystal a couple tries before she could speak. "Of course it's okay," she whispered.

"Alright," said Noah, and coughed a little. He walked forward to Krystal, and then past, keeping his eyes forward the entire time. His eyelids burned. Back ramrod straight, Noah managed to politely force out, "Goodbye." He didn't turn back, so he would never know if she watched him go.

His chest hurt, and tears finally fell.

CHAPTER 23

"That's rough, bro," Johnny Dormund said, tone sympathetic. He drove his large, red pickup truck, probably the only kind of vehicle that could match his huge frame. Noah sat in the passenger seat, staring dully at the Michigan trees as they whizzed by.

He nodded robotically. It had been a few hours since he'd last seen Krystal. He'd texted Johnny earlier while he'd still been a mess, and his best friend had picked him up and offered to drive him around the edge of town to help clear his head. The Sunday church bells rang clearly in the distance. After a moment, Noah let out a sigh and said, "She said we can still be friends."

Like any loyal friend would, Johnny made a pained face and sucked in air harshly through his teeth. "Girls, man."

"Girls," Noah agreed somberly. "Like, I get her perspective, I just don't understand why after all this time, she'd stick to her guns like that instead of, I don't know—" His voice tailed off.

A few silent moments passed before Johnny hesitantly said, "I don't think anyone is gonna be surprised about this, you know."

"What do you mean?"

"Well, you and Krystal have kind of obviously had a thing for each other for a long time. It's not like you two didn't have options for dances, but you'd always go alone, and always end up dancing with each other. You hung out all the time. Like, some girls at school were definitely into you but didn't think they had a chance. I actually know that one for sure."

"Really?"

"Yeah." The big boy sounded apologetic.

"Why didn't you say something?"

"I kinda just figured you were with Krystal like everyone else did, maybe on the down-low or something. She was always around, so it was really normal for you to be together. I mean, you're the smart one. If I could see it, you definitely would already know, right?"

Noah slowly closed his eyes and leaned his head back. *I can't believe this*, he thought. Finally he sighed and went back to staring out the window. Johnny gave him some space, and the two drove in friendly, if slightly awkward silence for a while.

After a few more miles, Noah realized that they were passing a familiar, abandoned office building. Johnny noticed too. His friend said, "Look, it's where your old internship used to be. I'm glad they moved offices to the other side of town. It used to be a pain for you to come out all this way, right?"

Happy to think about a new subject, Noah nodded and said, "Yeah, I think their budget grew or something."

Noah knew the truth, though. The Merriweathers' old office had been a dinosaur of a cold-war era location, originally built for a Merriweather genius in Michigan during that time. Noah had found this discovery extremely interesting. However, since the Merriweathers had begun regularly flying in to check on Noah, Burgess had thought the place was dated and too far away from the nearest airport.

Sometimes [Listen] really came in handy.

Noah glanced over at Johnny's titanic frame in his varsity letterman's jacket, and still saw the chubby-faced geek who loved to play video games. Under all that muscle, he was still a thick-headed, lovable goofball of a kid. Noah felt grateful for his loyalty.

The two talked about things that had happened in the last couple years, dredging up memories and dusting them off. Noah laughed more often than not, especially when his friend brought up the time one of their friends, Gregory Bist's pants had fallen down at a dance. Of course, Johnny remembered a few things that Noah couldn't recall, like Danielle Perkins following them around. His friend must have imagined that.

Johnny chuckled for a while, then said, "Remember last year when you told me about how all this preparing stuff you do is to secretly prevent humanity from all dying, like falling at the hands of alien space elves?"

Noah frowned. "Yes. Aelves. I know you don't believe me, but that's okay."

His friend shook his head with a grin. "You have some imagination, but I never saw you so serious then."

"What's your point?"

"My point," Johnny said, turning the wheel to the truck, "is even now, all messed up over Krystal, you don't have that vibe. See, when you told me about the aliens and that thing, the Shift? I believed you."

"You did?" Noah asked, shocked.

"Uh huh, but only for a second, and because you seemed so sure of yourself. Your eyes kind of glowed and you stood different," Johnny replied. "Since then, I've seen that focused look come up every now and then, and realized I've seen it in the past too. You usually slip off or look at something on your phone and just brood forever, then you act normal again like nothing ever happened. The thing is, with Krystal, I know you really liked her, but I don't see that look on you right now, that moody look." Johnny glanced over and Noah could tell his friend was trying to see if he had gone too far.

He didn't, of course–couldn't. Johnny was Johnny. After a moment to think about it, Noah said, "It's easier to say now with hindsight, but I guess I should have seen this coming."

His big friend shrugged and said, "I'm not a shrink, I've just known you forever. I'm not saying Krystal didn't matter to you, but like you said she said, you made her wait forever. Maybe she thought she wasn't your number one priority, and that's why she eventually let it all go."

"I guess I understand what you're saying. It just all happened so fast. Maybe if I'd been paying attention," Noah said but paused, "I don't know."

Johnny made a face. "Those times you get serious, man, you can get distant. For me, I'm cool with it because I know beneath that cool guy persona you put on for everyone, you're actually just a sappy little geeky emo kid underneath it all. Sometimes you just need a smushy hug."

Noah punched Johnny's arm, not hard, and he felt better. Something in his pocket buzzed and he pulled out his phone, pursing his lips at a text message from Burgess. It read: "Meet me at the main office. ASAP. Important. Not negotiable. I know you are in town."

"We need to make a detour," Noah said. "Can you drive me to my internship?"

Johnny checked his watch. "Sure thing, bro."

***

The red pickup truck pulled in front of a two-story office building with a sign in front that read, "Jolly Seasons Insurance Company." Like the previous Merriweather location, this one was located at the edge of town, just on the other side. The building stood in its own lot, separate from the nearby housing subdivisions.

Noah was glad the main office had moved. He'd been able to buy a nearby house to use as a stash spot, holding some weapons and gear. *When the Shift comes, my people with Log Cabin are the first people I want armed, to take control, but maybe if Burgess' people are in town, they could help too.*

Johnny parked the truck and asked, "Why is your boss' car the only one here?"

Noah shrugged, snapping off his seatbelt, guiding it past the Spyderco Bushcraft knife on his belt. He shrugged and said, "I don't know, Maybe because it's a Sunday."

He knew the real reason, though. Most of the other members of Burgess' team were away doing other things. In fact, Noah had planned to catch up on personal stuff over the week because most of the Merriweathers wouldn't be in town, and therefore wouldn't be bothering him. *So much for time off,* he thought. On one hand, he welcomed the distraction from what had just happened with Krystal. However, Burgess' tone in the text he'd sent had him a little worried.

Johnny unlocked the doors and asked, "You want me to wait here for you, or is your boss gonna give you a ride?"

Burgess probably just wants to hand me some paperwork or something, or give me prep materials for another assessment. Burgess had done it before. The man was a stickler for the rules, and never just hand-waved away the tests that Noah had to take, or the reports he gave–basically all amounting to the fact he was not a menace to society.

The Merriweather Division was a tight ship. If the boss said jump, the rest of the agents didn't ask how high–they'd just jump. From what Noah had seen, the organization was kind of strange, but all the agents from around the world took their jobs seriously, preventing kids with natural talents for mayhem from going bad.

Noah opened the truck's door and stepped out. "It should only be a few minutes. Wait here."

"Sure thing, bro. I'll just idle the truck and listen to the radio."

Noah closed the door and walked toward the office. [Listen] picked up the sounds of children playing nearby in the quiet suburban neighborhood. Neighbors chatted in their backyards while grilling burgers. Something rustled in the nearby bushes behind the building, probably deer.

Noah reminded himself to go hunting with Johnny again as soon as possible. His bow skills had all been levelled to five. Their next trip would probably be his last time with his friend before everything changed. He reached the door and pressed his hand against the glass window. It hummed with a faint light, scanning his fingerprints before unlocking.

It was easy to find Burgess' office, at least the one out in the open near the entrance. The public-facing office was spare and lit by overhead lights, a desk lamp, and a computer. Burgess leaned against the edge of his desk, his fingers drumming against the wood. *That's not a good sign*, Noah thought.

The door was open, but Noah still knocked and gave Burgess a friendly smile. He said, "Funny enough, I was hoping you'd call me in. I really need a distraction right now."

"Sit down, Henson," Goodrich said evenly, not a shred of humor in his voice. He looked grim.

Noah frowned and sat in one of the two chairs facing the desk. His boss didn't call him Henson unless it was serious, preferring first names when speaking. Something was wrong. Goodrich grabbed a pile of papers and handed them to Noah silently.

After blinking owlishly, Noah read through them and felt the blood drain from his face. What he saw were names, a long list of names, fake identities he had made over the years to help him prepare for the Shift. After the list of names were numbers indicating money spent in different countries by the identities. Additional pages tied these activities to Noah's whereabouts over the years and his publicly known companies. A couple pages detailed surveillance on Log Cabin, and additional pages outlined the hoops Noah had jumped through for free requisition privileges with both raw resource distribution centers, and weapon manufacturers.

Several more pages listed at least a few hundred locations that Noah owned through various channels. There was even a grainy satellite image of a row of arbalests standing outside a remote storage warehouse, being loaded into the hidden, locked armory. "I can explain," Noah managed.

Burgess frowned, the drumming of his fingers quickening. He looked like a tired father who had waited all night for his son, and had caught him sneaking home past curfew. The silver in his hair seemed duller, more of a grey. "I'm disappointed you didn't come to me with this when it could have been managed."

"Managed?"

"Yes, managed," Burgess said, anger in his voice. "If we were having this conversation four years ago, or maybe even two, and you came to me with the full truth about everything, I could have stopped the higher-ups from allowing this to happen. Now, it's too much at once."

Noah tensed, caution in his tone. "Stop what from happening? Too much what?"

Goodrich adjusted his tie and spoke evenly, "I've worked with you this entire time. I knew you've been hiding things from us, but I just didn't know what, or obviously how much. To be quite frank, I didn't really care that much. I just assumed it was more hacking, taking down corrupt CEOs during your spare time, or whatever it was you did for fun. Meanwhile, another division of Interpol acted on their own suspicions and obviously found something. A lot of it."

Noah's mind spun. He had definitely not been expecting any of this. In the clarity of extreme stress, his mind flashed through the last few years how he'd gotten lax, complacent. No new issues had arisen with any world government and with the Shift coming, he grew to care less. But now it was all biting him in the butt. It was time to level with Burgess. "Boss," Noah insisted. "I really can explain. In a few months—"

The stern Interpol agent cut him off with a snap of a finger. "Anything you say from here on has no credibility, not with Interpol and definitely not with me. Look at it from my position. If you saw millions, maybe even billions of dollars-worth of purchases in international real estate, doomsday prepping resources, and weaponry, no matter how weird, wouldn't you assume that person is either a terrorist, or at least dangerously unhinged? You are an eighteen-year-old and you literally own a mountain. One of the fastest growing security companies in the West actually belongs to you. At the very least, wouldn't it also be logical that you might be backed by some powerful, possibly dangerous people?"

Noah felt a flash of anger and slammed his hand against the arm of his chair. "I earned that money fair and square! From the time I was a little kid, I spent time other people got to sleep or watch TV to track stocks. Juggling so many businesses, even with help, it was exhausting. I worked hard for everything!"

Burgess' eyebrows raised, then lowered in suspicion. After inspecting Noah's face for a moment, he shook his head. "The worst part of all of this is that I want to believe you. We've done good work together, Noah. I've known you for a long time now, but this is just too bizarre, too...big. You messed up irrevocably. See, you're no longer a minor. That means you are technically not my jurisdiction anymore."

Noah heard the finality in the words, and he sat still. He didn't know what to do. First Krystal, now this. "What now?"

Goodrich grabbed the papers from Noah and set them back on the desk. "As you know, the original plan was for you to be a ward of the Merriweather Division until you graduated high school. Prosecution for your past crimes was put on hold, and you'd be pardoned once you graduated from probation. Now your status with the Merriweather Division has been revoked. You'll be on house arrest while the London office figures out what to do with you. If I don't call in to the regional office after you leave, there are teams prepared to raid the corporate office of your Log Cabin security company, occupy your home, and come after you. There is literally a committee occurring this very instant arguing whether or not they should just toss you in a cell and throw away the key."

"And you?"

Burgess shrugged. "My opinion doesn't matter."

Noah had never felt lower in this life. He looked away. "Why are you telling me all of this?"

"Mostly because I still don't really believe you're a bad kid. I honestly...don't know what to make of all of this. The level of organization and funding to pull off some of this bizarre stuff that's been pinned to you, it boggles my mind. You haven't committed any crimes since your cyber hacking days still, though, at least not that I've seen. Of course, the other teams are currently looking into that too.

"That doesn't answer my question," Noah mumbled.

There was a pregnant pause before the older man steepled his fingers and said, "As of this moment, you are the greatest failure of this program under my watch. All of this is going to reflect poorly on me and on my team. I wanted to talk to you first, to gauge your reaction. Obviously, if I thought you were a real threat, meeting alone would not have been wise, but I obviously took that risk."

"I don't understand."

Burgess cleared his throat and said, "For the moment, you haven't been incarcerated...yet. Deliberations are still ongoing. I may be the only ally you have in the near future. So while we still have time to talk, why don't you tell me what's really going on? Why...everything? None of it adds up. Things that don't make sense make people nervous."

Is it really that easy? Noah wondered. He had been tempted to inform Burgess and the Merriweathers about the Shift and Aelves for years, but always knew they'd just think he was crazy. Even his best friend Johnny hadn't believed him. There was no proof to back up anything he could say.

Now, even with Goodrich asking him outright, despite being so near the Shift, it was difficult for Noah to decide risking being seen more unstable than Interpol no doubt already labeled him. Could he still prepare for the Shift on house arrest? What would happen to all of his assets over the next few months? Would Log Cabin Security be left alone?

It's not like I have anything to lose, he realized. *I still have a few things left to take care of, too—house arrest, and especially being in jail would be terrible. But where do I start with something like this?* Telling Burgess the truth wouldn't be like dropping clues to the geniuses from Camp Firestarter.

Noah decided to take the leap. "Okay. Alright. Uh, I've been keeping a secret my entire life. It started wi—"

The lights in the office went out and Noah's heart sunk. *A power outage in Michigan during the day with no bad weather?* It was possible, but his skin crawled. With dread building in the pit of his stomach, he glanced through the window and noticed a car dead in the middle of the street. The driver, a middle-aged woman climbed out, confusion plain on her face even from a distance. Noah hissed and stood up in a rush. "It can't be," he whispered.

Behind his desk, Burgess sat back slowly and cocked an eyebrow. "Noah," the man said, an edge to his voice. "Do you have something to tell me?"

"No, oh, no," Noah rasped, his throat dry. "Not now. It's too early." He stood and woodenly walked to the door of the office.

Burgess seemed to pick up the fear in Noah's voice. The older man followed Noah out the hallway and growled, "Do you know what is going on? Is this more than a power outage?"

Outside, in the parking lot, Johnny had stepped out of his truck. The large young man circled his vehicle, scratching his head. Burgess' hand gripped around Noah's wrist. He demanded, "What is going on?"

The initial panic that had risen in Noah quickly died, overwhelmed by a lifetime of calm preparation. He had literally been born for this day, but he still had to make sure. "Pull out your sidearm and shoot it in the air," he asked. As soon as the words left his mouth, he felt foolish. A government agent wasn't going to fire a pistol in broad daylight at the request of a teenager.

Something about Noah's demeanor must have alarmed Burgess because his grip loosened. Noah's arms fell to his side. The agent shook his head, obviously confused. His wary eyes searched Noah. "Fire? Why? Is it a signal for something?"

Noah didn't have time for this. He turned from Burgess and began walking to his friend. [Listen] picked up all the noises around him. Cars had veered off the road. Families were stepping outside their homes, asking their neighbors if their power went out. He drowned out the noise with an effort of concentration and pivoted his attention back to Johnny.

"Johnny!" he yelled. "Turn on your truck!"

His friend, confused, took a step back. "What? It just died a second ago. It won't start. Like, I was about to look at the engine."

Noah quickly pulled out his phone—it was dead. "Is your phone dead too, Brawns?" Johnny checked his own phone and nodded. After closing his eyes for a moment, Noah sighed. He wasn't sure what was happening. Had he been wrong about the date? No, that was one thing he'd always been sure of. How could he remember the worst day of his life?

Behind him, something rustled and Noah turned. Burgess stood with his dead phone in his hand, holding it out like evidence. The man had drawn his pistol, what looked like a Sig 320. He hadn't done anything more than hold it at his side, but just the fact he'd cleared leather meant the man must have understood the implications of what was happening. "Noah, you seem to know what is going on. I am going to ask you about it like this, politely, exactly once," said Burgess. He pulled something from behind his ear too, probably his agent com system that also had to be dead.

A faint sound whipped Noah's head around, people nearby were screaming and pointing. Everyone looked up. A small plane in the distance had begun plummeting from the air. Noah heard Burgess breathe, "Dear God."

Noah knew there wasn't anything to do, no way they could help the people in planes all over the world. Instead, he took advantage of the distraction and darted forward, grabbing the pistol out of Burgess' hand. To his credit, the well-trained agent tried to slap his hand down and retain his weapon, but Noah had been too fast, too explosive.

The Merriweather leader grew very still and watched Noah warily. "This is the Shift," said Noah. He racked the slide of the pistol and a round extracted—the gun had been loaded. With an impersonal detachment, the youth pointed the pistol to the side and pulled the trigger. Burgess flinched, but no shot rang out, only a click.

As his boss blinked in confusion, Noah repeated what he'd just done, racking the slide, loading a new round, and pulling the trigger. After the second click, he handed the useless weapon back to Burgess. "It won't work anymore, no guns will. Technology is basically toast now."

From where he still stood by the truck, Johnny said, "That Shift stuff, that's not real, right? It's not real, right, Noah?" A tremor had entered his voice.

Noah calmed himself and focused with [Listen] again, his head down, ignoring Johnny's questions. Uncertainties rose in his head, but he pushed them aside. *Don't lose your cool. The plan. I need to stick to the plan.*

He had spent his entire life preparing for his day. As he took a breath, about to start filling Burgess in, [Listen] caught something odd in his hearing range. Something didn't belong.

Voices with strange tones, weird inflections were relayed clearly by Noah's supernatural hearing, and his breath stopped. He recognized the language. None of the words came from any tongue spoken on Earth, but somehow, he could understand what they were saying.

CHAPTER 24

"Reemeht, you know our orders. We are scouts, not a war party, or even explorers," a high voice said. "You must give a progress report via sat-flower in a fourth-cycle. We were not given permission to feed."

A guttural snarl replied, "Enough orders. We did what before, chase echoes of a human for local years? A speck of dust in the galaxy, a pointless endeavor. I am hungry! It has been sixth-cycles since I had any nourishment. Watch them, the humans. They are everywhere, panicked and lost, and soon there will be more disorder. I just needed this one. You can have the other, it is still alive." A faint sound, like a covered scream sounded, and in heavily accented English, the voice said, "Move and die."

The next soft whimper made Noah's heart beat faster, even as he tried to locate the direction of the voices.

Another more steady voice chimed in, "The Voice's word is

absolute."

"Devour the Voice," the snarling voice answered. "Kahlek isn't here. You two go, fulfill our useless task. Watching? We know how all of this works. An orb-attuned human? Pointless. Impossible. Go, try to find one human in billions for the thousandth time. I will catch up after I eat this one. If you do not have this other one, I will eat it, too."

Noah's head snapped up at the name. *Kahlek.* The Aelve who had helped the others kill Doc, Noah knew that name. A rage he had carried for two lifetimes surfaced in him, burning hotter than ever, narrowed to a needlepoint.

Listening for a while longer, he homed in on the voices, catching the sound of retreating footsteps. After they stopped speaking, he almost lost track of the direction they were coming from before [Listen] picked up a hiss, a snuffling sound, and another muffled sound of distress.

There.

With a feral growl, Noah broke into a sprint. Burgess and Johnny shouted behind him, but their words didn't matter. Nothing mattered now.

The Shift had come early. The Aelves were here, and one of them was going to kill an innocent person—that's what it sounded like, and that's what they did. *Not on my watch*, Noah thought. He had never run so fast in his life, not even in training. His body felt full of electricity, fueled by rage for the aliens, monsters that proved once again that they must be exterminated.

[Listen] told him he was only about fifty yards away.

A thousand thoughts went through his mind. The location he ran toward seemed to be a small wooded area, to the side of a housing development near the Merriweather building. Even as he ran, Noah realized it would be smarter to get weapons and more people. The Aelves weren't exactly pushovers. But even as that thought flashed through his mind, he heard another soft whimper and a wet cracking noise. No, even if this course of action was stupid, Noah wouldn't stand by, wouldn't be passive anymore.

He would never be Worm again, even if it cost him his life.

He drew his knife from its sheath, holding it in a reverse grip. Noah ran past the last house and broke through the bushes, dashing forward through the undergrowth to behold a scene of horror.

Danielle Perkins lay on her back, her clothing in disarray, as if she'd be dragged around like a piece of meat. A patch of a pale substance, like sickly clay, covered her mouth and bound her hands behind her. Her terrified eyes met Noah's, pleading silently. A broken camera lay next to her, its pieces scatter over the grass.

Nearby, Danielle's friend Brittany Macy lay on her back, at least Noah thought it had been her. The girl's head had been cut off, and the corpse's fingers spasmed even as the neck spurted blood to the grass. With the razor-sharp clarity of the moment, Noah noticed that the dead girl had been wearing purple socks and white shoes. One foot softly kicked against the forest floor.

Brittany's head floated in midair, partially obscured by a shimmering, faint luminescence. Noah wouldn't have caught it if he hadn't been staring right at it–and if it hadn't been blocking the view of a levitating, severed head.

As he crashed forward, the strange patch of air shifted, and Noah acted on instinct, grasping for his mother's lullaby. As soon as his mind filled with the melody, light peeled back before his eyes, like a hidden layer. After the unnatural concealment lifted, Noah saw the hunched silhouette of a tall, pale figure. The Aelve had pallid skin and long flaky white hair, almost plant-like. Just like the Aelves Noah had seen in his first life, the creature looked almost human except for his pointed ears and grey irises. The alien turned, and his clothing, or armor, seemed to be made of light blue leaves that moved sinuously, organically.

"Human!" the Aelve snarled in his language. In one narrow hand, he held Brittany's head by the hair. A...vine of the Aelve's armor, attached, arced up and into the alien's other hand. At the end of the vine, a hard leaf on the end was being used like a knife to cut the dead girl's skull open like a coconut.

Noah let his momentum carry him forward, actually picking up speed. Right before he collided with the Aelve, another knife vine detached from the alien's blue armor and whipped forward, straight for Noah's throat.

A spike of fear shot through his spine, but anger rose as well.

Noah hated the Aelves, and his burning blood made the lullaby in his head change, morph into something different, something darker. He used a combination of his level five [Parkour], [Gymnastics], and two martial arts skills, deftly springing into the air and rolling horizontally. As the knife passed beneath where he'd just been, Noah kicked out as hard as he could, catching the Aelve in the face with the edge of his boot.

This time, unlike with the Merriweather dog at fourteen years old, he put everything he had into the strike. Noah was a lot stronger now, too.

The Aelve dropped the dead girl's head and flew backward, slamming into a tree. Noah didn't relent, dropping to a crouch and springing forward, moving in for the kill. As he closed, the Aelve's vine knives flashed forward on their own, cutting through tree saplings like they weren't even there. Noah barely dodged the first one, and tried parrying that vine with his knife after the point was past. Whatever the thing was made of felt as hard as steel. Despite being so thin, it had almost as much strength as Noah's braced arm plus all of his momentum.

The other vine knife struck from a different direction, but Noah dropped to the ground, skidding forward on his knees, arched backward as far as he could go. A fiery line of pain erupted on his chest as the blue, leaf blade slashed over his body. Noah hissed, but popped up to his feet in one smooth motion, still moving forward, and stabbed at his pallid enemy's heart.

His knife stopped like it'd hit concrete. The wicked sharp Spyderco, carbon steel blade felt like Noah had tried stabbing through solid iron. He was close enough to feel the alien's breath.

The Aelve's startled eyes narrowed, and the creature smiled, showing off sharp teeth. One of the creature's hands shot out, and Noah barely managed to parry some of the force before the strike caught him in the shoulder and threw him back like a sack of laundry.

"That was well done, for a human," rasped the Aelve in his own language, "but you are nothing. You cannot compare; you are food."

The alien moved the arm that had pushed Noah back, moving it up, still extended outward. A few blue leaves lifted, and Noah realized too late that he was staring down the business end of a weapon. Light flashed, and Noah felt agony.

He'd lived in constant agony before, though, even after dying. Especially after dying.

Noah fought back, even as his skin felt like it was peeling away, and focused on his mother's lullaby, mentally adding more bass and some percussion, turning it into his war song. His world had turned violet, but Noah resisted, and vaguely remembered a similar situation at some point in his past. This energy felt familiar somehow. He railed against it, throwing all that he was against the pain, eventually even humming his war song out loud.

As he pushed back the attack, he realized that he'd been

surrounded by purple flames. The Aelve had been chuckling, but abruptly stopped. Noah gathered up all his will, and with a titanic heave, pushed outward with the energy roiling inside, swirled with the tempo of the war song he sang aloud now.

The Aelve stood still, stupefied, his eyes dilated in shock. "You are the one. You are real! The Voice—" With a hiss, the alien lowered his weapon arm and fumbled with a bag at the side of his armor. Noah could sense that the situation was dire. He was somehow not dead yet, but that might not last long. The Aelve drew something out from the bag and snarled before manipulating the new thing in his palm.

The Aelve was distracted, partially looking down. All or nothing, there would be no better time.

Noah narrowed his eyes. His body dumped massive amounts of adrenaline into his system, and his thoughts felt sharper, polished even further by his war song. Fear sang through his veins too, and he used it to feed the energy pumping through his body. He bared his teeth and flexed his knees before dodging a knife vine, then threw himself forward, hurling his knife.

With a sick thunk, Noah's blade slammed into the Aelve's head right through an eye socket. The murderous creature gasped, falling back and pawing his ruined face, his armor turning into a roiling mass of blue as it flared and moved like feathers.

Even as the alien fell, something in his hand, like a seed, began falling to the ground. Acting on powerful instinct, Noah dove forward, catching the pod even as it began opening, beginning to look like a flower. The object felt cold despite being organic in nature. Noah ignored the nearby thrashing Aelve, even as flashing knife vines tore apart the nearby trees, dangerously close. The knife vines were deadly, but Noah could sense that what he held in his hand was worse.

There was some sort of connection, felt right at the edge of his mind, but Noah didn't have the luxury to explore it. Instead, he changed his war song back to the lullaby, silently pleading the seed-flower thing in his palm to close. When it finally did, he sighed in relief.

As he stood, the dead Aelve's vine weapons had finally stilled. Noah turned and saw that where he'd been attacked by the purple flames, nothing but charred earth with a Noah-shaped shadow remained. Brittany's corpse had been damaged, half a leg burned away. Noah was covered in mild burns, scorch marks, and blood.

Danielle's whimpering brought Noah back to his senses. He cursed and tensed to run forward, but stopped and turned instead, cautiously approached the downed Aelve. Luckily, the knife vines stayed still and the scout stayed dead, but Noah still shuddered as he got closer. Finally, with a wet squelch, he pulled his knife from the murderous alien's face and jogged over to Danielle. Trying to be as gentle as possible, he knelt next to the girl and began cutting through her wrist restraints with his knife.

The stuff on her wrists was stronger, so he moved to her

mouth instead and was about to get the substance off. As soon as she could, Danielle thrashed and began screaming, but got less than a second of sound out before Noah clamped a hand over her mouth. "Calm down," he muttered. He knew such a thing would be easier said than done, though.

Noah shook his head at the terrible coincidence of knowing the first Aelve victim he'd ever seen in this life. He said, "Danielle, I can help you, but we are all still in danger. You need to get ahold of yourself before I can free you and get you out of here."

He looked into the girl's hazel eyes, showing her the knife and hoping she would calm. When Burgess and Johnny ran through the undergrowth a moment later, they found him crouched over a squirming girl, his hand over her mouth and a knife raised in the air.

Crap, he thought as Burgess predictably pulled his pistol.

"Noah, get away from her!" The Interpol agent's words came out calmly, evenly, but with an underlying strain.

At least Burgess isn't yelling, Noah thought.

Meanwhile, Johnny noticed Brittany's body on the ground. The corpse's head had been half burned. The entire scene was awful, on a level most normal people would never witness. Johnny licked his lips and pressed them together before darting into the bushes to be sick. It was one thing to clean animals after hunting, and quite another to see a murdered person. Noah knew from experience.

"Burgess, Boss, calm down. I can explain but we are all in danger."

"Noah!" The silver-haired man's eyes were growing wild. "Get away from the girl!"

"Your pistol doesn't work. Go ahead and pull the trigger."

Johnny stumbled out of the bushes and pointed at the alien corpse on the ground. "Is that an elf?"

"Aelve, and yes. They're here."

"So you were telling the truth before about all of this?" Dread filled the big teen's voice. He'd gotten vomit on his leatherman jacket.

"Yes."

"God I was afraid you'd say that." Johnny looked green and kept looking up at the sky.

Noah ignored Burgess and his shaking pistol, instead looking Danielle in the eyes. "Danielle, I'm really sorry to push you like this, but we don't have much time. Can you get it together?" The girl's eyes were still wild, but a shadow crossed her face and her demeanor changed. Iron entered her expression, and she slowly nodded. "Good," said Noah. He took his hand off of the girl's mouth and helped her up. "Keep your eyes on Johnny," he instructed her. If she saw Brittany's corpse now, she might start screaming again. She had to be in shock—hopefully it would keep her going.

"Okay," Danielle whispered. Noah noticed her glasses on the

ground, one of the lenses had popped out. He wordlessly bent down and picked them up for her.

With Danielle on her feet and slowly tottering over, Burgess had lowered his useless weapon. The Merriweather leaders' eyes flashed and he said, "A plane fell from the sky, Noah. There is a dead girl on the ground, you are wounded, and nothing is working. Why are planes falling from the sky, Noah? What is going on?"

His boss's words came as a demand, not a question. Noah studied the man who he had reported to for years. He knew how Burgess' mind worked. *With all the chaos he's confronted with right now, this must be really hard to deal with.* Somehow, through his adrenaline and the rush of still being alive, Noah felt the familiar tickle of his Charisma stat.

He said, "It's called the Shift. I didn't cause it, I just knew it would happen, and this is why I've been doing all the weird stuff your Interpol buddies dropped me from Merriweather for. I couldn't tell anyone before, not really. If I'd told you, would you have believed me before now?"

Burgess looked at Noah as if he were crazy. In response, Noah nodded at the dead Aelve on the ground.

Surprisingly, the exchange seemed to be enough for Burgess to collect himself. The man smoothed his short, silver hair and adjusted his tie. "Fine. And what do you suggest? What now? You are an expert, yes?"

"I'm going to need you to do something. In fact," Noah said, looking at both Johnny and the Merriweather agent, "you guys technically haven't met. Johnny, meet Burgess Goodrich, my boss. Boss, meet Johnny."

"Dude," Johnny replied, a little fear in his voice. "What do we do?"

Noah shook his head. "Info first, orders second. Long story short, the Shift means no electricity. Guns don't work. Explosions don't happen. Other stuff—basically technology is dead. The Aelves' mean danger for everyone here. There are still at least two left." He didn't tell them that he'd barely killed this one, and had just gotten lucky. He assumed that his Magic Resistance stat had allowed him to survive the flame weapon the alien had used.

Burgess pointed at the inhuman corpse. "Aelves?"

"Yes. All you need to know now is they're monsters with superior everything—technology, bodies, and magic."

"Magic? You've got to be—" Goodrich began but then looked at the corpse again, took a deep breath, and said, "Okay."

"Alright," said Noah. "We don't have a lot of time left. The other two could be back any minute—"

"Can we help?" asked Johnny.

Noah said, "You are going to help by taking Danielle and getting her to safety." Johnny already had his had his arm protectively around their school's top student. "Just follow Burgess. The Aelves are cloaked, you guys can't probably even see them right now, the living ones anyway."

Noah hustled over to the dead Aelve and took the strange, mossy bag off the corpse's armor, adding the seed pod he'd grabbed out of the air to the rest in the bag. By this point, he'd realized that they were communication devices of some kind. Noah desperately hoped the other Aelves didn't have any of their own. He jogged back to Burgess and handed him the bag. "Take these, take Johnny, and Danielle, and lead them into the protected area under your office."

"That's classified."

"Not anymore, and that is the strongest area for miles, probably. I believe the bag has Aelve coms devices. Keeping these things away from the others may be critical, and more important than anything else right now."

Burgess searched Noah's eyes with his own before saying, "You know, I still don't believe you are bad, kid. I am going to trust you." His mind apparently made up, Burgess holstered his pistol and put a hand on Johnny's shoulder, reaching up to do so. "Come on, young man, let's go. I don't understand this, but let's get the young lady to safety."

Noah felt deeply grateful for the man's decisiveness.

Johnny turned, his expression unnaturally serious. He said, "Be careful, Noah."

"Always."

"Alright. Later, Brains." The big boy looked like he wanted to say something more, but stopped.

"Later, Brawns."

As the other three humans left the tree line and hurried to the Merriweather office, Noah took off the other direction, toward the residential area. More people were starting to come outside, realizing that something was deeply wrong–by instinct if nothing else. Noah remembered the feeling.

He darted between houses and hopped a fence before running across a residential road. His current course of action would put people's lives in danger, but they were already in danger. At this point, risk for everyone in the world would kind of exist on a constant, sliding scale. Still, Noah's decision now would be one of many that would probably keep him up at night for years to come.

If he survived.

He was absolutely terrified, his guts roiling even as he ran. Worm would have been long gone, running away and hiding ages ago, but Noah Henson had people to protect.

CHAPTER 25

Noah ran around to the rear of his safe house, a hidden stash of gear hiding in plain sight. He'd learned a few lessons since Burgess had cornered him in a similar building years before. After he got inside using a key that had been hidden in a tree outside, the wounded youth ran to the upstairs master bedroom. Survival gear was located downstairs in the basement, but Noah needed weapons.

After reaching his destination, he grimly nodded. The room looked like any other sparsely decorated bedroom. Furniture was covered in plastic, like whoever lived here wouldn't be back for a while. Of course, Noah knew nobody lived here. The other rooms hid weapons too, but this one had gear specifically for him.

With a grunt of effort, he punched through the drywall in a few spots. He remembered stashing gear in this wall, but not exactly where. With the help of his knife, he tore apart entire sections, making a huge mess. The picture-perfect, showroom-style bedroom had been destroyed, but now Noah had a collection of shields and swords on the floor to choose from.

Out of the shields, he grabbed a round shield made of layers of thin plywood, a thin lattice of steel, and several layers of thick leather, all laminated with modern epoxy. The center boss was fairly thick steel.

For a sword, Noah chose a short, broad falchion with a knuckle guard. The blade wasn't much longer than a machete, so he could still move easily with the weapon slung, but it had some heft to it. The nasty little chopper could deliver staggering bows.

After securing his weapons, Noah attached the falchion to a baldric and set the shield to the side, adjusting its strap so he could hang it from his back later. Then he drew the sword and used it to cut up part of the ceiling. He worked quickly, feeling every second tick away, aware that the Aelves could find their dead comrade at any moment.

Finally, he managed to cut through the ceiling enough that the whole section crashed down, revealing a number of wooden boxes that had been stored in the attic. Insulation and dust continued to rain from the ceiling, further soiling the previously immaculate room.

Noah popped open all the chests and tried to decide on a weapon, eventually strapping on a brace of three heavy throwing knives that acted as a sort of bracer, secure in thick kydex sheaths.

A Venu-designed dazzler completed his ranged weapon loadout. Working as quickly as possible, Noah tensioned all the rubber bands and loaded all three cylinders of the dazzler with wicked bolts. Half the projectiles had nasty razor heads, and the other half were long, needle-like bodkin points. Then he loaded the dazzler itself, attached one cylinder magazine to the back of his belt, and set the last to the side to hand carry.

Last, Noah threw the empty dresser to the side and pried up two sections of floor. By this point the room was almost completely full of rubble. From the hidden space in the floor, he withdrew a chainmail hauberk of his own design, Dragon Mithril. Arms up in the air, he shimmied into it. After the armor was on, he hissed, realizing he'd forgotten to take off his belt knife–now it was covered in the armor's alternating titanium and steel links.

Noah had no idea how much time had passed. He breathed heavily as he relocated the Spyderco knife from his belt to his sword baldric. The Aelves could have already found their dead comrade. Anything could be happening outside—anything at all.

He'd killed an Aelve. The youth had expected to feel more after actually fighting. Ultimately, in addition to the stress and responsibility he felt, and anxiety from preparing to fight, he felt happy and thankful to still be alive.

Finally fully kitted, dressed for war, Noah grabbed the last of the weapons he planned to take, a cloth sack with three Molotov cocktails. The glass bottles had been filled with flammable liquid and pitch, making the firebombs extra nasty. Noah always kept a ferro rod in his pocket, just in case, and today it would come in handy.

He bounded down the stairs, and stopped when he heard a loud boom outside. After a pause, Noah hurried out the door of his safe house and his heart sunk when he heard Aelves speaking in the distance. The alien voice sounded like its volume had been enhanced, like through a megaphone. He could hear them without using [Listen].

One of the voices from before was speaking, hissing in fury. "—if you do not come, we will keep killing. There is no way a human of this planet could kill an Unaleshi, and in the first fourth-cycle after a planet-wide suppression? No, you must be the one that Kahlek, the Voice, sent us to hunt. You took the sat-flowers. We have nothing to lose, so we will just keep killing your kind until you scurry out like vermin. This is your fault, human."

Then in heavily accented English, barely understandable, the voice said, "You come or more humans die." The Aelve went quiet, and Noah reasoned that the creature would try taunting him again soon to call him out.

If Noah hadn't spent his entire life preparing for this day, the situation would have been jarring, surrealistic, and terrifying. But he just felt sick; rage and fear for the people in this neighborhood moved him forward.

His regular hearing could have lead him to the Aelves, but

using [Listen], he had a much more precise idea of where they were. People in the neighborhood were milling around, some of them heading toward the noise. Noah agonized, not knowing what to do even as he hid behind some bushes. If the people saw him, armed and armored like he was, they might raise a commotion and give him away, but they also might currently be walking to their doom.

For the first time in his life, Noah truly felt what it was like to hold immediate power over people's lives with a mere decision, and he hated it. Using [Listen], he could pick up muffled crying just like he'd heard from Danielle when she'd been restrained. Noah's lips firmed into a straight line, and he resolved himself to see this through.

The Aelves, or Unaleshi as they apparently called themselves, could not be allowed to do whatever they wanted. As he crouched, hiding, Noah reasoned through why the Aelves were still even here. They seemed to have orders to find him or kill him. Maybe if they returned empty-handed they'd get in trouble. That seemed to make sense.

He'd gotten lucky. If the Aelves still had the bag with the communication devices, they might be telling their alien friends about Steelton and attacking in force instead of calling out Noah now.

Fine. If they wanted a fight, they'd get a fight. The fact that Noah absolutely had to kill the two remaining Aelves weighed him down, but at least he could be fairly sure there weren't any others. If there had been more nearby, these two would have gotten reinforcements or just used the others' communication devices.

Actually, he took that back. He couldn't be sure there were only two left, but he decided to hope. If there were more, the town was probably doomed anyway. He needed to know what he was dealing with either way.

Noah couldn't believe his terrible luck to run into Aelves right after the Shift in this lifetime. Then again, it sounded like they'd been looking for him for a long time, so maybe in a way he'd gotten lucky that he hadn't seen any until now. The thought of near-invisible killing machines running around with freaky vine knives and magic flamethrowers among his family and friends made his heart stop for a moment. His resolve strengthened, though. The terrible creatures had started the fight, but Noah was determined to end it.

Crushing uncertainty and stress ran through his body as he crept from house to house, climbing over fences and proceeding unseen. Moving quietly was not easy while weighed down with over forty pounds of armor and weapons. [Stealth Travel] and [Stalking], both at level five helped him remain undetected. [Listen] picked up more muffled distress, so at least the Aelves weren't killing people right away… at least he hoped not.

Noah savagely shook his head. This was the Shift. There was no way he could save everyone. That thought made him remember his parents, Krystal, his friends…he knew that if he failed here, everyone he cared about would be in much greater danger.

The Aelve began shouting again in the other language, and Noah carefully watched the scene around him again. People from the neighborhood talked in groups, some of them speaking quietly, hushed. A few were loud. Obviously, most of them hadn't seen any planes go down and might still think the Shift was a power outage. Some moved toward the shouting, but a number didn't. They couldn't understand the voice, and people paying attention must have noticed the dead cars in the street and other weirdness surrounding them.

There. Noah saw a flicker of motion as a mother and her son disappeared around a corner. The thundering Aelven voice was ordering, "—must come to our location and give yourself up, human! Even now, we capture your people, and we will kill more of them the longer you take to show yourself! Come to the location of my voice, give yourself up. Return what you stole, and we will minimize damage to your kind!"

Noah rolled his eyes. *Yeah, right.* Now that he knew at least one of them was camouflaged, he started watching for the telltale shimmer, continuing to carefully move in a way that wouldn't rattle his gear. He managed to cross the street without being seen, and quickly climbed a house near where the Aelves were shouting from. His [Stalking] and [Stealth Travel] skills came in handy again, as well as [Climbing] and [Quiet Exertion]. He'd acquired the last skill at age ten, when he'd been practicing guitar without actually playing, all to avoid waking his parents. The name of the skill still seemed weird.

He wasn't going to complain, though.

Once up on the roof of the house, Noah lay flat and carefully set aside the Molotov cocktails against the chimney. The roof's grey shingles were rough against his palms but gave him excellent traction. While avoiding making too many scraping noises, he gingerly eased himself forward, and peeked over the edge of the roof.

The Aelves had set up shop in a large yard. Along one fence, Noah saw about a dozen people restrained and gagged like Danielle had been. Since they were at the bottom of the fence line, he couldn't see them all that well, mainly just the bottom of their shoes. The way they moved made him believe that they were all still alive—for now, and he breathed a sigh of relief.

A big male Aelve stood on the lawn in front of a concrete patio. His armor appeared to be like the Aelve that Noah had just killed. Noah didn't see any more of them and carefully watched.

He observed the male Aelve touch something on his armor before hollering another challenge. The reason for the big banging sound earlier proved to be because of the Aelves, at least Noah assumed so. A car had rolled down a hill and crashed into a house. *So I guess they know about cars.* Noah found that thought highly disturbing. At this point, based on the conversation he'd heard before among these Aelve scouts, they had been on Earth for a while, and the car proved they'd been studying humanity.

Noah carefully watched a while longer and checked behind him. A few people from the neighborhood were still milling around, but most were not approaching his direction anymore—the curious folks must have already been captured. Most people just seemed confused, and Noah was thankful for small favors. Nobody noticed him. People rarely look up, even while stressed—a fact that Noah had learned a long time ago through his self-study on stealth skills.

Suddenly, an immobilized middle-aged man got dragged through a gate and into the yard, seemingly by nothing. Noah narrowed his eyes, and spotted the strange, oily spot in the air where he knew the Aelve had to be. His heart burned and rage coursed through his veins as the restrained human got thrown against the fence with the rest of the people from the neighborhood. The sheer arrogance of the Aelves, brazenly announcing their presence after the Shift made Noah sick.

He wondered if the monsters had acted like this in his past life. If so, the main reason their existence had been rumors, not a well-known fact, must have been because of how fractured humanity had become, or how few survivors the Aelves had left behind. Both possibilities made Noah angrier.

The high voice that Noah had heard before seemed to come from the empty air. He could hear it clearly with [Listen].

"Fentesh, here is another one. This should be plenty to kill for some time. Do we really need more?"

"No, but you do not have much else to do, so it is a good use of time. Plus, if you keep moving, you might be able to spot the human before he makes himself known."

"How is that possible?" asked the cloaked Aelve. "We do not know what the human looks like other than the drawings that the Voice distributed."

"Perhaps, but staying mobile is good since we know of an enemy. He has already killed one of us. Plus, we are only scouts, and do not have war armor. We are alone so we must remain vigilant."

"It is only a human. Reemeht must have been incredibly careless. But even with your reasoning, why don't we just leave and report?"

"As I said before and you know, if we go back now after Reemeht has been killed, we will suffer great dishonor."

"Reemeht was a fool!" hissed the hidden Aelve.

"Yes, but all Unaleshi life is precious."

"That is true, but how do you know that the human will come if you keep yelling?"

The big male said, "I do not know anything for sure, but you have been watching these humans like I have. They alternate between caring nothing for life and being obsessed with it. I believe he will come. At least we will give it another fourth-cycle.

Then if we go back with nothing, we can say we tried. We can also take the element from these humans we have collected for sustenance."

"This is logical. I accept your reasoning."

"You did before as well," said the visible Aelve, a bit of what sounded like irritation in his voice. "I lead. Follow."

The hidden Aelve's distortion in the air stayed in one spot for a moment before moving again, heading back out of the yard. From another spot in the neighborhood, Noah noticed at least a couple men with rifles beginning to wander around, confused but checking on people. If they figured out that people were missing in the direction of the foreign yelling, they might come to investigate. *Oh no*, Noah thought. The Aelves weren't killing anyone yet, but if any people attacked, they probably would. What's more, people with guns would have no idea that their weapons were useless. Time was running out.

Noah prepared to act. He waited until the Aelve in the yard started yelling again, then scraped a small pile of shavings from his ferro rod, right on the roof. Next he placed the soaked cloth of all three Molotov cocktails in the powder. He organized his other weapons and mentally nodded. Everything was ready.

His plan was probably not perfect, but time was not on his side. This was the best he had. His guts roiled in fear, and he couldn't help but think about the Aelve he'd killed. The monster had been distracted and hadn't really taken him seriously, but

Noah had still only won by the skin of his teeth.

He breathed deeply, as silently as he could, using every stealth skill he had. If anyone noticed him on the roof now, and made a ruckus, his plan would be ruined. Every human in the neighborhood might die—including Noah.

Time seemed to crawl, and stress made Noah feel cold, even in his armor. Finally, about five minutes later, he saw the distortion in the air, where the other Aelve must be. It dragged another person, actually two into the yard. This window of opportunity wouldn't be large, so Noah prepared to act.

After manhandling a helpless young man and a little girl to the fence, the hidden Aelve moved back. Noah had been hoping that the second alien would stop and talk to the other Aelve again, but he had no such luck.

The anxious, focused teen called upon several more skills, including [Ricochet], [Fire], and [Throwing]. He hoped the surrounding, ambient sounds would cover what he was about to do, and used his ferro rod to spark the pile of magnesium shavings he'd created. The little mound immediately caught fire, and lit the Molotov cocktails.

Noah immediately grabbed all three bombs, said a silent prayer, and without popping his head fully over the roof, threw each glass bottle in quick succession, arcing high into the air.

The first firebomb slammed against the patio near the house and broke, throwing flammable liquid everywhere, including against the camouflaged Aelve. Unfortunately the weapon's fire had gone out, doused by the liquid. Noah silently cursed. The visible Aelve crouched and turned, quick as a cat. He whipped his head in multiple directions and held out an arm, probably a weapon. A flicker ran through the light distortion where the hidden Aelve moved to the side and began, "There is—"

The next bottle's aim was off and hit the roof, throwing liquid and shards of glass everywhere. A portion caught fire, but only on the top of the house, not the spray that had hit the yard. Noah suddenly realized too late that he might accidentally set the captive humans on fire, and his throat tightened in terror. *Uh oh.*

Both Aelves flickered back and forth, searching for the threat as the last bottle descended. Between fear of hurting the hostages, and terror at just how fast the Aelves could move, Noah couldn't breathe.

The last Molotov cocktail hit beautifully.

After shattering against the edge of the roof, the weapon's burning cloth caught some of the liquid on fire, and the blaze on the rooftop helped, resulting in a wave of crude, burning napalm and motor oil that cascaded over the male Aelve. Some of the fire splashed against the hidden monster as well.

Both aliens screamed, and the male Aelve frantically beat at himself. As the cloaked Aelve began losing optical camouflage, Noah took the initiative, using his power to rip the concealment away. The second Aelve was female, one leg on fire, frantically throwing handfuls of dirt on herself.

Noah hoped the flames wouldn't spread too much. The captives must be beyond terrified at this point. As he grimly aimed his dazzler, he thought about the salty advice he'd gotten from some of the dangerous people he'd trained with over the years.

Never fight fair, but especially against a superior foe.

With a heart full of terror, anger, and regret, but a mind full of ice, Noah began pulling the trigger. Powerful, tensioned rubber bands launched bolt after bolt at the screeching aliens—luckily their armor seemed ill-suited against fire. Unfortunately, though, it seemed to do well against dazzler bolts.

Two of Noah's projectiles slammed into the male Aelve, but bounced off, ineffective. The Aelve must have felt the attacks even through his confusion and agony. The big, armored alien blindly held out an arm in random directions, firing balls of crackling violet energy before running into the house, trailing a comet of fire and smoke in his wake.

Noah shifted his aim. Two more bolts bounced off of the female before she realized what was happening and began spinning in circles, searching, continuing to bury the fire on her leg with dirt. *Why do they have to be smart? Why can't they be like movie villains?* Noah thought savagely. He quickly fired his remaining bolts and didn't even wait to see them hit before ducking down, reloading another magazine of seven projectiles, ready to go.

Venu had really done a great job on these weapons.

He popped up again, took aim, and fired, his first bolt hitting the Aelve scout in the shoulder. It bounced off, but the force rocked her. She suddenly turned, looking directly at Noah. He swallowed and fired again, shooting as fast as he could pull the trigger. The Aelve scout moved her head to the side, avoiding one deadly bolt, and slashed her arm forward, blocking another. Noah fired everything he had, but the Aelve stared him down as she calmly blocked or evaded the rest of his attacks, then bent down, picking up a bolt to study.

Noah felt equal fear and determination as he ducked down again, but this time, he grabbed the last dazzler magazine before sliding off the roof to run away. He had a half-formed plan, crazy and risky, but the dazzler wasn't effective. As he ran, he glanced back and gulped, spotting the Aelve where he'd just been on the roof. Her leg smoked, but was no longer on fire, and she looked furious.

As she jumped down from the roof, as easily as a mountain lion, Noah somehow turned on more speed. People from the neighborhood gaped at him, either from windows or outside where they'd been talking. He was probably quite a sight, dressed in armor, bloody, and frantically reloading a strange wooden weapon.

"Noah!" somebody called.

"Everyone get inside! It's dangerous!" Noah yelled.

Up ahead, old Ms. Abernathy goggled. "What is going on! Why are the cars stopped? Who is that back there?"

Sprinting as fast as he could, Noah noticed more residents coming out of their houses, and his heart sunk. The Aelves had probably already killed plenty of people, but Noah wanted to prevent any more loss of life. He sucked in the largest breath he could and screamed, "Terrorists! They have guns and bombs!"

All around the street, nervous, curious people vanished, and Noah allowed himself a bit of relief...until he glanced back again. The Aelve had already almost caught up—she was ridiculously fast, even with a noticeable limp. With a [Running] skill of five and top physical condition, Noah had been timed at barely below Olympic running speeds. He'd also had a one hundred yard head start, but the injured Aelve had already almost caught up. She didn't even look like she was trying her hardest.

Luckily, Noah had reached his objective, a pink kick scooter at the top of a huge hill. He had a friend in this neighborhood he'd visited, and knew that little Lucy Smith loved to ride down the hill from her yard. She usually kept the scooter outside—Noah had seen it multiple times in the past. He silently thanked the little girl who unknowingly had saved his life.

Noah slung his dazzler as he raced forward with the scooter, then kicked off down the steep hill, quickly reaching screaming fast speeds.

There would be no traffic today, and no slowing down.

A quick glance back showed the Aelve was running faster now, but Noah was slowly pulling ahead. The little pink scooter vibrated and trembled under Noah's armored weight and the breakneck speed, but somehow held together.

In the distance, at the bottom of the hill, Noah spotted his destination—a local equipment rental company.

As he raced into the yard, he felt massive relief that there were no workers around. He was sure that an employee or two was still around, but if they stayed elsewhere, they might not get hurt. Using the momentum from the hill, Noah rode the abused scooter directly into a large warehouse on the company's lot.

The moment he made it past the door, Noah ran to one side of the huge metal building, using [Parkour] and [Climb] to scale high shelves full of heavy construction equipment. He made a lot of noise while moving, his armor jangling, but managed to reach the top and lie down, hiding, before the Aelve came tearing into the warehouse. She breathed heavily as she ran to the other end of the warehouse, realized that Noah likely had not left, and doubled back. The dangerous alien scout examined the scooter, one wheel still spinning, and growled.

Noah thanked himself for all the physical conditioning he'd done. The ride down the hill, while terrifying, had actually let him catch his breath. He stayed silent as the Aelve began prowling through the warehouse below.

Noah really hoped she didn't have heat vision or something. His only hope against the Aelves seemed to be catching them off guard or being sneaky and underhanded. He could live with that.

The Aelve began muttering to herself as she stalked through the warehouse, carefully moving around equipment on pallets, and searching among the rows of tall shelves. A knife vine detached from the Aelve's armor and began poking into crevices. A couple long, grass-looking blades extended from her wrist.

Noah carefully peeked over the top of his hiding place. The Aelve glanced upwards, probably because of the earlier ambush, but thankfully didn't see him. She kept walking through the large warehouse, looking behind and under things before she must have finally lost her patience. The Aelve leveled their arm before loosing a cone of violet fire. The magical attack demolished a large jumble of welding gear, scorched the concrete, and charred a few shovels. Some of the damaged equipment fell over with a crash. Noah wondered how the flame burned without catching things on fire.

Then his heart dropped.

"Hey, what are you doing!" A grizzled man jogged into the warehouse, waving his arms. His ruddy complexion and glasses didn't jog Noah's memory at first, but [Community] told him the man's name was Greg Campbell. He'd had a beard a before. Mr. Campbell said, "Get away from there! What are you doing?"

Too late, the older man realized that the person he'd been talking to wasn't a person. The Aelve whipped her head around as her vine knife slashed forward. The rental company employee fell back with a cry, and the Aelve took two quick steps, raising her wrist blades to strike. She attacked, and Noah put his head down before he could see the rest.

Sorrow warred with his determination to exterminate the Aelves. He wasn't Worm anymore. Sitting by and watching people get hurt was unbearable, but he had a plan, so he gritted his teeth and stayed silent.

As he hid and listened, he briefly wondered why she hadn't just killed Mr. Campbell with her flame weapon, then answered his own question. They ate people, which meant they had to leave the bodies at least somewhat intact.

New disgust and hatred flared in Noah's heart.

Sounds of the alien female moving again came from below, as if she were moving to the other side of the warehouse. This was Noah's chance. He silently fished in his pockets for something to throw, and regretfully settled on the ferro rod—he didn't really have much else to toss. He breathed in and out deeply before holding his breath, and threw the ferro rod to the far side of the warehouse. Now he knew he would need to act fast.

Luckily, the plan seemed to work. As soon as the object landed and made noise, the Aelve ran to that part of building, away from Noah.

He quickly but silently stood. Then bracing himself against the roof, he pushed on the shelves beneath him with his legs and the full weight of his body. Noah had noticed this group of shelves months before when he'd come to get a propane refill. Someone had removed heavy machinery from the lower shelves, but a lot of weight remained on top. This wouldn't normally be a problem…unless a determined, armored teen were to climb to the top and try pushing it all over.

After a few seconds of straining, the shelves creaked and began to tip. Noah kept pushing until the very last second, jumping backward to another group of shelving.

As he watched, the heavy structure of wood, steel, and machinery he'd set in motion fell, slamming into the next set of shelves, creating a domino effect. Noah suddenly caught sight of the Aelve female, and they locked eyes at the same time. She snarled, showing her teeth, but it was too late.

Thousands of pounds of shelving and equipment slammed down, generating a messy, dusty, hammer of destruction. Noah quickly used a number of mundane skills, including [Wall Climbing] to shimmy over and jump to another shelving unit. The one he'd just been on wobbled after getting hit with a cement mixer.

Noah lay down as the rubble continued to crash beneath him and stayed that way for a while even after it settled. [Listen] picked up voices of other workers at the rental yard. They hadn't gone home yet. They were probably waiting for the power to come back on. People didn't know about the Shift yet.

They would soon.

Noah was exhausted, but at least he was still alive. *Two Aelves down, one to go,* he thought.

Then he heard screaming in the distance, back in the direction of the houses he'd just come from.

Oh no.

CHAPTER 26

Noah ran. A couple men jogged towards him, pointing at the warehouse, but he ignored them, not even registering what they said.

People in the neighborhood were screaming.

He drew the dazzler from where it'd been hanging off his shoulder to run faster, and began ascending the hill he'd ridden down earlier on the pink scooter. Worry tied his guts into knots, and time kept moving—Noah could practically feel the seconds passing. Rushing up such a steep hill while weighed down with weapons and armor wasn't the easiest thing Noah had ever done, but compared to the guilt, stress, and underlying terror he felt, it was nothing.

The Shift had been the worst day of his life. His second Shift seemed to be living up to its legacy.

At the top of the hill, Noah didn't need to go far to see bodies.

His throat went dry. Lungs working like bellows, sweat rolled down his back and he wasn't sure where to go. Despite smoldering rage for the Aelves driving him forward, Noah wanted to cry. Sorrow made him tremble, not just for the people in this community who had been cut down, but for the millions, maybe billions of people all around the world who would die in the next few months.

It was horrible, all of it. And it was all because of the Aelves! Noah snarled, and ran toward a new scream.

He found the last Aelve, the big male, two streets over. As Noah closed the distance, a man from the neighborhood pointed a rifle at the burned, smoking Aelve. The bearded man's ballcap had a salmon on it, his rifle clicked again and again while the man worked the slide. With an air of finality, the Aelve pointed an arm and tensed. When he'd been on fire before, the monster had quickly shot several balls of violet energy, but this time, seemed to be struggling to create one. The Aelve's armor must have been badly damaged.

Noah knew what was still about to happen. "No!" he screamed, and fired two dazzler bolts, but they had no effect. He'd been too late. A burst of energy from the Aelve's weapon took the man high in the chest and he fell backwards. Noah loosed every remaining dazzler bolt he had.

The Aelve turned, but didn't otherwise move. He just looked away, and all of Noah's projectiles bounced off the charred, leafy armor on his body and the sides of his head. Noah threw the empty dazzler to the side, drew his sword and donned his shield before crashing into the Aelve...or tried to.

A damaged vine knife whipped out, diverting Noah's rush. The sharp head of the Aelve's weapon had been damaged, and instead of cutting into his shield, it just left a nasty gouge. Noah barely heard all the new screaming around him. The neighborhood's residents were obviously all terrified at this point, probably trying to dial the police over and over again on phones that wouldn't work. Their fear helped Noah deal with his own, and he spun, slashing with his falchion.

The Aelve danced back, or tried to. His legs had been too badly damaged, and he narrowed his eyes, blocking the attack with an armored arm. This close, Noah saw the extent of the Aelve's injuries and took sick satisfaction from it. Part of the alien's face had run like wax, and only one eye seemed to still be working. Some of his lips were gone.

Parts of his body had been more severely burned than others. The Aelve's other vine knife must have not worked anymore, if he'd even had another. His armor had saved his life, but had been badly burned itself. The creature was slower now, its body ravaged, but it was still faster than Noah.

With a low hiss, grass knives like the female Aelve's extended from the alien's wrist. The monster punched, and it was all Noah could do to divert the blow. Luckily, his shield held, but even with the glancing attack, and blocked at an angle, it felt like he'd been hit by a truck.

Noah retaliated, delivered a succession of lightning-fast cuts that would have made any of his trainers proud, but the Aelve blocked or evaded all of them with almost contemptuous ease. The monster grabbed Noah's shield with his other hand, fingers badly burned but still strong. He yanked down so hard, Noah's arm was almost wrenched out of its socket. Suddenly, new pain flashed, and Noah woodenly realized that the vine knife had slammed into his shield shoulder.

Luckily, his chainmail held against the damaged weapon, but the force of the blow knocked him back like he'd been hit by a sledgehammer and the entire side of his body lit up, nerves protesting.

Armed and armored like he was, Noah would be like a walking tank against normal people, a wrecking ball of destruction. Even against several men armed with knives or machetes, he would have been untouched. However, the wounded, burned, half-dead Aelve was picking him apart in seconds.

Noah gritted his teeth and chopped at the arm holding his shield. The attack must have done something through the charred, organic armor, because the Aelve winced and let go. His flat, remaining grey eye narrowed. In his alien language, the big male said, "I assume you killed Dirak somehow. That means along with Reemeht you have ended two Unaleshi. The Voice was right to warn us of you, and to hunt you. The Voice's word is law, and reward for killing you would be leaves and seeds from the garden, but even without that, I now see you are far too dangerous to live. It will be an honor and a service to end you. How did you get an orb?"

Noah was exhausted, but he stood tall. Some of the people from the surrounding houses scurried away, escaping. He needed to buy time for them.

So far, he had heard and somehow understood the Aelve's language. If his orb could do that, maybe he could turn it around, too. He opened his mouth and tried to let his thoughts form into the alien language. To his surprise, his throat uttered guttural noises and whistles, saying, "The Voice? You speak of Kahlek?"

At first, the Aelve obviously didn't know how to react. Noah breathed hard. He drew in another breath and said, "Your name is Fentesh, right? You aren't very intelligent, are you?"

Fentesh's disbelief shifted to confusion and then anger. His hand produced what looked like a seed, and it disappeared into his armor. Spikes formed on one shoulder. The alien snarled, "You have no right to speak our language, let alone the Voice's name. He has lifted the Blue Mountains to be of equal footing with the Silver Clouds. What do you, a barbaric primitive, know of Kahlek?"

Noah's mind raced, thinking of everything he could remember about his first encounter with the Aelves in his past life. When they had come to Doc's cabin, Kahlek had worn different colored leaves than the others in the group. They had cast disdainful looks at him. Noah coughed and croaked, "Kahlek told you to look for me, huh? From what I remember last time we met, he didn't seem to have much respect from the others."

The leaves on Fentesh's armor rustled, at least the ones that were not too burned to move, and the grass knives on his wrist grew. Noah eyed the blades warily. The Aelve said, "Enough talk. You are not worthy of speaking to, and your tongue spews lies!"

Noah barely got his shield up in time, and his injured shoulder screamed in agony. Grass blades punched clean through his shield. The blow had been solid and effective. The force of Fentesh's attack pushed Noah back, and his shield too. Just the tips of the Aelve's blade punctured Noah's arm, digging through the links of his armor, and he yelled in pain.

He called upon his mother's lullaby with added percussion and tempo, his war song. The heavy melody ran through his body, giving him a burst of energy. Noah had hoped not to use the song again for combat. He had a feeling there was a price to pay for the burst of power it provided.

With a kick, Noah created some distance. [Combat: Shield], and [Combat: Short Sword], both level five helped guide his body. The Aelve grunted trying to pull his blades out, but Noah tilted to shield to side to trap them and put his enemy off balance. He whipped a couple wrap cuts to the side of his enemy's body, and a chop at his opponent's face, but the inhuman monster was just too strong, too fast. An armored forearm caught all three attacks, but the last one had almost slipped through.

Roaring, Noah barely parried the injured Aelve's vine knife as it shot for his face. The blade of his falchion scraped against the chitin with a sound like a fork dragging across a seashell.

Suddenly, the Aelve reached up and grabbed at Noah's sword, but the youth managed to disengage and back away before losing the weapon. After retreating two more steps, Noah stared the Aelve down. The alien's elbow dripped—he was bleeding. Noah couldn't tell if he'd actually scored a hit on Fentesh or if the big scout had just opened a burn-related wound.

The Aelve hadn't used his ranged weapon yet, and Noah wasn't sure why. It was possible he was trying to conserve ammo, or had reasoned that Noah had somehow resisted the flame attacks of the other Aelves. It could just be a pride thing too. Noah wasn't going to complain. The blades and damaged vine blade had been enough to almost kill him several times already.

At that moment, Noah knew that he was probably going to die. As Worm, he could have just given up, run away, but Noah couldn't abandon other people to a creature like this. He'd fought hard, though, and had somehow killed two of them. He'd done his best to prepare humanity for the Shift and had even gone toe to toe with the Aelves without insta-dying.

But a deeper part of him refused to die a martyr. *I'm no*

warrior, he admitted. *But I'm a fighter. If this is how I die, I'm gonna take this monster down with me.*

The thought gave him power. *That's right. I'm not a warrior, I'm a bard! But seriously, it'd be nice to be a warrior right now.* His mundane skills were useless against the Aelves' superior abilities and weapons. All Noah had had to give him an edge were his core [Listener] skills.

[Jack of All] had created all of his mundane skills, but not only was the Aelve just too powerful, Noah was more tired than he'd ever been in his life. He thought of his other core skills. Even if he had his guitar, [Harmony] wouldn't have done him any good in this situation. Maybe [Stumble] would activate to help him avoid an attack, but the chance for the passive skill triggering was too low to count on.

But suddenly, [Listen] picked up a familiar set of stalking footsteps from behind. Noah felt a glimmer of hope, and knew he needed to stall for just a little more time. Vine knife poised to strike, and bladed arm held forward, the Aelve looked prepared to close again but seemed to be studying him. Noah chuckled and said in the Aelve language, "It must be embarrassing that I am still alive, right? I mean, I know that if this was a fair fight, I'd already be dead. But luckily it's not, and it wasn't for your two friends either."

The alien's bladed arm twitched.

Noah continued, "You have been looking for me for a long

time, right? Well, here I am! What are you going to do about it?" Charisma gave Noah a nudge, and he went with the flow, saying, "Your people, you called them the Unaleshi? The Unaleshi are weak."

"We are weak?" hissed Fentesh, dangerously quiet.

With a crash of a door slamming open, Noah noticed a girl burst from a house out the corner of his eye. He recognized her. Her name was Miscy Torres, a Junior at Washington High School, and she must have been born with the worst timing in the world.

"It causes you distress when I kill others of your kind, yes? You believe the Unaleshi are weak? Know despair before you die, Human."

The Aelve held up his arm with the ranged weapon and pointed it at the distant girl. The organic armor moved slightly and Noah launched two throwing knives in quick succession, but the Aelve barely even noticed, knocking them both out of the air with his grass knives.

Finally, [Listen] let Noah know it was time. In English, he yelled, "Aim for the face!"

Johnny Dormund's giant shadow stepped around the corner of a house, levelling his favorite deer hunting crossbow he kept in the lockbox of his truck. The sleek, modern weapon clicked before it thrummed, the sounds echoing through the street. Fentesh, the Aelven scout, never knew what hit him. His head slammed to the side, Johnny's expertly aimed bolt sticking out of his forehead.

The world seemed to slow as the alien whirled, his weapon arm extended, swinging in Noah's direction.

Stumble has activated

Noah found himself flat on his back, his ringing head resting on the road. Behind him, on the other side of the street, the towering figure of his best friend stood very still. Light from the setting sun poured over Johnny's back, framing him in a golden halo. Blood ran down his boots.

No, Noah thought, confusion turning to horror.

He replayed the last few seconds in his mind. The violet projectile that would have hit Noah had hit Johnny instead. With a rasping whimper, Noah shakily stood and ran to his friend's body. He knelt, holding Johnny's head in his lap. The wound was mortal, especially now with no ambulances and modern hospitals. Johnny's letterman jacket was already soaked in blood.

The big, gentle boy looked confused until he saw Noah's face. "Hey, buddy," he said weakly. He spoke as if it was Noah who needed comforting.

Tears fell from Noah's chin, landing on his friend's face. He said, "You were supposed to stay with Danielle."

Johnny looked at Noah as if he had just said the silliest thing in the world. "I knew you would need help. Also, I still feel bad about not believing you before. You know, about everything."

"Johnny—"

The big boy shook his head slightly. "Noah. Everyone said you were special. But...that's gotta be lonely, right? Even now, doing everything alone to help everyone. Just promise me something, man."

"Anything."

"Don't do everything solo. I hate seeing you push yourself away from everyone. Please. I know you really well, and you need people as much as they need you."

Noah wanted to say something, but the words caught in his throat. He had seen death before, and prepared his entire life for the Shift. He'd known that people would die, but not Johnny. Not like this. His friend's massive hand gripped Noah's, and he said, "Promise me, Noah. Whatever you do, do it with others."

"I promise. I will."

"You better. Thanks for everything–like, for being my friend when I was just a fat kid into video games. You were the best friend I could have asked for. I always wondered why you spent time with me, figured you would stop, but you never did, and now we are eighteen. Can I tell you a secret?"

Noah's lip trembled. "Sure."

"You always seemed lonely, and I know you're an only child. Sometimes I thought of myself like your brother. Kinda weird, huh?" He sighed, his breath rattling, then weakly said, "Anyway, I'm getting tired. Time to sleep. Later, Brains." Johnny closed his eyes and smiled.

The gamer-turned-athlete let out his last breath, and he was gone.

Noah's hand tightened around the big, honest boy's wrist. "Later, Brawns." He lowered his aching body forward and rested his forehead on Johnny's shoulder. "You were the best friend I could have had too."

CHAPTER 27

It took a while for Noah to regain control after the first wave of grief. He must have fallen asleep at some point, because he woke up with a handful of people standing protectively around him holding machetes and shovels. Burgess had been working with a group of other men, ignoring shouted questions, holding back a crowd from the body of the dead Aelve.

The next hour or so was a blur, but Noah vaguely registered Burgess calming down frightened people and organizing the removal of the Aelve body...and of Johnny's.

Respectful hands helped Noah up and he let himself be led to some shade. His armor clanked and he maintained a death grip on his weapon, but nobody said anything about it. If anything, some of the looks he was getting, at least the ones he noticed, made him a little uncomfortable even through his sorrow.

He sat, letting his mind go blank and letting time past. Finally,

Noah got ahold of himself, burying his sorrow for the time being. There would be a price to pay later, but he could think again. If this had been his first life, he probably wouldn't have been much good to anyone the rest of the day…but unfortunately he wasn't new to this sort of thing. The first Shift had been the worst day of his life before, but now he definitely had a new one. *Wonderful.*

After a long, shaking breath, he squeezed his swollen eyes shut tightly, and stood in an explosive rush. A little girl eeped and ran back to her mother. The people standing around Noah with garden tools continued to face outward, but their expressions flickered. [Listen] picked up one of the men mutter, "Tough kid."

Noah's body hurt—bad—but he could recover later. This was still the day of the Shift, and he had a job to do.

He marched over to Burgess. The older man was talking to some young kids on bikes, handing them handwritten notes and giving directions. Noah nodded in appreciation—the Interpol agent was smart and resourceful, and the Shift hadn't changed that.

"Burgess, is the bag safe?"

The agent's eyes flicked up and he gave an approving look. "Yes. Danielle is safe too, and the bag has been secured deep in the location you mentioned before." The stocky, silver-haired man raised an eyebrow at the sword in Noah's hand. "Are you going to keep walking around with the pig sticker in your hand?"

"Ah," said Noah and sheathed his sword. "Come with me. We

need to go."

Burgess raised both eyebrows, but then glanced around at the people taking control of the neighborhood, probably telling other people whatever Burgess had told them. Noah didn't have time to find out—there were only a few more hours of daylight–if that–and he had places to be. Finally, Burgess said, "Okay."

Noah led the older man to his safe house in the neighborhood. He'd noticed that Burgess had picked up a cheap machete from somewhere, but shook his head. That wouldn't do. The cache didn't have any armor that would fit the agent, but after arriving, he gave his old boss a dagger to hang off his belt, and a short, broad-bladed spear with a kydex sheath to sling over his back. The small, deadly spear was probably one of the most effective melee weapons that an untrained person could easily carry.

After that, Noah fetched a couple bicycles from the basement. As he left the house, he noticed that curious people from the neighborhood had followed them, and Noah figured there wasn't anything he could do about it. Burgess obviously thought otherwise, because he called over a man armed with a hoe. "Tony," he said. "Make sure nobody gets into that house, please."

"Is it dangerous, Mr. Goodrich?"

"Something like that. Tell anyone who asks that it's a matter of national security."

Noah made a face but kept his mouth shut. Time was critical. Next thing he knew, he and Burgess were riding down the street.

Noah had recovered his two other throwing knives before leaving, and was armed with his falchion and damaged shield. His wounds had stopped bleeding at some point, but they all felt like they could open at any time. He knew he probably looked horrible. Noah told the spear-carrying Interpol agent where he was heading.

"Lucy's Diner?" Burgess said. His voice still held a note of underlying dismay about the situation, but he had asked the question in a business-like manner. Noah's relationship with his former boss had changed, their roles somewhat reversed now.

Noah said, "Yeah. I know that at least one Merriweather agent is only one town over, right? If you can reach any of your people, tell them to rally in Steelton, we can fill them in later—the more people to help in the next few weeks, the better. Meanwhile, I have my own people, and the next few hours are important. Steelton will collapse into chaos really fast if we don't hurry. Communication will be terrible, so the bigger head start we have, the more chance will be able to build instead of rebuild."

Burgess studied Noah as the wheels of their bikes whirred. "I think one of the most surreal things about all of this is how you are acting now."

"What do you mean?"

"You are so serious, focused. Then there's how you fought those—things. It's like you're a different person."

"I've prepared my whole life for this," Noah said with a shrug.

They reached a four-way stop and Noah halted. He nodded east. "You're probably that way. I'm this way. Your people, Merriweathers, are a priority, but any more law enforcement or other emergency services people you can get, the better. Civil engineers and community leaders will be good, too. Bring them all here for a full briefing. I'll arm the ones that people can vouch for. Don't go too crazy, because time is not our friend right now, but even folks from only one or two other towns will be helpful."

Burgess adjusted his tie and turned to ride away, but stopped. He said, "I'm trusting you."

Noah didn't reply. There was nothing more to say. Then the older agent rode away on his mountain bike, dressed in a suit and carrying a spear. The scene would have looked comical if not for Burgess' no-nonsense demeanor, and the obvious lethality of the weapon on his back.

With one last glance at his former boss' vanishing back, Noah took off down the street toward his house. He'd always imagined that when the Shift finally came, he'd be working feverishly to ensure that all his careful plans were executed perfectly. However, since everything had happened early, many of his more complicated ideas were no longer possible. Thank goodness for his contingency planning, but right now, the only thing he could personally influence was what would happen in Steelton.

My town will be the beginning, he reminded himself.

He didn't see many people on the roads outside of town, and

eventually arrived in front of his house. A handful of people from the neighborhood stood on his front lawn, surrounding a group of twenty Log Cabin Security guards, all armed. The guards had pistol crossbows slung over a shoulder, riot shields, and clubs. Noah breathed a sigh of relief upon spotting them. He'd had disaster instructions in the company guidebook and in each Log Cabin location's individual orders.

During a power outage, there was a device at each Log Cabin site that Noah had cooked up, a simple device that only worked with great pressure. If the device didn't work, instructions had several other things for guards to check before instructing them to open a special box containing instructions for the Shift, and a few simple Shift-effective weapons. Not every Log Cabin guard on duty could be expected to follow the instructions, but these Steelton guards had performed perfectly.

Of course, they didn't know much more about the Shift than Noah's neighbors did at the moment, so they were mostly just saying comforting things. Uniforms usually meant authority to most people, so it seemed to be working.

As Noah approached, he heard rampant speculation, theories ranging from terrorist attacks to the possibility of a nearby power plant breaking down. Noah began pushing through the crowd of panicked people before one of them actually saw him and gasped. This was when Noah remembered he was beat up, battle-scarred, and covered in blood. Most of the surrounding people recognized him, trying to get his attention, demanding to know what was going on. Noah responded politely, telling them all to head to Lucy's Diner, but kept moving.

When he got through the crowd, one of the security guards saluted and opened the door for him. Part of the disaster instructions for Log Cabin personnel had been a reveal of who actually owned the company, and would be calling the shots from now on.

Noah's neighbors shouted, confused, trying to push past the guards. He shook his head as he closed the door behind him— their frightened, panicked voices carried right through the wood. Time was crucial, and making sure his parents were safe was important. The neighbors could learn about the Shift with everyone else.

In the hallway stood two guards, armed like ones outside had been. Both were Log Cabin officers, and one was the newly promoted Jamal. The tall black man glanced at Noah and his jaw firmed, like he understood something better now. Both guards snapped salutes.

Past them, Clark and Lana sat at the dining room table where their family had shared countless Chinese take-outs together. Noah had gone out of his way to make good memories with his parents at this very table, but that was all in the past now. It was time to move forward or die. His parents were about to experience a side of him that they'd never seen before, and his heart sagged a little at the realization.

Lana looked up as Noah entered before leaping from her chair, knocking it back to the tile floor. She rushed over, holding her arms out, but stopped short, gaping at his appearance. "What happened?" she whispered. Behind her, Clark stood slowly, holding a newspaper in his hand like a lifeline.

"We don't have time, Mom," said Noah and sadly shook his head. He held out a hand covered in dried blood, letting his mother approach him slowly, like a frightened rabbit.

"What is going on?" Lana repeated, slowly hugging Noah like he might break. "You have armor, and you are covered in blood," she stated the obvious.

Noah looked at his father, who seemed to be holding himself together fairly well except for the way he kept wetting his lips. Clark sighed and asked, "Is this what you've been hiding from us?"

Lana stepped back, joining her husband side-by-side, clutching her cardigan. Clark wrapped a steady arm around his wife, holding her tight. Noah said, "I'll explain more later. The gist of it is, this is the end of the world as we knew it. I knew it was coming, but not this early."

"Noah–" his mom whispered. Clark squeezed her closer, and she stopped talking.

Grateful for the chance to continue, Noah said, "No details right now. I need to do something now or else this whole town will be more likely to fall apart. I've worked really hard, but a lot of people are still going to die in the next few months. I've been preparing my whole life for this in ways you can't imagine."

"Like the millions of dollars you've been spending on the side," Clark stated as a fact. "You can't hide moving that much money from me." His wife gave him a confused look. Noah was startled too, shocked by the revelation that at least one of his parents had been aware of some of what he'd been doing.

"Billions of dollars, actually," Noah responded, businesslike. He had practiced this speech a thousand times. *I need to stick to the truth, but telling them about my reincarnation will just be too much for anyone to handle right now. Maybe I'll tell them in the future...but probably not.*

Lana slowly nodded. " I know there were more companies than we were told about."

"Yes," said Noah. "But all my business efforts were just to raise money for this moment. Everything I've done has been to protect the community and the two of you, preparing for this day. I'm sorry I couldn't tell you anything before, but you wouldn't have believed me, and would not have understood."

He paused and ran a soiled hand through his dirty hair. "I'm going downtown to Lucy's now. Don't worry, I'm ready for this, but I need you to do something for me."

Lana shook her head in disbelief. "You're hurt! You need to go to the hospital! Why are you—Why are these people following you? Are you going to do something dangerous? Are you into crime? I knew we shouldn't have let you go flying all around, doing who knows what!" Lana's voice had started to climb.

Clark adjusted his arm and held his wife's hand. Noah's father said, "No, look at him, Lana. He's not a boy anymore, not that he ever really was." The accountant shook his head and looked Noah in the eyes. "What do you need, son?"

"Thanks, Dad." Noah stepped forward and laid a hand on his mother's shoulder. "Mom, I promise I will do my best to stay safe, and I also promise I will explain what is going on soon. Please, trust me. Have I ever let you down before?"

Lana began to silently cry, but she shook her head. "No. You've always been a good kid, and you've always worked hard."

"Then trust me."

Noah's mother sucked in ragged breath. "We already let these people in here because they said you told them to come, and Jamal was with them." She seemed to be thinking out loud. "Are you really helping people? Are you trying to do good?"

"Yes," Noah answered honestly.

"Okay. Fine. But you owe us a full explanation as soon as possible."

Noah nodded solemnly. "That's fair." He turned to his father and said, "Dad, some Log Cabin guards, good people, are going to take you to a safe location, at least for the time being. I really need to know that you are safe. But on the way there, I need to you help me by telling as many people as you can to head to Lucy's Diner."

***

Noah arrived in downtown Steelton, a group of Log Cabin Security guards at his back. Most of the townspeople were too preoccupied, too worried to even notice the arrival of his group yet. A crowd had begun to gather in the distance, farther up the street, but plenty of people were aimlessly walking the sidewalks. If the Shift just been a power outage, people would still just be waiting it out, but everything was dead. The streets were full of stalled cars, and some kids talked excitedly about the planes they'd witnessed going down. Luckily, Noah didn't think any planes had actually fallen on Steelton itself. However, he could still see new garbage in the streets, people packing, and other signs of unrest.

Things hadn't gotten anywhere near as bad as they could, but order had obviously already begun to break down. It had been hours since the Shift, but the town's general civility was keeping most people from acting on their fears or uncertainties.

Most people.

Noah heard a crash, the distinctive sound of breaking glass and hurried forward. A couple men had broken the storefront of a closed sporting goods store and were busy filling bags with sporting gear. A few people from the street shouted and pointed, but none of them intervened. "Someone get the police!" shouted a woman. [Community] confirmed her name to be Sally Vernon. She owned the hair salon one block over.

Noah doubted any police would come. After the Shift, law enforcement had cars and guns that wouldn't work anymore. Anger about the Shift, the Aelves, his crying mother, it all exploded in Noah. The time for hiding was over. He'd worked too hard over too many years for selfish people to try ruining everything.

The two thieves were clever to have figured out the implications of the Shift so fast, but also foolish to have acted so quickly in front of others. "Hey, stop!" Noah ordered.

"Get lost, kid." Neither man even really turned to look. [Community] reminded Noah that they were Michael and Raymond Carver, brothers and town ne'er-do-wells that Noah only knew from the newspapers, rumors, and police reports.

Noah grabbed Raymond, the older brother by the arm. "Stop. Go to Lucy's Diner," he commanded.

He'd been expecting some more resistance, but when Raymond suddenly turned, swinging a machete, Noah was genuinely surprised. The man noticed Noah's appearance and his eyes widened even as the weapon hit Noah's shoulder with a dull whack.

The blow hurt a little, even through the quality chainmail. The attack felt like getting punched, not the cut it otherwise would have been. Noah's eyes narrowed. If he'd been a normal person, not armored, the blow probably would have been lethal. The man had obviously intended serious harm at the least. *So be it.*

The time for hiding was over.

Noah didn't even draw his sword, just punched out with the edge of his shield, catching the man in the throat. As Raymond staggered back, he tried chopping again with his machete, panicking. Noah expertly slammed the full weight of his shield into his opponent's elbow with a crunch. The scruffy man gasped a scream as Noah let his shield fall, delivering a savage chop to the side of the man's knee. As the would-be murderer fell to the sidewalk, Noah raised his shield for a killing blow, but slowly lowered his arm.

No. Not yet.

The downed man, despite his injuries, kept flailing with his machete until Noah caught the man's wrist and broke it, relieving him of his weapon. Surrounding people had begun screaming and yelling, but Noah ignored them.

The other Carver brother, Michael, stepped out of the store and gaped. Like his older brother, he wore a dirty flannel and a pair of holey jeans. He took one look at the bloody, armored, very angry Noah and ran away. From the other direction, Greg Stanton, one of Steelton's police offers rounded a corner, heading toward the commotion.

"Arrest that man!" shouted Noah, pointing.

"What? Noah?" The cop mimed a hand around his ear, and Michael Carver breezed past, sprinting for all he was worth.

Noah sighed. The officer jogged up the rest of the way and

looked Noah up and down. He glanced at Raymond on the ground and raising his eyes at the approaching Log Cabin Security guards. "You wanna explain all this?"

"Not really. I don't have time, either."

The cop glanced around at all the yelling, pointing people. A crowd had started to form. "Normally, I'd be arresting both of you and trying to make sense of everything, but this is just going to be one of those days, isn't it?"

The man's unflappable calm made Noah's lip twitch–even through his irritation–but he kept his face expressionless. "'Fraid so."

"Did you kill him?" The cop gestured down.

"I think he'll live. He might not be happy, though."

Officer Stanton spat to the side. "You really should come with me, Noah."

"I'm afraid not, Officer. In fact, I need you to do something for me."

The cop blinked. "Say what now?"

"You heard me. I'm really sorry that I can't explain right now, but I promise you'll understand soon. I know what is happening right now, and I want to help everyone."

"It's not a power outage?"

"Nope"

"I was afraid so. Okay, I'm listening."

Noah nodded. "Okay. Please help round up everyone and send

them to Lucy's Diner, everyone you can find. If you see any other officers, please ask them to do the same thing and eventually join everyone there."

"You sure about this? You know if you're pulling my chain, you're going to be in a lot of trouble, right?"

Noah sadly shook his head. "Officer, we're all already in a lot of trouble."

***

The area around Lucy's was packed, full of people shoulder to shoulder.

A Log Cabin guard stepped away from a ladder he'd just leaned against the wall of the Diner. The guards all knew about the Shift now. Noah had given them a quick class and instruction to help him with the townspeople. The guards, all being well-trained professionals, had been performing admirably.

It had taken all the guards and a half-dozen uniformed cops to quiet down the crowd, turning their frightened shouts to quiet murmurs. [Listen] picked up their words. *Right now, they're scared and a little panicked. I don't blame them,* thought Noah.

Most of the surrounding people stared at him. He wasn't trying to hide his battered, bruised, bloody appearance. A few boxes sat at his feet where he'd placed them visiting a nearby apartment, yet another of his safe houses.

His armor clinked as he moved up the ladder, a cone in his left hand to help amplify his voice. Noah had consistently made an effort with his Charisma and [Community] for nearly everyone in Steelton to know who he was. Today was the day that effort was going to pay off…or so he hoped.

At the top of the ladder, he gingerly climbed to the roof of the diner. It had been a long, horrible day, and even walking was beginning to feel like torture. The wounds in his arm had opened again and blood ran down his arm to this wrist.

Standing on top of the building, he could see the familiar faces of everyone he had grown up with. Lucy Perkins held her daughter Danielle protectively. Venu and his wife. Jamal Hendricks. Krystal and her family.

Johnny was notably absent.

Noah swallowed a fresh, savage avalanche of grief, letting the focus he had built over the years take over.

At his feet lay an acoustic six-string guitar that a Log Cabin guard had placed for him as per his instructions. If the next ten minutes went well, he'd need it.

Noah didn't ask everyone to quiet, he waited for the crowd to hush. Charisma had told him it was better this way.

All my life, I've been prepared for this. Noah thought. *Before I was reborn, I had no strength to speak out. Yet now, here I am speaking to my entire town.* He remembered Doc, and imagined his friend giving him a proud smile.

Yusef came to mind, too. Noah still had never successfully located him in this life, but he was sure that the kind man was still alive. He'd hopefully live more than another two years, not die at the hands of a scared, lost, pathetic young man who'd be named Worm.

I've come so far, Noah realized. Now it was time to put all of his lessons, his entire journey to the test.

He put the cone to his mouth and spoke loudly, confidently. "Most of you already know who I am. My name is Noah Henson. I know you have questions."

"You bet we do!" said one man, but his wife elbowed him the ribs, shushing him.

Noah could feel his Charisma at work, helping him control his tempo, his breathing, hinting when and how he should speak. He let his words flow. "I have answers for you, but please, just wait a second."

He nodded to Jamal who gave a signal to the Log Cabin guards and a number of emergency response personnel. All of them held stacks of paper, bound neatly together, taken from the boxes that Noah had fetched. The front page of each pamphlet was titled, "The Shift: A Guide to Our New World". The confused townspeople took them hesitantly and began rifling through.

Noah explained, "These are pamphlets for common questions you will have. For example, if you want to know why no electronics work and guns won't fire bullets, turn to page six. I'll give you a hint, though—nobody really knows and we just have to learn to live with it.

"Page eight will explain how to deal with garbage from now on. Page eleven will explain what I will be doing soon to try keeping the water running. Of course, the second page is everything I hope you all do to be good neighbors, like conserving water so we can postpone a crisis. The faster you use city water right now, the faster it is going to run out. Please use the instructions on page eight to flush your toilets, and do not use your home's running water for that.

"The entire pamphlet has infographic and notes that will guide you along."

The crowd stared at the paper in their hands, stunned by the words and pictures inside. Whenever someone raised their voice to ask a question, one of the Noah's security detail helpfully gave them a page to turn to which held the appropriate answer.

Noah let time pass without saying anything, allowing the people to process everything he'd just said. A lot of them would be in shock. He wanted them to move forward on their own. This was important–he couldn't, wouldn't be their savior. Steelton needed to be a shining example of hope, a unified humanity during the Shift. The people needed to work together, with or without him.

Noah's sight landed on Krystal. Her expression was much more complex than most others, confused, yes, but also shocked, sad, and maybe even a little awed. Noah looked away, unable to think about what was possibly going through her head. He pulled up the cone again and spoke, "Now that you have answers, this next step is crucial. If you could all please flip to page fourteen."

Rustles filled the entire area as paper turned.

Noah continued, "You will see a map of Steelton with several stars. These are aid locations where you can request supplies for survival. Page fifteen has a list of available resources like water purifiers, salt, and other items. Requisition officers will keep a list of Steelton residents, and we will be tracking everything closely. Over the next few days, town officials will also be moving resources from other places like businesses to centralized locations for safekeeping."

And weapons, he thought, keeping it to himself. *It's best that we focus on working as a town first, and then we can prepare for militarization and weapons training.*

"You mean you are going to steal all my stuff?" shouted James Red, a store owner.

"No," said Noah, shaking his head. "I believe in the goodness and community of Steelton. All donations by business owners and individuals will be voluntary."

Lucy Perkins, the owner of the diner, shouted, "What the heck is all of this for?"

Noah sighed. Of course Lucy hadn't even tried to read the pamphlet.

He said loudly, "It is important that we, the people of Steelton, work together to build a fort. Before you ask me what a fort is and why we are building it, feel free to turn to page twenty-one. You all need to remember that everything happening isn't just here, but all around the world." This was the part where he needed to tell a white lie. "I have suspected for a while now that this might happen, the Shift, and I tried to tell people in charge, but nobody would listen. But I did what I could, and now we need to work together to prepare for the terrible things to come."

Someone else shouted the question he had been waiting for since he began speaking. "Why you? Why do we have to listen to a kid like you? You are covered in blood!"

A tattooed man yelled, "Yeah! This is crazy! Why should we believe any of this?"

Noah gave a grave nod. "Great question. Turn to page twenty. But I'll tell you now that I received information in the past and acted on it. For proof, examine any electronics you like. Test the facts listed in the pamphlet or do your own experiments, don't just take my word for it.

"Your pamphlets will list every other possibility for the changes you are experiencing, and also explain why the Shift is unique. Different from an Electromagnetic Pulse, or EMP, firearms will no longer function properly."

The crowd muttered. People processed what had just been said, and some people murmured to others that it was true.

Noah held up a hand. "In another week or two if all is going well, there will be new pamphlets distributed for phase two. However..."

He paused for effect, fueled by the tingles of Charisma flowing through him. The crowd's growing murmurs stopped. "I am not your leader. I just have some answers and resources. Steelton already has a great leader."

This was a part of his plan he had not originally prepared for. Over the years, several unexpected things had occurred in Noah's life, for better and for worse—Camp Firestarter, the Merriweather Division, Anonymoose, and other things around town that he had influenced. One of those things, a simple seed that he'd planted had borne considerable fruit.

It had also made his mother feel proud and accomplished, which had been worth it by itself.

Noah pointed toward Krystal, and then a little bit to her left at her mother. He shouted through the cone, "People of Steelton, a leader we already have and can trust is Eileen Connolly, your mayor! She helped shine a light on all the past corruption in this town. Since she took over, Steelton has flourished, both its economy and community. Mayor Connolly did not know about the coming Shift, but my team and I will be working side by side with her to make sure Steelton and its residents are safe in the days to come."

He clapped slowly, deliberately, and thankfully the crowd eventually joined him, hopeful voices rising around the square.

Eileen looked surprised, but to her credit, her face steeled with resolve and her back straightened. Noah caught a frown from Krystal.

After the applause died down, he said, "I will not lie to you. These are dark times. Unlike in stories, there are no heroes to save us, we will have to do this on our own. We will all be following Eileen as our mayor, but right now, until she is up to speed, I ask that everyone study the pamphlets and please heed my words.

"We are a community, and that is our greatest strength. For now, if you feel safe you can go home, but we will be preparing community halls for everyone soon. Running water will likely be a problem within a few days, and if we have to turn off water to the rest of town, we can probably still keep water flowing in a few central locations. Please be patient, and be strong."

Noah still saw the fear in the eyes of the crowd, but rising determination as well. Not everyone from Steelton was present to hear him, not even close, but hopefully word would spread.

The town's cohesiveness came from something deeper than his speech just now. These people had trust and faith in each other, in part because of Noah's tireless meddling.

The battered, bruised, and aching young man grabbed his guitar before heading down the ladder. Log Cabin guards made sure he had plenty of space. Jamal came forward, shaking his head and clapped Noah on the shoulder. "It's time to do your mojo now I think."

Noah nodded. He strapped on his guitar over his shoulder and began to play lightly, recalling the names of every person he had ever encountered in Steelton. [Harmony] reverberated through him, guiding his thoughts.

[Community] called open each person's screen as they came to mind, and Noah assigned them to different groups before giving each group its own note. As he played, he moved forward, away from the milling crowd. They didn't need him anymore, at least not until tomorrow.

Noah lost himself in the music, but gave instructions to Jamal and his security team, assigning different guards to various collection points, giving orders for the guards who weren't present, either.

He kept playing, sparing encouraging smiles for the people he passed. Most of them had their heads buried in their pamphlets, in various states of shock, but those who looked up had varying expressions as they watched him go. He didn't linger with any one person to talk. With [Harmony] they were just notes to be moved and played.

Noah had never played a song this long and this complex before. All of his attention and focus were being spent—the best he could manage beyond [Harmony] was short, concise orders to the Log Cabin guards. Jamal in particular made sure his words reached the right person every time.

As he passed, townspeople did try to ask him questions now,

some even pressed forward. Thankfully, the surrounding guards stopped them.

He didn't know how much time had passed, but when his music finally ended, the stars were beginning to shine, brighter than ever before now that there were no more city lights to wash them out. Noah's fingers were cut, a few of them bleeding freely. He looked at them in confusion, realizing that he'd been so engrossed in his abilities that he hadn't felt the damage.

Noah noticed Jamal staring at him warily and also realized that they were far, far away from Lucy's at this point. His friend looked tired. Voice hoarse, Jamal asked, "What do we do about security now? You gave a good speech, but things are probably gonna get dicey soon. I've been willing to take things on faith for a while now, but it's time to level, Mr. Log Cabin owner boss man."

The young Marine set down his riot shield and folded his arms. "I know this has been a long day for all of us, especially for you," he eyed Noah's wounds, "But this is where the rubber meets the road. If we are gonna work together like this, you can't keep me in the dark about anything anymore. I think that's fair, because everyone else can sing kumbaya and trust in the mayor, but I know this is one hundred percent your show right now. I'm worried about my family. So are you gonna fill me in, now? Like, what is behind that big steel door in the back of the warehouse I used to work from?"

Noah's throat was parched. He set down the guitar and

studied his hands again. Somewhat distantly, mechanically he wondered how long it would take his body to heal. Noah wanted to sleep, to have time to grieve for Johnny, to adjust his plans for the premature Shift. He had so much to do, he felt overwhelmed. Crushing despair descended, but Noah pushed it away with feelings of accomplishment.

He had done it. The first day of the Shift was almost done, and Noah had set Steelton on the path of survival. *Within the month, Steelton might truly be a beacon of hope.*

But protecting his family wasn't enough, and wasn't his true mission. Noah couldn't just stay in town. This was only the beginning–the Aelves were coming. Noah had faced three monsters and had almost died, barely surviving. What's more, he was fairly sure that those three had been among the weakest of their kind. None of them had used magic like he had seen before.

The Shift had finally come, and he still had unanswered questions. *How did I understand the Aelves? Is there anything I could have done to save more people? What could I have done differently earlier today against the Aelves? Did I prepare myself enough?*

Doubts began to crowd his tired mind, but he remembered the first Shift he'd lived through. In his past life, he had cowered in his room as chaos broke out around him, growing worse every day. His parents had died in an effort to save his life, but now in this life, they were alive, safe. Worm was a lifetime away, only a memory.

Noah looked up and watched the stars. One of the constellations, the Big Dipper, was out of alignment, and for some reason, the odd sight gave him comfort. Some things hadn't changed, and the strange stars reminded him of Doc. The wise man's mission had been to unify humanity through communication. Despite all of Noah's efforts, he'd never been able to locate Doc. They had no way to create electricity in this life. Without his friend, Noah didn't have the crazy machine he'd invented, and didn't even have a physical orb—it was part of him now.

Noah blinked, and new screens appeared he had never seen before.

Modifier's alignment with the [Listener] Archetype has strengthened.

Modifier has gained one stat distribution point.

Modifier has gained one [Listener] ability point.

His jaw dropped.

Jamal gave him an irritated look. "Are you ever going to answer my question?"

Noah nodded absently. "Yes, sorry. I was planning to tell you everything anyway. Behind the warehouse is an armory, and we'll get you geared up by tomorrow at the latest. I've said several times now that you are a natural leader, and it's true—I am going to need you. Heck, the town needs you. I'll give you every tool I can. After that, I doubt you will even need my help anymore."

After the Marine reservist grew silent, Noah's thoughts turned inward again. Truly, had he done enough? Would he survive the days to come? Could he save the rest of his friends who were still alive?

Suddenly Jamal stressed and chuckled darkly. The tall, muscular man said out loud what was likely on the minds of most people in Steelton, probably most people on the planet. "I can still barely believe this is all happening. What do we do now?"

Noah let his mother's lullaby run through his body, making his mysterious power rise in response for a moment. The first song he'd ever heard in his life was still the only music that made his orb react that way. Noah turned and said, "We Listen."

EPILOGUE

"This is for you, miss."

Yoko warily watched the unfamiliar, uniformed guards. She had her own people nearby, but the world had obviously gone mad, just like the theoretical world changes Noah had always suggested in the past. The Firestarter group had played hypothetical, leadership simulation games with each other based on outlandish situations. As of two days ago, Noah's bizarre scenarios didn't seem so impossible anymore.

And now a strange woman was handing over a letter with a handwritten, "To Yoko, From Noah," on the envelope.

Yoko was a bit surprised at first when her hand shook as she withdrew the letter, but then merely accepted the reaction. Her hand stilled. Now was the time to think, not jump over every little thing.

The note read,

Dear Yoko,

By the time you receive this letter from one of my people, you will have already realized that the laws of physics have changed. The others from Camp Firestarter have also been sent similar letters like this one. This message and the ones like it are part of a contingency plan in case I am not able to properly speak to you about the coming disaster called the Shift.

On the last page of this note is a map with locations of warehouses I have set up in your country with supplies for your people. Additional instructions to open fortified, armored doors to more sensitive equipment (like weapons) is on the back of your map. Please guard this information carefully.

In the warehouses, you will find pamphlets created specifically for your people, and suggestions on how to unify them. Modify the plans and materials as you wish. If there is anything I've learned over the years, it is to not underestimate you.

Carlo's interest in old weapons has proven invaluable.

As for the Shift itself, I told you and all of our friends in the past that something was coming—something big.

Let me say now with grave sincerity: I told you so.

I know all of this may seem unbelievable, but I trust you to do what is right. You have hopefully not seen any in person yet, or even heard about them, but the Aelves, murderous aliens, are coming. I've attached everything I know of them, including my guesses about their social structure, technology, magic, and abilities. It isn't much, but hopefully you and the other Firestarters might be able to use what I can give you.

As for myself, I will be fortifying my town, Steelton, ensuring that I have a solid base of power and establishing a stronghold for civilization in my area. After that, I will probably travel, visiting other communities.

We will be largely travelling with horses. You already know about the horse stables I founded throughout the world. Japan has several. Travel and communication will be the key to keeping humanity unified. Please establish control of the stables as soon as possible, and you will control the information network. Horses are precious.

Enclosed with this letter is a sample of the pamphlets I created and printed for your country. These are meant to quickly and easily educate people about the Shift. I don't have to tell you the implications of the Shift or the terror it will bring. I suggest you build a power base if you haven't already, and assign people to establish order, create some sort of medical infrastructure, and control, then distribute food.

Good next steps will probably be securing roads between population centers to cut down on crime and prevent as many atrocities as possible. The hidden armory I have left you will help you initially arm your people with Shift-effective weapons and armor.

Please use everything I have left you with my blessing. Take any measures you can to save as many people as possible and prepare them to defend against human raiders...or the Aelves.

As I said before, if all goes well, I will travel my country, but international travel is unlikely, especially in the near future.

Even if we never meet again, always know that I feel fortunate to have met you.

Stay strong. Hope. Survive.

You friend,

Noah Henson

END OF FIRST SONG BOOK ONE

—First book of the Anthem of Infinity series!

Noah's adventures will be continued in the next book of Anthem of Infinity: First Song, Book Two!

Please read on for a note by the author, including multiple ways to connect on social media.

...And don't forget to review this novel!

ABOUT THE AUTHORS

Blaise Corvin served in the US Army in several roles. He has seen the best and the worst that humanity has to offer. A sucker for any hobby involving weapons, art, or improv, he's a fairly hard core geek.

He currently lives in Texas with enough geeky memorabilia to start a museum.

Being a professional author, he must sometimes talk about himself in third person within author biographies.

It's all very eccentric.

***

Outspan Foster can be found writing and reading on RoyalRoad.com, lurking on Discord chats, drawing and painting digitally, animating in 3D, flying kites, and talking about stories and the craft of stories with his friend Regan

Outspan is clumsy, stares at people too long, and likes weird people. He believes in the almighty power of love. He is not a hippy.

He has no great aspirations and lacks any real ambition. He just wants to eat ice cream and relax with friends.

To Readers,

PLEASE, PLEASE LEAVE A REVIEW!

You are wonderful and reviews are amazing for all authors, but especially indie authors like Outspan and I. Your reviews help me pay the bills. Seriously.

If all you can think of to say is, "I liked this book, you should try it too," that would still be awesome!

In 2016 I published my first book. Now I'm full time. This is pretty amazing, but also extremely scary. ...lol. A lot of writers won't admit to this. The uncertainty can be intense, wondering if everyone will like what you just wrote enough to help you keep the power on.

The Anthem of Infinity universe has been extremely fun to write so far, and Noah definitely has many more adventures in store.

Ways to connect with me:

1. My Facebook fan group

Amazon and other distributors are pretty terrible at letting you know when my new books come out. For the latest news and updates, join my Facebook group:

Blaise Corvin Reader group
http://www.facebook.com/groups/BlaiseCorvinBooks/

2. My website

If you're interested in checking out my website, the URL is http://blaise-corvin.com/. You can find news, Delvers artwork, and maps. In 2018, the site will have a store, too.

The site is still a work in progress so please be patient with me.

3. These are my social media pages. Connect with me!

Twitter – @Blaise_Corvin

https://twitter.com/Blaise_Corvin

Facebook – Leave me a like on facebook!

https://www.facebook.com/BlaiseCorvinWriter/

GameLit Society Facebook Group

https://www.facebook.com/groups/LitRPGsociety/

Blaise Corvin Reader group (best place for updates)

http://www.facebook.com/groups/BlaiseCorvinBooks/

My Patreon!

http://www.patreon.com/BlaiseCorvin

If you really love my work and would like to support me further, Patreon offers a great way to help out. I get a lot of support from readers there!

My email

If you want to drop me a line for any reason, you can email me at:

Blaise.Corvin.Art@gmail.com

Until next time (--and please leave a review!--)

Thank you for joining me on this adventure! I couldn't do it without all the knowledge and encouragement I get on a daily basis from everyone I interact with.

I can't wait to spend time with you again and with Noah in First Song, Book Two

:)

-BC

Special thanks to:
Frances Law
Lucas Luvith
Ryan O'Malley
Levena Lindahl

-Beta readers who really helped with polishing this book, making it better than it otherwise would have been.